Choosers
of the
Slain

CHOOSERS
of the
SLAIN

JAMES H. COBB

G.P. PUTNAM'S SONS
NEW YORK

G. P. Putnam's Sons
Publishers Since 1838
200 Madison Avenue
New York, NY 10016

Library of Congress Cataloging-in-Publication Data

Cobb, James H.
    Choosers of the slain / by James H. Cobb
        p.   cm.
    ISBN 0-399-14197-9
    1. Imaginary wars and battles—Fiction. 2. Twenty-first century—Fiction. 3. Antarctic regions—Fiction.
I. Title.
PS3553.0178C48   1996
813'.54—dc20   96-775
                                                  CIP

Printed in the United States of America
10   9   8   7   6   5   4   3   2   1

Book design by Junie Lee
Map by Jackie Aher

Dedicated to the members of "Task Force Cunningham"

To the Chief, as always

*To the two Kathys, who helped reacquaint me with
the English language*

*And to Sherrill and Laurel, who instructed me in
the care and feeding of a heroine*

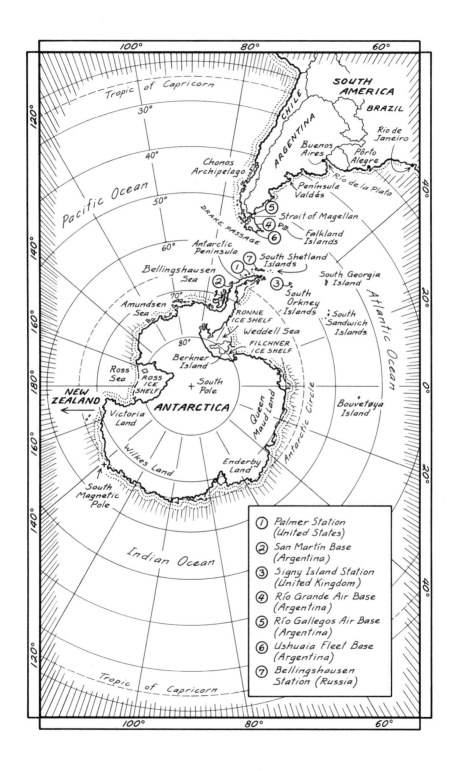

Choosers
of the
Slain

"Awake and about, woman! There's a hot plankton count to be done."

Captain Evan York peeled the covers off his first mate and applied a hearty slap across her bare bottom. She in turn responded with a squealed curse, yanked them back up over her head, and burrowed deeper into her corner of the double bunk. York smiled down at the curl of tousled blond hair that showed from beneath the heavy Hudson's Bay blankets. Roberta Eggerston had been sharing his life and bed for the better part of five years now and yet she maintained her own individuality. Among other things, she would never be a morning person.

"You know what you can do with your plankton count," she growled, "at least till the cabin is a decent temperature and the tea's ready."

"Shackleton never had to put up with this kind of sass from any of his subordinates."

"Shackleton never got to sleep with any of his subordinates either, at least not so's the history books mention."

York smiled again, rolled out of the bunk, and reached for his clothes: thermal long johns and a single pair of heavy wool socks, insulated jumpsuit, and the ubiquitous white plastic "bunny boots" of the Antarctic. He'd had his custom-made by Camtors of the Falkland Islands with full-length composite deck soles for shipboard use.

Topping off his outfit with a Day-Glo orange sea parka, he tucked a pair of mittens in his pocket. He left the master stateroom, heading aft along the narrow companionway to the wheelhouse.

Presently, he would kick the main cabin heater up to day temperature and start the breakfast brew-up, but first, the young master of the *Skua* wanted a morning's look around.

The big motor-sailor had been born out of the love both he and Roberta had for sailing and their mutual fascination with the Antarctic. She was a seventy-five-foot ketch with a reenforced steel hull, designed specifically for long-range ice cruising. They had built her using a small inheritance York had received upon his graduation from Cambridge plus every other penny they had been able to earn, beg, or borrow.

It had been worth it. Basing out of Port Stanley, he and Roberta had sailed south with college-student crews for the past three seasons, chartering out as a research vessel to the British Antarctic Survey. It was a rare thing to successfully turn a dream into a viable way of making a living, but they had done it.

While York had a passion for the southern polar seas, he also had a profound and wary respect for them. Even while lying at anchor off the BAS's South Orkney base at Signy Island, he had maintained a round-the-clock deck watch. At the moment, said watch didn't look too happy.

"Morning, Geoffery. How's the new day?" York asked, stepping out into the cockpit.

"Bloody cold! That's how it is!" the younger day replied miserably, surrounded by the frost haze of his own breath. "I had to be a total loony to ever get involved in this. 'Excellent field experience,' my frostbitten ass!"

"Shouldn't worry," York said, stepping to the rail and eyeing the slushy pancake ice that had accumulated around the hull during the long, late-season night. "That nip of frost in the air means that it's just about time for us to bugger off for home. Pack'll be closing in soon. Two weeks from now you'll be back in England, thrilling the ladies with your exploits."

"If they haven't frozen off by then," Geoffery replied, doing a little jig step to try to stamp some feeling into his feet. "At any rate, I was just going to shout you up. We've got company coming."

"Oh, where away?"

"Just coming into the channel. I think she's that Argy."

The *Skua* was holding some fifty yards offshore in the little cup-shaped harbor on the southern coast of Signy Island. Now a ship was just rounding the western headland and was slowly nosing into the steel-blue waters of the bay. She was an icebreaker, wide-hulled and buff-bowed, her high-stacked military-gray superstructure clearly outlined against the snow-shrouded hills on the farside of the inlet.

"That's the *Presidente Sarmiento* all right, but what the blazes is she doing here? She doesn't have any more calls scheduled this late in the season."

Frowning slightly, York ducked back into the wheelhouse and lifted a pair of binoculars from the rack beside the hatch frame. Returning to the cockpit, he surveyed the new arrival, being careful not to let the chilled metal of the eyepieces touch his face.

Same old *Presidente.* The Argentine naval vessel wasn't listing, nor did she show any outward sign of storm or fire damage. Engine trouble? Or maybe they were just dropping in for a chat. York hoped that they might have a little fresh produce to spare.

Suddenly he stiffened. There was something different here. As the icebreaker came around fully broadside in the channel, York could make out the smallish boxlike structure that had been added to her foredeck. A turret, and from it protruded the slim, bell-mouthed muzzle of an autocannon.

"What the hell?"

"Problem, Skipper?"

"The *Presidente,* she's mounting a bow chaser."

"A what?"

"A gun, she's mounting a gun!"

"So?" Geoffery shrugged. "She's a navy ship and all that."

"So remember the treaty. Heavy military weapons aren't permitted south of the Antarctic Circle."

There was other movement out on the bay. York hadn't picked

up on them at first in the thin, metallic light of the polar dawn. The icebreaker was being preceded by a flotilla of small craft; four big twelve-passenger Zodiacs were powering in toward the black-shale beach below Signy Station.

York brought his glasses up again, studying the forms huddling behind the low gunwales of the inflatables.

White! They were wearing white. On the ice, high-visibility Day-Glo colors were universal for outer clothing. In an emergency situation, you wanted to be seen, not concealed.

White could only mean camouflage.

"Geoffery, turn everyone out and get them into survival suits! You too! Then tell the first mate to get up here straightaway! Move!"

Startled, the younger man vanished below. York returned his attention to the events unfolding at the station, not disbelieving but not wanting to believe.

The Zodiacs had reached the shore and had ridden up over the dirty gray rime ice along the tideline. Disembarking swiftly and expertly, the troops they had carried sprinted upslope, unslinging their assault rifles as they ran. One figure dropped to his knee and began squeezing off precise three-round bursts at the green-painted huts of the Survey base.

For God's sakes, why shoot? York thought. The only weapon ashore was a single-shot .22 used for collecting bird specimens. As the sound of gunfire echoed across the bay, Roberta appeared at the wheelhouse hatch.

"Evan, what's happening?"

"It's the Argentines. Launch our Zodiac and the life rafts. Get everyone over the side."

"Why?"

"Don't ask questions! Go!"

Obediently, she dropped belowdecks. York ducked back into the wheelhouse and went for the communications console. He broke the seals on both of the *Skua*'s emergency transponder beacons and activated them, then turned his attention to the powerful sideband radio set.

"CQ, CQ, CQ. This is BASK *Skua,* calling BASG South Georgia. Do you copy?"

He lifted his thumb from the microphone key and was rewarded by a high-pitched warbling squeal from the speaker. Evan York had never heard cascade jamming before, but he could guess what it was. He swore and started to punch in an alternate frequency.

Up forward, Roberta Eggerston ran her people through the often practiced, but never before needed, drill of abandoning ship. Because she was a skilled mariner in her own right, she followed procedure and refused to be flustered or panicked. Swiftly, she got the life raft, survival packs, and crew over the rail. With her duty accomplished, Roberta acted for herself. She hurried back aft along the deck to the ketch's wheelhouse, a small fearful figure swaddled in an orange foam survival coverall.

York still leaned over the sideband transceiver, glowering at it as it squalled in electronic agony.

"Evan, please, what is going on?"

"The damned Argentines are attacking Signy Base. They're jamming all the BAS frequencies. I can't get through to anyone!"

"What do they think they're doing?"

"I don't know. We can't get out of the bay past their ship, and they'll likely have a boarding party alongside us in a few minutes. We've got to get word out about what's happening here!"

The jamming warble from the speaker was cut off to be replaced by a calm voice speaking a mildly accented English.

"Motor vessel *Skua,* motor vessel *Skua,* secure your radio transmitters and make no further attempt at communications. I repeat, make no further attempt at communications or we will be forced to fire on you."

York wasn't listening. Instead he had started to flip feverishly through the pages of the radio log.

"We still might have something here, Bobbie," he said, not looking up. "The Yanks use a different block of frequencies than we do. We might be able get through to Palmer Station before the Argys can figure out what's up."

York began to key a new setting into the transceiver.

"Evan, if you transmit again they'll start shooting at us!"

"I know, I know!" York brought himself in check. "Look, we have got to let someone know what's going on out here. For our sake, and for the sake of the people at Signy."

The two could sense that the world they had so carefully built together was coming to its end. Their dream was suddenly going to hell around them, and they had only enough time left to speak as captain and first mate. All of the things they had to say as a man and a woman had to be said with their eyes in the few seconds they had left.

"Bobbie, you take the crew and head for shore. You'll be safer there. You'll have to surrender to the Argentines, but there's no other choice. Leave me the small life raft. I'll make one try to reach Palmer, then I'll follow you in. Get going now, everything will work out."

She was crying as she went forward. For a moment, York considered calling after her that he loved her, then turned back to the radio.

"CQ, CQ, CQ. BASK *Skua* calling USARP Palmer. Emergency, do you copy?"

On the farside of the bay, the bow turret of the Argentine warship indexed around and the gun barrel recoiled. Simultaneously with the flat crack of the cannon shot, a thirty-foot plume of water jetted into the air off of the *Skua*'s bow.

"CQ, CQ, CQ. BASK *Skua* calling USARP Palmer. Emergency, repeat, emergency! Do you copy?"

Dead air, unjammed but dead air, and then . . .

"BASK *Skua*, this is USARP Palmer. We read you four by four. What is your situation?"

He could hear the droning of the outboard motor of *Skua*'s Zodiac and the sound of Roberta screaming his name. He could also hear the rhythmic coughing of the Argentine gun mount as it began to walk a stream of shells in on the anchored ketch.

"Palmer, this is *Skua* at Signy Station. The Argentines are landing here in force! I repeat, the Argentines are landing here in force! Armed troops are ashore at the station! It's a bloody invasion!"

York did not hear Palmer Station's reply. Nor did he hear the forty-millimeter shell that exploded through the side of the wheelhouse just inches from his head.

RIO DE JANEIRO
1630 HOURS: MARCH 20, 2006

Amanda Lee Garrett had long ago learned that she required a certain amount of time to herself. Given her chosen profession, however, such time was hard to come by. When a chance at a free afternoon had presented itself, the first in several weeks, she had set out to make the most of it.

She had lunched at one of Rio's finest churrascurias, the steak houses that served the spicy barbecued cuisine of Brazil's southeastern goucho country, a pleasantly old-school establishment where the staff apparently still considered a woman dining alone to be a little scandalous, or at least a pity. She had lingered for a time over a second glass of the good but rough local wine and then moved on.

She had wandered along the warm, tree-lined streets of the Ipanema district and had browsed in the shops and boutiques of the Rua Visconete de Paraja, looking at everything yet seeking nothing in particular. Eventually, gravitating eastward, Amanda had found herself on the famed black and white tiled promenade overlooking the beach at Ipanema.

The pale sands and low surf called to her, making the decision of how she would spend the rest of her afternoon an easy one. She hadn't really planned or prepared for a day at the beach, but it would make a good excuse to buy a new swimsuit.

That, in turn, had led to this soft and shaded patch of sand at the foot of the seawall. It was midweek and the seaside wasn't excessively crowded, just enough so that the air was filled with a happy jumble of samba and New Swing coming from a few radios and CD players. Her clothes, bundled into a plastic shopping bag, made a comfortable pillow and she was content to drowse lazily and people-watch.

Likewise, she was content to be watched. Aware of the occasional appreciative glances that came her way, Amanda gave the whiite satin one-piece she had chosen a surreptitious smoothing tug. The suit was staid compared to the locally favored tangas and monokinis, but the form that it sheathed was a good one, a trimly compact dancer's body, firm-breasted and flat-stomached. Her features were good as well, strong yet feminine, framed by thick, cinnamon-colored hair and dominated by her large—and, as one past lover had described them, dangerously hazel—eyes.

Amanda Garrett was an attractive woman, not classically beautiful, but attractive. At age thirty-five, she was also wise enough to know it. She was neither vain nor shy about the fact. She simply accepted it as a minor but pleasant part of her being. So she was neither surprised nor displeased when, out of the corner of her eye, she noticed another shadow flowing across the sand to merge with the patch of shade she was occupying.

"Hello, I really hope you speak English, because I think I'd like to get to know you."

Amanda came up onto her elbow a little faster than she had intended. Good Lord, this boy was beautiful!

"What would you do if I didn't?" she inquired curiously.

"Keep on trying, I guess." He shrugged and dropped down

onto the sand a couple of feet away. "Things would be a little more complicated, but it'd still be worth it."

She would guess his age as being somewhere in the late twenties, but he had that kind of boyish grin that made her think of high-school-grad-going-on-college-freshman. On the other hand, he had obviously been around enough to be just a little bit bored with some of the more conventional male-female approach-and-contact rituals, much as she was.

"That was an interesting opening. Direct and with a minimum of cute."

"I've found that cute seldom works with the class acts of this world. Honest does."

Amanda nodded. "True."

He wasn't overly tall, not many inches over her own medium height, and he had a hard body. Not a muscle builder, but lean and whipcord wiry. Mediterranean dark, maybe with some Greek lineage in that black and curly hair. His eyes, though, were a particularly penetrating shade of blue.

Those eyes were also giving her a frank survey. Not an ogling that she found offensive, but more of a connoisseur's complimentary consideration. Amanda did suspect, however, that her new swimsuit had been mentally peeled off and tossed into the nearest trash can. Well, fair was fair. She'd had her own momentary visualization of slipping down those well-worn denim trunks to see if that wonderful tan went all over.

"Okay, then, we'll go with honest. My name's Vince."

"Amanda."

"Amanda . . . Let's see, that means 'worthy of being loved.' It suits you."

"And what does Vince mean?"

"Vince, a contraction of Vincent, which means 'invincible.' "

"Which has yet to be proven." Amanda smiled.

"That's what I get for memorizing those name derivations out of the back of the dictionary. Gah! How bad am I bleeding?"

She chuckled softly. "Not too badly."

He could make her laugh, that was important, and honesty did work well with her. He wasn't exactly what she had visualized as the man of her dreams, but there might be definite potential here for a playmate.

"Stay and be welcome, Vincent, and let's see where doing some more honest gets us."

He returned her smile. They each understood the game they were beginning, and the beach at Rio on a late summer's afternoon was a wonderful place to play it. With luck, they both could win.

As it was, though, they were allowed only a few minutes. Both became aware of a disturbance out on the water, a rumble of engines and a chorus of perturbed voices. Something about the sound of those engines made Amanda sit up abruptly.

A ship's boat, a navy-gray, semirigid Zodiac with a stern steering station, was nosing its way inshore, pushing a scattering bow wave of swimmers and waders ahead of it. It rode up onto the sand and a slender figure in khaki hopped over the inflated sidehull and trotted up the beach toward them.

"Damn, damn, damn!" Amanda muttered under her breath.

"Begging the Captain's pardon, but your presence is urgently required back aboard ship."

Commander Amanda Lee Garrett, United States Navy, sighed and got to her feet, brushing off the sand. Time to herself was over.

"Okay, Lieutenant, what's going on?"

Lieutenant Christine Rendino's inquisitive pixie features, normally expressive to the extreme, remained carefully neutral. "I really couldn't say, ma'am. The executive officer just dispatched me to locate you."

"I see. Very well, then, return to the gig and stand by to shove off. I'll be with you in a second."

Amanda knelt down to retrieve the bag that held her uniform. Her new acquaintance had come up on one knee, looking wary and a little unnerved.

"We all have to make a living somehow," she said wryly. "It

was a very good pass. If it's any consolation, I think I might have gone out to intercept it."

Following an impish impulse, she leaned forward and lightly brushed her lips against his. Then, getting back to her feet, she started down to the waiting boat and her responsibilities.

The gig's twin outboards churned up a flurry of sandy foam as they backed off the beach. Slewing about, they went up on the plane and headed for Sugar Loaf Point and Rio's inner harbor.

Amanda rode one of the side benches while Christine Rendino stretched out comfortably on the deck, her back propped against the steering-station windscreen and her legs extended out ahead of her over the keel line. It was a rather casual stance in the presence of a superior officer, but then, that could sum up a great deal of Lieutenant Rendino's military career.

The lithe ash-blonde had entered the service via the University of California's NROTC. She had graduated with honors but had never quite managed to fit into the classic mold of "an officer and a lady." She survived and even prospered because of two things: one, that she was very good, if not brilliant, at her job, the other, the long-held belief within the naval community that intelligence officers were always just a little bit peculiar.

Beyond that, during the tour of duty she and Amanda had shared on the same Fleet staff in the Pacific, she had become a friend, comrade, and confidante. When Amanda had moved on to her own command, she had expended a considerable portion of her accumulated store of favors to ensure that Christine came along with her.

"All right, Chris. What's really going on?"

"Not sure, boss ma'am, but my sit-guess is that it's big, local, and we're being sent to do something about it."

Now that they had a degree of privacy, the intel had released the sober-faced control she had exhibited on the beach and was backsliding into her more usual state of casual frankness.

"Specifics?"

"Not many. A little over an hour ago we caught a rocket from high places. CINCLANT no less, Milstar, top priority. Commander Hiro took the call, then hit the Chinese fire drill button. Crisis one, find you. Crisis two, make all preparations for getting under way."

"Oh, glorious! Of all the days not to take my phone ashore with me. What else?"

"One other thing: my justification for thinking it's local. The Defense Intelligence Agency has asked for a download of all of our Sigint intercepts for the past forty-eight hours. We're dumping into the link now."

"Are they going to find anything interesting in there?"

Christine looked uncomfortable. "To tell you the truth, Captain, we haven't been breaking anything down since we anchored here in Rio. We didn't have any priorities on the threat board, so we've just been keeping the scanners and recorders running and storing the raw data. I've got my gang working on it now, and I'm sure we'll have something for you by the time you get back aboard."

"No need for explanations, Chris," Amanda replied, pulling her whites out of the shopping bag and shaking the wrinkles out of them. "We've all been keeping bankers' hours these last couple of days. Speaking of bankers' hours, how did you know where to find me? I didn't even know I was going to the beach when I left the ship."

"Heck, this is Rio. Someone with your sea and sand fixation would be bound to end up on the beach sooner or later. When Mr. Hiro put me in charge of the 'For Crissake, find the Skipper detail,' I just borrowed your gig and coxun and a good pair of binoculars and I cruised offshore, checking off redheads until I spotted you."

"Good thinking and good work," Amanda replied, buttoning her blouse on over her swimsuit.

Rendino delicately cleared her throat. "If I may be so bold as to say so, my captain was doing some pretty good work back there herself."

"No, Lieutenant, you may not say so. Not if you intend to hang on to those bars on your collar."

"I'll be the soul of discretion."

"Not likely," Amanda snorted, sliding back into her tailored skirt. "You'll have me taking part in a beachfront orgy five minutes after you hit the wardroom."

She tugged up the side zip and slipped her feet into her pumps. Glancing sideways, she cocked an eyebrow at her intel. "On the other hand, it might do certain mopheads around here some good to know that 'The Lady' still has a few moves left in her."

"Fa' sure, Skipper, fa' sure." Christine laughed, a hint of her old Valley Girl lilt coming back into her voice.

As the gig swept around the point, Rio's port district came into view, as did the ships lying off in the deepwater anchorage. Two of them were United States men-of-war. The more distant of the two was a FRAM-updated Perry-class frigate, a diving barge snuggled against its stern quarter. The closer and larger of the pair was Amanda's ship, DDG-79, the USS *Cunningham*.

Amanda moved in her seat to get a better view. She was new enough into her captaincy to still feel a surge of excitement and pride at the sight of her command. Likewise, she was not long enough into it to realize that those feelings would always be there.

A navy man of the old school, circa the Second World War through the 1960s, would have been somewhat puzzled by the same view. For one, he wouldn't have considered a ship of the *Cunningham*'s size to be a destroyer. Measuring 580 feet from her radically raked clipper bow to her short well deck aft, she was the length of a treaty-vintage heavy cruiser. She also would have displaced nearly as much, were it not for the extensive use of aluminum alloy and high-strength composite materials in her construction.

The blocky, angular superstructure and cluttered upperworks that had been the hallmark of American naval architecture for three-quarters of a century were gone. Instead, just aft of the midships line, there was a single, low, slope-sided deckhouse, like the flattened sail of a nuclear submarine. Inset in the curve of its upper forward facing was the transparent strip of the bridge windscreen, and belted around it were the rectangular planar antennae of the destroyer's SPY 2-A Augmented Aegis system.

Gone, too, were the tripod masts. Supplanting them was a freestanding mast array, a towering finlike structure similar to the vertically mounted swept wing of a jet airliner. Fared into the aft end of the deckhouse, its conformal radiating and receptor panels and "smart skin" segments replaced the old open-girder Christmas tree with its tangle of radar dishes and bedspring aerials.

The overall impression was that of uncluttered, Art Deco sleekness, like something off the cover of a 1940s science-fiction magazine. Even the usual deck fittings either retracted into or were fared into the hull. A closer examination would have revealed that there were almost no absolutely flat surfaces or abrupt right-angle joinings anywhere above the waterline. All structural edges and corners had been carefully coved or rounded. Even the weather decks had a very slight turtleback to them.

This had little to do with streamlining in the conventional sense. It had everything to do with electromagnetic propagation, for the "Duke" was the world's first blue-water stealth warship. Her radical hull design eliminated all of the clean reflective surfaces and "wave traps" that could return a clear radar echo. That hull was also sheathed in the latest generation of RAM (Radar-Absorbent Material) and contained almost a quarter of a billion dollars' worth of the most sophisticated electronic countermeasures technology available to military science.

The *Cunningham*'s stealth capacities extended into the visual spectrum as well. The traditional navy-gray paint job had given way to a duller, lower-visibility gray similar to that used on U.S.

carrier aircraft. Also stolen from carrier aviation had been the use of outline "phantom" lettering for her name and identity numbers.

In addition, wavering sooty bands of a darker shade striped her sides from railing to waterline, vertically down the length of her hull and horizontally up the height of the mast array. The veteran of the Second World War would have approvingly recognized this as a variant of his era's "dazzle" camouflage.

The overall effect was strikingly similar to the markings of a tiger shark. They served much the same purpose, breaking up the ship's silhouette and rendering her harder to see and identify under adverse weather and lighting conditions.

There would have been one further point of puzzlement for the hypothetical old navy observer. For a ship of her size, the *Cunningham* would appear to be very lightly armed. The only obvious weaponry were two small, single-mount gun turrets, one just forward of the deckhouse, the other aft on the well deck.

Appearances were deceiving. The Duke was hypothetically capable of sinking a small fleet, downing a small air force, or leveling a small city. If the "neither confirmed nor denied" option was taken, she could incinerate a small nation.

As the gig tucked in alongside the gangway, the ship's bell sounded its four clear notes and the topside MC-1 speakers replied tinnily, "*Cunningham,* arriving." Reaching the quarterdeck, Amanda faced aft and gave the traditional salute to the colors. As had many generations of captains before her, she used that moment to run a quick inventory of her ship's condition.

There was a faint vibration coming from deep within the hull, and a soft, rushing roar whispered down from the stubby, side-by-side exhaust stacks atop the superstructure. Engineering had one of the mains spooled up, hopefully testing that portside anti-infrared system.

Deck Division was busy striking painting and maintenance gear below, while back aft they were doing a hurried fix on the tricky weather seal around the helipad elevator. *Make a note on the to-*

catch-hell list, Amanda thought to herself. *That piece of work has been put off to the last minute once too often.*

She dropped the salute and was facing forward again when her executive officer emerged from a deckhouse hatchway. Lieutenant Commander Kenneth Hiro was a fourth-generation Japanese-American and the kind of XO captains pray for. He was an organizational animal, one who considered ship-operations management an all-absorbing challenge. Increase the load on him and the challenge just became that much more absorbing.

Now, as he approached her, he wore the headset of a mobile ship's interphone over his short-trimmed black hair and carried a computer pad tucked under one arm.

"Good afternoon, Captain. Sorry to wreck your day ashore. Just a second. I'll be right with you."

He leaned over the PVC-and-nylon-strap deck railing and yelled down into the gig waiting below. "Hey, De Lancy, get inshore and check in at the passenger pier. Start shuttling the liberty parties back aboard."

Hiro straightened and cast an approving look at Christine Rendino, who had joined them at the head of the gangway. "Good job, Lieutenant. You not only found the Skipper but you got back in time to save us from having to strike another boat topside."

"Our Christine is a very capable young officer who should go far, granted she's not hanged first," Amanda commented. "Okay, Ken, what are you doing to my ship and why are you doing it?"

"As the Lieutenant informed you, we've received orders to sortie under a potential theater-conflict alert. Beyond that, my only other instructions were to locate you as rapidly as possible."

"I'm located. Ship's status?"

"All in-port maintenance and service programs have been terminated and are securing for sea. Engineering reports that the problem with the intermix blowers of the portside Black Hole System has been corrected. They're buttoning things up now. Weapons Division was running a series of combat simulations on the secondary fire-control suites, but they should have the training programs dumped and the primaries rebooted within the next few minutes."

"What about the liberty parties?"

"I've got search details ashore and I've requested the assistance of the Brazilian Navy shore patrol."

Amanda considered for a moment whether Hiro had left any preliminary bases uncovered. She wasn't surprised to find that he hadn't.

"Very good, Ken. Buzz communications for me and have them stand by with a Milstar channel to CINCLANT in . . . ten minutes. I'll take it in my quarters."

"Aye, aye, ma'am."

"Chris, you get down to Raven's Roost and see if your people have picked up on anything. I suspect this will be a hot briefing, and I do not want to go into it blind."

"Aye, aye," the younger woman called back over her shoulder as she started for the hatchway.

"Ken, one other thing. Did the *Boone* catch the same sortie order we did?"

"No, Captain, they didn't. They aren't going to, either. I talked with her exec this afternoon. The divers confirmed that vibration was coming from a cracked propeller blade. They're out of it."

"Thank heavens for small favors. Going tactical with a Perry would have been like trying to dance *Swan Lake* with a bucket stuck on my foot."

Amanda turned and started for her cabin. "Advise all division heads that there will be an O group in the wardroom as soon as I've gotten the word."

The captain's quarters of a Cunningham-class DDG were a compromise that satisfied no one, especially the generation of naval officers who would occupy them. The intent had been to consolidate the traditional in-port and at-sea cabins into a single convenient suite. Accordingly, they were located one level below and directly underneath the bridge, leaving the sleeper totally at the mercy of a heavy-footed night watch.

Divided into equally minute office, sleeping quarters, and head, the forward bulkhead of the cabin followed the curve of the superstructure faring, rendering almost impossible the efficient and comfortable use of what space there was. Finally, the waste heat radiating in from the surrounding systems bays overwhelmed the air-conditioning, making the cabin stuffy in anything short of a North Atlantic blizzard.

Perspiration and a few missed grains of sand began to prickle under Amanda's clothing almost as soon as she had entered. For a moment, she wondered if the security of Western civilization could be left hanging in the balance long enough for her to take a quick duck under the shower. In the end, she compromised by undoing the top button of her blouse as she squeezed in behind the combination desk and workstation. Even as she did so, the interphone trilled.

"Captain here."

"This is Chris, down in Raven's Roost. My guys are starting to produce. I can confirm we have something big, local, and quiet, including or centering around Argentina."

"Particulars?"

"We've just finished rough-graphing the local military communications traffic, and there's a definite upsurge on the standard Argy bands. It's not a general mobilization, but the load is building."

"Anything from the Brits down at Mount Pleasant?"

"Negative, Skipper, that's beyond our effective monitoring arc. This stuff is signal intelligence coming in from the northern Argentine bases and the sidelobe off of their comsat links. We haven't interrogated any of our Elint sats yet.

"That's another thing, though, we're getting a whole shitpot full of orbital traffic pattern updates down here. It's all across the board: Air Force, Navy, National Security Agency, Elint, recon, weather, and communications. It looks like they're optimizing for

Southern Hemispheric coverage. You just don't retask satellite assets like this unless something pretty important is going down."

"How about the other locals?"

"No load-pattern changes noted on the Uruguayan or Brazilian nets. All quiet."

"How about the global media? Are they showing anything?"

"Nope, nothing on the local or international wires. Whatever it is, the lid's still on."

"Could it be the Falklands again?" Amanda inquired.

"Possibly, or something related. The only other thing showing on the graphs is that the civil sideband channels used by the United States Antarctic Research Program and the British Antarctic Survey threw one heck of a spike yesterday morning. Then they seem to have dropped off almost into radio silence. I don't know if this is significant or not. I'll be able to say better when we actually start listening to some of this stuff."

"Okay, stay on it, Chris. I'll see you at the O group."

Dropping the phone back into its cradle, Amanda tilted her chair back the few inches that it would go. She bit her lower lip as she reflected on what she knew of recent events in these waters and what role her ship might conceivably have in them. A faint shiver rippled down her spine, like the promise of an encounter with a new lover, half excitement, half fear.

She let the chair rock forward and reached for the phone again. "Communications, this is the Captain. I'm ready for that channel to CINCLANT."

She waited for the access tone, then spoke slowly and deliberately. "This is Commander Amanda Lee Garrett, authenticator Sweetwater-Tango-zero-three-five."

Her words were carried by an optical fiber link down to the radio room, and from there back up to a gyrostabilized laser projector at the crest of the Duke's antenna array. Via a modulated beam of coherent light, they were fired up to a Milstar B communications satellite holding in synchronous orbit high above the South

Atlantic and then across to a sister sat hovering over the Northern Hemisphere. From there, they were aimed down to a receptor on the roof of a certain building within the vast United States naval operations complex at Norfolk, Virginia.

As they were received, a security monitoring system matched Amanda's words against her digitized voiceprint held in a computer file along with similar prints from every other active and reserve naval and marine officer in federal service. A single glowing word appeared on a terminal: "Verified."

The reply began its return journey.

"Acknowledged. This is Vice Admiral Elliot MacIntyre. Authenticator, Iron Fist-November-zero-two-one.

"Good afternoon, Captain Garrett. We have a job for you. . . ."

WASHINGTON, D.C.
1720 HOURS: MARCH 20, 2006

For Secretary of State Harrison Van Lynden, the ending of one long journey marked the beginning of another.

He had disembarked from the United jetliner he had ridden from New Zealand to find Marine Three waiting on the tarmac for him, its rotors already turning. A ten-minute helicopter flight had transferred him from Dulles International to Andrews Air Force Base and to yet another waiting aircraft—in this case, a huge Boeing Seven Century SST.

It was the Air Force VC-31 variant, a VIP transport in the blue and white livery of the Executive squadron. Frequently assigned to the State Department's shuttle-diplomacy operations, they had earned the collective nickname "The Kissinger Express."

The Secretary was a spare and generally amiable New Englander. Into his mid-forties, he moved with the ease and vigor of a much younger man even when, as now, he was carrying a thirteen-hour accumulation of jet lag. Except for a short stint as a Marine officer, he had spent his entire adult life in the diplomatic service of the United States. He had reached the peak of his chosen profession because he was good at his job, and he was good at his job because he loved it.

To Van Lynden, international diplomacy was truly "The Great Game." The give-and-take of high-stakes negotiation, the formation of international policy, the creation of history around the conference table, he relished it all. It beat even a good hand of stud poker, his second passion in life.

Now, as he began to climb the mobile stairway to the transport's door, Van Lynden felt a familiar surge of adrenaline. Like a bird dog catching the first trace of a scent, he sensed the beginning of a challenge.

The Assistant Secretary of State for Latin American Affairs, Steven Rosario, was waiting for him just inside the hatchway.

"Good evening, Mr. Secretary. Sorry about your vacation being interrupted."

"No problem, Steve," Van Lynden replied. "I just hope someone was able to scare me up some fresh laundry. Other than this one suit, all I've got in my luggage is a week's worth of dirty fishing clothes."

"Taken care of, sir. Mrs. Van Lynden sent you a couple of suitcases. She also instructs me to tell you that she sends her love as well. She would have come down herself, except that she knew that you'd be making a fast turnaround."

"Ah, I guess I'm at her mercy when it comes to my selection of ties, then. So be it. I'll give her a call after we get airborne. Do we have a full crisis team on board?"

"Yes, sir. We're ready to roll."

"Good. Since you seem to be running the show, Steve, I suppose we must be bound for South America."

"Sir?"

Van Lynden chuckled at the younger man's puzzlement. "The inn I was staying at was on a party line, for God's sake. Thanks to having a madman as a driver, I was just barely able to catch the last direct flight stateside from Wellington this week. Since my recall, I haven't had a second's access to a secure phone or terminal. I don't have the faintest idea where I'm supposed to be going."

"Uh, Buenos Aires, Mr. Secretary."

Van Lynden gave Rosario a wry grin and a pat on the shoulder. "Well, that's a start."

With greenish flame flickering in the throats of its methane-burning scramjets, the big transport lifted off from Andrews and climbed out over the Atlantic and away from the setting sun. Leveling out at 75,000 feet, the Boeing accelerated smoothly through the sound barrier to its triple-sonic cruising speed and began tracking on the Speedbird South flight lane to Argentina.

In the airliner's comfortably appointed briefing lounge, introductions were being made.

"Mr. Secretary, this is Dr. Caroline Towers of the National Science Foundation, currently the director of the United States Antarctic Research Program."

Van Lynden found himself shaking hands with a slender, mid-fortyish, handsome woman in a conservative pantsuit. Her short brown hair appeared more sun bleached than graying and the hand he clasped was strong and work-roughened. Van Lynden suspected that whatever the doctor held her doctorate in, she wasn't of the test-tube-washing and paper-shuffling breed.

"Dr. Towers is the closest thing we have to a diplomatic representative to the Antarctic," Rosario added.

"Antarctic? As in the South Pole?"

"Yes, sir. That's our crisis point."

"Well, welcome aboard, Doctor. We don't often hear from your end of the world."

Dr. Towers gave an acknowledging nod. "Generally, we've

been able to keep our problems in the family, as it were, Mr. Secretary. At least until now. I just hope that you'll be able to help us contain this current mess."

"I hope we can too, whatever it is," Van Lynden replied, dropping into one of the padded captain's chairs slotted around the conference table. "Can you and Steve bring me up to speed on the situation? Just the basics on this first run-through."

"I'm afraid it gets rather complex very rapidly," she replied, drawing the briefing-room control pad in front of her from across the table.

She touched a series of keys and a flatscreen set into the forward bulkhead lit up, displaying a high-resolution map of the Antarctic continent. The touch of another key expanded the upper left quadrant of the map until it filled the screen, zooming in on a mountainous, glacier-covered extension of land, reaching out like a stumpy tentacle toward the tip of South America.

"Mr. Secretary, this is the Antarctic Peninsula. The name is a comparatively recent compromise. For years, the British called it Graham Land. The Chileans called it O'Higgins Land. The Argentines referred to it as the San Martin Peninsula, and we called it the Palmer. Each nation marked it so on their own charts. No one would acknowledge any of the other names for fear of also acknowledging the associated territorial claim. Many of us at USARP had hoped that this kind of political posturing was no longer relevant. It appears we were wrong."

She manipulated the control pad again. Fifteen glowing dots appeared along the peninsula coastline and on several of the offshore islands. Flanking each was a small national-flag symbol.

"As you can see, several nations currently maintain research installations in the area. We have Palmer Station, Russia has Bellingshausen, and the Republic of Poland has Arktowsky. The others are equally divided between Argentina, Chile, and the United Kingdom.

"Palmer and the European stations are all comparatively small, operating with, oh, between six and twenty personnel, depending on the season. They are oriented primarily toward pure scientific research. The South American bases are larger, small colonies really, intended to reinforce the territorial claims of their respective governments."

"Just a moment, Doctor. Didn't the Antarctic Treaty of 1961 abrogate all territorial claims in that area?"

"No, Mr. Secretary, that's a popular misconception. The Treaty of 1961 places all territorial claims in abeyance for the duration of the treaty. None of the signing powers, including the United States, have ever disavowed their claims. Nor does the treaty prevent the involved nations from taking actions to reinforce those claims."

"Such as?"

"Issuing postmarks, assigning magistrates, producing Antarctic citizens."

"What?" Van Lynden and Rosario almost chorused the exclamation.

"At the Chilean bases, Mr. Secretary, I have met young people in their teens who, barring the occasional holiday, have spent their entire lives on the ice."

"That's incredible, Doctor."

"Not really, not if you think about it. Chile and Argentina have always had a profound interest in the Antarctic, a sense of 'manifest destiny' if you will. They take their claims there very seriously, apparently more so than we even imagined."

She returned her attention to the wallscreen. "At any rate, at approximately eight-thirty Washington time yesterday morning, Palmer Station"—the American flag next to one of the station symbols near the lower end of the peninsula flashed—"received a distress call from a small British research vessel lying off the British Antarctic Survey base in the South Orkney Islands."

A U.K. symbol blinked beyond the northeastern tip of the headland.

"They reported that Argentine troops were taking the station by force. When Palmer tried to get confirmation, neither the research ship nor the South Orkney base replied.

"Further investigation revealed that all of the BAS bases on the peninsula had gone off the air almost simultaneously. The station commander at Palmer then declared an emergency and notified our main installation at McMurdo Sound."

Dr. Towers glanced across the table at the Assistant Secretary of State. "At this point, I believe Mr. Rosario should take over."

Rosario nodded and picked up the narrative. "Upon being advised of the situation, the commanding admiral of Antarctic Support Command launched an immediate investigation. VXE-6, the Navy's polar-operations squadron, had a C-17 outfitted for photo-reconnaissance on an ice-survey flight over the Weddell Sea and it was diverted to the South Orkneys. The aircraft was unable to contact the British either, so upon arrival, it descended to conduct a low-altitude observation pass over the base."

Rosario had taken over the control pad and now activated a second wallscreen. It began to flick through a series of film-frame blowups. There was a view of a scattering of white-clad men around a cluster of green-painted buildings. Another, closer view of a group of snow-camouflaged men, assault rifles clearly visible slung over their shoulders. A shot of a chunky, buff-bowed naval vessel, the autocannon on its foredeck up-angled and aimed at the camera. Finally, there was a photo of a small motor-sailor lying on its side in the ice-choked shallows, a line of shell holes punched into its hull.

"The troops are Argentine Marine Corps Buzo Tactico Special Forces. The ship is an Argentine navy icebreaker. Everything else should be pretty much self-explanatory.

"Our plane circled the area for several minutes, taking photographs and attempting to raise someone at the British station. Eventually, they were challenged and informed that they were violating Argentine national airspace. They were ordered to depart or be fired on."

"Just a minute, Steve. Dr. Towers, who would these islands belong to if the Antarctic territorial claims weren't in abeyance?"

The USARP Director shrugged her shoulders. "That's a very good question. Chile, Argentina, and Great Britain all claim the Antarctic Peninsula and its offshore islands. The British by right of first discovery and occupation. The South American states by proximity and occupation. Even the United States and Russia have potentially valid first-discovery claims. Conflicting boundaries and territorial-claim overlays are common throughout the continent, primarily due to the poor grade of cartography and record-keeping by the early explorers."

"At the moment it appears that possession is nine-tenths of the law," Rosario commented. "Our intelligence now indicates that Argentina has seized all four of the British installations on the peninsula in a well-coordinated military action."

Van Lynden frowned. "What's the status of the British base personnel?"

"That's one of the few straight answers we've been able to get out of Buenos Aires since the incident began. With one exception, all the British are alive and well. They will shortly be repatriated through Chile. That one exception is the captain of the British research ship. The Argentines claim he was killed when they were, and I quote, 'forced to take defensive actions.' "

One of the briefing-room printers began to buzz and rasp softly. Rosario swiveled his chair around and accepted the sheet of hard copy it produced.

"It's a new estimate on Argentine force deployment from the Defense Intelligence Agency, Mr. Secretary."

"Let's hear it."

"Estimated platoon-strength units of the Buzo Tactico at each of the captured British installations and at each of the secondary Argentine bases. At their main San Martin base, they've airlifted in a full mountain-infantry battalion, plus additional light artillery, combat support, and heavy-lift helicopter elements. Currently, they have over two thousand combat troops deployed on the peninsula."

The Secretary of State remembered his days as a Marine butter bar second lieutenant and what he had learned about the logistics of hostile-environment combat operations. Whatever the Argentines were up to, they were going for broke. An operation of this size and complexity was probably pushing their capacity for long-range power projection right to the limit.

"My instinctive first question is why?" Van Lynden said. "Why launch a military action that will no doubt scar Argentina's relations with the major powers for years? Why all this over an area that's primarily a scientific curiosity?"

"Possibly because Antarctica is also the last great untapped pool of natural resources on the surface of the Earth," Dr. Towers replied soberly. "Our mineralogy surveys have discovered in-dications of a wide spectrum of valuable metals, copper, ti-tanium, iron, silver, even uranium and gold. The South Americans have been concentrating on this line of research far more than we have. They could very well have located commercially viable deposits.

"In addition," she continued, "we know that the Antarctic has the world's largest deposits of coal, and, we suspect, oil and gas re-serves over three times the size of the Alaskan North Slope fields."

"But what good are they if no one can get at them?"

"Until recently that has been the case, Mr. Secretary. The Antarctic's nearly impenetrable ice pack and extreme climatic con-ditions have made commercial development impossible. That's what has preserved the continent in its nearly pristine environmen-tal condition."

"Probably that's why we were able to get the Treaty of 1961 in the first place," Rosario commented. "None of the signing powers really had anything to lose."

"Quite right," Towers agreed, "but times and technologies change. In Alaska, Canada, and Siberia, oil drilling and mining operations are routinely being conducted north of the Arctic Circle. Soon, it will be just as feasible to operate in the Antarctic."

"Such things are currently against international law down there, aren't they?" Van Lynden inquired.

"Yes. The Wellington Accord of 1991 extended the Antarctic Treaty's ban on mining for a further fifty years." An element of anger and frustration crept into her voice. "Many of us in the Antarctic community wanted something more permanent. And, damn it all, until this thing came up, I thought we had it."

"The international park?"

"Exactly, Mr. Secretary. For decades, the Treaty states have been considering the concept of having the Antarctic declared an international park under the protection and administration of the United Nations. The entire continent would be held in perpetuity as a wilderness area and a scientific preserve with all commercial exploitation, barring a degree of tourism, banned."

"But hasn't that always been just a concept, Doctor?" Rosario asked. "I know that in recent years, the United States has come to favor the park idea but that there still wasn't a solid consensus among the Treaty states yet."

"As I said, Mr. Rosario, times change. Some low-profile but very intense lobbying has been going on within world science circles these past few months. At last we've succeeded in turning several key obstructionist governments. At the next full meeting of the Antarctic Treaty states this July, we were sure that we would have the majority needed to get the act passed and the park created."

Dr. Towers leaned forward across the table and her voice took on intensity. "Next year, 2007, has been named the second International Geophysical Year. A major Earth sciences program is being planned that will involve almost the entire global scientific community. It will be the premier international research project of this half of the twenty-first century.

"The original Antarctic Treaty was a direct outgrowth of IGY One back in 1957. The committee we've had working on the park project couldn't imagine a better tribute to the concept of international scientific cooperation than to be able to take the next step with the actual creation of the park."

Dr. Towers leaned back into the padding of her chair. "Or at least that's how we thought the scenario would go."

Van Lynden cocked an eyebrow. "Is it necessary to ask who the opposition was?"

"Argentina and Chile fought us every step of the way. Brazil too, to a lesser extent. Their stake in the Antarctic is somewhat smaller and of a lower national priority. Apparently the Argentines are willing to fight us with more than words."

"You can almost see their point of view," Rosario mused. "For the last couple of centuries, exploitation has been the name of the game. Then, just as they get ready to do some exploiting of their own, somebody changes the rules on them."

"Point of view or not, Steve, the Argentines have used armed forces against a close ally of the United States. They have also put their foot through a treaty to which we are a signatory. If I know our boss, he isn't going to take this lightly."

"He's not, sir."

Rosario lifted his briefcase onto the surface of the table and thumbed the security lock-check pads. He popped the latches and passed Van Lynden a dark blue folder bearing the embossed golden seal of the presidency.

"Your instructions, Mr. Secretary. In summary, you are to proceed to Buenos Aires and seek to consult directly with President Sparza. You are to ascertain the intent of the Argentine action and you are to express in the strongest possible terms the opposition of the United States to these acts. You are to request that the Argentine government withdraw their troops and that they abide fully by the Antarctic Treaty of 1961."

"I gather that those are to be firm requests?"

"Yes, sir. The President has also sent along an official note of protest to be delivered by you to President Sparza. A copy of the text has been included in your briefing file."

"Very good. Now, has there been a military response ordered?"

"Yes, sir. Atlantic Fleet Command has been ordered to dispatch forces south. There is a major British deployment under way as well. CINCLANT will be ready to update you on that situation at your pleasure."

"Again, very good." Van Lynden opened the file on the table before him. Settling his wire-framed glasses a little, he began to skim the opening paragraphs. After a moment, he looked up.

"By the way, have the Argentines made any hostile gestures against any of the other peninsula installations—ours, the Chileans', the other European powers'?"

"There has been nothing overt, barring that one threat to our plane," Dr. Towers replied. "The Chileans seem to be working with them. At least they're maintaining normal station-to-station communications. They've broken off direct contact with everyone else and they are refusing to allow foreign aircraft to land at San Martin or at any other of their bases. This is another major violation of the Antarctic Treaty—" Dr. Towers brought herself up short. "Pardon me, I'm going to have to get used to the fact that the treaty doesn't mean all that much anymore."

"Oh, I don't know about that, Doctor," the Secretary of State replied, returning his attention to the folder. "We shall see, as the blind man said."

RIO DE JANEIRO
1800 HOURS: MARCH 20, 2006

As with all of the world's warships, the *Cunningham*'s wardroom served her officers as a combined dining area, lounge, and auxiliary work space. It was home, all that they had while they were at sea.

Accordingly, they had contributed generously to their mess fund to ensure that home was a comfortable place.

The traditional gray linoleum decking had been covered with navy blue carpeting, and the single, long wardroom table had been supplemented by several comfortable-looking pieces of Danish modern furniture in russet leather. One bulkhead mounted an entertainment center, complete with stereo and video system and ranked CD and LD cabinets, while the others were sheathed in "redwood" paneling, handsome despite being a safety-cleared fireproof synthetic.

The bulkheads also displayed a growing collection of memorabilia. Launching and commissioning photographs, a nearly empty deployment plaque, and a meter-wide enlargement of the *Cunningham*'s official ship's patch: a circular sigil divided across, with light blue sky above and dark blue sea below and with a phantom outline of the Duke's silhouette sailing on the horizon. Her name and Fleet Identification Number arced across the top of the patch in gold, while her motto, "Strike in Stealth," curved along the bottom in silver.

Flanking the hatchway leading aft were two special items. To port was a small glass case containing a worn pair of naval aviator's wings. They had been a commissioning gift, bestowed by the man whose name the ship now carried: Rear Admiral Randy "Duke" Cunningham, the Navy's legendary first ace of the Vietnam era.

Mounted on the bulkhead to starboard was another commissioning gift: a painting, done by a seafarer for seafarers, in blues, grays, and misty silvers.

It was a presentation of a rather unusual destroyer squadron, running in echelon formation across a foam-streaked sea. In the foreground was the *Cunningham* herself, leading the line. Holding position on the Duke was a big, slab-sided Spruance-class DD. Beyond her was a rakish Charles F. Adams from the 1960s, and beyond that, the five-turreted silhouette of a World War II–vintage

Fletcher. In turn, almost lost in the horizon haze, were the pole mast and slender funnels of a First World War four-piper.

At the bottom of the white oak frame was a small bronze plate bearing the last verse of Rudyard Kipling's poem "The Destroyers":

> The strength of twice three thousand horse
> That serve the one command;
> The hand that heaves the headlong force,
> The hate that backs the hand:
> The doom-bolt in the darkness freed,
> The mine that splits the main;
> The white-hot wake, the 'wildering speed—
> The Choosers of the Slain!

Among its other uses, the wardroom was the usual setting for the ship's O groups.

The operations-group command style had been a concept developed by the armed forces of Great Britain and brought to its fullest fruition by that nation's Special Air Service during the 1970s. Consisting of the commanding and executive officers and the senior division heads, the O group was convened to confer and brainstorm over mission planning and operational and tactical developments.

Many officers of the old school disapproved of the O group. They claimed it eroded the captain's authority and pushed perilously close to command by committee. Amanda Garrett, however, preferred it, never having been the kind of officer who believed a captaincy automatically conferred omnipotence.

As she glanced around at the little cluster of men and women gathered at the wardroom table, she realized again that she had been blessed with a good team. Certain of them, like Ken Hiro and Christine Rendino, she had served with before and had been able to select. With the others, she had just been damn lucky. One would have to be a fool not to take advantage of their input, and Amanda wasn't a fool.

"... In short, that's the situation. Once we complete preparations for deployment, we are to proceed immediately to Drake Passage and establish a patrol station. Once there, we await reinforcements or new orders, whichever come first. Any comments?"

She watched intently as each division head digested the orders and considered how they would affect his or her particular area of responsibility.

Hiro was the first to speak. "Without tender support, I don't see what kind of deployment preparations we can make. We have to go with what we've got, unless the Brazilians are willing to loan us some compatible gear and stores. Either that or wait for the stuff to be airlifted in."

"There's another option, Ken. We've got the *Boone* sitting right next door. We can interface with their stores list and requisition anything they have that we can use. Then we sling the stuff over using the helos."

"Commander Stevens isn't going to like having his paperwork messed up like that, Skipper."

"I can't help that, Ken. I'm going to the South Pole. He's limping home with a busted prop. If he throws too much of a snit, remind him that I have four months in grade on him. If that doesn't work, refer him directly to me. CINCLANT will back us on this."

"Does that include fuel, Captain?" Chief Engineering Officer Carl Thomson inquired.

Lieutenant Commander Thomson was a big, quiet, shambling man who had likely grown a little tired over the years of being compared in appearance to John Wayne. In his early forties, he was the oldest of the *Cunningham*'s officers, overage in grade because he had always displayed more interest in ship's systems than he had in career planning.

"How do we stand on bunkerage, Chief?" Amanda inquired.

"Sixty-seven per."

"I don't think we want to fuss around with a ship-to-ship transfer. See if the Brazilians can provide us with a fueling barge on short notice. If not, we'll pay a call on the Brits and top off down at Port Stanley. How's the plant otherwise?"

"She's holding together."

Amanda smiled a little. Translated from Thomson-ese, that meant that the drives were in as close to perfect a condition as human dedication and ingenuity could bring them.

Her attention moved on to her tactical action officer.

"Okay, Dix, can Weapons Division report the same?"

First Lieutenant Dixon Lovejoy Beltrain did not at all fit the popular image of a computer geek. In fact, the sandy-haired TACCO looked far more like the first-string quarterback he had been at the University of Alabama.

Nevertheless, he was one of that first generation to be raised interacting with computers from kindergarten on up. He plugged in to the guided-missile destroyer's fire-control matrix as effortlessly as one of his own black boxes and played the master missileer's console as if it were a cheap video game.

"The Aegis Two system and all secondary surface and air sensors are four-oh, ma'am. Same with the ASW suite. All fire-control and weapons systems are up and on line."

"Ordnance loads?"

"Full warloads in all torpedo tubes. Phalanx magazines are also full. From ordnance testing, we're down about forty rounds of seventy-six-millimeter, fore and aft, for the Oto Melaras, but I guess we can top up from the *Boone* on that. As for the Vertical Launch Systems . . ."

He consulted his computer pad, calling up a weapons payload listing. "All cells loaded and operational. Current loading, surface-to-surface: thirty-six Harpoon Twos, twelve Standard HARMS, twelve Sea SLAMs, and twelve SCMs. ASW: thirty-six Vertical Launch ASROCs and four Aquahawks. Surface-to-air includes forty-eight LORAINs and twenty-eight ESSM quad packs. Special-mission loads include four BRAVE drones and a Zenith round."

Beltrain looked up. "We also have the standard block of alternate warheads and guidance packages in the magazines. The only glitch we have is a check yellow warning on one of the 'Poons last testing cycle. Might need some work."

"Don't fool with it, just pull it and send it home with the *Boone*. While you're about it, pull the Aquahawks too."

"There's nothing wrong with the 'hawks, ma'am," Beltrain replied contritely.

"Nothing except that they still don't work half of the time, even when they do check out green. Look, Dix, I know that you and General Dynamics think those contraptions are the antisubmarine wonder of the age, and I'd like to indulge you. However, this is a potential combat deployment, and I'm simply not going to waste cell space on iffy ordnance. Swap them with the *Boone* for whatever you think we can use, just so long as it works."

Beltrain admitted defeat. "Aye, aye, ma'am." He grinned back with an acknowledging nod.

Amanda moved on around the table from offensive to defensive systems.

"How about your people, Mr. McKelsie?"

"We're up, Captain."

"How about the Black Hole Systems?"

"Like I said, we're up."

Lieutenant Frank McKelsie was the ECM and stealth systems officer, holding sway over the *Cunningham*'s arsenal of active and passive electronic defenses. He was an abrupt, gingery man, nervously slender with thinning red hair. He had an abrasive, bullying command style that Amanda didn't particularly like. She also suspected that he was something of a closet chauvinist as well.

On the other hand, he knew his job and got performance out of his systems and personnel. That counted for a great deal, given his area of responsibility. Besides, he had never directly challenged her authority . . . yet.

"Ensign, how about Air Division?"

Through no fault of her own, Ensign Nancy Delany was the

O group's current weak link, her primary problem being an almost painful lack of experience. Fresh out of flight school, this had been her first blue-water deployment. As the sole helicopter pilot currently attached to the Duke, she was also the sole officer in charge of the ship's tiny air group. She had been struggling throughout the cruise to bring herself and her unit up to speed.

"We're operational, Captain," she replied softly. "I'm sure we can use some extra spares, but I'd have to check with my crew chief to get an exact list on that."

"Don't worry about it. We're going to pull the whole aviation section right off the *Boone*—helo, personnel, parts bin and all—and take it aboard. Ken, is that going to present any problem?"

"Not really, Captain, we're set up for two-helo operations. The only thing is, we've been using the spare berthing spaces and gear lockers for general storage."

"Well, get 'em unstored and ready for habitation."

"Aye, aye."

She returned her attention to the younger woman. "There is one thing, Ensign. The *Boone*'s helo detachment is from your squadron and the pilot is probably going to have rank on you. I'm sorry, but it looks like you're going to get bumped off this august council."

"That's okay, ma'am. I'll survive." If anything, the rather harried-looking little brunette appeared relieved.

"Chris, how about your people?"

"We're good, Skipper," the intelligence officer replied from the end of the table. "I've got the word on the current mission database."

"Go with it."

"Okay, gang, here it is. We're putting the standard mission database together down in Raven's Roost. DIA is giving us the usual download of the usual stuff: climatics, geo- and oceanography, military TOE of the involved powers, plus all the latest chart and sat photo files.

"State is providing a political situation report on the theater of operations and a current crisis update. Oh, and one other thing. I've contacted both Antarctic Support Command and the Coast Guard to provide us with files on the South Polar operational environment and how to stay alive in same. We should have the full menu up and running in another couple of hours with standard access available through all ship's terminals."

Amanda nodded her approval. "Very good, especially those polar data files. We're going to need them. Now, can you give us a brief op-force rundown?"

"Sure thing." The intel nodded. Of all the group seated around the table, she was the only one without an active computer pad in front of her. Christine was that one-in-a-thousand individual who had been born with an eidetic memory. She hardly ever resorted to the artificial props of notes or reference material and her shipmates rarely ever doubted her declarations. They'd seen her win too much money in too many Officers' Clubs by wagering that she could quote extemporaneously and verbatim any national entry out of the latest *Jane's All The World's Warships.*

"Okay, people," Christine began, "our potential black hats here are the Argentines. These guys are a definite power to be reckoned with down in this part of the word. It will behoove us to act accordingly."

"I thought the Brits kicked their butts back in '82," Beltrain commented.

"They did, but their unit performance during the Falklands War varied between the pathetic to pretty darned good, depending upon the unit involved and the situation. Junior officers then— company commanders, deck officers, and flight leaders—are now senior command cadre. We have got to presume that these guys may have learned a few things.

"The four strike arms we have to be concerned about are their air force, their naval surface and submarine forces, and their naval air wing.

"The Fuerza Aérea Argentina is good. In fact, they are probably the best, most professional air force in South America. These guys made the British sweat blood. They sank five ships and shot up ten others during the course of the campaign. Current operational strength is around three hundred and fifty aircraft, about one hundred and fifty of which are combat capable. The majority of these planes are the domestically produced Pampas attack aircraft, a very typical, third world jet trainer–turned–light strike fighter. Limited range, limited air-to-air, very limited night and all-weather capability. You're not likely to see these aircraft out of sight of land.

"On the other end of the spectrum, they have about forty Dessault Rafale E's, the top-of-the-line export variant of the standard French tactical fighter. This is a very bad-ass aircraft indeed, boys and girls. Good range, good sensors, good ECM, day and night, all-weather capable, and it can deliver large amounts of all kinds of very nasty ordnance with unnerving accuracy."

"*Vive la France,*" somebody down the table muttered.

"Moving right along to force multipliers, the Argys have no dedicated Wild Weasel or Raven aircraft, but those lovely Rafales can carry HARMs and jamming pods. Tanker assets consist of a single flight of Lockheed Hercules modified for air-to-air refueling. Airborne Early Warning assets are built around a couple of converted Boeing 737-400 airliners tricked out with Israeli Elta Phalcon phased-array radar."

"Are any of their squadrons mission-dedicated to antishipping?" Amanda inquired.

Christine shook her head. "Nope, that's left to the Aeronaval Argentina. Fortunately for us, that World War Two–vintage British flattop the Argys had finally fell apart on them a few years ago. To date, they haven't been able to afford a replacement. Instead, they've opted to develop a land-based maritime strike capacity. They picked up a squadron of ex-Kriegsmarine IDS-model Tornadoes and had them rebuilt by Fiat of Italy. The airframes have been zero-timed, uprated engines installed, and all internal systems updated to current spec. These are your premier ship killers, the weapon of choice being the AM-44 advanced-mark Exocet missile."

Amanda lifted an eyebrow. "Any other good news for us?"

"Oh, lots and lots. One of the Aeronaval's weaknesses during the Falklands War was its lack of long-range search aircraft. They corrected that little problem by picking up a half-squadron of Dessault Atlantique ANG patrol planes. They routinely work up with the Tornadoes, and both aircraft types have full date cross-link and targeting capacity. It's a neat setup."

"It sounds like the Argentine armed forces have been undertaking a major modernization program," Ken Hiro commented.

"They have. Argentina has been riding high on the South American economic recovery and their current administration has been supporting increased military appropriations. It's starting to show in all of their services."

"Does that include the submarine and surface forces?"

The intel nodded an affirmation to her captain. "It does. Sub-wise, they're converting from German designs to the new Swedish export boats: the Kockums 471-B. They've got two in commission along with three of the old Thyssen 1700s. The Thyssens are reaching the end of their hull lives, though, and are probably not really fit for serious combat deployment."

Amanda frowned a little as she recalled what she knew about the Kockums. Anechoic antisonar hull sheathing, diesel electric propulsion with fuel-cell auxiliary, six twenty-one-inch torpedo tubes with launch capacity for surface-to-surface missiles.

"I reckon it could be worse," Dix Beltrain said, reading her mind. "A diesel boat will have problems in the kind of crappy weather we can expect in Drake Passage."

"Um-hmm. And the more sea room we have, the less effective they'll be. Let's make a note to try and lay as well off the coastline as is feasible. Carry on, Chris."

"The core of the Argentine surface force is also German built. This consists of four Meko 360–class destroyers and half a dozen 140-class frigates. These are twenty-year-old hulls, but they have recently undergone a full service-life extension and systems modernization.

"There's some new stuff as well. Three Italian-built Animoso-class destroyers. Two of them are antiair–oriented DDGs with the Aerospatiale/Thomson-CSF Aster area defense missile system. The third is a modified helicopter carrier with flag capacity and an enlarged hangar, capable of handling either two EH-101 Merlin or four Lynx Mark V helos. These units generally operate together as a single squadron and are considered the local first string."

"Shit, Rendino," McKelsie commented dryly, "those are Italian hulls optimized for Mediterranean operations. An outfit that would buy them for use in the South Atlantic doesn't impress me a whole hell of a lot."

A flash of annoyance crossed Christine's face and she leaned forward across the table, her eyes narrowing. "These are good ships and good aircraft, manned by people who, Mr. McKelsie, we must presume know how to use them. To do otherwise is to ask to be popped right into the body bag."

"Belay that, Chris," Amanda said, frowning. She had been able to cope with McKelsie, but Christine and the stealth boss struck sparks off each other as inevitably as flint and steel. She had some growing fears about how the two would be able to work together under an operational load.

"Lieutenant Rendino's point is well taken, though, Mr. McKelsie," she continued. "Ships, battles, and wars have been lost because an enemy no one expected to be able to fight, did. Arrogance is a weakness I will not tolerate aboard the *Cunningham*."

McKelsie flared and looked as if he had something more to say. Amanda met his gaze levelly, and after a few moments he gave a curt acknowledging nod. "However you want it, Captain."

Amanda contained a sigh. She didn't have an immediately available solution for this problem, and there wasn't time to look for one. "Go on, Chris. Is there anything else to report?"

"They've still got a couple of old French A-69–class escort frigates in commission, and they've picked up a couple of those new Sparviero 1,200-ton hydrofoil corvettes. Those last are pretty much inshore stuff, though. I doubt you'd see them deploy blue-water."

"What about strategic reconnaissance assets?"

"The Argys have one dedicated military reconsat in polar orbit. A Mitsubishi vehicle frame with Thomson-CSF and SOFMA systems packages. It's an opticals platform with some secondary Sigint and Elint capability. It doesn't have realtime downlink capacity. It does have thermographic imaging."

Amanda sat up a little straighter. "Enough to give us trouble?"

Christine gave an apologetic shrug. "I'm not sure. I've got a query in with DIA for further data on the systems package. I'd have to say that a lot would depend on our tactical situation and the transient environmental conditions."

"What else?"

"That's about it. The Brazilians have an Earth resources satellite with some imaging capacity, and then there's the French SPOT commercial system available for charter. They hang pretty much in the plane of the equator, though. Once we get down south a little more, they shouldn't be able to get a line of sight on us."

Amanda nodded. "Very well, then, ladies and gentlemen. I think that should about do it for the housekeeping. We will commence cross decking as soon as we get a stores list in from the *Boone*. Check with Commander Hiro for your individual division assignments. Remember, I intend to be ready for sea by 2400 hours."

She started to push her chair back from the table, then hesitated. After a moment, she spoke again: "This is something of a milestone for the Duke, our first real operational commitment. I suppose I should be making some kind of big rah-rah speech, but I can't think of anything more that really needs to be said. Over these past months, as we've worked her up, I have seen you all give one hundred and ten percent to this ship. I have a hard time imagining any of you doing anything less now. So let's get on with it."

NORFOLK, VIRGINIA
2000 HOURS: MARCH 20, 2006

Beyond the mile-long row of graving docks and piers on the Elisabeth River estuary, within the confines of the Norfolk Naval Shipyard complex, there is a very special building. A four-story structure, only two of which are above ground, it covers roughly the same area as a football field. Several acres of Second World War–vintage warehousing had been demolished to accommodate its construction. Windowless and bunkerlike and flanked on all four sides by reinforced blast-deflection walls, it was built to be able to survive anything up to a near miss with a tactical nuclear weapon.

Its roof is studded with half a dozen different kinds of antenna, and belowground armored land lines radiate outward, direct-linking to other key federal command and communications centers. Its two entryways are protected not only by steel doors and ever-scanning television cameras but by quietly alert Marine sentry teams. This is a measure of the value placed on this particular building and its contents. The only other facilities routinely guarded by the men of the Fleet Marine Reaction Force are the Navy's nuclear weapons depots.

For all of the security measures, for all of its imposing appearance, there is a careful anonymity about this building and its purpose. There is only a single, white-painted acronym beside the main entrance: OPCENT LANTFLEETCO (Operations Center, Atlantic Fleet Command).

The Commander in Chief Atlantic Fleet, Vice Admiral Elliot Mac-
Intyre, stood at the railing of the duty officer's balcony overlooking the Second Fleet's Operations Room. Below him, dimly
illuminated by the cool glow issuing from the monitors of two
dozen different workstations, the flag watch went about their duties in the worry hole. Across from him, at the far end of the room,
the huge main display screen sketched out in luminous lines of red,
blue, and gold the parameters of his zone of responsibility: an area
that extended from the Panama Canal to the Strait of Gibraltar,
from the North Pole to the Antarctic coastline.

Target hacks numbering in the hundreds crawled across the
vast map in a stately, glacial-velocity dance. With a single sweep of
his eyes, MacIntyre could note the position of every major identified surface vessel, submarine, and air- and spacecraft moving
within Second Fleet's hunting ground.

That was what this Center and its twin facility at Pearl Harbor
were all about. They had been born out of the "Flag Crisis" of the
1980s and '90s as the complexity and sophistication of combined
air–surface and sub–surface fleet operations had continued to grow.

Growing in a geometric parallel had been the demand for im-
proved C3I: command, control, communications, and intelligence.
Soon, this demand was outstripping the ability of sea-based systems to cope with the load. Even dedicated command vessels such
as the Mount Whitney class could not provide for the needs of
larger flag staffs, additional communications channels, and more
computer processing power.

The land-based operations centers had been the answer. State-
of-the-art facilities built around two of the most powerful computer suites in government service, they could provide a Fleet
Admiral's staff with every possible fragment of data available about
any potential trouble spot. They could grant a Fleet Admiral a
situational awareness unimaginable ten years before.

Be that as it may, the CINCLANT sometimes rather wistfully wished that he could at least see the ocean from this new "flagship" of his.

"Admiral, Secretary of State Van Lynden is on-line for you, sir. In regards to the Argentine deployment."

"Right, Maggie, I'm coming."

Square-set and craggy, with thick brown hair just turning to gray, MacIntyre moved from the vista of the operations room and followed his Chief of Staff, Captain Margaret Callendar, the few steps back to the communications desk.

The Secretary had elected to use an audiovisual link, and the desk screen was already glowing with the standard Milstar test pattern. MacIntyre authenticated himself to the security system, and a moment later he was looking into the briefing lounge of Harrison Van Lynden's aircraft and into the face of the man himself.

"Hello, Elliot, how are you doing?"

"I can't complain, Harry. How was New Zealand?"

"The scenery was magnificent and the fishing was pathetic. I should have taken those wild stories of yours with a grain of salt."

MacIntyre grinned back at his old Annapolis classmate. "I was always taught that when you got skunked, it was usually the angler's fault, not the fish."

"What the hell does a Navy man know about fishing anyway?" Van Lynden leaned in a little closer to the screen. "Let's get down to it, Elliot. I need the word on our military reaction to Argentina's move into the Antarctic."

"We're moving too. We caught the President's deployment order down here about noon, and we've got the basics sorted out and rolling."

"Can you give me a rundown?"

"No problem. Our primary response at this time is the deployment of a carrier task force into the South Atlantic. The *Theodore Roosevelt* group has been working up around Bermuda, and we've already got her turned around and headed south. She'll rendezvous with an ammunition ship out of Mayport and take on a full set of warloads, then proceed directly to the crisis zone. The British also have a task group deploying into the Falklands. We'll be working in coordination with them."

"Do you have a time on station for me?"

With her usual foresight, Maggie Callendar had had the required data dialed in on a computer pad. Unobtrusively, she slid it across the desktop to MacIntyre.

"We're estimating ten to twelve days, depending upon the sea states en route."

Van Lynden frowned. "I was hoping for a faster response time, Elliot."

"Sorry, Harry, that's the best I can do. The *Eisenhower* is in the middle of a refueling cycle. The *Constellation* came in from a long Mediterranean deployment last week. She's got half her engineering plant torn down and two-thirds of her crew on leave. *Washington*'s in the North Sea on fleet exercises with NATO, damn near as far away as you can get from Argentina without using an icebreaker."

"Couldn't you second a carrier from Sixth Fleet?"

"All we've got in the Med right now is the *Kittyhawk* group. Pulling her out won't give you an appreciably shorter response time. Besides, with those flare-ups along the Algeria-Tunesia border, I don't think this is the time to leave Sixth without a flattop."

"True. What about that new Sea Control Ship of yours? Isn't it operating in the Caribbean?"

"The *Coral Sea*? I considered her, but she's only into the third week of her shakedown cruise. In my judgment, she's just not ready for an operational deployment, especially into a hostile oceanic environment. Given our long-range weather projections, Drake Passage is going to become just about as hostile as it can get very soon.

"That doesn't apply to her escorts, though. She's got two Burke-class destroyers operating with her, the *Clancy* and the *Brown.* I've got them detached and headed across to rendezvous with the Brits' *Ark Royal* group. Our English cousins are bound to yell for Aegis cover sooner or later."

"You're a mind reader, Elliot. I've got the Admiralty's request for a couple of Aegis-equipped escorts right in front of me. Now, what else do you have available?"

"A couple of subs. The *Louisville* is diverting south from the mid-Atlantic, and *Sea Serpent* will haul out of Savannah later this evening. They'll be arriving on station a day or so ahead of the carriers, if that'll be any help."

Three thousand miles away, the Secretary of State frowned and shook his head slightly. "Every little bit helps, but what I really need is somebody out there showing the flag right now. The Argentines seem to be playing hardball, and I'd like to be able to show that we're willing to get out there and pitch right along with them."

"The South Atlantic isn't one of our usual zones of operation, Harry. As a rule, we just don't keep anybody down that way. However, by a rather weird set of circumstances, I can provide you with your flag-shower. We've got a ship practically sitting in the Argentines' front yard."

"Only one?"

"Yeah, but if I had to choose any one vessel out of the fleet to be there, this would be it. She's the *Cunningham,* the lead ship of our new guided-missile destroyer class. She's been designed from the keel up for independent operations, and she carries enough firepower to be a significant presence in the area."

"The *Cunningham?* She's one of the new ghost ships, isn't she?"

"I wouldn't use that 'ghost ship' line in front of any of the stealth crews," MacIntyre replied. "They don't much care for it, but yes, that's her. She'll sortie out of Rio de Janeiro tonight, and proceed into Drake Passage. Time in transit will be about three days."

"They'll be running right down the Argentine coast," Van

Lynden mused. "That should do it. Couldn't be better, in fact. How did this miracle come to pass?"

"As I said, a rather weird set of circumstances. I borrowed her from Seventh Fleet to work up with the *Coral Sea* group in a series of stealth-doctrine exercises. They routed her around the Horn instead of through the Panama Canal specifically to show the flag in South American waters."

"Someone in the E ring has been using a Ouija board."

"Weirder still, she's supposed to be way the hell up in the Caribbean by now, but the ship she was running with suffered an engineering casualty in the South Atlantic. They had to divert into Rio for repairs. Sheer dumb luck, Harry."

"I'll take it whenever I can get it."

Van Lynden looked up and spoke briefly to someone off-screen and out of the audio pickup's focus. As he did so, his image faded and pulsed for a moment before restabilizing. The transmission platform at the far end of the telecommunications link had started to maneuver.

Returning his attention to the video monitor, Van Lynden said, "Elliot, we're starting our descent into Buenos Aires. Thanks for the sitrep, and thanks for coming through for me."

"No problem, Mr. Secretary. I'll have a detailed hard copy of the deployment TOE on the datalink to you shortly. Now, if you can give me another second, I need a question answered."

"Go ahead."

"What's the hostility quotient here? Are we just making faces at each other, or could we end up going to guns with these guys?"

Van Lynden shook his head. "I honestly don't know, Elliot. And that's just one of a hell of a lot of things I don't know about this situation. I can't see Argentina actively seeking war with the United States. On the other hand, this is no fly-by-night land grab. It's becoming obvious that they've been planning this for a long time, and that they are deadly serious about it. They're working to some game plan that, as yet, we can't recognize. I don't know how deeply the other major South American powers are involved. I don't know what the Argentines will do if we back them into a corner. I don't even know specifically what they want yet.

"What I do know is that they have launched a major military operation against an ally of the United States, and that a civilian has been killed as a direct result of that operation. Beyond that, I think I'll leave it to your best judgment."

"Very good, Mr. Secretary. We'll keep you advised."

"I'll do the same, Admiral. Take care."

The screen blanked back to a test pattern.

MacIntyre looked up at his Chief of Staff. "Okay, Maggie. What do you think?"

Captain Callendar crossed her arms and rested one still-shapely hip against the edge of the desk. "Well, sir, I think I know what I'd do in this situation, but then I'm a very staid and conservative person."

"So am I. Get a signal off to all Fleet units committed south. They are to proceed under the assumption that they are deploying into a potential combat zone. All rules of engagement are to be applied accordingly. As of now, this is a fangs-out operation."

RIO DE JANEIRO
2035 HOURS: MARCH 20, 2006

Night had fallen over Rio. From the observation point atop Sugar Loaf Peak, a scattering of tourists and Cariocas looked down upon the starblaze of the city and the darkness of the harbor beyond. Centered in that darkness were the two American warships, glowing blood tone like twin rubies on a black velvet sheet. In the distance could be heard the faint, persistent thudding of rotors.

Closer in, the view was far more hard-edged and prosaic.

Cross-decking operations were in full swing aboard the Duke. SAH-66 Sea Comanche helicopters came bellowing in across the water, cargo pallets slung beneath their sleek, fishlike fuselages like pendulous growths. Coming to a hover over decks illuminated by red-lensed floodlights, they eased their payloads down onto the replenishment hardpoints. Cargo handlers dashed in, braving the hurricane-velocity downdraft to trip the manual shackle releases so the helicopters could lift clear and cycle back for the next run.

From that point on, it was all on the backs of the *Cunningham*'s sailors. Munitions, spare parts, lubricants, rations, ship's stores of all descriptions had to be sorted out, hogged over to cargo elevators and shell hoists, or packed down companionway ladders. She was a big ship with a comparatively small crew, lacking the luxury of a horde of deck apes and warm bodies. All hands were turned to and would stay that way until the job was done. The destroyer was engaged in a cannibalistic fete at the expense of her smaller sister, gorging herself in preparation for what was to come.

"Begging the Lieutenant's pardon, but what in the hell was he thinking of!"

"I was thinking that she was a pretty sharp-looking lady."

"But she's the fuckin' captain!"

"She wasn't wearing her oak leaves on her swimsuit, Gus," Lieutenant Vince Arkady commented mildly to his systems operator, Petty Officer 1st Class Greg "Gus" Grestovitch. The aviator and the AC-1 had been flying together for some time now and were accustomed to speaking the truth.

"Yes, sir. But begging your pardon again, she has to be at least a three-striper. She's gotta be ancient!"

"Haven't you ever heard of the mystique of the older woman?"

"Oh shit . . . sir."

Their helo was down on the *Cunningham*'s landing pad for fuel and a fast round of tactical servicing between cross-decking runs. Accordingly, the two naval aviators were taking the opportunity to report in to their new duty station. In the light of certain recent events, even Arkady was willing to concede that it might be a rather sensitive task.

Going forward, they climbed an interior companionway ladder to the second level of the destroyer's deckhouse. Down a short stretch of passage they found the door that bore the ominous designation, "Captain's Quarters."

"We're dead."

"Shut up, Gus. Here . . ." Arkady shoved his flight helmet into his SO's stomach. "Hang on to that while I go in to do the honors. It'll give you something to do with your hands besides chewing on your fingernails."

Vince approached the gray-panel door, lifted his hand, and hesitated. Damn! Why couldn't that fine lady have been a schoolteacher or a cocktail waitress or a nuclear physicist. Anything on God's green, but his new CO? He took a deep, deliberate breath and knocked.

"Come in," a husky alto replied.

The last hope was gone. He couldn't mistake that voice. Vince flipped the door handle and stepped through briskly. Coming to attention, he fired a precise salute to the figure seated at the desk.

"First Lieutenant Vince Arkady of Heloron sixteen, reporting aboard for duty, ma'am."

Steady, boy, keep those eyes focused on nowhere. Keep that face in neutral. One hint of a grin or a smirk and you are dog meat.

She coped well. Those incredible eyes widened and her jaw dropped slightly, but then she caught herself.

"At ease, Lieutenant," she replied, half rising and returning his salute. "Welcome aboard the Duke. My name . . . my full name is Commander Amanda Lee Garrett."

She said the latter with a slight, wry smile. Suddenly Vince decided that things were going to be okay.

"Pleased to be aboard, Captain," he replied, peeling open the

Velcro flap on the thigh pocket of his flight suit and removing the data disk case he'd been carrying. "Here are my service records, and those of the rest of the aviation detachment. The hard copies are still being processed aboard the *Boone* and should be across shortly."

"Thank you, Lieutenant. Have a seat. I'll be with you in a second."

She dropped back into her chair and snapped the disk case open. It was obvious that any dismay or embarrassment she may have felt over this second encounter was already well behind her. She removed a file—Arkady noted that it was his own—slipped it into the access slot of her workstation terminal, and activated the system with a precise, three-key finger dance.

She read silently and intently for a few minutes, leaving Arkady free to discreetly glance around the small, odd-shaped compartment. There wasn't much to be seen at first, beyond standard government issue. Then he began to note the personal traces Amanda Garrett had overlaid on her surroundings. The faint scent of cologne and baby powder mingling with the neutral, painted-metal warship smell. A thin, golden chain necklace coiled in a compartment of a desk organizer. A flash of unmilitarily bright clothing showing through the partially open door of an overloaded locker. Then there was the picture.

It was a small oil, mounted on the bulkhead behind her desk. Vince was no art expert, but he could recognize that it had been done by the same skilled hand as the larger painting he had seen in the destroyer's wardroom. It showed a white-hulled Cape Cod sloop running free before the wind, a young woman at the tiller. Her features couldn't be made out, but that distinctive red-brown-gold hair was easy to identify.

"That's impressive."

She had said just exactly what he had been thinking, and Vince mentally floundered for a moment until she continued.

"The Sea Comanche hasn't been with the fleet that long. I

didn't think anyone had been able to accumulate four hundred hours in it already."

"I've been with the bird pretty much from the start," Vince replied, rather relieved to find that his new captain wasn't a mind reader on top of everything else. "HS Sixteen was the first squadron to get the SAH-66, and for a while before that, I flew with the operational conversion unit assigned to the type. Some of those hours are in standard Army RAHs, but essentially, there's not much difference."

"None of those hours are off of a Cunningham, though?"

"No, but I've flown the Cunningham-class approach-and-departure program a lot of times on the simulator. I've been checking the positioning points and approach angles just now while we've been cross-decking. They seem to match up pretty well. I don't see any problem."

"How about stealth doctrine?" she inquired.

"I'm current on the standard package and I've done some studying on my own. The Sea Comanche LAMPS and the Cunningham-class destroyer were intended as mated stealth systems, so I figured I'd pull duty on one sooner or later."

"Well, it looks like now will be the time. Are your people aboard yet?"

"No, Captain, they had to pallet up our maintenance kit and our spares. They should be coming across inside the hour."

She nodded approvingly. "Good enough. Commander Hiro should have your billeting assignments ready by then. Now, what kind of an outfit am I inheriting?"

"They're solid, Captain," Arkady replied with certainty. "I've got a good air detachment and a first-rate systems operator."

"Good, I'm glad to hear it. Now, what about you?"

"Me, ma'am?"

"Yes, how good are you at what you do? An accurate personal assessment, please. Excessive modesty is of no more use to me than excessive machismo."

Arkady noticed that Amanda Garrett was one of those rare individuals who look directly at a person when they speak to them. Most people were uncomfortable doing that, they angled their line of vision slightly to one side or the other. She didn't. She fixed those big hazel eyes right on you, alert and calmly demanding of all pertinent information. He decided there and then never to play poker with this woman and never, ever, attempt to lie to her.

"I'm good, Captain. Just about anything you want done with a helicopter, I can do."

"All right." She nodded. "I'm glad to hear it, because as of now you're my new senior air group officer.

"I think you'll find that basically we have a sound outfit here on the Duke as well," she continued. "It might be a little ragged around the edges, primarily because our current pilot is still a bit of a nugget. Nancy is a competent officer, but she desperately needs more shakedown time."

Vince nodded. "I know Ensign Delany from the squadron and I can concur with that. She got a raw deal when she got dumped out on her own like this, first crack out of the box. Do you think there'll be any problem with me bumping her out of the group leader slot?"

"My guess is that you'll be greeted with considerable relief. There shouldn't be any trouble."

She stood up behind her desk. "I suppose that should do it for now. I know that you've got more loads to fly and that you've got your people to get bedded down. We can finish the paper chasing tomorrow."

As Vince got to his feet, Amanda extended her hand out to him. "I say again, Lieutenant Arkady. Welcome aboard the *Cunningham.*"

There was a formality to the way she spoke, like a queen accepting a retainer into her court. Vince almost found himself bowing over her hand instead of shaking it.

"And I say again, ma'am, glad to be aboard."

They exchanged parting salutes. Vince had turned for the door when she called him back.

"Arkady," she said levelly. "There is one other thing. I don't think I really have to say this, but just for the record, what happened on the beach today doesn't cut either of us one millimeter of slack on the decks of this ship."

"I never figured that it would, Captain."

Gus Grestovich straightened from his slouched position against the bulkhead as his pilot exited the Captain's cabin. He looked on as the aviator stood in the passageway for a moment, an odd, thoughtful smile on his face.

"How did it go, Lieutenant?" the SO asked apprehensively.

"Hm ... Oh, it went just fine, Gus. No problem. We're all dialed in."

As they started back down the passageway, Vince threw his arm around his SO's shoulder. "In fact, pal, I think we're gonna like this boat."

Amanda gazed at the door for several seconds after Arkady had left. Eventually, a small snicker escaped her. It grew into a full-fledged gale of laughter that tilted her back into her chair until her head thumped lightly against the bulkhead.

Of all the total improbabilities of the world. No wonder the poor guy had looked as if he'd been struck by lightning this afternoon on the beach. Good Lord! What if Chris hadn't found them when she did and the topic of mutual professions hadn't cropped up until later? Say, as pillow talk at about two in the morning.

The concept was intriguing. She bit her lower lip in amused consideration for a moment, then shrugged and returned to the work at hand.

However, she soon found that she couldn't get back into the mission data scrolled up on her terminal. Her concentration had been broken. There was another task, though, that she had wanted to tend to. Now would be an excellent time to take care of it.

The *Cunningham* had been granted a direct microwave link into the Rio telecommunication net, so it was a matter of simply tapping the fourteen-digit international calling code into her desk communications deck. A quarter of a minute later, an old-style wall phone began to ring in response in the kitchen of a sea-gray ranch house outside of Norfolk, Virginia.

Amanda visualized the lean, angular figure that would come slamming in from the converted garage studio, still sea-tanned and with a white crew cut, likely clad in his usual paint-smeared Levi's and sweatshirt.

Four rings and a curt "Yo!"

"Hi, Dad."

Rear Admiral Wilson Garrett, USN (Ret.), grinned into his end of the circuit. "Hi, Angel. How's it going?"

"It's going fine, Dad. How about you?"

"Stinkin', but what's unusual about that? You still in Rio?"

"For the moment."

"How is it? Rio is one liberty port that I never had the chance to hit."

"It's a beautiful city, Dad. I only had this afternoon to wander around, but I enjoyed myself. How's the latest masterpiece coming?"

"Like I said, stinkin'. I've shaken my sources down for every photo and model of the South Dakota–class battleship they can come up with. I've been sketching all week and I still can't find what I want."

"I wouldn't worry. You'll nail it down sooner or later."

"I had an idea. When you get into Mayport, why don't you see about getting a couple of days' leave? I could drive down and pick you up and we could go over to the *Alabama* memorial in Mobile. We could poke around her for a while and maybe I can find the feel I'm looking for."

"It sounds fine, Dad. The thing is, I won't be getting into Mayport for a while. We've been diverted."

"They're finally putting that gold-plated spit kit of yours to work, huh? What have you got?"

"I can't say."

"CNN just broke a story about things going to hell between Argentina and Great Britain in the Antarctic. Are you getting a piece of that action?"

"Sorry, Dad. I can't say."

"Okay, I get you. Can you at least tell me when you're going to sortie?"

"In a couple of hours. I don't know when I'll get back in anywhere. I . . . well, I just wanted to talk a little."

"I know the feeling, angel. At least the phones work better now. Sometimes back in the good old days it would damn near require an act of God and Congress to get a call in stateside from Bahrain or the PI."

"We're almost in the same time zone, too. Mom and I would sometimes wait up till two or three in the morning for one of your calls to come in. We never minded, though."

"No, you never did."

There was a remembering kind of silence at the other end of the line, then Wils Garrett went on briskly. "Well, Captain, is that special-effects barge ready to go or not?"

"Admiral Daddy Sir, the Duke came off the ways ready."

"Good enough, just don't let those black boxes do any of the thinking that you should be doing. And another thing . . ."

In the passageway outside, the MC-1 speakers blared. "Security detail! Lay topside to the quarterdeck. On the double!" Simultaneously, the watch officer's circuit began to blink urgently on the phone control pad.

"Hang on a second, Dad."

Amanda switched across to the new call. "Captain here."

"Ma'am, we've got a problem with the refueling. Could you please come topside?"

"I'm on my way."

She went back to the land line. "Dad, something's come up. I've got to go."

"Okay. Listen, real fast. Project High Jump, 1946. A study was done on destroyer operations in the Antarctic. It's dated, but it's the only one of its kind ever made. Get a transcript!"

"Will do, Dad. I've got to go. I love you."

"Love you too, angel. Be careful."

Hanging up the phone was one of the more difficult things Amanda had done that day. Like the end of one of those three A.M. phone calls from the Persian Gulf, it was the cutting of a slender thread that had momentarily connected her with someone she held very dear. Only, this time she was the one taking a fast ship into harm's way and her father was the one who had to wait for the next call. She found herself rather urgently wishing that her mother were still alive. Waiting was a little easier when you didn't have to do it alone.

She shook off that train of thought and got to her feet. She had her command to tend to.

Amanda shuddered a little as she stepped out onto the weather deck. She didn't like the blood-colored illumination of the battle lights. She knew that there was a superb reason to use the red-lensed arcs. Red light doesn't destroy night vision. However, there was something eerie and unnatural about standing in that glare and still being able to see the stars.

The Brazilian navy had been exceptionally helpful and efficient about the *Cunningham*'s request for fuel. Just as dusk had settled in, one of their harbor tugs had brought a heavily laden tank barge alongside to receive the destroyer's replenishment hoses. Fueling operations had been going on for some time, but now apparently something had gone extremely wrong.

The deck officer and the gangway watch were peering down over the side and the security team was standing by at the head of the gangway itself. Amanda noted that they had the Velcro retaining tabs on their holsters pulled open.

She took her own quick look over the rail. There was obviously a confrontation of some kind going on aboard the barge. A cluster of blue-coveralled destroyer hands were facing off a smaller group of dungaree-clad Brazilian sailors. At the foot of the gangway, Chief Thomson was apparently having it out with a short, heavyset officer.

"What's going on here, Stewart?"

"I'm not sure, ma'am," the deck officer replied. "There was some problem with the refueling and Commander Thomson yelled up to get you on the double. There was some yelling and shoving going on between our people and the tug crew, so I also called away the security team."

"Right. Stand by, I'll check it out."

Amanda clattered down the gangway to stand beside the engineer.

"Okay, Chief," she demanded quietly, "what's going on?"

"These sons of bitches were trying to sabotage us!" Thomson snarled, as angry as Amanda had ever seen him before. The Brazilian tug skipper replied with a barrage of Portuguese backed by a flurry of gesturing.

"Dammit! You spoke English five minutes ago!" Thomson exploded.

"Stand easy!" Amanda snapped. "What do you mean by sabotage?"

"They tried to slip us a load of contaminated fuel."

"Are you sure?"

"Yes, ma'am. I was checking the fuel quality before we took it inboard, like I always do. You know the kind of . . . stuff you can get in these third world ports. Everything went fine while we were loading from the first four cells, but when I start to test the fifth cell, this . . . gentleman climbs all over me. He tells me to knock it off and keep loading because he's behind sked or something. I tell him to take a hike and I run my check."

"And?"

"Take a look."

The Chief hunkered down beside an open POL testing kit and picked up a half-pint glass beaker. Standing erect again, he took a pencil flash from his shirt pocket and played a beam of white light on the little container.

It should have contained a high-density kerosene compound, optimized for use in marine gas turbine engines and mixed with an explosive-suppression agent. Amanda was surrounded by the waxy, raw petroleum scent of it. It also should have been a clear fluid with a pinkish tinge. The substance in the beaker was murky, except for a half-inch-deep colorless layer at the bottom where fuel and contaminant had started to separate out.

"Water?"

"Uh-huh. The next four cells are all just like it."

Amanda took the beaker from Thomson and turned to confront the Brazilian officer. "I want an explanation for this," she demanded quietly.

The tug captain was taken severely off guard. As the product of a culture where women still deferred to men, he had discounted the arrival of this woman who thought she was a naval officer. Too late, he realized that indeed she was a naval officer.

She faced him now with her back arched, eyes narrowed, and with the air around her practically crackling with controlled anger. The Brazilian fervently wished that he had never heard of this assignment and groped for his rusty English.

"The water in the tanks may have come from damage, Capitão. An accident—"

"Bullshit!" Thomson exploded. "That water isn't leakage."

He gave his testing kit a sideways tap with the toe of his deck shoe. "It's fresh and chlorinated. They were too damn lazy to pump it up out of the bay, so they contaminated those cells with a dockside hose."

Amanda glanced over her shoulder at the engineer. "Chief, could you and your people handle the entire fueling operation?"

"Sure. The valving and fittings are pretty much standardized."

"And is there still usable fuel aboard this barge?"

"Begging your pardon, ma'am. But they likely didn't piss in it all."

"Then bypass the contaminated cells and continue the refueling. Indicate to the Brazilian personnel that they are to stay out of our way until we've finished topping off. Also put the duty security team in the wheelhouse of that tug. Keep them off their radio-telephone until we're done."

"Aye, aye, Captain."

"This is not authorized!" the agitated Brazilian officer said, stepping forward. "There must be investigations! This is not authorized—"

"Silence!"

Amanda continued in an ominously low voice. "Mister, you—and, I presume, the government that you represent—have just tried to disable my ship. I am not pleased about this."

With great deliberation, Amanda poured the contents of the beaker down the front of the Brazilian's uniform.

"An official protest will be filed, but until then, you may inform your superiors of this. You do not ass around in this fashion with the United States Navy. You do not ass around in this fashion with the USS *Cunningham,* and you most definitely do not ass around in this fashion with me!"

RIO DE JANEIRO
2343 HOURS: MARCH 20, 2006

The last transfer flight had been made, the last ton of stores had been secured, and Deck Division was rolling up and striking below the last of the heavy rubber matting used to protect the Plessey

LA-1 RAM tiling that sheathed the destroyer's weather decks. Amanda glanced down at the luminescent hands of her old Pusser's Lady Admiral wristwatch and then up at her exec.

"Eighteen minutes to midnight, Ken. I said we'd take her out by twenty-four hundred hours. Think we can do it?"

"We can give it a good try."

"Then let's make it happen."

As she started topside from the quarterdeck, the word was relayed to all compartments.

"Station sea and anchor details! All hands, make all preparations for getting under way! The officer of the deck is shifting the watch to the bridge!"

"Captain on the bridge."

"Carry on," she said, brushing through the light curtain that covered the entryway.

As with everything else aboard, the big destroyer's bridge was cutting-edge technology, its centerpiece being the helm control station. Like something transplanted out of the cockpit of a state-of-the-art airliner, two comfortable-looking contoured chairs faced a bank of multimode telepanels, the lever-studded pedestal of the lee helm's propulsion controls set between them.

Instead of a set of aircraft joysticks, there was only the single dial of the main helm controller on the console's centerline. Here, too, was a little human sentimentality. The issue black plastic knob had been replaced by a stainless-steel miniature of a sailing ship's spoked wheel.

Forward, there were twin rows of monitor screens, one above the transparent curve of the bridge windscreen, one below. The upper row provided navigational data: low-light television images of the ships surroundings, fore, aft, port, starboard; chart and positioning displays; tactical situation; depth soundings; meteorological information.

The lower tier covered ship's systems: engineering, sensors, damage control, communications, ordnance. Every fragment of data a watch officer might require to make a critical decision was there, instantly accessible, vastly reducing the number of seconds squandered in having to ask for information.

The officer of the deck and the duty bridge crew had already been on-stream for some time, running down their predeparture checklists. From below came the whispering wail of the big Rolls Royce/Westinghouse turbogenerator sets load-testing up to full output.

Amanda lifted herself into the elevated captain's chair to the right of the helm station. Disconnecting her command headset from the little transceiver clipped to her belt, she jacked it directly into the interphone system, then activated the personal telepanel built into the chair arm, calling up her own procedures listing.

"Okay, Lieutenant," she said, "go get yourself a cup of coffee. I'll take her out."

"Aye, aye, ma'am." The OOD lifted his voice slightly. "The Captain has the con."

"All right, ladies and gentlemen. Ready for final departure checklist. Helmsman?"

"Helm control is on the bridge. Rudder has been tested on primary and secondary steering systems. Stabilizers are set to standard. Autopilot is off. Ready to maneuver."

"Lee helm?"

"Engine control is on the bridge. Power Rooms One and Three on-line. Power Room Two on cold-start standby. Primary throttles and propeller controls tested. Hydrojet propulsors to standby mode. Main engineering reports all boards green. Ready to answer bells."

"Interior integrity status?"

"Condition Zebra set in all spaces. All watertight doors and hatches are secure."

"Navigation?"

"SINS and GPU systems checked, cross-referenced, and tracking. Position locks verified. Fathometers tested and verified. Navigational radar on-line. Ship's siren tested . . ."

Overhead, the *Cunningham*'s distinctive twin-tone air horns squalled, sending echoes rippling off of Rio's shoreside mountain peaks.

". . . departure course plotted and on the boards."

Projected from the quartermaster's station at the right rear of the bridge, a computer-generated chart of Rio's outer harbor appeared on one of the brow monitors and on a telepanel in front of the helmsman, displaying water depth, shipping channels, and maritime traffic. A blue ship-position hack for the *Cunningham* appeared a moment later, along with a white course plot that would guide her out to the open sea.

Underlit by the glowing surface of the main chart table, the senior quartermaster of the watch looked up inquiringly.

"Begging your pardon, Captain, but what about the port pilot and sailing clearance from the harbor master?"

"Chief, after that incident with the refueling barge, anyone who thinks I'm letting any of the locals anywhere near the helm of this ship is sadly mistaken. We'll take her out ourselves.

"As for the harbor master, he can figure out we've gone when he looks out tomorrow morning and sees the hole in the water."

Amanda tapped a call number into the interphone and a filtered voice sounded in her headset. "Capstan room, aye?"

"This is the bridge. Ready to heave 'round?"

"Affirmative, bridge. Ready to weigh anchor at your order."

"You may proceed."

Three hundred feet forward, a boatswain's mate peered down the narrow shaft of the anchor well with the aid of a flashlight as the great, gleaming links of chain began to rise out of the churning water. Over the roar and clatter of the capstan, he chanted the traditional litany.

"Showing twenty fathoms at the waterline. . . . Chain is up and down. . . . Anchor is breaking ground. . . . Anchor's aweigh!"

Moments later, the massive, submarine-type mushroom anchor slammed into its recess in the keel.

"Anchor retracted and secured for sea."

"Very well. All engines ahead slow."

"All engines ahead slow." The lee helm echoed, rolling her throttles forward.

The *Cunningham* utilized an integrated electric drive as her primary propulsion system. Her main engines were carried outboard of the hull on the stern quarters in pylon-mounted "propulsor pods," not unlike those of a dirigible airship.

The massive, twin 45,000-horsepower electric motors drew their energy from the power room turbogenerators and spun contrarotating sets of propellers mounted tractor-style at the forward end of the pods. Now, smoothly, those great tribladed screws began to cut water.

"Engines answering ahead slow, ma'am."

"Helm, bring her around to marked departure headings."

"Steering to marked departure headings."

The helmsman delicately spun his controller. Beyond the windscreen, the lights of Rio de Janeiro began a slow drift to port.

"Ship is answering her helm, Captain. Coming about to marked departure headings."

"Very well. Navigation, shift from anchor to running lights."

Amanda looked across the width of the bridge to her exec lounging at his own station. "What time is it, mister?"

She caught the pale flash of Ken Hiro's grin in the screen-glow dimness. "I make it twenty-three, fifty-nine, and thirty-two seconds, ma'am."

"So do I. Close enough for government work."

She buzzed the communications room. "This is the Captain. Get the following off to CINCLANT, please: 'Departing Rio as per schedule. Proceeding as per orders.' "

"Aye, aye, ma'am. Be advised we have just received a blinker message from the *Boone*. Personal, Captain to Captain."

"Read it."

"Good luck and good hunting, you lucky little bitch."

Amanda chuckled. "Send the following to Captain Stevens, personal: 'I take strong exception to your last message. I do not consider five feet seven little.' "

"Will do, ma'am. We're getting a second blinker signal from the Brazilian shore station. They are requesting we respond."

"Ignore it. I've got nothing to say to those gentlemen."

Once clear of the port approaches, the *Cunningham* put on speed and ran to the southeast, opening the range from the coast. Soon, Rio de Janeiro was nothing but a fading sky glow astern. As she began to angle into the deep ocean swells of the South Atlantic, the big warship started a smooth, slow, pitch and roll, like a great hunting cat stretching out into an easy run.

There is a special intimacy about the bridge of a ship at night. Rank can't be made out in the darkness, and the watch seems to draw close within itself. There is a low murmur of conversation, talk about homes, families, and inconsequential things, interspersed with an occasional, quietly given order. Now and again, an outsider will come up from below, "to see how she is doing," and to look out at the star fire burning in a great arc over the bow.

Amanda liked the night watch, and she had remained bridgeside even after returning the con to the officer of the deck. She half-drowsed in the captain's chair, lulled by the feeling of the sea beneath her.

The bitch box broke that tranquillity. "Bridge, this is the CIC. Is the Captain still up there?"

She came erect and keyed in her headset. "Captain here. What's the problem?"

"Check your tactical display, ma'am. We have an airborne radar contact, a slow mover, just coming over our horizon at medium altitude. Range two hundred and ten miles, bearing one eight three degrees."

Amanda leaned back slightly in the chair and her eyes sought the appropriate monitor. "I see him."

"Target is apparently working north in a surface-search pattern. Elint indicates that the target's emission patterns match that of a Dessault-Breguet Atlantique ANG maritime patrol aircraft, the same-standard model used by the Argentine navy."

Amanda did a fast mental calculation. They had cleared Rio two hours ago. A phone call to the Argentine Embassy in Brasília, another one from Brasília south to Argentine Fleet GHQ in Buenos Aires, a fast conference, and then an order issued to their base at Esporu to scramble a search plane. That would be just about right.

"Have they painted us?"

"Negative. Their ECM may be picking up our radar, but they don't have a skin track yet. Do you intend to go full stealth, Captain?"

Amanda allowed herself a long moment of contemplation before replying. "No. In fact, put a blip enhancer on-line. Standard image."

"Standard image it is, ma'am."

The blip enhancer was an electronic-warfare system that amplified the return "echo" of a radar wave, allowing a small target to masquerade as a much larger one. In this case, it would be used to mask the fact that the Duke, even passively, had a vastly reduced radar cross-section. The observers at the far end of the radar beam would see an appropriate return for a conventional warship of the *Cunningham*'s size and tonnage. With equal ease she could have mimicked the return of anything from a cabin cruiser to an aircraft carrier.

Amanda settled deeper into her chair and gazed out into the darkness beyond the repeater screens. She would keep the Duke's bundle of secrets to herself just a little longer.

Benito Mussolini had a method for intimidating those who wished
to confer with him. He had his public office located in a vast, mar-
ble-walled chamber, decorated in an aggressively neo-Romanesque
style. A dignitary forced to trudge across that chilly stonework ex-
panse to stand before Il Duce's desk frequently developed the unnerving feeling of being a sacrificial victim meeting his destiny in
some ancient temple of the gods.

Certain lesser individuals endeavored to get the same effect by
placing their desks on a low platform so that official guests were
forced to look humbly up at them. President Antonio Sparza of Argentina would have none of such crudity.

Instead, his public office in the Casa Rosada had been turned
over to a skilled team of interior decorators, who, by the deft use of
furnishings and decor, had focused the entire room on the presidential desk and the man seated behind it.

Harrison Van Lynden was grateful for this. It would help to remind him not to take his opponent for granted.

As Van Lynden and Steve Rosario were ushered in, Sparza
came to his feet. He was not a tall man. Rather, he was solid and
stocky with few indications of middle-age softness.

Likewise, there was little gray in his thinning black hair and
narrow mustache. There was a hint of ruddiness beneath the olive
of his complexion. This was another warning to take this man very
seriously. In a nation that still prided itself on being the most
"European" of the South American states, a politician who could
overcome the prejudice against "Indio" blood would be most
remarkable.

"Mr. Secretary, it is an honor." Sparza's handshake was dry-palmed and firm, and his English was faultless. "Mr. Rosario, it is a pleasure to see you again. Gentlemen, please be seated."

As Van Lynden settled into the silk damask upholstery of the chair he had been offered, he sensed that the great game was about to be played.

"Thank you, Mr. President. I wish that this first meeting could have taken place under more favorable circumstances."

"As do I, Mr. Secretary," Sparza replied, leaning back into his own chair. "And I shall be the first to admit that your nation has every right to be concerned about certain, rather draconian actions that Argentina has taken recently. I hope that I might be able to explain them to your full satisfaction."

"I hope so as well, Mr. President. However, before we delve into that, there is a formality that I must attend to. Mr. Rosario . . ."

The junior State Department man lifted his briefcase to his knees, unsealed it, and removed a flat, cream-colored envelope bearing the Great Seal of the United States. He passed it to Van Lynden, who in turn handed it to Sparza.

"President Sparza. I must present to you this official note of protest from the President of the United States concerning the following points:

"Point one being the Violation of the Antarctic Treaty of 1961, of which the United States and Argentina are both signatories, by the deployment of armed forces to the Antarctic continent.

"Point two being the forcible occupation of installations belonging to the United Kingdom, an ally of the United States, and the detainment of the installation personnel in violation of international law.

"Point three being the death of a British citizen at the hands of Argentine troops in the process of this occupation."

Sparza didn't bother to open the envelope. Instead, he gazed at Van Lynden with a carefully maintained look of concerned interest.

"Again, I understand. Earlier this morning, I received a similar, somewhat more pointed note from the British Ambassador. Firstly, I would like to assure you that the death of Captain York was a terrible accident. The preliminary report I have received indicates that our people believed his ship to be fully abandoned when they opened fire on it to silence its radio beacon. We accept full responsibility and we promise full reparations to the Captain's family and crew."

Van Lynden kept up his own expression of sober neutrality. An interesting opening. No weaseling and a ready accepting of the blood blame. What did they expect to trade off for it?

"We're pleased to hear that, President Sparza. However, we're also strongly concerned about the fate of the other British citizens involved."

"Understandably so. I am pleased to be able to inform you that the situation is being resolved. All of the British Antarctic Survey personnel displaced when we assumed custodianship of the British bases are being flown out by the Chilean Air Force even as we speak. All are in good health, all have been well-treated. They will be turned over to the British consul in Punta Arenas this afternoon."

"That is very good news, sir. It clears the way for us to get down to the core of the matter." Van Lynden let a carefully metered amount of steel creep into his voice. "Why has Argentina violated the Treaty of 1961 and launched an armed invasion of the Antarctic continent?"

Sparza refused to cross blades. "Please, Mr. Secretary, hear me out. We ask that you consider our actions not as an invasion as much as an act of deliberate civil disobedience on an international scale. A protest against an injustice done to Argentina and to all of the developing nations of the world."

"I don't follow you, sir."

"As you must be aware, we are on the verge of the second International Geophysical Year. A number of the signing states of the Treaty of 1961, including your own, have been campaigning strongly to have Antarctica declared a world park. Their motives are no doubt most admirable, but in their rush to bring about this idealistic dream, the differing opinions of other signatory states have been ignored, if not suppressed."

"States such as Argentina," Van Lynden replied.

"There is certainly no reason to deny our concern over this matter. My nation invests a far larger percentage of its national budget on Antarctic operations than the United States does. The Antarctic is our closest overseas neighbor. It is not surprising that we would be strongly interested in its future."

"Argentina isn't alone in that interest," the Secretary of State replied. "For decades the Antarctic Treaty states have been discussing its use and development. The clear consensus now is that the Antarctic continent be maintained as a natural preserve."

"That is because the majority of the Treaty states consider the Antarctic as a scientific curiosity, something to be put up on a laboratory shelf and studied at their leisure!"

For the first time, Sparza's control loosened just a little. Van Lynden noted the extra intensity in his speech, the spark in his eyes. Now he wasn't just speaking words, he was speaking beliefs.

"Argentina has long planned for the development of the Antarctic. Not a massive, destructive development, but a carefully controlled utilization of the rich natural resources available on the southern continent. It will be a program that will benefit not only Argentina but the international community as a whole, while leaving ninety percent of the Antarctic untouched. That is our dream."

"And you feel this dream justifies a military takeover?"

Sparza made an impatient gesture. "Mr. Secretary, as I have stated, we will be the first to admit that our actions have been drastic. However, it was necessary to halt this impetuous rush by the Treaty states into a well-meant but ill-considered pitfall. I assure you, we desire a rapid solution to this situation and a rapid return to the status quo."

"But?" Van Lynden inquired, looking over the frames of his glasses.

"But we ask for one thing, and one thing only. A true international hearing on the future of Antarctica. Not just among the rather insular Treaty states, but before the world community as a whole. We wish to take this question to the United Nations and put it before the General Assembly for open debate and a vote. That is all. You have my word personally, and the word of the Argentine government."

"That's all?"

"That is all, Mr. Secretary."

Van Lynden gave himself a five count to consider before speaking again. "I can see no overt problem with U.N. involvement. Any final decision, however, will require consultation with my government."

"Of course."

"Now that you've made your 'demonstration,' what about the withdrawal of the Argentine military, and the return of the occupied facilities to British control?"

Sparza smiled benignly. "There is every reason to hope that the British may soon be allowed to resume their scientific operations. We desire not to keep a single combat soldier on Antarctic soil a moment longer then necessary. However, my government feels these matters are best dealt with through United Nations channels. Do not worry, Mr. Secretary. We have no intentions of taking any hostile actions against any United States installation in Antarctica."

"I'm pleased to hear that, President Sparza," Van Lynden replied slowly. "Because I am authorized to inform you that a United States Fleet Marine Force Recon Company is being airlifted in to Palmer Station on the Antarctic Peninsula. They are fully equipped and trained for polar warfare and they have been ordered to resist any armed incursion made against that facility."

Put that in your pipe and smoke it, smart boy.

The Argentine snapped taut, but just for a moment. When he spoke again, his voice was as carefully modulated as ever.

"This action was unnecessary, but understandable. We acknowledge the right of all nations to safeguard their national interests, just as we are doing."

Van Lynden didn't reply beyond levelly meeting Sparza's gaze.

The tautness returned to Sparza's demeanor as he broke the silence. "In a related matter, it has been reported to us that a United States naval vessel is currently off the Argentine coast, apparently en route to the Drake Passage area. I trust that since we are in agreement as to the desirability of a negotiated settlement, your nation is not contemplating some additional, unnecessary escalation."

"President Sparza, ships of the United States Navy routinely deploy to all corners of the world for a wide variety of reasons. As long as those operations are conducted within the confines of international waters, they are solely the concern of the United States and the Commander in Chief of our Armed Forces. However, I'll mention your concerns to my government."

The sword tips had crossed; the opening gambit was over. Sparza glanced down at his wristwatch. "Thank you, Mr. Secretary. That will be greatly appreciated. And now, gentlemen, you must excuse me. Other matters of state require my attention."

On the limousine ride back to the U.S. Embassy, Steve Rosario made the first tentative comment.

"The Argentines appear willing to negotiate. That's hopeful."

"It's easy to be magnanimous when you think you're winning, Steve. Through the major part of that meeting, Sparza was acting like a man with four kings and an ace-high kicker."

"You think so?"

"I know so. He had a pat answer ready for any question we could ask. Hell, I was tempted to look over my shoulder for the TelePrompTer. He's got a game plan going here, and so far, we're wired right into it."

"You don't think they're playing straight with us, then."

Van Lynden shook his head. "No, this whole line about 'international civil disobedience' is bullshit of the rankest kind. It's a justification for a blatant land grab that they hope will play well to the global media. Argentina is a member of the United Nations. They could have brought the Antarctic question up before the General Assembly at any time they desired. Dr. Towers indicated that that's where it would have ended up anyway.

"There is something else going on here, Steve. Another entire level to this situation that we don't comprehend yet."

"Where do we start?"

"I'm not sure. I did notice one thing. Sparza expressed concern about that ship we have off his coast, yet he didn't even mention the fact that half of both the Atlantic Fleet and the Royal Navy are roaring down on him."

The Secretary of State was quietly thoughtful for a moment, then he continued. "If we can figure out why one ship now is more critical than twenty next week . . . Well, we might just have something."

EIGHTY-SEVEN MILES EAST OF PÔRTO ALEGRE
1257 HOURS: MARCH 21, 2006

The topic of the day during lunch had been sports. Dix Beltrain was pushing his usual premise that football now reigned supreme as the true national pastime of the United States. Vince Arkady provided a new rallying point for the wardroom's baseball traditionalists, while Christine Rendino maintained her one-woman radicalist party in favor of ice hockey.

Amanda, who loathed all team sports with equal intensity, kept her peace and listened with amused interest. Arkady was fitting in well with her crew, and that pleased her.

Eventually, she dropped her napkin across her plate and said,

"If I might bring this edition of 'Saturday Afternoon in the Locker Room' to its conclusion, we've got a little business to attend to. Chris, how do we stand on fixing the Argentine submarine force?"

"We have solid fixes on four out of the five," the intel replied, spearing a last forkful of strawberry pie. "Currently, one of the Kockums 471s and one of the old TR 1700s are tied up at the main Argy sub base at Mar del Plata. A second TR was caught running on the surface in the Golfo San Jorge by our last reconsat pass about half an hour ago. Finally, a couple of Brit helos have been working a contact down around the Burwood Banks natural-gas fields all morning. Mount Pleasant Control gives me an eighty percent probability that that's our third TR."

"That leaves the other 471."

"Yeah, the last we have on her is when she submerged off Río de la Plata four days ago. Tactically, she could be anywhere by now."

"That's what I'm afraid of," Amanda replied. She glanced across at her new air group leader. "Arkady, I'd like to use the helos to sanitize an antisubmarine corridor for us right down the Argentine coast. How about it?"

He shrugged. "I can give you a conditional okay. Given the rate of knots we're turning and the fact that those new Swedish boats are quieter than a shark wearing sneakers, it'll require both helos up and operating in tandem most of the time to really scrub things down. That and clearance to drop sonobuoys on spec. Is that how you want it?"

It was, but as one great military mind had phrased it, "The balloon of theory is anchored by the lead weight of logistics." How many hours could she afford to pile onto her aircrews and equipment, and how many days would it be before a supply ship loomed over the horizon?

"Negative. Alternate your flights and stick with your MAD gear and dunking sonar. Drop sonobuoys only to verify potential contacts. Stay in fairly close, right along our course line. I just don't want to run over this guy without knowing about it."

"Aye, aye, Skipper. Do you want us to load torpedoes?"

That question triggered a sudden, intent silence around the table. After a moment, she shook her head. "No, it hasn't come to that yet. We've just got some people around here who have started playing sneaky. I don't intend to leave them any openings."

Arkady gave her a quick nod. "Right. C'mon, Nancy, we've got an operations sked to put together."

The two aviators shoved their chairs back and rose to leave. Already Arkady and his junior officer were moving as a well-coordinated team with no apparent sign of resentment or friction.

The majority of the other officers also trailed out over the next few minutes, returning to their respective duties. Soon, only Amanda and Christine remained at the table, lingering over a last cup of coffee.

Christine watched the last of the others leave, then produced a theatrical sigh. "I always suspected you had pull in high places, but now I know you must have a hot line to the Father, Son, and Holy Ghost."

"What are you talking about, Chris?"

"Our new rotor rider, the one who was conveniently available to transfer aboard back in Rio. My, he is sweet to look upon."

"Chris!" Amanda set her cup down with a clatter. "It's a good thing I know you to be basically irrational. Anyone else making a suggestion like that would get this ship dropped on them!"

The intel produced a mean little-girl snicker. "I knew that would be good for a small explosion. Don't get fussed, boss ma'am. I know you're so straight they could use you as a test standard for pool cues."

"A commanding officer can't even afford jokes about things like that, Lieutenant."

"I know, I know." Rendino leaned forward and cupped her chin in her palm. "But come on, God's honest, you and our Mr. Arkady were busy building a thing back there on that beach."

Amanda couldn't control her half-smile. "Well, we weren't

exactly throwing rocks at each other. However, that is no longer relevant. I didn't know he was Navy, and I most certainly didn't know that he'd be placed under my command. From here on, he's just another of my officers."

Christine muttered something into her hand.

"I didn't catch that?"

"Nothing, ma'am. Just commenting about likely stories I'd heard recently."

Whatever Amanda's response would have been, it was cut off by the overhead speaker. "Captain, contact the CIC, please."

Her command headset was lying beside her plate, and it took only a moment to whip it on. "Captain here."

"We have two fast movers closing on us from the southwest. Contacts identified as Argentine."

"I'm on my way. Chris, stick close."

Amanda was out of her chair and halfway to the hatch before she finished the second sentence.

The *Cunningham*'s Combat Information Center was one level down, below the main deck and almost directly underneath the wardroom. The big compartment was roughly octagonal in shape, with the four subsystems bays extending off from the angled corners. Communications, starboard side forward. Electronic-intelligence gathering, starboard aft. Stealth systems and electronic countermeasures, port aft. Sonar and antisubmarine warfare, port side forward.

Spaced around the remaining bulkheads were other work-stations: engineering, damage control, fire control, and sensor support. Right forward was the "Alpha Screen," the primary display of the destroyer's Aegis II radar system. A softly glowing topaz tele-monitor, eight feet wide by four high, it was etched with a computer graphic representation of the ship's surroundings.

One critical aspect of the "New Age" Navy was that more and more captains were abandoning the bridge, the traditional seat of command authority in a battle situation, in favor of the Combat Information Center. Here, through the media of their ship's sensors, they could better "see" what was actually going on out to a tactically useful range of several hundred miles.

The *Cunningham* had been designed with this in mind. Centered in the compartment was a "command cluster" of specialized workstations. The captain's chair with its bank of multimode flatscreen monitors was located directly alongside the tactical officer's master fire-control console. Just forward of these were the primary operator's station for the Aegis systems and the "battle helm," an abbreviated, one-man combination of the helm and lee helm stations on the bridge.

This latter stemmed from the realization that the speed and ferocity of naval combat was steadily increasing, in some ways resembling aspects of aerial dogfighting. The old system of captain-tells-talker-who-tells-another-talker who-tells-watch-officer-who-tells-helmsman was becoming catastrophically cumbersome. Direct hands-on control of the rudder and engines could save time that could save ships.

Because general quarters hadn't been sounded, none of the command-cluster stations had been manned except for the duty Aegis operator. The captain's chair was facing aft, awaiting her. Amanda dropped into it and gave the sideways flick of her foot that rotated it 180 degrees and locked it forward. One fast look at the big Alpha Screen told the story.

The image displayed wasn't produced by any one system; rather, it was a computer composite, generated by combining the data flow from the sensor systems with oceanographic and geographic map overlays from the Global Positioning Unit and the navigational data banks. At the moment, two bat-shaped air contact hacks, glowing yellow to signify potential hostility, were clearing the northern Argentine coastline. A course-projection plot extended out from them to intersect the *Cunningham*'s line of advance a few miles off the bow.

Christine had split off to confer with her people in the Elint bay. Now she returned to stand at her captain's shoulder.

"What have we got, Lieutenant?"

"Definitely Argy. They've been chattering away with Pedro out there, getting a position fix on us."

"Pedro" was the nickname that had already sprung up in reference to the relay of Argentine Atlantique patrol planes that had been shadowing the Duke through the night. The current incarnation was orbiting now thirty miles off to port.

"What are they?" Amanda inquired.

"Given their performance characteristics and the size of their returns, they're strike fighters. If they're Fuerza Aérea they'll probably be Rafale E's. If they're Aeronaval, they'll be the Panavia Tornadoes."

A slow quarter hour passed as the targets closed the range. Twenty-five miles out, the Duke's Mast Mounted Sighting System was brought on-line. A derivative of the same McDonnell Douglas targeting unit used aboard the U.S. Army's scout helicopter fleet, it consisted of a high-definition television camera with 12× magnification and a FLIR (Forward Looking Infrared) scanner unit, both mounted on a gyrostabilized platform atop the mast array.

Now, under radar guidance, its lenses swiveled around to lock on to the incoming aircraft. Down in the CIC, the image it picked up was windowed into the upper right sidebar of the Alpha Screen.

The two women studied the sleek, delta-winged forms shimmering slightly with air distortion. "Rafales," Christine said finally.

As more detail became apparent, the intelligence officer called up a media copy of *Jane's Battlefield Surveillance Systems* on a secondary screen and referred to it.

"No ordnance apparent and the flight leader is carrying a photoreconnaissance pod on his centerline," she commented. "It looks like a Kodak run."

The Argentine jets turned in toward the *Cunningham* and

boomed overhead, crossing fore to aft at 5,000 feet. Dropping down to 2,000, they swung wide and came in again on the destroyer's flank, their engines smoking slightly at the lower altitude. Then, their mission apparently completed, they climbed away to the southwest, heading for home.

The CIC duty watch relaxed marginally as the Rafales pulled out of engagement range.

"I guess they just wanted a few pictures," Christine said.

"This time," Amanda agreed quietly.

BUENOS AIRES
1925 HOURS: MARCH 21, 2006

SECURITY*SECURITY***SECURITY***SECURITY***
*

ALPHA LOC 5-AUTHENTICATOR*GREEN CHECK VERIFY
***************** MODE TERMINAL-TERMINAL
*

**SECSTATE-BRAZILCONSUL
*

**SECSTATE GO
*

QUERY: WHAT IS SITUATION REPORT ON SABOTAGE ATTEMPT OF USN CUNNINGHAM?
*

MILITARY ATTACHE HAS MET WITH BRAZILIAN ASSIST. SEC. NAV.
  POINT ONE: DENIES ANY ATTEMPT AT SABOTAGE. BRAZILNAV
      REPORT CLAIMS INCIDENT DUE TO ACCIDENTAL
      FUEL CONTAMINATION DURING DOCKSIDE
      LOADING.
*

POINT TWO: PROTEST FILED OVER UNSCHEDULED DEPARTURE
OF USN CUNNINGHAM. VIOLATION OF PORT
PROCEDURES CITED. REQUEST INSTRUCTIONS.

*

DISREGARD PROTEST.
REQUEST UPDATE ON BRAZILGOV ATTITUDES RE. ARGENTINE
ACTIONS IN ANTARCTIC?

*

ONLY AVAILABLE OUTPUT AS PER MINISTRY OF INFO PRESS
RELEASE CALLING FOR "REASONABLE ATTITUDES AND NEGO-
TIATIONS."
BRAZILPRES, BRAZILVICEPRES, BRAZIL MINISTER OF STATE UN-
AVAILABLE FOR CONSULTATION FOR PAST 24 HOURS.
CIA STATION CHIEF REPORTS AS FOLLOWS:
POINT ONE: SPECIAL ARGENTINE MINISTRY OF STATE LIAISON
GROUP HAS BEEN ON SITE IN BRASILIA FOR PAST
72–96 HOURS.
POINT TWO: BRAZILPRES, BRAZIL MINISTER OF STATE HAVE
BEEN IN CONSULTATION WITH SAME.
POINT THREE: EXTENSIVE MOVEMENT OF DIPLOMATIC COURIERS
BETWEEN BRASILIA AND MAJOR OVERSEAS
EMBASSIES.
QUERY: WHAT IS GOING ON, MR. SECRETARY?

*

*

*

WE STILL AREN'T SURE.

Vince Arkady double-timed up the 'tween-decks ladder to Air
One, the *Cunningham*'s flight-control center. A small triangular
compartment located right aft in the trailing end of the superstructure, it was the only compartment on the ship other than the bridge
with a direct exterior view, a vee of stealthed Plexiglas looking out
over the helipad. In addition to the windscreen, it contained a pair
of repeater terminals, a small communications console, and, at the
moment, Chief Petty Officer Frank Muller, Retainer Zero Two's
crew chief and the Air Division's senior NCO.

"What do we have, Frank?"

Muller passed his boss a headset as he replied. "Zero Two's just
declared an in-flight emergency."

"Where is she?"

"About fifteen miles south-southwest and inbound."

The Aegis system's tactical display had been dialed up on one
of the repeaters and Zero Two's beacon hack could be seen, warning flagged in glowing red.

"Right, what's she on?" Arkady asked, settling on the
earphones.

"Tac Three."

As Arkady keyed in to the ship-to-air circuit, he shot a quick
look at the sea and weather states. The Duke was running under a
mixture of blue sky and broken cumulus cloud. However, she was
also running through a sharp, choppy swell with plenty of white-
caps showing. The wind sock on its snub mast beside the helipad
was whipping in an ominously suggestive manner. It was not a
good day to try swimming away from a sinking helicopter.

"Gray Lady to Retainer Zero Two, do you copy?"

"Affirmative, Gray Lady, I read you."

Beyond the carrier hiss in his earphones, Ensign Nancy Delany's voice was tense but still level.

"Hi, Nancy. This is Vince Arkady. What's happening out there?"

"I'm not sure, sir. I'm getting a power surge and fade real bad. I can't maintain a constant engine RPM."

"What do your diagnostics say?"

"I've been getting a green board except for a fuel-flow variance. I've tried switching back and forth between the primary and backup fuel-feed pumps and between the interior and exterior tankage. I've also tried some fuel transferrals and I still can't isolate the problem, or get it to smooth out."

Vince glanced over at Muller. He'd worked with the man for less than two days, but he had already judged that the Chief knew his business. Currently, the burly, balding CPO was hunched over the other terminal, intently studying the stream of telemetry flowing in from Zero Two's systems.

"Was she running on her internal fuel or the drop tank when she started to pack up?" he inquired thoughtfully.

"I'll find out." Vince keyed his microphone again. "Ah, Retainer Zero Two, were you on internal or the drop tank when the problem started?"

"Gray Lady, I was on the drop tank. I'm sorry, sir, but she's lost power so badly a couple of times we've almost gone in the water. Nothing seems to help, so I figured I'd better bring her in."

"We concur one hundred percent. Bring her home, Retainer."

Vince turned back to Muller. "What do you think?"

"I think she's got air contamination in the fuel system, probably through a fault in the hardpoint connector. You get a slug of air in there, get some bubbles under a filter, and you can get surge and fade like this."

"That ain't supposed to happen with the Comanche anymore, Chief."

"There's a lot of stuff that ain't supposed to happen anymore, Lieutenant, but it still does. They only got a partial fix on that problem. It still crops up every once in a while. Just rare enough so that the diagnostic program for it was deleted from the onboard software. These kids aren't being taught what to look for.

"As it is, Ensign Delany went right along and followed all of the proper procedures for a standard feed-flow problem and managed to involve the whole damn fuel system instead of just the drop tank feeds."

"What can we do about it?" Arkady inquired.

"Not a whole hell of a lot beyond getting her on the deck as fast as we can. In the next thirty seconds the bubbles could work out of the system and she could be right as rain, or she could have a total blockage and fall right out of the sky. I'd give you even money on it going either way."

"Okay, let's bring her straight down."

Arkady went back on the circuit. "Retainer Zero Two, we've got your problem spotted. Just bring her on in. We'll sort it out once you're down on the deck."

As he talked, Vince called up Zero Two's stores list on his terminal. It was the package he had authorized, the suspect 110-gallon drop tank, an SQR/A1 dunking sonar pod, and a half-load of sonobuoys.

"Hey, Nancy. Do you still have your stores onboard?"

"Yes, sir."

"Well, get rid of 'em. Lighten yourself up."

"That's okay, Lieutenant. I think I can bring them home."

"Jettison your stores, Ensign. That's an order. We can buy you more toys later. That's what we keep the taxpayers around for."

"Damn kid's trying to conscientious herself to death," Arkady muttered as he dialed up the bridge. "I guess we'd better let the boss know what's going on."

"Bridge, aye," Amanda Garrett answered the call herself a moment later.

"Captain, this is Arkady back in Air One. Retainer Zero Two is inbound with a fuel-feed problem. She'll be in position to recover in about five minutes. I request we go to emergency flight quarters."

"I concur," she replied coolly. "We've also been monitoring the situation up here. I'll be putting the ship across the wind at this time and we'll be bringing the stabilizers up full.

"Also be advised we've got a flight of Argentine jets moving in on us. We're not sure what they want, but they'll be overhead about the time we'll be making recovery."

"Joy for fucking ever unconfined."

"I'll worry about the Argentines. You take care of our helo. If I can assist you by maneuvering, let me know."

Amanda's voice became a little less professional and a little more concerned. "Do you think you can get them home, Arkady?"

"Talk to me again in about five minutes, Skipper, and I'll have an answer for you."

"Flight quarters! Flight quarters!" the MC-1 circuit thundered. "Aviation Fuel Repair team and Crash and Salvage teams lay to on the double! All compartments set Condition Zebra!" All to a background of honking alarm klaxons and slamming watertight doors.

Down on the helipad, landing lights began to flash rhythmically at the four corners of the main elevator. Around the outer perimeter, containment barriers rose up out of their belowdeck slots and flared open like the petals of a nylon strap and aluminum flower. Aviation and damage-control personnel, many swaddled in silvery firefighting rig, stood by, watching for the first sign of their troubled charge.

In Air One, Chief Muller pointed and said, "There she is. I got her strobe. She's swinging out wide to the west."

Arkady dumped the Alpha Screen image on his workstation and called up the MMS system. Laying one of the cameras on the approaching helo with the terminal joystick, he engaged the auto-track and zoomed in on the little aircraft.

"Damn, she's in worse shape than I figured."

He could see the power fades hitting the aircraft every few seconds. The Sea Comanche would sag down out of level flight as it lost turbine RPMs and Delany would firewall her throttles to stay airborne. Then the surge would hit, gray smoke would smear out of the exhausts, and the helicopter would buck and lunge forward and upward.

Muller shook his head. "Lieutenant, if she drops off like that comin' over the rail . . ."

"Don't draw me pictures, Chief. The thing is, what the hell else are we going to do? Let's just apply the KISS protocols here and bring her straight on in."

Arkady keyed his mike. "Retainer Zero Two, we have you visually. The ship is thirty degrees across the wind and we are showing twenty-eight to thirty knots over the deck. You are cleared for a standard quartering approach. Recovery teams are standing by. Take your time, Nance. If you go bump, we'll have a pillow under you."

"No sweat, sir. I got a handle on it."

Could have fooled me from the sound of your voice, kid, Arkady replied silently.

She came in high, not daring to get too close to the sea too soon, trying to find a pattern or rhythm to the power fades, seeking the few moments of full control necessary for a landing pass.

She went into a station-keeping hover fifty yards off the starboard quarter. The landing-gear bay doors flipped open in the Sea Comanche's sleek belly and its wheels lowered. Slowly she started to angle in toward the helipad.

A voice blared in Arkady's earphones. "CIC to Air One! Descending traffic turning in on us! Range closing fast! Oh, Jesus! Watch it!"

In Air One, there was a blur of motion to starboard, literally at eye level. Arkady was able to snap his head around fast enough to catch and mind-freeze a single clear image: a pair of dark blue Panavia Tornadoes, each bearing an azure and white roundel and the word ARMADA on its flank. Both strike fighters had their wings swept full back and had shock-wave-studded flame spewing from their afterburners. The point-blank thunderclap of their passage hit with the impact of a hard-swung two-by-four across the chest.

Riding the concussion of the first brace of Tornadoes, a second pair blasted past to port. Pulling up into the near vertical, all four aircraft climbed out of sight in mere seconds.

If the Argentine flat-hatting run had startled Arkady and Muller, it had nearly killed Nancy Delany and her systems operator. Not only had her concentration been shattered but Retainer Zero Two had been hammered by converging streams of jet wash.

The helo staggered and torqued almost a full 360 degrees around its rotor mast. A power fade hit and the pilot wildly tried to compensate. She overpitched and the aircraft plunged out of the sky.

At the last possible instant, the fade cleared and the turbines shrieked back up to flight power. The Sea Comanche pulled out, so low that one of the landing-gear trucks ripped through a wave top.

"Who were those guys? Just damn it! Who were those guys?"

"Take it easy, Nancy. They're just some of the local boys ass-ing around."

"What do they think they're doing! Damn it, *Cunningham,* they could have killed us!"

"Settle down, Ensign! Retainer Zero Two, climb out and set up for another approach. We'll take care of these clowns. You're gonna be okay, babe."

Arkady turned the handling of the helicopter over to Chief Muller and started scanning the UHF surface-to-air frequencies for the one being guarded by the Aeronaval fighters. Someone down in the CIC had beaten him to the punch, and he dialed into their outgoing transmission.

"... SS *Cunningham.* You are interfering with an emergency recovery operation. Clear our airspace! I repeat, clear our airspace!"

The voice that replied spoke a fluent, almost accent-free English. It also spoke with a lightly restrained arrogance.

"United States Ship *Cunningham,* this is Tigre flight leader. It is necessary to advise you that you are near the territorial waters of Argentina and the Malvinas. These are our sea and air spaces, Norteno."

"Tigre flight lead, this is the USS *Cunningham.* We are currently operating in international waters. We say again, we have an in-flight emergency. Please stay clear of our flight pattern while we recover our aircraft."

"*Cunningham,* this is Tigre flight leader. You do not understand." The Argentine pilot sounded as if he was enjoying himself. "As you are operating near our territory, it is necessary for us to investigate all such intrusions and all such unusual events, such as your emergency. We shall proceed to do so."

Muller was bending over a call-up of the Alpha display.

"They're pitching in again ... descending. Aw, man! They're going right for Zero Two!"

"I don't believe this!" Vince snarled, cutting back to the Duke's operating frequency. "Retainer Zero Two, you got fast movers coming in on you again. Watch it!"

There wasn't time for more.

The Argentine Tornadoes flashed into view, converging on the crippled Sea Comanche. Viciously, they whipsawed it with a series of near-supersonic close-range flybys. It was a deliberate effort to blast the helo out of the sky with the shock waves of their passage.

Arkady forgot to breathe as the wildly bucking helicopter fought to survive again, and won.

"Retainer Zero Two, you guys okay up there?"

"Okay for now," the faint reply came back. "But one more like that, and we're in the water."

Another readily identifiable voice cut into the radio band. "Ah, *Cunningham*. I believe I have identified your problem. Inferior aircraft flown by inferior pilots. You should tell your young ladies to stop playing at being naval aviators, *Cunningham*."

Arkady nearly broke his thumb on the transmitter key. "Don't talk about inferiority, asshole. You've just earned yourself a lesson in it!"

He switched over to the ship's interphone. "Hangar bay! Get Zero One on the elevator with a full air-to-air ordnance load. Sidewinders and gun pods. Expedite!"

"Belay that order!" Amanda Garrett's voice cut in sharply. "Lieutenant Arkady, what are your intentions?"

"I'm launching, and I'm going to escort my pilot in. Right over the top of those macho bastards, if I have to!"

"Negative. Getting Delany caught in the middle of a dogfight isn't going to help matters any. Have her drop back, and go into a holding pattern off to starboard, until we get this sorted out."

"Captain . . ."

"I'll take care of it, Lieutenant." The tone of her voice didn't brook any protest.

"Aye, aye, ma'am." Arkady took a slow, deliberate breath and began to relay her instructions up to the helo.

The bridge had patched in to the ground-to-air frequencies and Amanda came on-line a few moments later.

"Tigre flight leader, this is Commander Amanda Lee Garrett of the United States Navy, currently commanding the USS *Cunningham*. To whom am I speaking, please?"

The cool dignity of her words took the Argentines by surprise. There were several seconds of dead air before the reply came in.

"This is Capitán de Frigata Alfredo Cristobal of the Aeronaval Argentina, commander of the First Naval Fighter and Attack *Escuadrilla*."

"Captain Cristobal, this situation is unnecessary. It is placing the lives of two of my crew in jeopardy, and can only serve to further inflame the tensions existing between your nation and mine. As one officer to another, I respectfully request that you please withdraw and allow us to recover our aircraft."

For a second, Vince thought that she had pulled it off, that an appeal to simple, bald-faced sanity might end it. Maybe it would have, too, if Capitán Alfredo Cristobal hadn't been born with an apparent critical imbalance between brains and bullshit.

"Of course, Captain Garrett." The jocular arrogance crept back into the Argentine's voice. "But first, I must insist on one more flyby, to salute the lovely ladies of the Norteamericano Navy."

"As you wish." Amanda Garrett's voice was no longer cool, it was cold. Vince Arkady had a sudden mental image of a pair of hazel eyes narrowing ominously.

"Here they come again," Chief Muller reported. "This time it looks like they're going to scrape the paint off the top hamper."

Suddenly, the deck speakers came on-line again. "Alert on deck! Rig for live-fire ordnance testing. Clear the RBOC launchers!"

Arkady and Muller exchanged puzzled glances as the kerosene-fired thunder of the approaching aircraft began to grow.

On the foredeck and the forward facing of the superstructure, hatches swung open, revealing clusters of launcher muzzles. With a rippling roar that eclipsed the sound of the jets, the RBOC defense system salvoed a full spread of chaff rockets. The sky over the destroyer was suddenly filled with interlocking airbursts of smoke and metal foil, and the Argentine fighters found themselves driving right into the heart of it.

The Aeronaval strike fighters scattered like a covey of startled quail, pulling up and pitching out wildly to evade. Tigre lead didn't make it. Captain Cristobal's Tornado ripped through the edge of the cloud, and as it did so, a partially dispersed chaff packet was ingested by its starboard air intake. A fragment of a second later, several million dollars' worth of Turbo Union turbofan engine began to disintegrate.

Arkady caught the distinctive thud of a jet power-plant shedding a flame bucket. He was watching with considerable interest as the plane came crashing out of the chaff cloud, smoke streaming from the right engine exhaust.

Grant him his due, Cristobal was a superb airman; anyone less would have lost it totally. As it was, his Tornado did a complete slow roll at wave-top height before he could get the wings motored forward and the right side of the aircraft shut down.

Finally, he got his crippled plane leveled and coaxed into a slow climb. When he came back on-band, his arrogance was gone. He had cycled through shock and fear, and now was running on raw rage.

"Puta nortena! We will not let you get away with this! The Tierra San Martín belongs to Argentina! The Southern Ocean belongs to us! We will send you to hell!"

Amanda Garrett failed to conceal the contempt in her voice. "If the performance you put on out here today is an example of the professionalism of your services, I wish you luck. This is the *Cunningham,* over and out."

"Now, there goes a man," Arkady commented as the damaged aircraft limped off to the east, "who ain't going to be able to get it up for a month."

"Air One, this is the bridge." His captain's now more amiable voice filled his headset. "The Alpha Screen indicates all Argentine aircraft now departing the area. You may resume recovery operations as soon as we clear the chaff cloud."

"Aye, aye, Captain. Will do. By the way, Air One requests permission to applaud."

A soft chuckle echoed back over the comm. "Permission denied, Air One. Let's just get our sick child back aboard."

They ran the Strait of Malvinas between the Falklands and the Argentine mainland that evening, with the con in CIC and the ship cleared for action.

Possibly it was an unnecessary precaution. Beyond "Pedro" circling at a respectful distance, that stretch of sea miles had proved to be empty. The Duke's sensors reacted only to the vigilant sweeping of search radars far to east and west.

It was near midnight before they passed back into the open waters of the South Atlantic. Running fast over a mild sea, the *Cunningham* held her course for the approaches to Drake Passage.

After standing the ship down from general quarters, Amanda returned the watch to the duty officer, then headed for her cabin. By rights, she knew that she should be feeling tired. However, the events of the day had built up a massive backlog of nervous energy within her. She had to move before she could rest.

She changed into her old brown leotard and ponytailed her hair with a band. Slipping on a beach jacket, she picked up her portable CD player and disk case and padded forward to the ship's gymnasium.

This was far from her first late-night visit to the gym. She favored this hour because she almost always had the compartment to herself. So she was startled to find the place already occupied as she came through the hatchway.

"What are you doing here?" she blurted out before she could catch herself.

"Pretty much the same as you, Captain," Arkady answered amiably. Clad in those same denim trunks and a T-shirt, he was just straightening up from setting the load lever on one of the tread-mills. "Between one thing and another, this is the first chance I've had to get down here for a workout since I came aboard. If you'd like some privacy, I can come back another time?"

"Oh, no, go ahead."

Damn, damn, damn! She never danced in front of anyone any-more. On the other hand, she couldn't just turn around and walk out after lugging all of this paraphernalia down here.

When she had first come aboard the Duke, she had ordered cer-tain modifications made to the gymnasium. All of the exercise and weight machines had been moved over against one bulkhead, leav-ing the other clear for the installation of a ballet bar and a full-length dojo mat. There had been a little grumbling over that, but then rank has some privileges.

She selected a disk that contained one of the mixed programs she had chosen and edited herself and fed it into the player. Then, feeling shy for the first time in years, she dropped her robe to the deck, took a deep breath, and started her bar exercises. By the time the "Young Prince and Princess" theme from *Scheherazade* had run its course, she had lost herself to the music and movement and had forgotten the steady whirring of the treadmill at the other side of the compartment.

The program changed from Rimsky-Korsakov to Richard Rodgers and she smoothly translated the sweeping tango of "Be-neath the Southern Cross" into classical ballet. The next selection was more difficult, an involved, light electronic jazz piece by Ryuichi Sakamoto. She shifted from ballet to modern improvisa-tional and began working her way through it. Twice she was dissat-isfied and twice she replayed that segment of the disk, modifying the patterns she drew with her body until they flowed properly with the feel of the orchestration.

The last cut was another stylistic shift, Belinda Carlisle's old rock hit "Valentine." Amanda accepted the challenge and let herself take on the driving, elemental edge of the music, dancing the song out to final release and freedom.

The music ended and Amanda dropped to her knees, panting softly and coming back into herself.

"You're very good," Arkady said. He was sitting on the end of one of the exercise tables, regarding her intently.

"Not really," she replied, suddenly finding that she didn't feel quite as self-conscious as she thought she would. "I started ballet when I was eight and modern dance when I was in junior high. Ever since the Academy, though, I've just fooled around with it. It's more fun than doing push-ups."

"I guess you know more about it than I do, but it sure seems to me like you know what you're doing."

"Thank you."

"By the way, while we're on the subject of talents, the signature on the big painting in the wardroom reads 'Garrett.' Is that another one of yours, Captain?"

"I can't draw a straight line. My father did that. It was a gift from him when I received command of the *Cunningham.*"

"He knows what he's doing too. Ex-Navy?"

She nodded. "Yes, that was his Charley Adams in the picture. We're Navy from way back."

"At least four generations' worth, according to that picture."

"Farther than that. Dad was just recounting the destroyer branch of the family. What about the Arkadys?"

"Hmm, seagoing yes, Navy no. Back when the fishing fleets were a big deal in San Francisco and Monterey, the Arkadys were a big deal in the fishing fleets. Other than an uncle of mine whose claim to fame was being busted from petty officer first to seaman more often than anyone else in fleet history, I'm the first of the clan in living memory to join up."

"You made a good choice. You've run up a very impressive service record." Amanda rested her back against the bulkhead and tucked her feet under her. "There is one thing I'm curious about, though. According to your file, you started out in fixed-wing aviation before going to helicopters. You were near the top of your class when you transferred. Why? This isn't anything official. You don't have to talk about it if you'd rather not."

Arkady shrugged. "No big deal. I did start out intending to be a fighter jock and I was doing pretty good at it, right up to when I had to try my first carrier landing. You ever make one?"

"Once, in a C-2 COD transport. There weren't any windows in the cargo bay, so you couldn't really see anything. I just remember a long period of being scared silly followed by an almighty crash. My first priority after disembarking was a dry pair of panties."

"Seeing what's going on doesn't help matters much. When I tried it, it was in a T-45 out of Jacksonville with an instructor in the backseat, and I was shooting my first trap on the old *Kennedy.* That was a real interesting experiment in reverse optical physics. The closer you got to the flight deck, the smaller it looked."

Arkady angled his arms behind him and leaned back against the tabletop. "An actual carrier landing is like nothing else in the world. You can do all of the dry-land training, all of the simulator hours you want, but until you are actually out there, in the slot, riding the meatball down to the deck, you don't know what it's all about.

"The old-timers tried to explain it to us. How you have to put everything you have into getting from Point A, approach, to Point B, touchdown. Total concentration, zero error, no room for anything but absolute perfection."

Arkady chuckled. "I didn't do too bad. I nailed both of my traps first time around. No problem with my catapult launches, either. Then we flew back to Jacksonville, and that night I turned in my request for transfer to helo training."

"Why?"

"That's what my senior instructor kept asking. He also kept trying to tell me that everyone was a little scared during their first carrier op.

"I kept trying to tell him that fear had nothing to do with it. I've never been scared of, or in, any aircraft in my life. It was a matter of knowing myself and my own capabilities. Once I'd actually shot a carrier landing, I realized that I'd never be able to maintain the necessary mental focus to fly fixed-wing off of a flattop day in and day out.

"I'd done it. I could do it again once, twice, a couple of hundred times. The thing is, I knew that sooner or later I'd let my concentration slip for that one-tenth of a second necessary to kill myself. Probably I'd take some other guys and a big chunk of ship with me. No way. I got out while the getting was good."

"Did you find helicopters an easier go?" Amanda asked.

"It's not easier. Rotor-wing aviation, especially off of a small-surface platform, is just about as hairy a way to make a living as you can find. It's just that there are a different set of operating parameters. Like the Brit Harrier pilots say, 'It's easier to stop the airplane and land on the ship than it is to land on the ship and then stop the airplane.' "

"This time, I won't argue the point with you. It takes two Tylenol washed down with a stiff brandy and soda just to get me on the D.C.-to-Norfolk shuttle. At any rate, that was a tough call to have to make."

"Hell, it was just common sense."

"I find that 'common sense' is a rather rare commodity these days."

Amanda used the bar to pull herself to her feet, took a step away from the bulkhead, and not quite fell flat on her face. A muscle had knotted up in her right leg and was screaming in white-hot agony. She clung to the bar, trying to maintain her balance. Arkady was up in a second, steadying her with a hand on her shoulder.

"Hey, are you okay?"

"Just a cramp. Ow . . . ouch, dammit that hurts!"

"You cooled off too fast and you're locking up," Arkady said, guiding her down to the end of the exercise table. "Lay back and I'll work it out for you."

"No, it'll be okay. I just have to stand on it."

"If your leg doesn't fall off first. Captain, ma'am, will you please just *lie down!*"

He gave her a gentle push on the shoulder while lifting her legs. Amanda overbalanced and thumped back on the soft foam padding. Arkady swiftly positioned the heel of her cramp-stricken limb against his shoulder.

"Okay now, push with your leg. Not hard, just a steady pressure."

Arkady encircled her thigh about midway down with the thumb and forefinger of each hand. Then, slowly and deliberately, he drew upward, coming back over her knee and then down to the ankle. Returning his hands to their starting place, he repeated the process.

Amanda wasn't exactly certain how she found herself in this position, and she wasn't exactly sure if it was a proper one for her to be in. On the other hand, in an amazingly short time the knotting muscles began to relax and the burning pain subsided.

"That's better." She sighed. "Where in the world did you learn how to do that?"

"Well, I could say that my old high-school football coach taught me, but actually it was this Japanese girl I was going with when I was stationed at Yokosuka. She was a professional masseuse and she knew how to manipulate muscles that medical science hasn't even discovered yet. Okay, switch sides."

Arkady released her right foot and brought her left up to his shoulder.

"Pardon me, Lieutenant, but I don't have a cramp in that one."

"Preventive maintenance."

"Oh."

As he set to work, he said, "Now can I ask one, Captain?"

"One what?" The strong and sure movement of his hands was making it a little difficult to concentrate.

"A question?"

"Sure, go ahead."

"I was looking through the latest issue of *Naval Institute Proceedings* down in the wardroom, and in the letters section I noticed that a couple of carrier officers were taking your name in vain.

"They seemed to be taking strong exception to an article you'd written. I couldn't find the number they were talking about, though, and I was just wondering what you'd said to kick their puppy so hard."

"Oh, that." Amanda shrugged as best she could from her horizontal position. "It was an article relating to a doctrine paper that I did for the Naval War College. Basically, I was saying that the United States can no longer depend on the aircraft carrier as its first line of overseas crisis intervention."

"Is that all? My, you do enjoy spitting in other people's holy water."

"Those two airedales missed the point entirely. I was talking in economic and operational terms, not in tactical effectiveness. The classic flattop is still a very viable weapons system, although this may be the last generation that this will be true. The problem is that there just aren't enough of them to go around anymore.

"Currently, the United States maintains a ten-carrier active-duty fleet. That's just barely enough to regularly forward-deploy one task force each into the Atlantic, western Pacific, and Mediterranean. The new Sea Control Ships we're building will help, but that'll be offset by the decommissioning of the *Enterprise* and the last of the oil burners. We're losing the ability to cover all of the potential global trouble spots with a fast-reaction carrier force."

"So, what's the fix?"

"What I call 'raider deployment.' We use stealth ships like the *Cunningham,* operating alone or in small, widely dispersed task groups. They'll cover the forward-deployment zones while the carriers are held back in reserve in a centralized oceanic area.

"For example, say with the Seventh Fleet. The raiders would deploy out and cover the current hot spots—the Persian Gulf, the Maldives, and the China coast. The carrier would park itself somewhere—say, off the north coast of Australia. If a flare-up occurs, the raider vessel on station will hold the line until the carrier can move up in support."

Arkady released her leg. "Sounds interesting, but what if the natives get really restless? Given the firepower available to third world states these days, one ship wouldn't have much of a chance. Flip."

Distracted by their developing conversation, Amanda obediently rolled over onto her stomach. "Not necessarily. Up until the Second World War, a fast ship operating alone and trying not to be found was a hellishly hard thing to do anything about. Oh, Lord, that feels good!"

Arkady was firmly running the heels of his hands up either side of her spine from the small of her back to her shoulder blades. Amanda abandoned her last lingering concerns about propriety and considered learning how to purr.

"I guess that ended when radar and long-range search aircraft came along?" he commented.

"Hmm? Oh, yes, and later recon satellites were developed and made things even worse. If they can see you they can hit you, and if they can hit you they can kill you. The surface Navy became locked into a big-fleet mentality. You assumed that eventually you would be spotted, and that the only way to survive was by the massed area defense of a big-ship formation, backed by a carrier air group."

"Sounds reasonable to me."

"Not necessarily." Amanda semi-stretched and tucked her hands under her chin. "A single ship that can strike, disappear, and then strike again at will can raise havoc out of all proportion to its size. Read your history; Sir Francis Drake and the *Golden Hind* shattered the Spanish Imperial economy with their raids on South America. During the American Revolution, England was thrown into a panic by the presence of a single U.S. sloop-of-war off of their coasts. And right in these waters during the Second World

War, the German pocket-battleship *Graf Spee* kept an entire Allied fleet pinned down for months hunting for her.

"The key to the whole thing is stealth technology, and the ability it gives you to escape and evade long-range detection. If the seas become a place you can hide in again, then, as the saying goes, the solitary raider can once more kick ass and take names."

"That sounds sort of like sub doctrine."

"True. The submarine was the first stealth warship. The thing is that undersea craft have inherent problems with their ability to collect and react to data outside of their primary operating environment. Their main sensors are effective only under water. The surface ship has the edge because it can fully interact with all three of the maritime combat environments: air, surface, and subsurface."

"Interesting," Arkady commented. "It looks like your doctrine is about to get a field test with this Argentine job."

Amanda abruptly rolled over onto her side, a thoughtful expression coming to her face. "You know," she said slowly, "it hadn't struck me before, but you're absolutely right. That's funny."

"Not really," Arkady replied. "It's like me and that first carrier landing. Things can look a whole lot different than you expect when you make the transition from theory to reality. How do you feel?"

Amanda stretched again experimentally and yawned. "Pretty good. I think you've got all the kinks worked out. Thank you."

"No problem. Anything I can do for the Captain."

He gave her a slow smile, and she felt his gaze linger on her for a moment. "I guess I'm about ready for a shower and some sack time," he continued. " 'Night, Skipper, see you in the morning."

"Good night, Arkady."

He tossed off a quick half-salute before ducking out the hatch.

She put off her own leaving for a while. Instead, she lay back on the exercise table and drowsily considered the last few minutes. She wasn't quite sure if her new air group leader had just taken advantage of the situation or had just taken advantage of her.

On the other hand, she had been the one who had allowed herself to be massaged—no, damn it, practically caressed—in that fashion. And, shame the devil, she'd enjoyed it, along with the surge of physical desire that had accompanied Arkady's touch.

He was an extremely attractive man, that she couldn't deny. She also suspected that he was unwilling to abandon what they'd inadvertently started back in Rio. Sooner or later, she would have to clear the air with him.

However, as she savored the fading warmth of Arkady's hands on her back, she decided that she wasn't going to worry about it for the moment.

NORFOLK, VIRGINIA
0930 HOURS: MARCH 23, 2006

In the Second Fleet Operations Room, the huge primary monitor had been reconfigured. A tactical display of Drake Passage and its environs now took up half of the screen space, just as the situation in the South Atlantic was now taking up a growing slice of FLEET-LANTCOM's time and attention.

As was usual when something was on the burner, Admiral MacIntyre found himself spending more and more of his time down on the command balcony. He could have stayed on top of events just as easily via the repeaters in his office, but he didn't like the sense of detachment that went along with working that way. The Ops Center still wasn't the same as the flag plot of a cruiser, but it was something.

"Maggie, what the hell are the Brits playing at?" he demanded irritably. "I've got half a squadron of Orions sitting on the ground in Puerto Rico wasting their time and mine. When can we start deploying them south?"

MacIntyre had taken admiral's privileges, with the coat of his "Blue Baker" uniform draped over the back of his chair and his tie yanked down comfortably a couple of inches.

"It's going to be a while, sir," Captain Callendar replied. "I've been in communication with my opposite number in the British Admiralty on that. It seems we're bucking a monumental traffic-control problem."

"What do you mean?"

"None of the South American states are granting us basing or overflight rights. Everything staging south has to go through Wideawake Field on Ascension Island. The problem is that Wideawake is just a support facility for the Atlantic Missile Range. They've only got a single jet-capable airstrip and apron space for exactly twelve aircraft. The Brits have activated their Falklands defense plan and they're trying to move the Parachute Regiment, a couple of fighter squadrons, and Lord knows what amount of support and logistics through there. Wideawake is fully saturated."

"So we bypass," MacIntyre responded. "The P-3s have long legs. We send 'em directly into the Falklands using aerial refueling."

"I proposed that, sir. Things are almost as bad down at Mount Pleasant. In addition to the British military trying to bring their people in, Shell and BP are trying to get a couple of thousand of their gas-field workers and their dependents out by chartered airliner.

"On top of that, we're starting to get weather lockouts down there. The fall storm fronts seem to be breaking early in the South Atlantic. I gather that its developing into one hellish mess. The Admiralty says that they won't be able to slot our aircraft in for at least another seventy-two to ninety-six hours minimum, and I'm calling that an optimistic estimate."

"Then will the Brits guarantee to provide air support for our people?"

"They promise to do what they can, but the *Cunningham* is moving out of their effective range. They aren't deploying any of their heavy stuff south until later, either. Defensive systems have the priority for the moment."

"God damn!" MacIntyre muttered. "We're sticking our people out on a limb."

The Admiral scowled out across the low-lit length of the operations room at the Alpha Screen. Maggie Callendar leaned back against the workstation desk, her arms crossed. She sensed that her commanding officer wasn't finished with her yet.

Finally he spoke again. "Maggie, what kind of information do we have available on the captain of the *Cunningham?*"

"The standard service records, sir. Is there anything specific you wanted to know?"

"Just who I have down there and what I can expect out of her. When I issued that kid her orders, she sounded almighty young."

His Chief of Staff lifted an eyebrow. "This wouldn't have anything to do with the fact that she's a woman, would it, Admiral?"

"Hell, Maggie, at the moment it's irrelevant if she's man, woman, or Martian. She's senior officer present at a major flashpoint. Furthermore, she's being sent into that hole without a solitary rag of cover or backup. I like to know a little bit about the owner of any neck I'm ordering stuck out that far. I owe her that much."

The corner of Callendar's mouth quirked up and she slipped a zip-disk case out of her pocket. "Here you are, sir. I was checking over her files myself earlier today and I pulled a copy on the chance you might be interested."

"Have you always had this capacity to go around predicting my future wants and desires, Captain?"

"Of course, sir," she deadpanned. "It's a prerequisite for the job, right along with ironclad infallibility."

MacIntyre accepted the case and turned in to face the desk's workstation. "What did you think?"

"Interesting. I think you'll be suitably impressed."

"We'll see," he replied, powering up the terminal. "In the interim, go shake the Bureau of Personnel's tree. See if they have the situation paper on our NCO shortfalls ready yet."

"Aye, aye."

As Callendar went about her task, MacIntyre fed the zip-disk into the workstation's scanner and leaned forward, studying the screen intently.

* GARRETT, AMANDA LEE   COMMANDER USN   771-25-6657-ST-038*

The Admiral found himself looking at a sober-featured young woman in navy uniform. He set aside his professionalism long enough to note that, despite the ID-grad photography, she was a compelling lady. A touch of Lauren Bacall, he decided, back from the glory days of "The Look." There was something vaguely familiar about her as well.

> * AGE: 35   BIRTHDATE: 8/9/71*
> * HAIR: AUBURN   EYES: HAZEL*
> * HEIGHT: 5'7"   WEIGHT: 130*
> * FAMILY AND DEPENDENTS: GARRETT, WILSON M. REAR
>   ADM. U.S.N. * RET.*

MacIntyre suddenly made the connection. "Well, Jesus to Jesus and nine hands 'round," he muttered. "So you're Wils Garrett's kid."

He must have seen a younger variant of her picture an uncountable number of times back in the Persian Gulf, sitting on the desk of his old CruDesRon Commander.

"I hope there's something to this genetics business, honey, because your old man was one righteous destroyer driver."

* GRADUATE U.S. NAVAL ACADEMY: CLASS OF 1992*
* 23RD OUT OF GRADUATING CLASS OF 997*

A fellow ringknocker.

* SERVICE HISTORY*
* U.S.S. *SHENANDOAH AD-44:* 7/19/92-7/21/94 ORDNANCE DIVISION
  +LETTER OF COMMENDATION FILED: C.O. *SHENANDOAH.*
  +PROMOTED LT. J.G. 6/1/94
* NAVAL SURFACE WEAPONS CENTER, DAHLGREN VIRGINIA: 8/1/94–6/27/95 * ADVANCED SURFACE COMBATANT PROJECT.
* T.D.Y. NAVAL SHIP WEAPON SYSTEMS ENGINEERING STATION, POINT HUENEME, CALIFORNIA: 6/27/95–9/6/95.
  +AWARDED NAVY ACHIEVEMENT MEDAL 5/1/95

Obviously a fast-track kid. She was one of the new breed of gundeckers too, coming up the ladder from the ordnance divisions instead of from engineering, as the bulk of his generation had done.

* T.D.Y. U.S. COAST GUARD: 9/20/95–1/20/96, ANTI-DRUG INTERDICTION OPERATIONS.
  +LETTER OF COMMENDATION: C.O. U.S.S. *SPENCER*
  +LETTER OF COMMENDATION: COMMANDANT U.S. COAST GUARD
  +AWARDED BRONZE STAR FOR VALOR: 1/11/96
  +AWARDED PURPLE HEART: 1/11/96

"Whoa!" MacIntyre stopped scrolling and called up the particulars on the file.

*   ON THE DATE SPECIFIED, LT. J.G. AMANDA GARRETT, SECONDED TO U.S.C.G. AND SERVING ABOARD THE MEDIUM-ENDURANCE CUTTER U.S.S. *SPENCER* AS SENIOR BOARDING OFFICER, LED THE INSPECTION PARTY DETAILED TO INVESTIGATE THE ECUADORIAN-FLAG TUNA CLIPPER *BERNARDO GUZMAN* OFF THE COAST OF BAJA CALIFORNIA.

POST-OPERATIONAL ANALYSIS WOULD REVEAL THAT THE *GUZMAN* WAS, IN FACT, A CARTEL SMUGGLING VESSEL TRANS-PORTING A CARGO OF 18 TONS OF RAW MORPHINE BASE WITH A STREET VALUE IN EXCESS OF 8 MILLION DOLLARS.

AS THE BOARDING PARTY CAME ALONGSIDE, THE CREW OF THE *GUZMAN* OPENED FIRE IN AN APPARENT ATTEMPT TO SEIZE HOSTAGES. DESPITE BEING WOUNDED IN THE FIRST EXCHANGE OF GUNFIRE, LT. GARRETT RALLIED THE BOARDING PARTY, AND THEN LED THEM IN THE STORMING OF THE *GUZMAN*'S WHEELHOUSE. SHE AND THE OTHERS THEN HELD THEIR POSI-TION UNTIL THE ARRIVAL OF REENFORCEMENTS FROM THE *SPENCER.*

* MEDICAL LEAVE: 1/20/96–3/3/96

* T.D.Y. NAVAL SURFACE WEAPONS CENTER, NORFOLK, VIR-GINIA. 3/4/96–6/1/96

* NAVAL SURFACE WARFARE SCHOOL, NEWPORT, RHODE IS-LAND. * 6/2/96–6/1/97
  +PROMOTED TO LT. 6/1/97

* ASSIGNED: C.O. FLEET OCEAN TUG U.S.S. *PIEGAN* 6/20/97–7/5/99
  +*PIEGAN* AWARDED LANTFLEETCOM "E" FOR EXCELLENCE 1998–99
  +LETTER OF COMMENDATION, COMMANDER, ATLANTIC FLEET SUPPORT FORCES.
  +LETTER OF COMMENDATION, COMMANDANT 5TH COAST GUARD DISTRICT.
  +AWARDED NAVY AND MARINE CORPS MEDAL 12/18/98.

MacIntyre again dialed up specifics.

*   ON 11/22/98, WHILE OPERATING UNDER FLEET SER-
VICE FORCES COMMAND, U.S.S. *PIEGAN* WAS ONE OF SEVERAL
VESSELS CAUGHT OUT IN OPEN WATER BY THE UNEXPECTED
DEVIATION OF HURRICANE "ARCHIE" TOWARDS THE ATLANTIC
COAST OF THE UNITED STATES.

AFTER RIDING OUT THE FIRST PHASE OF THE STORM OFF
HAMPTON ROADS, LT. GARRETT ELECTED TO RUN FOR SHELTER
AT NORFOLK AS THE EYE OF THE HURRICANE CAME ASHORE AT
THE MOUTH OF CHESAPEAKE BAY.

HOWEVER, OFF OF FORT MUNROE, A FREE-DRIFTING BARGE
WAS OBSERVED JUST BEYOND THE SURF LINE. COAST GUARD
TRAFFIC CONTROL IDENTIFIED IT AS A BULK PETROLEUM CAR-
RIER EN ROUTE FROM LOUISIANA TO NEW JERSEY WITH A FULL
CARGO OF HEAVY CRUDE OIL, THE COMMERCIAL TUG AS-
SIGNED TO IT HAVING ABANDONED THE TOW UPON THE IS-
SUANCE OF THE HURRICANE ALERT.

LT. GARRETT IMMEDIATELY ORDERED *PIEGAN* TO CLOSE
WITH THE BARGE AND COMMENCED PREPARATIONS TO PLACE
A LINE ON IT. WITH CONSIDERABLE DIFFICULTY DUE TO THE
HEAVY RESIDUAL SEAS RUNNING AND THE BARGE'S CLOSE
PROXIMITY TO THE SHORE, THE TOW WAS REESTABLISHED
WITH THE HEAVIEST AVAILABLE GEAR AND *PIEGAN* BEGAN AN
ATTEMPT TO HAUL THE POL CARRIER CLEAR OF THE BEACH.

AT THIS TIME, HOWEVER, THE EYE OF THE STORM HAD
OVERRUN THE AREA AND THE FULL FORCE OF HURRICANE
ARCHIE'S SECOND PHASE STRUCK THE CHESAPEAKE AP-
PROACHES. FIGHTING WHAT WERE ESTIMATED TO BE FORCE 15
SEAS, *PIEGAN* WAS UNABLE TO GAIN GROUND WITH THE POL
CARRIER. WITH HER ONLY OTHER OPTION BEING TO CUT THE
BARGE LOOSE AND ALLOW IT TO GO ONTO THE BEACH, LT.
GARRETT ELECTED TO MAINTAIN THE TOW. FOR THE NEXT
EIGHT HOURS, *PIEGAN* HELD STATION JUST OFF OF THE SURF
LINE, UNTIL THE HURRICANE HAD PASSED AND THE POL CAR-
RIER COULD BE TAKEN IN TO A SAFE MOORAGE.

POST-EVENT ANALYSES BY THE ENVIRONMENTAL PROTEC-
TION AGENCY CONCLUDED THAT: "A MAJOR HEAVY OIL SPILL
AT THE MOUTH OF CHESAPEAKE BAY WOULD HAVE HAD CATA-
CLYSMIC CONSEQUENCES FOR THE VIRGINIA AND MARYLAND
TIDEWATERS. THE SWIFT ACTION OF LT. GARRETT AND HER
CREW UNDOUBTEDLY PREVENTED A WORLD-CLASS ECOLOGI-
CAL DISASTER."

IN ADDITION, THE COMMANDANT OF THE 5TH COAST
GUARD DISTRICT STATED: "THE ACTIONS OF THE U.S.S. *PIEGAN*
AND HER CREW REPRESENT ONE OF THE OUTSTANDING PIECES
OF FOUL-WEATHER SEAMANSHIP IN A CRISIS SITUATION EVER
OBSERVED BY THIS COMMAND."

MacIntyre nodded thoughtfully. Okay, the bloodline does
breed true. You aren't just a test-bench sailor.

* STEALTH SYSTEMS DIVISION, DAVID W. TAYLOR NAVAL SHIP
RESEARCH AND DEVELOPMENT CENTER, BETHESDA, MARY-
LAND: 7/15/99–6/3/00
  +PROMOTED TO LT. CMDR 6/1/00
* ASSIGNED EXEC. OFFICER U.S.S. *JOHN ALLEN PRICE DDG-68* *
6/10/00–7/15/01

* NAVAL WAR COLLEGE, NEWPORT, RHODE ISLAND:
8/1/01–6/25/02

* STAFF ASSIGNMENT, OPERATIONS OFFICER, FLAG GROUP,
TASK FORCE
* 7.1, U.S.S. *ENTERPRISE*: 7/20/02–6/5/04
  +NAVY COMMENDATION MEDAL 1/17/04
  +LETTER OF COMMENDATION, C.O. COMSURFORCEPAC

+U.S. NAVY LEAGUE CAPT. WINIFRED QUICK COLLINS AWARD FOR INSPIRATIONAL LEADERSHIP 2003.

* SPECIAL ASSIGNMENT, NAVAL WAR COLLEGE/DAVID W. TAYLOR SHIP
* RESEARCH AND DEVELOPMENT CENTER, ANNAPOLIS LAB DETACHMENT, ANNAPOLIS, MARYLAND: 6/20/04–5/21/05.
  +PROMOTION TO CMDR. 1/1/05
* ASSIGNED, C.O. U.S.S. *CUNNINGHAM DDG-79:* 6/7/05.

MacIntyre leaned back and stared into space thoughtfully. Eventually he became aware that his Chief of Staff had returned and was standing at his side.

"You're right," he said. "I am impressed . . . to a degree."

"I thought that might be the case. I definitely was when I had the chance to meet Commander Garrett at a Navy League symposium last year. She was speaking on naval power projection in the twenty-first century. She struck me as a woman who was going to make her mark on this man's Navy."

"Okay, I'll grant you that on paper this kid reads out like Arleigh Burke in a skirt. And I can see how they'd consider her qualified to take out the lead ship of the Cunningham class. But she's short into her first major command and she doesn't have anything like line combat experience."

"That's endemic with a lot of our people, Admiral. It's been some time since the Navy has fought a real blue-water war."

"That may be about to change."

Captain Callendar frowned. "Has something new developed down south, sir?"

"No, not anything concrete. It's just that if I were one with you and Captain Garrett here, I'd say that my female intuition was kicking up."

MacIntyre let his chair swivel back around to face out across the worry hole to the network of lights on the Large Screen Display.

"I think that we're going to have that overdue blue-water war, Maggie, and I suspect that it is going to be a pisser."

DRAKE PASSAGE
1400 HOURS: MARCH 23, 2006

Almost by accident, the *Cunningham*'s designers had produced one of the most seaworthy vessels in maritime history. Because of her minimal upperworks, the bulk of her displacement was carried low in her fine-lined hull. Combined with her sophisticated pitch-and-roll dampers and her outriggerlike propulsor pods, this made her an exceptionally stable and easy riding platform in heavy weather.

Her crew had reason to be grateful for this. Five hours before, under skies the color of lead, the Duke had cleared the lee of Islas de Los Estados and had entered Drake Passage.

Now, with sleety rain lashing her bridge windscreen like buckshot, she quartered into an unending series of steep-sided rollers that came booming in from the west. Dirty white foam exploded from under the flare of her bow as she pitched into each of the oncoming swells. Intermittently, a seventh wave would break cleanly over her forecastle and the big destroyer would shudder as she shook tons of seawater off of her decks.

Slouched comfortably in the bridge captain's chair, Amanda Garrett was content. This was her brand of seafaring.

"Heads up, Skipper." A flight-suited arm carefully snaked a steaming mug over her shoulder.

"Thank you, Arkady," she said, accepting it and taking a quick sip. "Mmm, you got it right."

"Earl Grey, one creamer, two sugars," he replied, bracing himself against the roll of the ship between her chair and the outer bridge bulkhead. "I checked with the wardroom messman on the way up."

"Thank you again. How are things back aft?"

"Hangar bay all secure. We won't be launching again until this weather moderates." He hunkered down a little to peer out into the murky sky. "God, it's rotten trending towards shitty out there."

"That's a matter of opinion, Arkady. If you plan to serve on stealth ships, you'd better get used to it. This is where we live."

"More of your raider doctrine?"

"Yes. When we go full stealth, we duck from one weather front to the next, like an infantryman zigzagging from one patch of cover to another. Nothing much can protect you from the old Mark One eyeball except Mother Nature."

She tilted the flat screen monitor mounted on her chair arm toward him and called a repeater image up off of the navigational radar.

"Take a look at this. We're picking up Cape Horn."

Arkady nodded his agreement, mentally comparing the glowing repeater image with the charts he had been studying. He glanced across at Amanda, noting the intentness with which she studied the monitor.

"This is kind of a special deal for you just now, isn't it?"

"It is. I've only sailed these waters once before, when I brought the Duke around from the Pacific, but I've read about them since . . . forever."

Her voice softened and her eyes drifted back up toward the mist-shrouded horizon. "You know, Arkady, this is a very unique and special area. The Atlantic and Pacific meet and merge here. This is the one place where you have no land at all to east or west, just one continuous belt of water encircling the entire planet. The true world ocean."

Arkady felt a shiver ripple down his spine. Damn, this woman could make you feel things.

"No wonder we're bucking heavy seas," he said.

"For Drake Passage and Cape Horn this isn't heavy. It's average. Two months from now, during the winter storm season, then you'll get the heavy stuff. You'll have twelve thousand miles' worth of water, all being driven by hurricane-velocity winds, trying to crash through these straits. Our radar sats have tracked waves two hundred feet high on occasion."

"Holy hell! What do you do if you run into a monster like that?"

Amanda cocked an eyebrow at her Air Division commander. "You sink."

"Once, just once, couldn't this country fight a war off of Long Beach?"

"You have no romance in your soul, Arkady. Some very illustrious people and ships have come through here over the years. Remember talking about Sir Francis Drake last night? These straits are his. He was the first to transit them on his round-the-world raid against the Spanish.

"The USS *Oregon* came through here as well, on her race around South America to rejoin the fleet off Cuba during the Spanish-American war. The clipper ships too, racing the other way, back when it was ninety days to hell or California."

"You sound like you wouldn't have minded commanding one of those old square riggers."

"A clipper ship? Oh no. While their aficionados won't admit it, most of those old clippers were rickety damn affairs, oversparred and underhulled.

"No. If I had my choice, I'd have taken one of those big old Brandenburg freighters the Germans built around the turn of the last century. Those were the real apex of sailing technology. They were bark-rigged, four- or five-masters mostly. They had steel hulls, steel masts, and steel cable standing rigging. You could drive a ship like that, drive her till the canvas exploded right off the yards."

Her words trailed off and just for a moment she was far away, feeling the Cape winds of another time whip her hair.

The moment was broken by the click and rasp of the overhead

squawk box. "Captain, this is Sonar. The hydrothermograph has just recorded that sudden sharp drop in water temperature that you asked us to watch for. You wanted to be notified."

"Yes, thank you, Sonar," Amanda replied into her headset.

"What's that about?" Arkady inquired.

"More uniqueness. We've just crossed a thermocline called the Antarctic Convergence. It's an actual, physical demarcation in this ocean reach that marks the parameters of the South Polar seas."

She keyed a new address code into the interphone. "Communications, this is the Captain. Please transmit the following to CIN-CLANT: 'The USS *Cunningham* has arrived on station.' "

BUENOS AIRES
1930 HOURS: MARCH 23, 2006

The United States Embassy in Buenos Aires was not a particularly large facility, and out of consideration Harrison Van Lynden had endeavored to put as small a strain on their resources as possible. Accordingly, he had converted the sitting room of his second-floor suite into his ad hoc command post.

A desktop computer terminal and its associate printer had taken over the coffee table. The telephone had been supplemented with a modem and a security-locked fax machine. Most of the room's other usable flat surfaces were gradually disappearing under a growing accumulation of books, files, and hard-copy printout.

Earlier on, Van Lynden, Steven Rosario, and Dr. Towers had released the Embassy Staff personnel assigned to them for the day. Following a brief break for dinner, they returned to the task at hand. Slacks and sport shirts had replaced more formal businesswear.

"Have we gotten the final word on the Bogotá meeting, Steve?" the Secretary of State inquired, settling himself onto the couch.

"Yes, sir, as we suspected, they had the Organization of American States wired. Our proposed vote of censure against Argentina was rejected in favor of a motion calling for the involved parties to act with restraint and seek a diplomatic solution."

"What's the latest from the U.N.?"

"The Argentine ambassador has requested a seventy-two-hour delay before the General Assembly initiates debate on the Antarctic situation. He claims he has to return to Buenos Aires for direct consultation with his government. Do you think he'll be able to pull it off, Mr. Secretary?"

"Cuba, Chile, and Uruguay currently hold temporary seats on the Security Council. I'd call the odds about fifty-fifty."

Van Lynden turned his attention to the USARP Director. "How about you, Doctor? Do you have anything encouraging to report?"

"Not really," she said, sighing. "I've received a transcript of the minutes of yesterday's meeting of the Antarctic Treaty Commission in Brussels. The Argentines presented a six-hour history lesson on Argentina's polar research program. Whenever anyone else tried to get a word in edgewise, Chile tripped them up on points of order. Nothing concrete was accomplished."

"There's been quite a bit of that going around lately," Van Lynden commented sardonically. "The Argentines appear quite willing to talk, just as long as that's all that's being done."

The Secretary of State picked a pencil up off the coffee table. Rotating it slowly between his fingers, he appeared to minutely examine it as if it had suddenly become vitally important. After a few moments, he snapped it back down violently.

"We're being sandbagged! They're stalling. Their entire intent has been to stall from the very start. For what reason, though? What are they waiting for?"

Dr. Towers dropped into the easy chair across from Van

Lynden. "At this time of year, the only thing that you wait for south of the line is winter," she replied.

"All right, let's go with that. What exactly does 'winter' mean in the Antarctic? What changes?"

"Well, let me see." Dr. Towers sat back in the chair, instinctively slipping into the tone of a practiced lecturer. "Winter, or more exactly fall, marks the end of the Antarctic operations season. Environmental conditions that are difficult to cope with during the summer become absolutely unlivable during the remainder of the year. The weather deteriorates. Hurricane-velocity winds become almost a daily occurrence. Temperatures plummet. Up on the plateau you can get still-air surface temperatures in excess of one hundred and eighty degrees below zero.

"Everything shuts down except for absolute top-priority projects. All nonessential personnel, the 'summer people,' we call them, are evacuated. Sea transport becomes impossible as the ice pack freezes solid. Air and surface travel is attempted only in extreme emergency."

"Sweet Christ!" Steve Rosario muttered. "Why would anyone want anything to do with a place like that?"

Dr. Towers gave a little smile. "It's an acquired taste. Some of us old USARPs find wintering over . . . exhilarating. The point is, during winter down there you don't do much of anything except hunker down in your station and ride it out."

"How long does this state of affairs last?" Van Lynden asked slowly.

"It varies. Generally about seven to eight months, from the end of March or early April into November."

"That's it, then. Sparza, you clever bastard! That's it!"

The USARP Director and the Assistant Secretary of State exchanged blank looks.

"I beg your pardon, sir, but what's it?" Rosario inquired.

"The Argentine game plan. They're freezing us out, literally. They intend to stall until winter shuts everything down in the Antarctic and kills any possible action we can take against them."

"That wouldn't have any effect on diplomatic efforts."

"Oh, yes, it would. Sure, we can talk ... and talk and talk, and that's all. We can't even effectively threaten diplomatic and economic sanctions. They'll just grin at us and say that it's physically impossible for them to withdraw their garrisons at this time and they'd be telling God's own truth."

"They'll have two-thirds of a year free of outside interference. They can use that two-thirds of a year to stir up dissension within the Antarctic Treaty states and the U.N. Also, our government and that of Great Britain are bound to be distracted by other developing problems within that same time frame. By next November, it will be near as damn all impossible to regain any kind of political and diplomatic momentum on this. The occupation of the Antarctic Peninsula will be accepted as a fait accompli."

"Yes," Dr. Towers added, "and once one nation grabs a piece of the pie, everyone will have to grab for a piece. All of the Treaty nations will be staking out their territories. The United States will have to activate its claims out of sheer self-defense."

"Exactly. Given the poor geographic definition and the overlapping nature of these claims, this could trigger repercussions with the European Community, Russia, Japan ... Hell, this could open the biggest geopolitical can of worms since the Yalta Conference. By this time next year, we could see military garrisons springing up all across Antarctica."

"With drilling rigs and mining operations following shortly afterwards as the occupying states try to financially justify their presence," Dr. Towers said bitterly. "The Argentines and their allies will be left holding the richest and most readily accessible claim. They'll reap the profits while the rest of the continent is torn apart. There must be something that can be done about this!"

"Offhand, I can't see what. Even if the United States or Great Britain opted for a counterinvasion, we could never equip, train, and deploy a polar warfare force before winter closed in. It looks like a done deal. Sparza is holding four aces."

The Secretary of State pushed his glasses up onto his forehead and tiredly massaged his eyes with the heels of his hands. "God, I'm going to hate briefing the Boss on this one."

A defeated silence filled the room, the kind of silence that makes those submerged in it ache for something to do to fill the void. Steve Rosario began to self-consciously organize one of the accumulated stacks of hard copy. Van Lynden sat back on the couch with his eyes closed. Dr. Towers flipped aimlessly through a folder of satellite reconnaissance photographs.

Then she paused, looking intently at one of the photos.

"Steve, when were these pictures of San Martin Base taken?"

"I don't know. Let me see the folder."

She held up the file for his examination.

"Oh, that's the latest set. We just got them in this afternoon."

"Do we have some of the other Argentine bases that are this current?"

"I think so. They're around here somewhere."

In moments she was riffling through the other photo files like a busy pack rat.

"The British stations. I need the ones for the British station too."

"Uh, I suppose they're down in the military attaché's office."

"Get them for me, please," she requested crisply.

Rosario exchanged puzzled glances with his superior and went about the task.

When he returned, he found the Director of the United States Antarctic Research Program on her hands and knees, spreading photography out across the sitting-room carpet while the Secretary of State looked on in total mystification.

"Pass those down to me, Steve," she said confidently. "I think I may be onto something."

A quarter of an hour later, she sat cross-legged in the midst of a carefully selected accumulation of photographic blowups.

"I was right."

"About what, Doctor?" Van Lynden demanded.

"The Argys don't have a pat hand, Mr. Secretary. They're bluffing like crazy while they try to fill out a bobtail flush."

"What in the world are you talking about?"

She gestured around her. "Less than a month ago, I visited every one of these installations as part of the standard yearly tour of inspection made by the Antarctic Treaty Commission. At that time, the Argentines had just completed their resupply operation for the coming winter. I noticed nothing out of the ordinary. As usual, they had fully stocked for one full year's operation plus a six-month emergency reserve, the Antarctic standard.

"That, however, was for a total staff of maybe five hundred personnel. Now they have over two thousand additional troops down there and, according to these photographs, their supply dumps are no larger than when I visited.

"It's even worse at the captured British stations. The Argentines have brought practically nothing with them. They have garrisons of forty or fifty people drawing on supply bases meant to sustain six or seven."

"Are you sure about this, Doctor?"

"I'm positive. You don't become involved in Antarctic operations without becoming something of a fanatic about logistics. Antarctica is the only terrestrial environment where the human species cannot live off the land. You have to bring everything in with you, every gallon of fuel, every mouthful of food, every square foot of shelter. Even your drinking water if you factor in the extra fuel needed to melt ice. Some of my colleagues at NASA have said that it's simpler to maintain Space Station Alpha than it is Scott-Amundsen Base at the South Pole."

Van Lynden leaned forward intently. "What amount of supplies would be necessary to cover their shortfall?"

"Oh, a ballpark figure would be between eight and twelve tons per man."

"Let's round that out at ten tons per man. For a two-thousand-man garrison, you'd be looking at twenty thousand tons of supplies."

"Mm-hmm, and they're going to be needing more hard-sided housing down there as well. A lot of those new troops seem to be living in tent bivouacs at the moment. On the ice, you just don't winter over under canvas and come out of it in any kind of decent shape."

"I'm wondering why our intelligence analysts missed this huge shortfall," Rosario said.

"Probably overcompartmentalization," Van Lynden replied. "I gather that polar logistics is a rather specialized business, and I suspect someone forgot to invite in the appropriate specialist at the appropriate time. If it wasn't for Dr. Towers here, it might have slipped right past us."

The Secretary of State leaned back into the couch. "Twenty thousand tons," he said thoughtfully. "The Argentines don't have the airlift capacity to move that amount of matériel. It'll have to come in by sea."

"And soon," Towers added. "I'd say they have only two or three more weeks at most before the ice pack becomes impassable."

"What will happen if those supplies don't arrive?"

"The Argentines would have no choice. They'd have to withdraw their garrisons, or watch them freeze and starve in the dark during the polar night."

Van Lynden considered for a few moments more, then reached for the telephone and keyed for the Embassy communications center.

"This is the Secretary of State. I'm going to need a direct line to the President, please."

Antonio Sparza breakfasted alone in the small residential dining room of the Casa Rosada. Normally, this would be a sacrosanct time for the Argentine President, an hour to be shared with his wife and three children before taking up the duties of the day. However, prior to the beginning of the Conquistador South operation, he had sent his family out to their country home in his native Catamarca Province. It was an instinctive precaution given the traditional volatility of South American politics.

This morning, his only companions were the international fax editions of the *Washington Post* and the *London Times.* In addition, a small, portable television tuned to CNN's "America Sud" service played quietly in the corner, ignored except when key words such as "Argentina" or "Antarctica" were mentioned.

He had permitted himself a second cup of chocolate and was just lifting it to his lips when his Minister of State hesitantly appeared in the open archway that led into the room.

"Come in, Aldo," Sparza said amiably. "You appear not to be having a good morning."

"We may have a problem, Mr. President. The United States Embassy has contacted us. Their Secretary of State desires to see you at once."

"Our Norteamericano guests sound impatient. We'd best see about giving them an appointment this morning."

"You don't understand, sir. They did not ask for an appointment. Their Secretary of State has demanded to meet with you immediately. His motorcade has already left the U.S. Embassy."

A warning bell sounded in Sparza's mind. "Do we have anything else on this?"

"National Security reports that their sources within the North American media have been informed of a presidential press conference to be held at approximately ten-thirty this morning, Washington time. There is also to be a follow-up conference involving both State Department and Pentagon personnel."

Sparza nodded grimly and touched his mouth with his napkin.

"The Conquistador South supply convoy was scheduled to sail this morning. Contact the Naval Ministry and have them hold the departure until further orders. I think you are correct, Aldo. We may very well have a problem."

DRAKE PASSAGE
1005 HOURS: MARCH 24, 2006

"Attention, all hands. This is the Captain. We have just received the following orders from the Commander in Chief, Atlantic Fleet.

" 'Effective as of 1200 hours, March 24, 2006. Naval forces of the United States and Great Britain will commence a total maritime blockade of all Argentine installations on the Antarctic continent. Until further notice, all Argentine-flag vessels, civil or military, or any foreign-flag vessels acting under Argentine charter or orders, endeavoring to cross the Antarctic Circle are to be intercepted and turned back. Blockading forces are hereby authorized to take whatever actions necessary to maintain this exclusion zone.'

"As most of you are probably aware, for the moment we're all the blockading forces there are. As a result, we're going to have a challenging time ahead of us. However, it's a challenge I believe the Duke can meet.

"As of 1200 hours, we'll be closing up to Condition Three, full wartime cruising mode, and we'll be staying there until we are relieved on station. Blue and Gold watches will be set in all divisions.

If you have any odd jobs to take care of, do them now. If you need help, ask for it.

"Plan for the long haul, because it's going to be at least a week before the fleet can come up to support us. A special briefing package on the blockade will soon be available on your crew access terminals, and I advise you to acquaint yourselves with it.

"Technically, a blockade is an act of war. As yet, however, nobody has started to do any shooting. Hopefully, no one will. We are not going to take that for granted, though. Let's stay alert, people."

BUENOS AIRES
1445 HOURS: MARCH 24, 2006

President Sparza maintained two offices within the Casa Rosada. One was the large and impressive reception office where foreign dignitaries, the press, and other such transients were greeted. The other, much smaller, and set well back within the residence, was where the real work of state was done and the decisions made.

Its furnishings were solid and comfortable and not excessively expensive. The bookcases that lined its walls were filled with a varied assortment of titles covering history, geography, current affairs, and the military sciences. There was also a scattering of personal mementos, a few family photographs, a sports trophy or two, and a delicate antique case clock, an heirloom of Sparza's grandmother.

At the moment, the presence of the President, the Minister of State, and the Chiefs of Staff of the three Argentine armed forces crowded it, overheating the little room. In the face of the warmth, however, the thoughts of the five men were on the cold.

"All of the reports from our Peninsula Met stations confirm that we have an early freeze coming in," General of the Army Juan Orchal stated. "The average daily wind velocities are increasing.

We are seeing a steady drop of temperatures and the rapid development of sea ice off all coastal installations. The demand on our supply reserves is growing, and those field units that have only tent shelter are starting to have problems."

Sparza nodded and slipped a cigarette from the flat twenty-pack of Players resting on his desk blotter. Kindling it with an old-fashioned silver pocket lighter, he turned his attention to Air Force General Marcello Arco. "What is the status of the airlift?"

"As good as could be hoped for. As described in the deployment plan, all available Air Force, Navy, and civil heavy-lift transports are standing by to sortie as the opportunity presents itself. Our problem is that the weather at San Martin Base is starting to close in. We are operational maybe twenty-four hours out of every forty-eight. We are also limited as to the number of aircraft we can handle on the ground at San Martin at any one time. Also our aviation fuel reserves on the ice are dwindling. I am sorry, sir. We are getting stores through, but we are not working miracles."

Chief of Naval Operations Admiral Luis Fouga cut in irritably, "If we had built our supply depots up to an adequate level prior to launching this operation, we wouldn't be confronted with this crisis."

"You were involved in the planning sessions for Conquistador South, Admiral," Arco replied, an edge coming to his voice. "A logistical buildup of the size necessary might well have aroused the suspicion of the other Antarctic Treaty powers. At the time we deemed it an unnecessary risk, all of us!"

"Stand easy, gentlemen," Sparza said quietly. "We are not here to find fault with each other. There is no fault to find. All of the services have performed admirably during this operation."

Sparza made no mention of the overreaction of one of Fouga's officers that had led to the unnecessary sinking of the British research ship and the death of its captain. He had to keep these men functioning together as a team, and damaging Fouga's excessive pride would not help matters. When this crisis was past, however . . .

"The problem with which we are confronted stems from an unfortunate coincidence, the presence of a North American warship in our waters when none was expected, not from a failing on anyone's part. Admiral Fouga, what is the status of the supply convoy?"

"The ice-operations vessel *Alferez Mackinlay*, the fleet oiler *Luis A. Huergo*, and the tank landing ship *Piedrabuena* are all fully loaded and standing by to sortie from Río Gallegos. The First and Third Destroyer Squadrons and elements of the First Escort Group and the fast coastal attack force are standing by to provide convoy cover."

"General Arco, status of the opposition?"

"No major changes, sir. The British defensive buildup in the Malvinas continues. Elements of two additional fighter-bomber squadrons and the Paratroop Regiment have been positively identified. A small British task group consisting of the Port Stanley guard frigate, the ice-patrol ship *Polar Circle*, and a small fleet auxiliary are currently covering the offshore petroleum facilities.

"The United States naval vessel is apparently holding on station in Drake Passage, three hundred and fifty kilometers south-southwest of Islas de Los Estados. Their nearest reinforcements are still more than a week's steaming time away."

"Thank you. Admiral Fouga, what are the chances of slipping the convoy past this single-ship blockade?"

"We don't need to slip past anyone. The fleet is fully capable of driving off this Norteno pest, or of sinking it, if necessary."

Sparza drew on his cigarette and sighed. "Admiral, I did not ask if you could sink this ship. I asked if you could get past it undetected."

The heavyset naval officer wilted. "No, sir. Given the Americans' extensive spy satellite network and their advanced seaborne sensor systems, it is unlikely we could reach the San Martin Peninsula without being observed and intercepted. As I have stated, however, if we sortie now, we could provide an escort of such overwhelming force that we could blast the Americans out of the water in seconds if they dare to interfere."

"I am not so certain," General Arco said flatly. "This vessel, the USS *Cunningham,* is the most sophisticated warship of what is still the most potent naval power in the world. Its systems are at least a full generation in advance of the best that we have. We should not take its potential capabilities too lightly."

"For God's sake, General. The damned thing is commanded by a woman!"

"A gun does not care who pulls its trigger."

"Gentlemen, let us leave the question of this ship's capabilities open for the moment," Sparza said, rotating his chair slightly to face his Minister of State. "Aldo, what is your opinion? Will the United States maintain the blockade? Will they open fire if we attempt to run a convoy through to our Antarctic bases?"

Aldo Salhazar marshaled his thoughts before replying. He sensed that his next words might be critical, if not apocalyptic.

"The United States is taking these events very seriously, very seriously indeed. Perhaps more so than we expected. Their deployment of a massive naval force, their attempts to mobilize world opinion against us, the presence of their Secretary of State in our capital, all indicate the depth of their concern. No doubt they perceive the political dislocation caused by our actions in the Antarctic contrary to American global interests.

"The current U.S. Administration has shown itself willing to use armed force if required to defend those interests, as it has recently demonstrated in Peru and in Central Africa. I believe that the captain of that United States naval vessel has, or will have, authorization to stop our convoy using whatever means necessary."

Sparza nodded. "General Orchal, a final question. Is it at all possible that we could carry through Conquistador South with the supplies available to us on the ice, plus what we can bring in by air?"

"I would say that it is not feasible," the Army officer replied.

"At best, our personnel would undergo extreme hardship. At worst, there could be a catastrophe of monumental proportions. Given a late spring, we could have dead and dying at every one of our outposts.

"You do not play games with polar logistics, Mr. President. If we do not receive adequate supply, we must abandon the operation and recall our garrisons. There are no other options."

Sparza found that he had about three good draws left on his cigarette. He decided to give himself that long to make the final decision. Deeply inhaling the rich smoke of the first of those draws, he considered the future of his nation and himself.

Antonio Sparza was a fighting man. Throughout his life he had fought against poverty, against the prejudice triggered by the touch of Indian blood in his veins, and against the corrupt and deeply entrenched political machines that did not wish to make a place for the hard-driving outsider from the northwestern goucho country.

He had learned the secret of victory in the boxing ring of the amateur athletics club of the small parochial school he had attended as a teen. Always go on the offensive. Explode out of your corner and drive into your enemy, no matter what his size, no matter what blows you might receive in return. The defender is the loser. Only the attacker can win.

That principle had stood him in good stead over the years. It had won him this seat in the Casa Rosada. He would not change his ways now. Deliberately, he snubbed out the butt of his cigarette.

"General Arco, have an air strike readied. Sink the American warship."

Shock rippled through the circle of men. Minister of State Salhazar half rose out of his chair. "Antonio, are you mad? That would be tantamount to a declaration of war on the United States!"

"No, not necessarily. The United States is quick to anger, but slow to take action over a single incident. Consider the historical precedents: the *Pueblo,* the *Liberty,* the *Stark.*

"I have no doubt that this will deepen the crisis, but we shall be able to perform damage control. We can claim it was an accident of some nature, a communications breakdown. Possibly we can shift some of the blame onto the American vessel itself.

"Afterwards, we can issue a formal apology and an offer to make reparations. The important thing is that we will be able to get those supplies through to our garrisons and the Americans will be unable to stop us."

"And what if they do not accept this apology, Mr. President? What if reparations are not enough!"

"Even if this is the case, Aldo, the San Martin Peninsula will belong to us and the Antarctic winter will have locked and barred the gate. Even a superpower such as the United States will be unable to contest that."

"The winter will not protect Argentina itself, sir," Arco said quietly.

"No, General, but world opinion will. During our attempt to reclaim the Malvinas, Great Britain did not strike at our military installations on the mainland, even when it was to their military advantage to do so. They knew that such an escalation would turn the diplomatic tide against them.

"The North Americans know this as well. Those actions they can take, the trade and economic embargoes, possibly a blockade of our coasts, we have expected these things and we have already made preparations to deal with them."

Sparza looked around his circle of advisers. "Gentlemen, when we were forced to conceive of this venture, we knew that we would be taking grave risks. However, we also knew that if we did not, everything our nation has worked for and dreamed of in the Antarctic for sixty-five years would be lost. This situation has not changed. If any one of you has some new option to present, I will listen."

His advisers could offer only silence.

The Argentine President nodded. "Very well, then. We simply must dare a little more. Admiral Fouga, you will order the supply convoy and its escort to sail upon verification of the sinking of the American destroyer. General Arco, you will plan and execute the attack on this warship, the *Cunningham,* as soon as possible.

The conference concluded and its attendees dispersed. As the Chiefs of Staff of the Army and Air Force descended the main stairs of the Casa Rosada, Juan Orchal glanced across at his compatriot.

"You do not look happy, Marcello."

"I'm not. It's happening again, Juan. Just like in '82, we are doing it to ourselves again. First, we assume that everything will go just as we have planned, and it does not. Then we assume that we will not have a fight on our hands and we do."

"Yes, but it's still not quite the same. We have learned a few things since Port Stanley, my friend."

"Maybe. But there we were only tweaking the tail of the lion. Here, I suspect we may be biting an elephant in the ass."

"I know that you were never as ardent about Conquistador South as some of the rest of us, Marcello. But you agreed to the strike commit at the last planning session. What else can be done now?"

"Nothing, I suppose. Nothing but to live with it."

As they reached the foot of the stairway, General Arco felt a sharp stab of pain across his lower back. He recognized the spasm as the flare-up of a spinal injury he had received many years ago, ejecting from a Rapier-blasted Skyhawk over San Carlos Bay. The Air Force officer grimly found himself wondering if its return might be an omen.

Some meteorologists theorize that the Antarctic continent doesn't have weather in the conventional sense. They believe that the prevailing South Polar climatic patterns are actually one titanic superstorm that has been raging continuously for the last ten thousand years—sometimes with greater intensity, sometimes with lesser, but perennially since the last ice age.

Occasionally, though, rents and eddies form within its structure, and for the moment the USS *Cunningham* cruised within one such patch of calm.

Corkscrewing easily through a steel-blue sea, the big destroyer ran beneath an open sky lightly streaked with frost-colored mare's tails. Twice that day, ice had been sighted to the south, great flat-topped burgs riding low on the horizon, sea smoke of their own creation swirling mystically around them.

The winds carried the mark of the Pole as well. They were the katabatics, gusting in from the southwest, fresh off the Antarctic Plateau. Chill, pure, oxygen rich, and seemingly denser than common air, breathing them was comparable to breathing the outflow of some icy mountain spring.

Amanda Garrett relished the experience. Parka-clad, she had spent most of the morning out on the wings of the bridge, enjoying the sight of the snowy foam peeling away from the cutting edge of her ship's prow. However, the clear weather also brought with it a faint feeling of unease.

"Hey, Skipper," Ken Hiro's voice sounded in her headset. "Have you decided about diverting south under that next storm front yet?"

Amanda glanced up at the glowing sun and hesitated. They had been running under heavy weather for almost two continuous days, and certain maintenance tasks were best done on a stable deck. Besides, a rest would be good for all hands.

"Negative, Ken. Hold your course. We'll be socked in again soon enough."

Two hundred and forty miles to the northeast, over Isla Grande, the fair weather had already broken. Heavy cloud cover and turbulence were complicating an already difficult air-to-air refueling operation. Flying under total radio and radar silence, a flight of four Fuerza Aérea Rafales had located and made rendezvous with their C-130 Hercules tanker aircraft as it churned along just above the overcast.

The flight elements were armed alike. The leaders mounted a drop tank beneath each wing and a slender, cigar-shaped pod on their centerline. The wingmen carried a single larger tank beneath their belly and a pair of 1,000-pound laser-guided bombs on their inboard pylons.

The first element tucked in under the elderly Lockheed. Guided in by light signals from the pump boss's station amidships, the fighters skillfully coupled into the refueling drogues trailing aft from the tanker's wingtip pods.

As they did so, a second strike flight closed and joined up. Two dark blue and gray Aeronaval Tornadoes. Like pale remora clinging to a shark's belly, each carried a brace of Exocet anti-shipping missiles.

"Hey, Captain." This time, Hiro appeared in the bridge-wing hatchway. "I think you'd better come take a look at this."

"Sure, Ken, what have you got?"

She followed him back into the wheelhouse, flipping back the hood of her parka as she did. Inside, she found her exec and Vince Arkady intently studying the largest of the monitors mounted above the bridge windscreen.

"We've got Lieutenant Beltrain on the squawk box from CIC. He says he has a funny contact on the board."

"What's so amusing about it, Dix?" she inquired, raising her voice slightly to trip the sound-activated microphone of the com system.

"It's funny peculiar, not funny ha-ha, ma'am. Have a look at your bridge repeaters."

The flatscreen showed a computer stylization of the southern-most tip of South America and the Drake Passage environs, the Duke's position hack glowing blue in its center. Half a dozen other identified and innocuous surface contacts were scattered across the display, none of which were within a hundred miles of the destroyer. In the sky to the north, a Chilean passenger jet was descending toward Punta Arenas. To the northwest, "Pedro," the Argentine Atlantique shadower aircraft, circled repetitively. To the northeast, there was a third airborne target.

"It's that new slow mover, ma'am. The one coded Contact Charley. He came into our coverage area from the north, turned southwest at Isla Grande beacon, and aimed himself right at us. Since then, two separate flights of fast movers have overtaken and joined up with him. Radar cross-section variance indicates a lot of close-in maneuvering, probably an air-to-air refueling operation."

"Target identification?"

"The big guy has to be an Argy KC-130. No doubt about it. No make on the small stuff yet. Could be two to four aircraft per flight and they're too far out to get a skin-track silhouette. These guys are being real quiet. Sigint indicates they're maintaining total EMCON. No radio, no radar, no transponders. Miss Christine's gang over in Raven's Roost says this is pretty damn unusual for this outfit."

"Maybe it's just some kind of training exercise," Hiro commented. "None of the other Argy harassment flights have used aerial refueling. Their aircraft have range enough to reach us without it."

"Not if it was an armed strike package," Arkady said soberly. "You'd be carrying ordnance on some of your hardpoints instead of drop tanks. You'd also want to top off on fuel before you went in over your target, so you'd have a big maneuvering reserve in case you had trouble. . . . Hey, check this out."

On the flatscreen, Contact Charley had fissioned just as it crossed the 180-mile ranging line.

"Bridge," the squawk box sounded. "The fast movers have separated from the tanker. Estimate three two-plane elements, now coded as Contacts Delta, Echo, and Foxtrot. New targets have accelerated to six hundred knots and are closing the range. Target Charley is now turning away to the north."

"He's not the only one. It looks like Pedro is bugging out."

"I see it, Arkady," Amanda said. "Dix, what's going on with that Argentine Atlantique?"

"He transmitted a nonscheduled position fix on us just before conducting his breakaway. He's descending and he's increasing speed."

"He's hauling ass before he gets it blown off," Arkady murmured under his breath.

On the repeater, the three fighter-bomber flights had fanned out into a broad triangle, an arrow fired from the Argentine mainland dead-on at the *Cunningham.* It would arrive on target in approximately sixteen minutes. Amanda shot a glance at each of the two officers that flanked her.

"Gentlemen, I need your evaluations, right now."

"We haven't seen anything like this before, Captain," her exec said quietly. "Something's up."

"Arkady?"

"If this isn't an armed Sierra strike, it's a helluva good imitation."

"Right. Mr. Hiro, I'm shifting the con to CIC. You have the bridge. Sound general quarters."

From bow to stern, all decks of the Duke were filled with the flat metallic honking of the GQ klaxons, the hammering of running feet, and the slam of watertight doors. Over all came the emotionless voice of the duty quartermaster. "General quarters. General quarters. All hands proceed to your battle stations. This is not a drill. I repeat, this is not a drill."

Down in the Combat Information Center, the systems operators began reciting the techno-litany that brought the destroyer's weapons arrays fully to life.

"Main turret indexing check, fore and aft."

"I have green lights, fore and aft, elevation and traverse."

"Phalanx safety interlocks off. Cycling to full autofire mode."

"Confirm helm and lee helm control shifted to CIC. Bridge and Main Engineering control to ready-use standby."

"All power rooms fully lit off and on-line."

"Alpha, Bravo, and Charley ESSM flights selected and armed. VLS cell doors opened and visually verified. Confirm hot birds on the rails!"

Amanda strode into the CIC to find her command chair empty and waiting for her. "Tactical Officer, status?" she demanded.

"The ship is at general quarters, Captain," Beltrain replied. "All weapons and defense systems up and on-line. Condition Zebra set in all spaces. Awaiting your orders, ma'am."

"What's the situation with the bogeys?"

"Bogeys have descended to wave-top altitude and are currently below our radar horizon. As of last contact they were continuing to close the range. Given no change in speed or heading, Contact Delta will be reacquired in approximately twelve minutes. Targets Echo and Foxtrot will be reacquired and will cross our bow and stern respectively at about a five-mile range at about one-minute intervals thereafter."

"Right. Where's our nearest heavy cloud cover?"

The tac officer dialed a weather overlay in on the Alpha Screen. "The nearest squall line is about twenty miles to the southeast."

Damn, damn, damn! A stealth warship must always seek out

protective weather cover. She had helped to write that doctrine. Then, first crack out of the box, she had allowed herself to be seduced by a patch of blue sky.

"We going to try and go stealth and evade, ma'am?"

"It's too late, Dix. They have us fixed. We'll have to take it as it comes."

"Aye, aye."

"When the bogeys close to an estimated one hundred miles range, go to tactical on the primary display."

"Will do."

"Communications, anything from those aircraft yet?"

"No, ma'am."

"Then get on their standard frequencies. Warn those planes off!"

"Aye, aye."

"Then get a link with CINCLANT. Tell them that we have Argentine aircraft in our vicinity, maneuvering with possible hostile intent. Inform them that we have gone to general quarters and that we will keep them advised."

The Argentine strike fighters had dropped down to within fifty feet of the ocean's surface, down where the jet wash of their engines flattened the wave crests and the spray pinged off their windscreens like pebbles kicked up off a gravel road. The aircrews knew that this zero-altitude approach granted them a temporary reprieve at best. They didn't need to hear the Duke's transmitted warning to know that they had already been detected. Their threat boards had reacted to a radar sweep of a kind they had never before seen. Sooner or later, they must pull back up into the sight of their enemies. There was nothing for it but to hunker a few feet closer to the sea and delay the inevitable for as long as they could.

"I do not believe that they are doing this," Beltrain murmured.

"They might not be," Amanda replied. "These guys could still be playing mind games with us."

"At what point do we decide that it isn't a game?"

"Well, Dix. That's the question now, isn't it?"

Amanda's instincts were all telling her that this was the real thing. However, when you are about to commit your nation to war, you dare not trust to instincts alone.

"We will be reacquiring Contact Delta within the next ten seconds, Captain," the Aegis operator reported quietly.

The MMS system activated, the image from the masthead camera windowing into the corner of the Alpha Screen. Just above the juncture line of sea and sky, there was a faint smudge of kerosene smoke with two gleaming metallic dots centered in it.

"Contact Delta is over the horizon. Line of sight and fire established."

Okay, Captain under God, fish or cut bait.

"Tactical Officer, designate the Tornadoes."

"Aye, aye. Designating Tornadoes now."

On the main display, a diamond-shaped targeting box blinked into existence around the closest flight of Argentine aircraft. On the outer skin of the superstructure, phased-array cells energized and a pair of tightly focused radar beams lanced out to paint the oncoming jets.

Aboard the Tornadoes, threat boards screamed as the *Cunningham*'s fire-control systems locked on. The Argentine element leader was startled. His mission profile had called for him to push in closer before commencing his own attack. However, he hadn't expected that his intended target would react so swiftly. After a split-second hesitation, he snapped a command to his systems operator in the rear cockpit and pulled up into his launching maneuver.

As the Tornado climbed through 120 feet, the systems operator powered up his own surface-search radar. Establishing a targeting lock, he gave his Exocets a look at their prey. As the "Missile Ready" lights went green on his ordnance panel, he called a launch warning to his pilot and pressed the release keys.

The first four-and-a-half-meter-long missile unshackled and fell away from beneath the wing. Ten feet beneath the aircraft, a braided wire lanyard snapped out the last safety pin and the Exocet's rocket engine ignited with a flair of orange flame. At one-second intervals, the other three missiles carried by the flight dropped and fired. Trailing streamers of milky smoke, they blazed away into the distance.

Within the CIC, the tracking teams called it out.

"Contact Delta is executing a pop-up maneuver . . . Tornado fire-control radars lighting off. . . . Active seeker heads! We have active seeker heads! . . . Missile launch! . . . Confirm multiple Exocet launch! . . . Missiles closing the range! . . . Impact in twenty-eight seconds . . . twenty-seven . . . twenty-six . . ."

Amanda Garrett's voice rang sharply clear over it all.

"Initiate full-spectrum stealth and ECM! All weapons systems commence firing!"

Throughout the CIC hands slammed down on actuators, unleashing the Duke's arsenal of physical and electronic firepower.

Dixon Beltrain had been standing by, poised over the armed firing triggers of his Main Tac Ops console. At his captain's word, he hit the launch sequence of the first ESSM flight.

Up on the *Cunningham*'s foredeck, the slender, eleven-foot length of the first missile lanced into the air, hurled out of its storage cell by the gas charge of the Vertical Launch Array's cold-fire system. Clear of the weather deck, its motor ignited, hurling it on its way in a boosted high-g arc to the north. With machine-gun rapidity, the three other rounds in the quad-pack canister followed.

The ESSM (Enhanced Sea Sparrow Missile) was a descendant of the original NATO Sea Sparrow surface-to-air interceptor system, crossbred with technology taken from the U.S. Air Force's AMRAAM (Advanced Medium Range Air to Air Missile). Like its predecessor, it was compact, reliable, and lethal.

The Argentine Tornadoes had reversed course instantly after

releasing their ordnance, sweeping their wings back and lighting off their afterburners in a desperate supersonic dash back to the horizon and safety. They activated their internal ECM jammers and spewed chaff and anti-IR flares into their wakes to throw off the swarm of Mach-4 killers overtaking them. The element leader succeeded; the wingman failed.

Steered into position by the gathering beams of the Duke's fire-control system, the ESSMs pitched over and dove. Seconds later, the trailing Panavia caught the sledgehammer blow of a missile hit. Its upper fuselage shattered, the big fighter-bomber plowed into the sea, its high speed and minimal altitude not granting even the fragment of time necessary for a clawing hand to reach an ejector seat handle.

Even as the Tornado was destroyed, a second battle was being joined—what Winston Churchill had once referred to as "the wizard war": the death struggle of the black boxes.

The *Cunningham*'s Wetball system came fully active. Derived from the Ironball stealth paint developed by the United States Air Force, the Duke's exotic polymer hull coating held billions of microscopic iron spheres in suspension. By shifting the polarization of these metal particles at ultrahigh frequencies and in irregular patterns, incoming radar waves could be distorted and dispersed.

Aboard the departing Aeronaval Atlantique patrol plane, systems operators watched in amazement as the *Cunningham*'s return faded off their scopes like a snuffed candle flame.

Other defensive systems engaged as well. Decoy launchers, like old-style K guns, hurled foxer pods off the destroyer's stern quarters. Some of these burst open upon striking the ocean's surface, ejecting a fast-inflating mylar balloon that carried a false radar target into the sky. Others bobbed upright in the wave troughs and extended waterproof antenna, broadcasting impulses that might be mistaken for the electromagnetic signature of a Cunningham-class destroyer by a simpleminded guided missile.

The Duke's own defensive radars jittered wildly up and down

their frequency spectrum, shifting operating channels a score of times a second to throw off homing antiradar guidance. Scanners hunted down the Argentines' operational radio and radar channels, and linked cascade jammers flooded them with electronic white noise. Seduction jammers spawned a flotilla of false radar targets around the *Cunningham*'s true position, blending them with the chaff clouds and flare clusters being scattered by the RBOC launchers.

The advanced-model Exocets responded in kind with counter-counter measures. Burning in at transonic velocity, a bare ten feet above the wave tops, their guidance packages cycled rapidly between active radar, passive radar homing, and infrared modes, cross-referencing the data inputs to try to penetrate the clutter and seek out the real target.

Despite their sophistication, two of the four missiles were overwhelmed in seconds, staggering away in cybernetic confusion. One of the remaining pair, by sheer chance, chose to fixate on the faint, true, ghost image of the *Cunningham* amid all of the ECM chaos. The last locked on the thermal flare of sunlight reflecting off the Duke's bridge windscreen. Stubbornly, they continued to close the range.

Dix Beltrain watched the sparks of light crawling across his tactical display. They looked just like the symbols he had battle managed in a thousand combat simulations. There was a difference, though. These were no computer-generated simulacra. These were the actual weapons boring in to kill his ship and his shipmates . . . to kill *him*. He tried to control the tremor of his fingers as he dialed up the second ESSM flight.

He drew the date wand and prepared to designate the next set of targets. He found his eyes being drawn back to the track of the Exocets, now only inches away from the *Cunningham*'s position hack. Abruptly, he stabbed downward with the glowing tip of the wand, encapsulating the incoming missiles in targeting boxes. He slapped the firing keys again, not recognizing until a heartbeat later the catastrophic error he had committed.

A second flight of Enhanced Sea Sparrows blazed out of their launch cell. However, before these rounds had even reached the peak of their booster climb, the Exocets were cutting underneath the interceptor missiles. The ESSMs pitched over at an ever-increasing angle, vainly attempting to acquire their targets. They failed, and the salvo plunged, wasted, into the sea.

The secondary lines of defense engaged. The RBOC launchers shifted from decoy to concealment mode, trying to bury the ship in the heart of a concealing chaff cloud. Fore and aft, the two Oto Melara "Super Rapid" mounts opened fire, spewing out their streams of 76mm shells at a rate of a round per second, seeking to blanket the incoming Exocets with proximity-fused airbursts.

Amidships, atop the superstructure, the portside Phalanx Close-In Weapons System came on-line. An advanced Mark II model of the original General Dynamics "Sea Whizz," the single Vulcan 20mm Gatling gun of the first-generation weapon had been replaced by a battery of four 25mm rotary-breech cannon and augmented with quad clusters of RAM light surface-to-air missiles mounted on either flank of the squat, stealth-sheathed turret. A fully autonomous robotic system, it required no human input beyond its activation.

Now, as it perceived the incoming threats with its millimeter-wave radar and infrared trackers, its artificial-intelligence circuits coldly assessed the possibilities. Opting for missile engagement, it salvoed four RAMS at the closest Exocet.

Two miles out, the heat-seeker rounds bracketed and killed their target, whipsawing the lead AM-44 with a shotgun blast of fragmentation and tumbling it into the sea in a flurry of spray.

The Phalanx mount was incapable of feeling relief or exaltation over its victory. It merely began hunting for the next foe, its multiple barrels indexing jerkily as it sought for a favorable firing solution.

In the *Cunningham*'s Combat Information Center, there was nothing left to be done. The Duke was operating in full Armageddon mode now, more and more systems cycling over to full automatic as the light-speed war of computer, sensor, and jammer was waged. This was a battle she must fight out alone; the men and women who crewed her could only come along for the ride.

"... seven ... six ... five ... Jesus! It's gonna hit!"

Topside, the Phalanx fired with a droning roar like a titanic chain saw, its quad gun muzzles blurring with recoil, a hundred rounds being expended before the first empty shell casing could fall to the deck.

A single slug caught the Exocet head-on. The tungsten penetrator core of the hypervelocity round had been intended to pierce the armor of a main battle tank. It simply ignored the far flimsier structure of the antiship missile, punching cleanly through the guidance package and the warhead to fracture the casing of the solid-fuel rocket motor.

The last Exocet exploded a meager hundred yards off the *Cunningham*'s portside flank, sending a long horizontal plume of scarlet and silver flame licking out toward the destroyer.

Amanda felt a series of faint thuds ripple through her ship's structure.

"We've got dropouts on the planar arrays, portside forward," the Aegis operator called out. "I think we have shrapnel damage."

"The bridge has been hit," a second voice chimed in from the battle-damage stations. "Bridge requesting corpsmen and damage-control parties. Repair Four responding."

No time to worry about it now. The mast cameras were panning aft to pick up the next attack wave.

The first flight of Rafale E's were coming in on the stern, anti-IR flares glowing in their wake like golden snowflakes. Already in too close for area defense systems, point defenses were shifting fire to engage the new threat. The aft turret was dappling the sky around the Argentine jets with shell bursts, and the smoke trails of RAM rounds reached out toward them.

Suddenly, a dazzling point of blue-green light appeared beneath the belly of the element leader. A warning horn blared from the CIC overhead.

"Laser lock!"

Amanda didn't need to look at the exterior monitors to know what the intent of their attackers was. Somewhere on the weather decks of the Duke, a small dot of brilliant illumination was dancing. The ordnance-carrying aircraft of the attacking flight would now execute a sharp half-loop at a range of two or three miles, pitching a stick of heavy laser-guided bombs at the warship in a high parabolic trajectory. As the bombs came over the peak of their arc, their sensors would pick up the laser energy being reflected off the target by the illuminator aircraft. They would home in on it unerringly.

The drop aircraft was already pulling up into its release maneuver.

"Helm! Crash turn! Hard right rudder!" Amanda snapped. "RBOCs, fire full concealment pattern!"

The sailor at the helm station spun her controller fully around against the safety stop, then forced it the extra click more to engage the crash-turn sequencer.

The Duke moaned throughout her framing as her rudder swung hard over and the propeller blades of the starboard propulsor pod feathered automatically. Despite the best efforts of her stabilizers, her deck started to tilt outboard as she drove into the tightest of minimum-radius turns. Her own wake overtook her, bursting over the well deck and rolling up her right flank in a knot of green water and foam.

As she pivoted around, her chaff launchers began to ripple fire again. The grenades, bursting at close range all across the destroyer's forward arc, produced not only metal foil but thick, white streamers of multispectral chemical smoke. The Cunningham plunged headlong into an artificial fog bank of her own creation.

The bawling of the warning horn wavered and fell silent. A few moments later, a double thunderclap sounded from beyond the bulkheads and the Duke shuddered heavily. Their guidance lock lost, the bombs had fallen off target into her wake, kicking up mast-high domes of seething water.

Someone produced a relieved whoop of victory.

"Steady down!" Amanda snapped. "We aren't out of this yet! Dix, where's that last flight?"

"Target Foxtrot coming in on the port side, bearing two-sixty degrees relative. Range, ten thousand yards and closing. Point defenses are engaging!"

"Helm, turn into him. Hard left rudder!"

The *Cunningham* burst out of her smoke screen, trailing rags of vapor from her superstructure. The MMS cameras picked up the last pair of French-built deltas almost at once as they slashed in from the east, going for the destroyer's flank.

As the ship clawed around to face her new attackers, Amanda realized that something was wrong. The bow Oto Melara, a key facet of their forward arc defenses, was still silent. A fast glance down at her weapons-status telepanel showed that the gun had been toggled out of the Aegis defense system's computer loop to manual control.

"Number-one mount! What the hell are you playing at?" Beltrain roared from the Tac Ops console.

Across the compartment, the young gunner's mate manning the bow turret control station was leaning forward over his console, intently reconfiguring the system settings.

The laser lock warning horn blared again as the Argentine element leader illuminated his target. His wingman started to pull up into his toss-bombing run . . .

The bow turret crashed out a single round and the lead Rafale dissolved into a smear of flame.

Dumbfounded, the CIC crew watched the fragments of burning wreckage tumble into the sea. The sole remaining strike pilot was also stunned and demoralized. Releasing his ordnance in a wild patch that put the bombs into the sea a comfortable half-mile from the *Cunningham,* he broke hard around and fled.

"All surviving Argentine aircraft are disengaging and withdrawing," Beltrain reported. "Reentering area defense engagement zone. Designating ESSM flights—"

"Negative. Check fire, all systems," Amanda cut in. "Save our rounds for the ones coming at us."

Swiftly, Amanda called up the damage-control report on her personal repeaters: Light splinter damage to superstructure. Efficiency of the forward SPY-2A arrays down to 94 percent. Diagnostics indicating damage to bridge systems.

"Damage control, any word on casualties yet?"

"None reported except for the bridge area, ma'am," the DC officer called in from his station. "Corpsmen have been called onsite. That's the last word we've had."

She scanned the threat boards. For the moment they were clear except for the retreating blips of the Argentine air strike. There was no sign of an immediate follow-up.

"Helm, bring her around to a heading of one seven oh degrees. All engines ahead standard."

"Aye, aye, ma'am. Steering one seven oh degrees. All engines ahead standard."

"Communications, get this off to CINCLANT, flash priority: 'USS *Cunningham* has been attacked by aircraft positively identified as belonging to the Argentine armed forces. Two attacking aircraft downed. Ship has taken light damage but remains fully operational. Until otherwise advised we are acting under the assumption that a state of armed conflict exists between the United States and Argentina.'

"Then prep a data dump from the Aegis memory system covering the attack. They'll be wanting that."

She turned back to her tactical officer. "Dix, I'm turning the con over to you while I go topside and check out how badly we're hit. Keep us on this heading until we get back under the slop and keep your eyes open for another strike package. Oh, and find out what was going on with that forward gun. Any questions?"

The younger officer took an ineffective swipe at the sweat accumulating on his forehead. "Captain, I need to tell you about something that happened during the attack. . . ."

"I know, Dix. You're okay. We'll talk about it later."

The damage was less than it might have been, and far less than she had visualized. The bridge had been spattered with a bucketful of high-velocity metal fragments from the exploding Exocet. The heavy composite materials of the superstructure had absorbed most of them. A couple of the smaller chunks were still embedded in the bridge windscreen, each surrounded by a gray, bubbly patch of heat-marred acrylic. The spray door leading out to the portside bridge wing had been blown inward, spraying the interior of the wheelhouse with flying shards of thermoplastic. Half a dozen flatscreens had been smashed and the deck was crunchy with bits of safety glass. The control consoles themselves appeared to be more or less intact, barring a couple of impressive shrapnel scores. Less could be said for some of the personnel who had been manning them.

The first thing Amanda saw when she entered the bridge was her exec holding a blood-soaked first-aid dressing to the side of his face as he leaned weakly against the chart table.

"Ken, are you all right?"

"Yeah, I'm just cut up a little."

"Let me have a look."

"Honestly, Captain. I'm all right."

"Damn it, Ken, Misa will give me hell if I bring you back any less pretty than you were. Now, let me have a look!"

Amanda eased back the dressing and winced inwardly at what she found. "You're going to start a fine collection of stitches there. What about the rest of the bridge crew?"

"Minor stuff except for the helmsman. Robinson's working on him now." Hiro painfully nodded toward the farside of the bridge where a cluster of people were hunkered down around a motionless form.

Hospital Corpsman 1st Class Bonnie Robinson was a quiet and rather plain black woman from Detroit, Michigan. Now, though, as she worked over her wounded shipmate, her intensity and concentration gave her a kind of knife-edge beauty that onlookers would recognize only after the fact.

The subject of her attention had already been eased into a basket stretcher, his blue uniform coveralls laid open and a mass of blood-soaked gauze packing taped down across his chest. His eyes were closed and he was still except for his labored breathing. A cannula fed oxygen into his nostrils and an IV bag was tucked under his shoulder, its contents being pressured into his arm by his own weight.

Amanda recognized him as she knelt down by his side. Petty Officer 2nd Something-or-other Erikson, twenty years old, from some little place in South Dakota. He had come aboard at Pearl just prior to this cruise. As usual, she had talked with him a bit when he had signed on, and probably hadn't exchanged a dozen words with him since. He had seemed to be a good kid with a good record.

"What have you got?" she asked.

"I'm not sure yet," the Corpsman replied curtly. When she had her hands on a serious patient, Robinson tended to let all thoughts about military formality slip from her mind. Her captain understood and made no comment.

"He was unconscious when we got here and he's shocky as all hell. There's penetrating chest trauma, and I think there's some shrapnel in there. There's no sign of hemorrhaging from the lungs, but I'll bet we've got some going on in the chest cavity. As soon as he's stable enough for it, we'll hump him down to sick bay and I'll get some X rays. We'll know more then."

Amanda held back all of the trite little phrases like "Do the best you can" and "Keep me informed." She simply gave an acknowledging nod and got to her feet.

She looked down into the young seaman's pale face for a moment more and a strange chill rippled through her. She stepped back abruptly and took a deep and deliberate breath. She had seen wounded before, as well as the dying and the dead. There was no sense in its getting to her now.

She went back to the bridge captain's chair and jacked her headset directly into the MC-1 circuit.

"All hands, this is the Captain. Here's the situation. We have been attacked without provocation by aircraft of the Argentine Air Force and Navy. We have sustained minor damage and a couple of our people have been wounded. Two of our attackers, one-third of the enemy strike force, have been destroyed. For our first action, we have acquitted ourselves well.

"At this time, we do not know what triggered this attack or what the current political situation is between the United States and Argentine. You will be informed as soon as we learn anything further. Until then, we must assume that we are at war and we must act accordingly on that assumption. From here on out, ladies and gentlemen, it's the real thing."

DRAKE PASSAGE
1420 HOURS: MARCH 25, 2006

Amanda was alone in the wardroom. All other hands were still at general quarters as the ship fled southward toward the weather fronts.

Her instincts were to remain in the Combat Information Center, hovering over the radar repeaters. However, she had forced herself away. Her command headset would give her an instant link with events there, and she must trust in her crew and her systems.

She heated a mug of water for tea in the countertop microwave and spread peanut butter on a piece of toast. Then, with great deliberation, she sat down and began to eat.

She wasn't particularly hungry. In fact, there was a massive leaden knot where her stomach should have been. She couldn't afford to yield to that, though. From this point on, she would have to run maintenance on herself, just as she would on any other key ship's system. She dare not squander her reserves of energy and mental focus.

She took another sip of the strongly brewed tea without tasting and stared down the length of the table without seeing, mentally following event probabilities into the future.

"Begging your pardon, ma'am?"

She glanced up to find one of the CPOs from Weapons Division and an enlisted man standing just inside the open wardroom door. She recognized the EM as the gunner's mate who had been on the forward Oto Melara mount. He was now holding a rather uneasy parade rest beside his chief.

"This is Gunner's Mate Second Danny Lyndiman, ma'am," the CPO said, shooting an ominous *You're gonna catch hell now* glance across at the younger man. "Mr. Beltrain said you wanted to talk with him."

"I do," Amanda replied, pushing her chair back to face the two men.

"Well, Lyndiman," she said, lowering her voice just enough so he had to concentrate on her words. "You scored a very spectacular one-shot kill on that Rafale this afternoon. Would you care to tell me how you went about it?"

The lean young gunner shifted his weight uneasily. Everywhere else he had ever served, when the CO got loud, things got bad. On the Duke, though, when "The Lady" got quiet, that's when you started to worry. Suddenly, his brilliant improvisation didn't seem quite so brilliant.

"It was like this, ma'am. When the Argys started using laser-guided ordnance on us, I figured why not use it right back at them."

"Go on."

"When that first Rafale flight illuminated us like it did, it occurred to me that if we had the chance to fire one of our own laser-guided rounds back up their designation basket, our shell would ride their own beam right back into the illuminator pod. Then, when the second flight started to come in, the angle looked good, so I took my gun out of the Aegis loop, went over to manual control, and reloaded with laser-guided munitions. I got it set up in time and I took the shot. I guess it worked."

"I guess it did," Amanda replied softly. "Did you clear the change-over with the tactical action officer?"

"No, ma'am. There just wasn't any time. I was barely able to recycle and reload the system and get the round off."

"I see, and what made you sure that our systems would be interactive with theirs?"

"I've been reading up on the briefing package for the mission, ma'am. The Argentines use a Thomson CSF designation system. It's fully NATO standardized and operationally compatible with all of our stuff. It had to work."

"No, it didn't. Not if the aircraft in the second flight had been carrying an ordnance load other than laser-guided munitions."

Amanda watched the play of expression across the seaman's face. First the moment of confusion, then the gut-lurching realization. She let him dwell for a while on the image of a gutted and blazing ship. It wouldn't be necessary to crucify Lyndiman further. He was a conscientious and intelligent young man and he was doing a fine job of it on his own.

"I'm sorry, Captain. I thought I was doing the right thing," he said miserably.

"You were. You thought clearly and quickly in a crisis situation and you spotted a potential vulnerability in an enemy. You knocked down an attacking aircraft and you just possibly saved this ship.

"It's my belief that one of the strengths of our Navy has always been that our ships have been crewed by intelligent, innovative people who can think for themselves in an emergency. I do not want or need mindless robots aboard the *Cunningham*.

"However, what you did down there today was a classic calculated risk. When you call something like that right, you get to be the hero. But if you call it wrong, you get to watch your shipmates die. Should you ever have to make another call like that, you make sure that you are as right then as you were today."

"Okay, Captain," he replied, giving her a sober nod. "You got it."

"Very well. Chief, this gentleman here seems to think he needs a little more responsibility in his life. We will oblige him. Gunner's Mate Second Lyndiman is now a gunner's mate first. He's also our new first-stringer on the forward gun. Please inform Mr. Beltrain about it and see that the paperwork gets to my desk when the opportunity presents itself."

"Aye, aye, Captain."

"Is that suitable for you, Mr. Lyndiman?"

"Yes, ma'am! Thank you!"

She cocked an eyebrow. "Thank you. Dismissed."

After the two men had disappeared back out into the passageway, Amanda had just enough time for another gulp of cooling tea before her headset phones went active.

"Captain, you'd better get back down here to the CIC."

"What's happening, Chris?"

"Offhand, I'd say we're up shit creek and the guy who's rented us the boat has just called time."

Lieutenants Rendino and McKelsie were hunkered down together in front of a computer terminal as Amanda reentered the dimness of the CIC, their close proximity giving them an odd air of intimacy.

"What's the situation?" she inquired sharply as she joined them.

"It looks like we might have to eat another air strike," Christine replied.

"Why? We've broken contact."

"It's that damn Argy satellite. It'll be making its next pass in about"—Christine glanced up at the digital clock on the overhead—"forty-five minutes. The spook meister here figures it's going to tag us."

"What about it, McKelsie? Are they that good? Can't we stealth it?"

He shook his head. "I've been running some computer models on the capabilities of the Argentine sat, specifically its thermographic scanning. It doesn't look good. We got a real contrast problem going here."

"More than our insulation and Black Hole systems can cope with?"

"Yeah, a lot more. We've got a still-air atmospheric temperature of nineteen degrees Fahrenheit out there and a surface-water temperature of thirty-one degrees. Even if we start an immediate emergency drawdown of our internal temperature and cut power completely while the sat is overhead, we're still going to show up like a lightbulb on black velvet on any kind of halfway decent infrared imager. The only way we can kill that kind of temperature differential is by using the misting system."

McKelsie referred to the system of high-pressure water jets built into the *Cunningham*'s weather decks and upper works. Primarily intended as a purging mechanism to clear the destroyer's topsides of radioactive or biochemical contamination, it could also be used to mask her thermal signature under a cooling and concealing cloud of spray.

"I can't use the water jets now," Amanda protested. "I'd have six inches of solid ice built up on the weather decks inside of half an hour. We'd have to use the deck heaters to clear it off."

McKelsie nodded. "Yeah, and that would magnify our heat signature so much that a nearsighted rattlesnake could track us."

Christine rose from behind the terminal and stretched. "Here's how I figure it. We've got about three hours of daylight left and about forty minutes until the next satellite pass. The Argys probably have another strike armed and on the runway, ready to launch the second they get a fresh fix on our position. Give them twenty minutes to the strike airborne and an hour's flight time from Rio Grande Base. That will put them over our last known location with an hour of daylight left.

"Currently, we've got two thousand feet between the bottom of the available cloud deck and the ocean's surface. Probably they'll drop down through the overcast at our last position fix and spiral outward in a visual search pattern. Figuring that they use a tanker on the way in, they'll have enough light and gas to have a pretty good chance of spotting us."

Amanda let the breath trickle out of her lungs in a soft hissing sigh. "They've got an absolutely solid chance of spotting us. If they can work in that close, we don't dare maintain full EMCON. We'll have to bring up the air-search radars to keep from being bushwhacked entirely, and they'll home in on our emissions. Unless we can find some little localized snow squall or fog bank to hide in, you're right, we will have to eat the strike."

"Maybe we could avoid a whole lot of unpleasantness by doing something about that reconsat before it can spot us," the intel pointed out hopefully.

"The Zenith round? It takes a minimum of two hours to stack it and prep it for launch. We just don't have enough time now. Later tonight, though, I intend to make good use of it."

Granting we're still afloat, Amanda added silently.

"I think we have an alternative."

Vince Arkady had been standing back in one of the bay's shadowy corners. Now he pushed away from the bulkhead and stepped forward. He was clad in full flight gear, including survival suit and Mae West life jacket, and his helmet was clipped to his harness by its chin strap.

"May I talk with you for a moment, ma'am?" he asked formally.

"Of course." Amanda nodded to her intel and her countermeasures man and moved over to the waiting pilot. "What have you got, Lieutenant?"

"It's not a good idea to let them move in on us like that, Captain."

"Tell me about it. More importantly, tell me what we can do about it?"

"We go after them."

"An ambush?" Amanda frowned thoughtfully. "We could run north and try to set up an over-the-horizon missile trap with the LORAINs."

"That could work, but I was thinking of something more up close and personal."

"Such as?"

"I want to try an intercept with an air-to-air armed helo."

Amanda's eyebrows shot up. "Arkady! Going after a fighter-bomber strike with a helicopter is turning macho into foolhardy."

"Not the fighter-bombers, Captain. The tanker."

"What do you mean?"

"I mean I take Retainer Zero One out along the incoming flight path of this next Sierra strike. Once I get out about where I figure they'll be running their refueling operation, I'll go stealth and wait for them to overfly me. Then I pop up underneath them and kill the tanker.

"That should not only break up this strike, but given their limited air-to-air refueling assets, it should go a long way towards screwing up any future ops they might want to launch against us."

Amanda frowned again. "How are you going to know what their line of approach is going to be?"

"I won't for sure, but I can make a pretty good educated guess. I figure the Argys will apply the KISS principle on this next strike just like they did before. When they launch, they'll fly a straight bearing out from the Isla Grande navigational beacon to our last fixed position. I just have to fly north, back along that bearing far enough, and I should be in pretty good shape to bushwhack 'em.

"While I'm running the intercept, we'll have Retainer Zero Two up with an Airborne Early Warning pod. She'll transmit an open-band downlink of what her radar is imaging that both the Duke and Retainer Zero One will be able to patch into passively. I'll be able to build a tactical display out of that without having to give away my position. The Argys won't know I'm there until they run right over me."

Amanda suddenly found herself wishing that he weren't making so much sense.

"All right, then," she said, "how do you plan to get out afterwards?"

"Same way I got in. Fully stealthed, and down on the deck. With a little luck, by the time they sort out what's happened, I'll be over the hill and far away."

"If you're not lucky, you'll end up alone out there with a bunch of very angry Argentine fighter pilots."

He gave her a half-grin. "If you don't bet, you can't win. That's how the game's played."

"Okay," she replied, grabbing for a last argument, "answer one more thing, then. What's the advantage of risking an aircrew over doing the same job with the LORAINs?"

"Surprise, and the probability of success. We have to assume that the Argys will be paying close attention to their threat boards as they come in. They probably won't worry too much about our air-search sweeps, but the second you bring up the fire-control radars, they'll scatter. Even a C-130 can do a whole lot of shuckin' and jivin' during the couple of minutes it would take for a SAM to get out that far. With my way, they won't realize they've got a problem until it's too late to do anything about it."

Arkady watched as Amanda slipped into what he was coming to recognize as her "heavy studying" posture: her arms crossed over her stomach, her head tilted down with her thick fall of hair flowing along her jawline, her lower lip lightly bitten in thought.

Finally she looked up. "Okay, Arkady, we go with it."

DRAKE PASSAGE
1630 HOURS: MARCH 25, 2006

They committed to the intercept. The Duke held her course to the southeast as the Argentine spy satellite arced overhead. The moment it dropped below the horizon, however, she came about to the north, closing the range with her potential foes with every beat of her racing propellers.

Both of her helos scrambled, each lifting into the sky on its assigned mission. Retainer Zero Two, with the radome of a Clear Water Airborne Early Warning pod bulging beneath one snub wing, took up its point station twenty miles ahead of the destroyer's bow, matching her course and speed. From here, serving as a mini-AWACS aircraft, her radar coverage would provide the sole link between the *Cunningham* and Retainer Zero One as the latter ranged ahead along their enemy's potential line of attack.

The *Cunningham*'s first team was fully closed up in the Combat Information Center. Amanda slouched in her command chair and used the sidearm keypad to flip the Large Screen Display from augmented computer simulacra to live radar and back again. The image being received from the hovering helicopter lacked the range and definition of the ship's big SPY-2A arrays. They were just barely pulling in the ghostly outline of the coast of Isla Grande and Cape Horn.

Dix Beltrain rested his hand on the back of her chair and quietly asked, "Captain, may I speak with you privately for a moment?"

Her normally amiable tactical operations officer had been quiet and indrawn ever since the Argentine attack. Amanda had sensed the crisis building and she'd been preparing for it.

"Sure, Dix," she replied, sliding out of her chair. She led Beltrain to the quiet rear corner of the compartment next to the ubiquitous Navy-issue coffee urn.

The younger officer was holding himself almost at parade rest as he began to speak in a low voice. "Captain, I need to confer with you about something that happened during the Argentine air strike."

"Presumably the total hash you made of our ESSM area defense during the engagement?"

"That's it, ma'am. I bitched it! I bitched it really bad. I saw that those Exocets were crossing into the point defense zone. The warning flags had come up on my tactical screen. I knew that they were passing out of a successful engagement envelope and I still tried to set up a shot instead of shifting fire to the Rafale flights. I . . . I have no excuses or explanations, Captain."

"You don't, Lieutenant?" Amanda replied mildly. "I do. It's a phenomenon my dad would have called 'buck fever,' probably mixed with a little whiff of raw terror."

"Not just a whiff, ma'am. I was scared shi— I was scared so badly that I made a critical error and I endangered the ship. I believe it's my duty to point this out to you, and to give you the option of pulling me out of the command loop."

"Dix, a short time ago, some very capable people were trying very hard to kill us. They came very close to succeeding. The individual who wasn't scared under those circumstances would be the one I'd be inclined to pull out of the loop, primarily because it would be plain that they'd become detached from reality."

Beltrain shook his head emphatically. "That isn't the point. I locked up so bad that I fumbled it. I should have been engaging those other bomber elements. I could have broken up the strike before they got within kill range. Instead, all I could see were those damn missiles coming in on us. I screwed up, ma'am!"

Amanda shrugged. "I won't argue the point, Mr. Beltrain. You most definitely screwed up. Realistically, though, wouldn't that same potential have existed for anyone I might have put on the main console?

"Someday, when you and he both have a little spare time, ask Chief Thomson about his experiences during Desert Storm. He was aboard the old *Sacramento* at the time, and he will vividly describe to you what it was like tending a fire room in the Red Sea in one-hundred-and-twenty-degree weather for six straight months. He's the closest thing to a combat veteran we have aboard this ship.

"Come to think of it, I believe this was the first instance of a United States naval vessel coming under air attack since the Persian Gulf tanker war. So, if I pulled you off the main console, I'd be bouncing the most experienced missileer currently serving in the United States Navy. That would be a rather stupid thing to do, in my opinion."

Beltrain ran his hand through his perspiration-damp hair. "That doesn't cover for the fact that I still committed a major error, ma'am."

"Join the club. I imagine that when we conduct a post-action analysis on this furball, we're going to discover that a lot of people made errors. I'm willing to concede that I made mine. The thing is, we survived and we learned. We're blooded now. We won't make so many mistakes next time.

"Don't get me wrong, Dix. I'm not tossing off what happened today. I just believe that you're still the best man available for the job. Now, push all of the guilt-trip cow hockey aside and give me a straight answer. If I leave you on the main console, will this happen again?"

He took a deep, deliberate breath. "No, ma'am. It will not."

"Okay, then." Amanda grinned and made a quick cross-shaped gesture in the air. "I grant you absolution. Go forth and sin no more, my son. Now get back to work."

"Aye, aye, Captain." Beltrain grinned back, the weight on his shoulders starting to lift.

From up forward, the Aegis systems operator called out sharply, "Distant contact! Slow mover turning south-southwest off Isla Grande beacon. Range two hundred and twenty miles, altitude eighteen thousand feet, bearing zero degrees relative off the bow. Multiple contacts!"

Three fast steps took Amanda and her TACCO back to their workstations. A single fast look fixed the location of the air-target symbol drifting out of the Isla Grande ground clutter. There was no precise position hack for Retainer Zero One being displayed. The Sea Comanche was running fully stealthed and radio and radar silenced, invisible even to the *Cunningham*'s advanced sensors. There was only an outlined block of space, indicating its estimated position, dead-on between the Duke and the advancing Argentine strike. A phantom guardian waiting for its enemies to cross its path.

"Bring up your LORAIN flights, Mr. Beltrain." All trace of humor and warmth had left Amanda's voice. "Fight's on."

One hundred and fifty miles off the *Cunningham*'s bow and a meager fifty off the Argentine coast, Retainer Zero One circled just above the wave tops, her low-visibility paint merging into the color of the sea.

Arkady used the trackball on the end of his collective-control stick to call up the fuel-status chart on his engineering telepanel.

"Okay, Gus, fuel transfer complete. Internal cells to one hundred per. Stand by to get rid of the tanks."

"Rog."

Vince slid the cursor across the monitor face to the actions menu and into the "Exterior Tank Jettison" detente and squeezed the actuator trigger. He was rewarded with the clank of releasing shackles. The drop tanks scarcely caused a splash as they hit the water.

"Green indicators. Verify me."

In the air cockpit, the AC 1 twisted in his harness to port and starboard, peering aft and down at the helo's snub wings. "Tanks are clear, sir. Can't see any system leakage."

"Okeydoke. How's the downlink look?"

"Pickup is nominal and a clear board, and I hope it stays that way."

"Show a little spunk there, fellow. Here we are, a couple of Uncle Sam's fighting bluejackets, out 'mid wind and wave, volunteering to do some of that hero shit for Mom, apple pie, and the girl next door."

"Volunteer! I didn't volunteer for nothing!"

"You were busy. I did it for you."

"Fuck you very much, sir."

"What was that, sailor?"

"I said, 'Thank you very much, sir!' "

"You're welcome, Gus."

Grestovitch went back to brooding over his systems displays. He liked Lieutenant Arkady and enjoyed flying as his SO more than with any other pilot he'd ever been teamed with. The Lieutenant was a mustang; he'd started out as an enlisted man himself. He'd laugh and talk with you like you were both real human beings, and as long as you did your job, he wouldn't get in your face over the small shit.

The downside was that you could find yourself doing foaming-at-the-mouth crazy stuff like this.

For a moment, the AC considered the possibility that Arkady might be studding off for the benefit of their new lady captain, then he rejected the notion. If the Skipper had been fifty years old, male, and as ugly as a bucket full of assholes, they'd still probably be out here.

LAMPS systems operators didn't get the chance to train in air-search mode as often as they did for other missions. So it took Grestovitch several seconds to recognize what was taking place on his screens.

"Airborne contact! Just coming off the coast. Bearing one eight seven true. Altitude one eight triple oh. Range forty-eight miles."

"Speed, Gus?"

"Uh, one hundred eighty knots."

"Relative bearing?"

"Oh two five, relative bearing off the nose. Second target just coming on-screen, closing with the first."

"Okay! That's our boy! Tallyho!"

Arkady slewed Retainer Zero One around onto a course that would intersect with that of the Argentine strike.

Captain Alfredo Cristobal applied the last-minute burst of thrust that socked his Tornado's refueling probe into the drogue basket of the Hercules. The control lights on the tanker's wingtip shifted pattern to indicate "Solid Connection" and "Transfer On." A flick of his eyes downward to the fuel-transfer panel verified that jet propellant was cascading into the fighter-bomber's cells.

Another glance took in the threat boards, currently showing that the sky around them was clear except for a distant trace of American search radar. It was safe to back his concentration down a level. Cristobal relaxed into the padding of his ejector seat.

Obviously the problem with the first strike had been the involvement of the Air Force. This was a job best dealt with by the

Aeronaval alone. He would personally command this operation to ensure its success. At the same time, he would take the opportunity to heal his own wounded pride.

Cristobal came from a culture that still primarily believed that women were to be protected, cherished, but above all else, dominated. This female Norteno captain had almost knocked him out of the sky during the harassment flight he had flown against her. She had humiliated him in front of his squadron and the entire fleet, and that brand had burned deep.

Amanda Garrett had come to both enrage and fascinate him. He had pulled the dossier that the intelligence section had assembled on her and had spent hours studying it. The photographs told him more than the text. One of them was currently taped into an odd corner of his cockpit control panel. A red-haired woman in naval uniform peered out from it, sternly beautiful, coolly sensuous, totally self-confident.

Alfredo Cristobal wanted to shatter that self-confidence more than he desired anything else on earth.

This time, they would send their Exocets blazing in behind a wave of Matra STAR antiradar missiles. It would be more than enough to suppress the Americans' point defenses and assure at least one hit.

For a moment he considered whether he should have incorporated another element of aircraft into the strike, one armed with iron bombs to finish the job the missiles might start. Too late now. Besides, all four of his Tornadoes were carrying a full load of armor-piercing incendiary ammunition for their 27mm Mauser autocannon. More than enough to give anything left afloat a good beating.

There might be survivors. That would be interesting.

With Cristobal's rage and fascination had come an unbidden fantasy. One in which he took this Garrett woman as his own personal captive, as the conquistadors of old would have done. He had visualized taming her as one would a fiery mare, stripping her of her air of authority and self-control, heating that cool sensuality into hot passion.

He shook his head regretfully. This modern day and age no longer permitted such things. He would have to be content with merely killing her.

"Raven's Roost is confirming the emission patterns of Tornado-type aircraft," Beltrain commented from his console. "Arkady called it right. They're coming right down the turnpike."

"Um-hmm," Amanda replied absently as she studied the Alpha display. The Argentine target hack was just crawling across the line into the estimated intercept zone. A few miles more and they would pass into the range of the Duke's long-range SAMs. She would wait, though. She had promised Arkady the first shot.

Amanda sank back into her chair and lightly bit her lower lip in thought. In her experience, there were two kinds of individuals capable of volunteering for a mission like this.

One was the kind who believed in their own invincibility, that death only happened to the other guy.

The other was the kind who were quite aware of their own mortality but who were still willing to surrender it to the cause that they served. Amanda found herself hoping that she would have the time and the chance to learn which defined Vince Arkady.

Grestovitch's fingers were sweat-sticky inside his Nomex flight glove as he called up the latest batch of intercept data.

"Target speed over ground still one eight zero. Altitude still eighteen thousand. Range six miles. Rate of closure sixty knots."

"We still in the groove, Gus?"

"Rog. Target bearing zero degrees relative off our tail. They'll be overflying us in about four minutes."

Arkady reflected that beyond this being the first helo-versus-jet intercept he had ever heard of, it was probably also the first ass-backward one where the bogey overtook the interceptor.

"We still being painted?"

"Negative, Lieutenant. They went active again on their radar a second ago, but all that we're getting is sidelobe."

"Okay, that means we're under their search cone. Time to take her up, ol' buddy."

Arkady squeezed the throttle trigger on the pitch lever and the twin LHTEC T800 gas turbines howled in reply. Rolling back on the collective, he lifted the little helo into a maximum power climb.

This pop-up maneuver was critical. The twin Sidewinder X missiles the Sea Comanche carried under its snub wings were state-of-the-art weapons, but they had a range of only twelve miles, a range that would be greatly reduced if they had to climb after their targets. Retainer Zero One would have to do some of that climbing for them if they were to make a kill.

"There they are, Lieutenant."

Arkady tilted his head back and looked up through the cockpit's overhead Plexiglas panel. The Argentine tanker formation was passing almost directly overhead. Eighteen thousand feet was normally low for contrail effects, but in the chill polar atmosphere, all five of the aircraft drew thin streamers of ice-crystal vapor behind them. They were clearly silhouetted against the royal-blue sky. They were also clearly pulling too damn far away.

Vince checked his altimeter and his airspeed indicator. His forward velocity was fading fast in the climb and he was falling behind his pursuit curve.

"Gus, heat 'em up!"

The air-to-air targeting reticule appeared in the center of his heads-up display and the high-pitched arming tone of the Sidewinders sounded in his earphones.

The tanker flight was opening the range, and they still didn't have the altitude Arkady wanted. There was no help for it. He flared Retainer Zero One back, lifting its nose above the horizon until the helicopter shuddered on the verge of rotor stall. Laying the death pip of his sights into the center of the enemy formation, he squeezed the actuator to give the missiles a look at their target.

The arming tone became a squalling growl.

"I got good locks! This is it! I'm taking the shot!"

Arkady squeezed the actuator again, and then again. At half-second intervals, the Sidewinders sliced off their launching rails trailing fire. He and Gus had done their best. Now it was in the hands of the gods and Ford Aerospace. Arkady dropped his helo's nose, dumped pitch, and dove for the sea.

Fully topped off, Captain Cristobal and his wingman had dropped a quarter of a mile back and to starboard of the Fuerza Aérea Hercules, clearing the way for the next element. Those two aircraft were now tucked in close beneath the tanker's wings and were taking on fuel, a task that would be completed in another minute or so.

Cristobal had been thinking ahead, mentally reviewing the next phase of the operation, when a flickering yellow light and a warning buzzer yanked his attention back to the here and now.

Tail warning radar! Cristobal jinked hard right and twisted around in his seat to check his six. He saw nothing but empty sky and a distant cloud bank.

He eased off on his controls and came back on course.

"Carcel, did you catch that?"

"Sí, Capitán," his backseater replied. "A momentary weak contact on the tail guard system. I am receiving nothing at the moment, however."

Cristobal frowned. His threat board was clear again, but now the warning was sounding in the back of his mind. He keyed his transmitter. "Tigre two, this is Tigre lead. Do you have any air-to-air contacts?"

"Negative, lead. No activity."

Cristobal acknowledged. He was about to shrug off his premonition when his tail warning system sounded again. An infrared return.

He jinked left, wildly searching the sky. This time he spotted a pair of flickering orange sparks, each pulling a faint smoky trail behind it, arcing up beneath the tanker formation. Cristobal crushed down on the transmitter button, groping for words that might avert the coming disaster. He could find none.

The Sidewinders were almost at the end of their range, with their fuel nearly exhausted and their velocity peaking. During the last second of its flight, the multiple targets presented by the C-130 and the two fighters holding formation with it confused the guidance system of the lead missile, making it bobble slightly. Instead of homing on an engine pod, it struck the tanker's belly. Punching through cleanly, its twenty-five-pound fragmentation warhead detonated amid the half-empty fuel bladders in the cargo compartment.

The Hercules dissolved into a ball of flame, a sun-colored blister against the sky that swelled to engulf both of the accompanying Tornadoes and then burst to rain a cascade of blazing wreckage down toward the ocean far below.

Buffeted by the shock wave, the surviving Argentine airmen stared in horror at the churning firestorm falling away beneath them. Someone whispered a supplication to God into the radio circuit.

Cristobal forced his shock-numbed mind to work, analyzing the attack, reconstructing how it must have been set up. The bitch had done it to him again! His curse came out almost as a sob.

His left hand stabbed at the ordnance-control panel, jettisoning his missile load and arming his cannon. Ordering his wingman to do the same and to follow him down, he rolled his Tornado into a split-S maneuver and dove for the sea. His honor had been shattered along with the air strike. This time Cristobal intended to demand a blood price in exchange for it.

"Primary target has blown up!"

Every hand in the Combat Information Center could see and recognize the distinctive "blossom" and rapid fade of a midair explosion on the Large Screen Display.

"Massive RCS dropoff on the target," Dix reported. "Looks like a couple of the fast movers were taken out along with the tanker. Way to go, Vince!"

A ragged cheer started to grow, only to be cut off abruptly.

"Belay that!" Amanda's voice rang out like a rifle shot. "Save it until we get our people home."

Retainer Zero One fled southward out of the intercept zone, its composite frame shuddering from the overload of its racing turbines. Officially, the LAMPS IV Boeing/Sikorsky SAH-66 Sea Comanche helicopter was rated at a maximum airspeed of 195 miles per hour at full war power. If the aircrew was scared badly enough, it could reach 200.

"Pick up your visual scanning, Gus. We still got a couple of fighters out there."

"I know it," Grestovitch replied. He was twisted around as far as his harness would allow, attempting to peer aft past the helo's fantail into their blind spot. "Begging your pardon, Lieutenant, but just how did you figure on getting us out of this?"

"Well, speaking frankly, Gus, I was hoping that the bad guys would just sort of go home."

"Begging your pardon again, sir, but I don't think very much of your friggin' plan."

"I'm willing to concede that this may be a definite flaw in an otherwise sound concept."

Grestovitch's threat board began to flash a warning. "Heads up, we're being painted. Two Tornado air-search systems. No locks, but they're coming up fast."

"Right, I'm going to fishtail. Try and spot 'em."

Vince rocked his rudder pedals, slewing the helo slightly to give his systems operator a better view aft.

"I got 'em, Lieutenant! Two fast movers at seven o'clock descending . . . Hell! They're turning in on us! They got us spotted!"

"Right. We're going evasive."

Arkady enabled and lit off his own radars and radios. No sense in fooling around with emission control now. He started tracking the incoming bandits on his HUD and tried to call up what he could remember of the Army's helicopter air-combat course he had taken TDY at Fort Rucker.

"Engagements with enemy fixed-wing assets are not to be undertaken lightly . . ."

No shit, Dogface.

Arkady continued to seesaw lightly on his rudder pedals, maintaining his wavering flight path as the Argentine jets bored in. If they had missiles, he could counter with flares and his anti-IR systems. If they went to guns, all that he had was his maneuverability.

As the range closed to critical, Arkady flared the Sea Comanche into a hard right pitch-out. He held the rackingly steep turn for a couple of heartbeats, then dumped gee and reversed back onto his original heading.

Whom! Whom! The Tornadoes blazed past overhead, buffeting the helo with their passage as they pulled out of their run. A short distance off to port, a quarter-mile-long curtain of spray was starting to disperse. It had been struck off the ocean's surface by the cannon shells of the strafing Argentine fighters.

"They're starting to come back around, Lieutenant!"

"Rog. Stay on 'em and call 'em out. I'm going to start yelling for some help."

"Retainer Zero One to Gray Lady. Be advised we've got a problem out here." Arkady's voice rasped from one of the overhead speakers. "I confirm one tanker and two fast movers are down. I also confirm that I've got the two survivors all over me. I am on the deck and fully defensive. Can you give us some cover?"

"Push the primary and Airborne Early Warning arrays to full output," Amanda snapped. "Give me a tactical of the engagement area. I want to see what's going on out there!"

An electronic outline appeared around the block of space on

the Alpha Screen that contained the air battle winding up. The image showed Retainer Zero One's beacon hack crawling southwest with agonizing slowness, while the blips of the two Argentine fighters buzzed around it like angry hornets.

"Dix, do we have range on those aircraft yet?"

"Yes, ma'am, they are within the LORAIN engagement envelope."

"Very well, then. Designate the Tornadoes and commence firing."

The Missileer bent over his console. Seconds passed, too many of them.

"Dix, what in the hell is the problem?"

"She won't lock up!" Beltrain replied feverishly, his hands playing across the fire-control matrix. "They're too damn low. They keep dropping out of our line of sight and we lose designation."

"What about Zero Two? Can we target over the horizon through her?"

"Negative. Her AEW pod is search-capable only. It doesn't have designation capacity and her integral radar systems don't have enough range."

Amanda slammed her palm down onto the arm of her chair in frustration. Overhead, the speaker came on-line again.

"Retainer Zero One to Gray Lady. The Argys just made another run on us. I don't want to be an alarmist, but we could really use some help out here."

Amanda had the answer to her question. Arkady's voice was level and controlled, yet she could hear the fear underlying it. He knew that he could die. At that moment, he was expecting to.

She let her reasoning mind race, assessing potentials and assembling possibilities.

"Dix, fire a flight of LORAINs across the engagement zone. Four missiles at ten-second intervals launched on fixed bearings at medium altitude. Fan them out across the entire area."

"Captain, I don't have target designation!"

"Just do it, Dix! Communications! Give me a patch through to Retainer Zero One."

Arkady slammed up on both the pitch and collective levers. The helo flared back like a startled partridge, using the full lift of its main rotor to kill off its forward speed. A split second later, the sea ahead of it boiled into foam under another storm of cannon fire. The Aeronaval jet veered off like a disappointed barracuda.

"*To evade fighter attack, execute a tight figure-eight flight pattern around two adjacent hilltops . . .*"

If somehow he got out of this alive, Arkady was going to kick the living hell out of the next army flight instructor he ever laid eyes on.

He nosed the Sea Comanche down and started to regain his airspeed, trying to ignore the flashing "Transmission Overheat" warning. The Argentines had split up and were coming in on him independently, reducing the time he had to recover between attacks. Sooner or later, one or the other of them had to get lucky. The SAH-66 had Kevlar armor protecting most of its critical systems, but it was proof only against rifle-caliber gunfire. It wouldn't take many hits from an autocannon to knock them down.

"Retainer Zero One, this is Gray Lady." Pushed by the *Cunningham*'s powerful transmitter, Amanda Garrett's voice came through into his helmet phones with amazing clarity. "We can see your situation and we are sending you something to fight with. We are launching a flight of LORAINs over your position. You will have to provide target designation and terminal guidance. Time to target will be about three minutes. Do you understand me, Arkady? You have got to stay alive out there for another three minutes!"

The small solid-fuel booster of the Raytheon/General Dynamics LORAIN (LOng RAnge INterceptor) ignited as it shot clear of its VLS cell. Six seconds and six hundred miles per hour worth of acceleration later, the booster burned out and was jettisoned.

Bat-ear air intakes opened at the base of the missile's forward set of cruciform fins and the sustainer engine fired. A high-efficiency, high-thrust ramjet, burning an exotic boron-slurry fuel, it smoothly pushed the missile through the sound barrier and up to its 3,000 miles per hour cruising speed.

The LORAIN was one of the showpieces of the current American arsenal, the most advanced, naval area defense SAM in operational deployment. But as it arced out over the South Polar sea, followed at intervals by three of its sisters, its sophisticated hunter/seeker systems were inert. It was only a machine. It still required a human to aim it and to tell it to kill.

Captain Cristobal had found the American helicopter to be a frustrating target. First, he had discovered that its stealth characteristics had rendered his radar gunsight useless, and then its pilot had proven to be a superb combat aviator.

Repeatedly the Norteno had reversed back under his fire streams, or had danced his machine laterally out of his sights. Already Cristobal had expended over half of his ammunition futilely.

It was time to shift tactics. He ordered Tigre Two to orbit above the copter, keeping it in sight while he swung wide to the north. Bringing the wings of his Tornado full forward, he dropped his flaps and landing gear and throttled up to full war power, converting the strike fighter into a comparatively slow and stable gun platform. Dropping down low over the waves, Cristobal began his final run in.

"That's the game plan, Gus. The Duke will give us a countdown as the missiles come in overhead, then we turn into the Argys and designate them with our own radar."

"It'd help if we had more altitude, Lieutenant."

"Yeah, but that would turn us into a sitting duck. You'll have to do the best you can."

"Aye, aye, sir. They seem to have backed off a little. Do you think they might be packing it in?"

"Nope. More than likely they're setting up something new."

Arkady gave himself a second to sweep the horizon ahead, another to check his instrumentation, and a third to try to analyze the vibration starting to feed back through his controls. *Feels like a possible rotor hit. Sure hope a blade doesn't go.* Then a check of the tail guard radar.

Somebody was back there, but he was coming in slower than before. Arkady skidded the helo a little and took a look aft. There was a pair of glowing landing lights on the horizon, aimed dead-on at them.

Uh-oh, he thought, *this guy's been staying at home, reading his manuals, when he should have been out chasing the hot women.*

A hundred and fifty miles away, Dix Beltrain reported. "First missile closing on engagement zone. Time to give them the count."

"Make it so," Amanda replied tonelessly.

"Gray Lady to Retainer Zero One. First round coming in. We are giving you a ten count."

Arkady didn't bother to acknowledge, he just threw the helo into the tightest possible pedal turn it could make. Instead of the 20mm Gatling gun carried in the nose of the Army's RAH-66 attack helicopter, the SAH-66 Sea Comanche mounted a variant of the same Hughes APG-65 multimode radar used by the F/A-18 Hornet strike fighter. The system had search and target-designation capacity, but it covered only a 270-degree forward arc. They had to face their enemy to fight.

"Okay, Gus, light him up as soon as she bears."

In the rear cockpit, Grestovitch stared into his tactical display, struggling with his joystick controller to lay a targeting box on the blip of the attacking Tornado. Succeeding, he keyed in the lock and heard a confirmation tone.

"We got designation!"

"All right! Now let's see if we can get us a missile!"

Over the radio circuit, the distant TACCO droned down the count.

"... four ... three ... two ... one ... zero."

"Shit! Missed it!" Grestovitch yelled.

"Second round coming in. Three ... two ... one ... zero."

"No capture! Still no capture!"

The combined speed of the two aircraft annihilated the distance between them. There was no pursuit curve to cut inside. No jinking or dodging that would make the least difference now. The Tornado would open fire in a matter of seconds.

"Third round coming in. Three ... two ... one ..."

"Shit! Shit! Wait a second. ... We got capture. We got capture!"

Twenty-five thousand feet up and five miles to the southwest, the LORAIN detected a familiar precoded pattern and frequency of radar impulses reflecting off an airborne target. Its onboard guidance package activated and fixed on it. The target's close proximity to the moving wave pattern of the sea complicated the lock. The LORAIN compensated with Doppler shift scanning and by sensing the passive microwave emissions radiating from the Tornado's own metallic structure. Its nose dipped and the missile dove.

The combined pull of gravity and the thrust of its engine pushed the LORAIN to the near hypersonic. The leading edges of its composite fins were starting to char as it punched down into the lower atmosphere. So great was its velocity that the warhead's proximity fuses didn't have the chance to function properly. It made little difference. The missile scored a direct hit.

There was a blue-white glare like a stroke of heat lightning and Cristobal's Tornado disintegrated, shredded wreckage spraying out across half a square mile of ocean.

Arkady got rid of a long-delayed breath. "Got capture? Offhand, Gus, I'd say you killed that puppy."

"Gray Lady, this is Retainer Zero One. Splash the third Tornado. The sole survivor is bugging out for home, and so are we. Resuming EMCON and proceeding to point item for recovery."

Amanda made no attempt to stop the cheering this time.

In the fading gray glow of the Antarctic twilight, Arkady spotted the *Cunningham*'s distinctive shark's fin silhouette ahead of him. As he circled it, the big destroyer turned across the wind and the marker strobes outlining the helipad began to pulse, welcoming him home.

He popped his landing gear and got three green indicators down and locked. As he began to ease in over the rail, he saw the slender figure in the heavy duffel coat watching from the top of the superstructure, her red-amber hair whipping in his rotor wash. He grinned and flared his landing lights at her, and she replied by lifting a clenched fist over her head in a salute of mutual victory.

BUENOS AIRES
1920 HOURS: MARCH 25, 2006

"Bullshit, sir!"

Harrison Van Lynden's words exploded within the Argentine President's office like a hand grenade.

"The proposition that your aircraft were acting in their own self-defense deserves no politer terminology."

"I do not enjoy being called a liar, Mr. Secretary," Sparza replied stonily from behind his desk.

"I do not enjoy calling a national leader and statesman of your caliber a liar, Mr. President. Could it be possible that your own military command has failed to fully inform you of the reality of this situation?"

"On the contrary, Mr. Secretary. I am quite aware of what has occurred off our coasts, and I completely stand behind the press release issued by our Ministry of Defense. Allow me to quote . . ." Sparza lifted a sheet of paper from his desktop and read aloud from it: " 'Realizing that the United States vessel was taking hostile action against them, the flight leader ordered his aircraft to open fire.'

"Those are the facts, Mr. Secretary."

Van Lynden's voice was controlled as he replied. "I have been informed by our own Department of Defense that a complete data download of the attack has been received from the USS *Cunningham*'s Aegis computers. Analysis of that data will show that your warplanes and not our ship initiated aggressive action. The *Cunningham* did not return fire until she was fired upon and was in imminent danger of being sunk."

Sparza let the press release flutter back to the desktop. "Perhaps we have a problem in semantics here. Our pilots did indeed see your ship conducting hostile acts against them. They are Argentine, and your ship has been interfering with Argentina's lawful freedom of the seas. This is clearly an act of aggression against their homeland; thus their actions were taken in defense."

"You might be able to sell that particular brand of sophistry to your own people, but the United States government isn't buying. I must warn you, President Sparza, that you have greatly escalated an already serious situation. My government will not accept having its ships fired upon and its sailors endangered!"

"Then withdraw your ships from waters where they do not belong! It was the United States that triggered this escalation with its reckless and unlawful blockade of the San Martin Peninsula!"

Sparza caught himself. Taking a deep breath, he cooled his temper. Van Lynden grimly waited for him to continue.

"Mr. Secretary," the Argentine finally said. "This kind of shouting match is as futile as the clash between our armed forces.

This is a matter best dealt with by open and honorable negotiations among all of the involved nations. Argentina desires this above all else. Can we not put aside this childishness and proceed along more constructive paths?"

"The United States would welcome open and honorable negotiations, if they were in fact 'open and honorable.' However, we are aware of your plan to sow discord among the Antarctic Treaty states, and of the scenario by which you intend to seize power in Antarctica. It won't work, Mr. President."

Van Lynden rose from his chair and picked up his briefcase. "I have been in communication with my President. He wishes me to inform you that he condemns the Argentine attack on our vessel in the strongest possible terms. He also wishes me to inform you that he is authorizing the captain of the *Cunningham* to utilize whatever force is necessary to defend her ship and to maintain the blockade.

"Good day, sir!"

DRAKE PASSAGE
1941 HOURS: MARCH 25, 2006

"Sorry to keep you waiting, ma'am," the Duke's senior Hospital Corpsman said apologetically, brushing through the curtained doorway that separated the small, four-bed ward from the equally tiny sick bay office–cum–examination room.

"Forget it, Chief," Amanda replied. "How's he doing?"

"He's stabilizing. I think we've got the shock under control. His blood pressure is up, and his heart action looks good. There are signs that he's starting to come around again. I think that, for the short term, he'll be okay. No immediate danger."

Amanda noted both Bonnie Robinson's words and her grim

expression. "You're qualifying yourself all over the place, Chief. What's the full story?"

"Erikson has suffered a deep puncture wound to the chest cavity."

"That sounds bad."

"It is, ma'am."

Robinson turned to the printer unit of the sick bay's compact X-ray unit and punched the processing key. After a moment, a fresh negative was extruded into the Chief's hands with a soft whir. She stepped to the rear bulkhead and clipped the negative to a glow plate.

"Come here, Captain. I'll show you."

Amanda stood at the Corpsman's shoulder as she outlined the problem. "He took the hit almost dead center in the chest. There was a clean penetration into the chest cavity, but we've got that sealed off without getting a collapsed lung. There was some damage to the right pleural sac. That sort of shadowy area indicates that there was some hemorrhaging within the pleural cavity, but not too bad. The big problem is right here."

Robinson's slender fingers moved to outline a jagged black silhouette.

"A shrapnel fragment?"

"Yes, ma'am. Drilled right in among the major blood vessels above the heart. It's a certifiable miracle that nothing critical was directly involved."

"He lucked out."

"Not by all that much, ma'am."

"You're qualifying again, Chief."

"Yeah, I am. That fragment could shift, cut through an arterial wall. It could still kill him very easily."

"What can you do about it?"

"Nothing. This is a job for a full surgical team. We've got to get Erikson medevaced out to one as soon as possible."

"Chief, the closest medical facilities we have access to are over a thousand miles away in the Falkland Islands, way off station. We've got to deal with this with what we have available right here."

Robinson shook her head with great deliberation. "I don't know what I can say, Captain. I've had the basic indoctrination into emergency surgical procedures and, with a real doctor coaching me over a video link, I might be able to pull a hot appendix if I had to. This kind of operation, though, is so far over my head, I might as well be cutting his throat directly. I'm sorry, ma'am, but that's how it is."

Amanda nodded a reply. Turning, she took the two steps to the ward doorway. Pushing aside the curtain, she looked in at the still form lying in one of the lower bunks, bound down by his web of IV tubes and oxygen cannulas. Somehow she felt it was important that she be looking at him when she made this next decision.

"What about the alternative, Chief? The fleet will be up with us in about a week. Can you hold him stable until they arrive?"

"Captain, the book says that the faster this kind of wound is treated, the better. His general physical condition is bound to deteriorate. There is danger of infection, and that fragment could shift at any time."

"I'll grant you that and more, Chief. Can you keep him alive?"

"Well, maybe if I can be advised by Fleet medical—"

"No joy. We'll be going full EMCON soon. You'll be on your own. Now, what about it?"

Chief Robinson sighed. She was one of the Duke's plank owners, having been aboard since the commissioning. During that time, she had learned that her captain never demanded miracles. She just quietly required the absolute best that was humanly possible.

"We'll try, ma'am. We'll really try."

Powered back to dead slow, the Duke crept through a night that was nothing but varying textures of blackness. The low-lying overcast smothered even the faintest trace of starshine, and the only illumination in the whole world seemed to issue from the small cluster of hooded work-lights on the destroyer's bow.

The Zenith was the largest single piece of ordnance carried aboard the *Cunningham*. Twenty-five feet in length and triple the diameter of a LORAIN, it took up four of the cells in the forwardmost Vertical Launch System. It also required the most preparation before it could fly.

The missile and its launch rail had to be lifted hydraulically to deck level. There, its four strap-on boosters, each nearly the same length as the main vehicle, had to be struck up from belowdecks, hogged into position with the missile-loading crane, and shackled onto their respective hardpoints. Heavy steel flame deflectors were positioned under the exhaust ventures and thick, insulated Fiberglas matting had to be deployed and secured to protect the RAM-tiled decks. Then the real work of systems checkout could begin.

The katabatics still raked the destroyer's decks like an icy spray of machine-gun fire. Heavy Navy-issue parkas helped to blunt the edge of the cutting wind, but many of the more delicate connections and adjustments simply couldn't be made by workers wearing gloves. The men and women of Weapons Division did the best they could. They worked until numbed fingers simply refused to respond anymore, then they swore and backed off, tucking frozen hands into pockets and armpits. When feeling returned, heralded by an agonizing tingling and burning, they swore again and got back on the job.

"How's it going up there, Dix?" Amanda inquired sympathetically into her headset.

On the low-light deck monitor that was covering the work party, she could see the Lieutenant look aft.

"We're back on the timeline, Skipper. Everything looks good. All hands-on tests read green, and there don't seem to be any parts left over."

Amanda glanced across the CIC to the Zenith operations station and its master readouts. "We concur with that. How much more time do you need?"

"Maybe five more minutes for final-phase checks and to button things up out here."

"You've got ten. Well done to all hands involved."

"Better wait till we see if this thing works first, ma'am."

The Combat Information Center had taken on the aspects of a miniature NASA mission control. The main screen had been reconfigured as an orbital positioning display, and Christine Rendino was overseeing the systems operators as they prepared to switch over to space operations mode.

"How are we looking, Chris?"

"Last update from Aerospace Command says that the Aquila B is still right in the groove. She'll be above our horizon in about twelve minutes and thirty-four seconds."

"Close, but we're in under the wire. Anything new from the Argentines?"

"Intermittent low-grade radar emissions to the north and west. Air-to-surface search stuff, but way out of range. Some operational chatter on their standard air force and navy frequencies. Nothing critical."

"Nonetheless, when we light off at maximum power to track that satellite we're really going to be calling attention to ourselves. How long will we have to radiate?"

"Maybe sixty to ninety seconds to acquire and confirm the orbit and to allow the Zenith system to set up the intercept solution.

Then we can shut down. I'd suggest, though, that we go active again briefly to monitor and confirm the kill."

"Sounds reasonable. Then we go back to full stealth and do a sprint away from here. Let's do it."

As the last seconds ticked away, every spare monitor in the CIC was dialed in to the topside cameras.

"... three ... two ... one ... Target is above the horizon."

"Initiate orbital scan."

The starboard radar arrays energized and sprayed the skies to the south with a silent microwave thunderclap.

"Tallyho! Target acquisition! Right on the numbers!"

On the Large Screen Display, a target hack and designation appeared at the bottom of the screen. It began to crawl slowly upward toward the blue triangle that marked the *Cunningham*'s position.

"Zenith operator, start your engagement sequence."

"Aye, aye, Captain. Going for firing locks now. System is tracking ... System is tracking ... Zenith system has integrated. Confirm good locks and firing solution."

"Enable system to fire."

"Final-phase safety interlocks are down. System is enabled."

There was no immediate reaction. The Zenith had been designed as a seaborne system. Within its guidance package, gyros gauged the pitch and roll of its launch platform, waiting for a moment when the vehicle was aimed at the near-true vertical before issuing the ignition command.

The air crackled. Suddenly, orange flame blanketed the Duke's foredeck. Then the ASAT had cleared its launching rail and was climbing away fast, holding the ship and the sea around it under a dome of pale golden light.

In seconds, it had reached and punched into the overcast and the sudden flood of illumination was extinguished. All except for a faint flicker like a lightning bolt buried in the belly of the clouds.

At 45,000 feet and Mach 2, explosive bolts sheared the booster packs away and the main stage ignited. At Mach 7 and 165,000 feet, its job was done. The upper quarter of the vehicle, containing the payload and a low-thrust sustainer engine, separated and went on its way. Also discarded was the plastic nose shroud, no longer needed with the bulk of the atmosphere penetrated. Exposed now, the onboard sensors took up the search for the target.

Once upon a time, there had been a brave hope that space need not be militarized. Attempts had been made to ban antisatellite weapons such as the Zenith by international agreement. However, as more and more nations developed orbital launch capacity and began to put near-Earth space to a growing number of uses, not all of them benign, the brave dream was replaced by a grim reality, one that was first stated by a revered Chinese warrior long ago: *"You must hold the high ground or you most certainly will perish in the valley."*

The major powers began to treat ASATs much as they did combat shotguns. Everyone signed impressive documentation banning them. Everyone had them. Everyone politely ignored the fact that everyone else was lying about it.

Arcing two hundred miles above the Earth's surface, Argentina's Aquila B reconnaissance satellite trimmed its billboard-size solar panels to catch the light of the low-riding sun. Circling the world from pole to pole in a "ball of yarn" reconnaissance orbit, it had conducted a lateral transition burn some fifty minutes previously over the northern ice pack, allowing it to repeat the same trajectory it had flown earlier that day.

As per the programming it had received on its previous pass, it again brought its sensors to bear on the Antarctic Peninsula, Drake Passage, and the surrounding environs.

Now, suddenly, those sensors reacted to the appearance of a powerful radar-emissions source near the center of its search zone, followed by the heat plume of a rocket climbing toward its flight path.

Had it been one of the big American Key Hole 13 reconsats or a Russian Sentinel Cosmos, it would have had artificial-intelligence circuits capable of recognizing the potential threat, and it would have taken evasive action or activated countermeasures. As it was, the Aquila B was a simpleminded device. It merely continued to record the details of its own death for a download it would never make.

The heart of the Zenith system was a kinetic kill weapon developed from the U.S. Air Force's "Intelligent Tomato Can" ASAT of the 1980s. It consisted of little more than a wide-angle infrared sensor, a ring of maneuvering thrusters, and a small, very high speed computer, all fit into a cylindrical package roughly the size of a gallon of paint.

After staging from its sustainer motor, the ASAT had searched for, and located, the sun-warmed metal of the Aquila B against the frigid emptiness of space. Now it delicately began to steer itself directly into the path of the Argentine satellite. There was no warhead per se. Given the kinetic energy involved in a five-miles-per-second collision, explosives were redundant.

"Aaaand . . . nailed it!" Christine exclaimed. "Argentina is out of the satellite business."

"Are you certain, Chris?" Amanda asked.

Rendino swiftly conferred with the Zenith operator.

"Yeah, Captain," she replied after a moment. "We have a solid kill. The target has displayed an abrupt orbital deviation, and the reflectivity variance indicates that it's tumbling. We're also tracking a dispersing debris cloud, and we lost the Zenith's transponder at the moment of intercept. There may still be a hulk up there, but it's not going to be doing anybody any good."

"Is there any chance they can put up a replacement?"

"Doubtful. None of the South American states have a domestically produced launch vehicle with enough steam to hit a polar orbit with that size of payload. The Argys contracted with Arianspace to put this one up.

"Even if they had a spare sat in storage, and if they could find a civil hauler somewhere willing to buck the sanctions on against Argentina, it would be months before they could get a slot on a launch schedule. Fa' sure, these guys are blind for the duration."

"Good enough. Helm, get us out of here. All engines ahead flank. Steer zero nine seven degrees."

"Aye, aye, ma'am. All engines ahead flank. Steering zero nine seven."

"All stations, secure radiating and set full EMCON. Establish full stealth protocols."

"Aye, aye, setting full emission control and full stealth."

"Communications, before you secure your transmitters, please dispatch the following, Milstar Flash priority: 'DDG 79 to CINCLANT. Zenith launch successfully executed as per previously transmitted plan of operation. Target destroyed. Now going full stealth. This will be our last transmission. Signature, Garrett, commanding.'"

The radio watch did a read-back and Amanda cleared it for sending. That dealt with, she slipped off her headset and settled back more deeply into the padding of the command chair. Closing her eyes, she let the ordered murmur of the CIC crew and the soft creaking of the hull flow around her.

That was a major piece of the load removed. Her enemies were still out there, hunting her, but now her options had widened. Now she could hide as well as run and fight.

"Coming up on the end of the break. Buenos Aires link is up and hot. Stand by to cut to the Embassy. Three . . . two . . . one . . . and go!"

The master screens in the control room of the media center flickered and filled with multiple images. One was the urbane and well-known features of the moderator of the news feature program. The second was an intense-looking, middle-aged Latino with graying hair and a pencil-line mustache, sitting centered in one of the studio's interview sets. The third was Dr. Caroline Towers. She was seated in a straight-backed chair in the U.S. Embassy's reception lobby, a light microphone clipped to the lapel of her suit.

"Good evening, Doctor." The moderator's smooth voice overlaid the imaging. "I believe you were able to hear the comments made by the Argentine Minister of Trade here in our New York studios about his nation's program for Antarctic development. Do you have any response to them?"

"Yes I do, Mr. Douglas," she replied. "With all due respect to Mr. Anaya, Argentina's plans for Antarctic development are a prescription for almost certain ecological disaster."

The Argentine shook his head impatiently. "That is the same hackneyed phrase we have heard from environmental extremists for decades. I can assure you that Argentina intends to make the protection of the Antarctic environment one of its primary concerns. In recent years, given the proper safeguards, industrial development has taken place in numerous ecologically sensitive areas without causing undue harm. Antarctica is no different."

"No, sir! This is not the case. It's true that over the past decade global industry has made vast strides in developing ecologically protective procedures and technologies. However, much of this development is simply not applicable to the Antarctic environment. There, you are dealing literally with another world, one as alien to terrestrial norms as something orbiting in another star system.

"The Antarctic ecology is unique. It's vast in extent, sophisticated in its dynamics, and yet basically simple in structure. This simplicity renders it perilously fragile."

"How is that so, Doctor? Could you elaborate?" the moderator inquired.

"There isn't a great degree of multiple redundancy available within the biosphere."

"Multiple redundancy?"

"Yes," Dr. Towers explained patiently. "Allow me to state an example. Around the turn of the last century, the wolf was all but wiped out within the confines of the continental United States. The elimination of such a key predator from within an ecosystem could have caused a serious dysfunction. However, the hardier, more survivable coyote moved in and took over most of the wolf's niche. The system was able to adapt and self-repair.

"This critical kind of diversity is lacking in the Antarctic. In many instances, you have only one specific species filling one specific slot in the food chain. Do something to impact that one species and the entire system could crash.

"That's why the Antarctic is such an all-or-nothing proposition. The southern continent and its surrounding waters must be kept intact and pristine. As I said before, anything less is a prescription for ecological disaster."

"Come now, Doctor. Even if other nations choose to exercise their sovereignty in the Antarctic and elect to develop its resources, how much of the continent will be involved? Five percent, ten?"

"Mr. Anaya, how big does a cancer have to be to kill its host?"

"Those are strong words, Doctor." The moderator smoothly intervened before Anaya could initiate a heated reply. "Back here at home, however, we are hearing some other strong words. People are expressing concern as Argentina and the United States appear to be edging closer to open warfare over the Antarctic question. While not yet confirmed by the Pentagon, there are reports that at least one military engagement has been fought in the South Atlantic. In all probability, there will be more.

"The question is, is it really worth it? Are polar bears and penguins worth the potential loss of human life?"

Dr. Towers smiled quietly and removed her glasses. "There are no polar bears in the Antarctic, Mr. Douglas. I am a scientist, and the study of ethics and social morality isn't really my field. My stock-in-trade is the accumulation of factual information.

"I can tell you this. The Antarctic seas pour millions of tons of protein into the global biosphere yearly. Disrupt that flow, and you will disrupt oceanic ecosystems all over the globe. Antarctica is also the premier weather generator of the planet. Disrupt its climate, and you disrupt the climate of every other continent as well.

"I can tell you one other thing. The cold polar environment greatly slows the natural processes the Earth uses to repair ecological damage. Whatever mistakes we make in the Antarctic today, the human race will have to live with for the next thousand years."

DRAKE PASSAGE
0210 HOURS: MARCH 26, 2006

The hours just past midnight were a favorite time for Amanda to prowl the Duke's passageways and compartments. It wasn't an inspection in the classic sense, but more a chance to attune herself to her ship's state.

She moved quietly through the dim, red, night lighting, extending a hand out occasionally to a bulkhead to catch herself against the destroyer's pitch and roll and stopping now and again to listen to the whisper of air through a duct, or to feel the faint vibration of a pump. Once, she paused near the partially open door of a berthing bay to listen to the low murmur of conversation coming from within. It wasn't eavesdropping; she had no interest in the contents of the conversation, just in its tone. Angry? Uneasy? Confident?

A burst of bantering laughter came from the darkness. Amanda smiled and moved on.

She exchanged a few words with the duty security patrol and the junior officer of the deck as they made their rounds. She hit the CIC to check on the latest weather states and intelligence updates, then went down two decks to Main Engineering for a look at the fuel-consumption projections.

Under normal conditions, that would have been enough of an early-A.M. walk-around. She would have dropped by the galley to sample tomorrow morning's batch of cinnamon rolls, then turned in for another couple of hours' sleep before rising again to be on the bridge at first light.

Not this night, however.

"Good morning, Terrel."

The Corpsman striker who had the night watch in sick bay scrambled to his feet from behind the desk in the small office/ examination room.

"As you were," Amanda said quietly. "I just came down to see how your patient was doing."

"Yes, ma'am. Pretty much no change. Chief Robinson is concerned about fluid buildup around his lungs, so we're keeping an eye on that. He threw a fever spike earlier in the evening, but it seems to be coming down now."

"Thanks, Terrel. Carry on."

Erikson's medical file was sitting out on the corner of the desk. She picked it up, flipped it open, and began to study the latest entries and evaluations.

"Begging your pardon, Captain," the striker asked hesitantly, "but are you going to be here for a couple of minutes?"

"I imagine so. Why?"

"I just finished the sick-bay supply inventory, and we're short on a couple of things. I've got orders from the Chief not to leave Erikson alone, but if you were going to be around for a while, ma'am, I could make a run down to the medical-stores room and get us restocked."

"That'll be fine. Go ahead."

The striker departed on his task. Amanda returned the file to the desk and stepped across to the entrance of the ward bay. Pushing aside the curtain, she peered in.

She didn't like hospitals, especially in the still, close hours of darkness. Such places reminded her of the night she lost a large part of her family.

It had been an automobile accident. Amanda's mother and eight-year-old younger brother had been driving in to Norfolk to pick her up after an evening dance class. A drunken driver had crossed over the road's centerline and had hit them head-on. Despite the best efforts of the trauma teams, they had died the same night, within two hours of each other.

Her father had been in the western Pacific when it had happened. It would be almost two days before he would be able to get home. Amanda had been fourteen years old and alone. The hospital staff had tried to get her to leave, but she had refused. She had been at each of their bedsides at the end, because that was where she needed to be.

"Terrel? Hey, Terrel, you there?" Erikson's voice came weakly from out of the dimness and he shifted a few painful inches in his bunk. Moving swiftly, Amanda entered the bay and dropped down at his side.

"Are you all right?"

The young seaman must have been startled at having his commanding officer suddenly materialize at his call.

"Uh ... yes, ma'am, I'm okay. I was just trying to get the Corpsman."

"He's out for the moment and I'm minding the store. What can we do for you?"

"It's nothing, ma'am. Just a little thirsty. I was wondering if I could get some more of that ice they've been letting me have."

"No problem."

Amanda got to her feet and filled a plastic cup from the ice dispenser on the forward bulkhead. Returning to the wounded man, she carefully fed him a few of the ice chips.

"Thank you, ma'am," he said, easing back down onto his pillow. "I didn't mean to cause you any trouble."

"You didn't. I did come down here to see how you were doing, after all."

"That was nice of you, ma'am. I'm doing okay. They're taking pretty good care of me, I guess." The seaman shifted in his bunk in weak discomfort. "It's just that I don't much like having to be taken care of in the first place."

"I know what you mean," she replied, sitting down on the deck and tucking her feet under her. "I hate being fussed over myself."

"Yeah. I guess I won't be able to get around for a while. This just lying here is gonna drive me crazy."

"I seem to remember that you were big into sports. Football, wasn't it?"

"Yes, ma'am. Fullback. My senior year, my team was runner-up for our state triple-A championship. I tried out for a couple of athletic scholarships, but I never made the cut. That's how I came to join up. Mom and Dad are divorced, and neither one of 'em have all that much money. I figured that the Navy would be my best chance for college."

"The Matching Funds Program?"

"Yes, ma'am. I've got a couple of thousand bucks riding the books already. I'm going to be signing up for some of the college-level correspondence courses, too. I'd really like to be a building contractor someday. Run my own outfit, you know. I figure that becoming an architect is my best first step.... Sorry, ma'am. I didn't mean to start carrying on like that."

"It's all right," she replied, letting her gaze drift off into the middle-distant darkness. "I've been there. When it's the middle of the night and you're hurting, sometimes you want to talk."

"Yeah.... Captain?"

"Yes?"

"Have my folks been notified that I've been wounded?"

"I'd guess so. We notified Second Fleet about our damage and casualties before we went EMCON. Why?"

"I was just wishing that there was some way that I could rig it so they'd know that I was okay, that everything was going to be all right, you know?"

"I wish we could, but it's just not possible."

"I understand, ma'am." The young sailor hesitated for a moment, then went on. "Captain, could you do me a favor?"

"Like what?"

"If anything happens, could you tell my folks that I was okay, that I wasn't hurting or scared or anything?"

"I've got a hunch that's not exactly the truth."

"No, ma'am," the young seaman replied tightly. "It isn't."

Amanda came up onto her knees and took Erikson's hand in both of her own. "Look, you can tell your family yourself, because we are getting you out of here. I've never lost anyone under my command yet, and I'm not starting with you. You remember that, sailor. I'm taking us all home."

A brace of Fuerza Aérea Rafales blazed down the main runway at Rio Grande as President Sparza descended the short stairway from the door of his plane, the crackling roar of their afterburners echoing across the base. An Antarctica-bound C-130 followed within moments, its four powerful turboprops moaning as it lifted into the rain-swept sky. The backlog of aircraft that had accumulated on the taxiways while the Executive jet had been on approach were moving out, expedited by wartime urgency.

At Sparza's own insistence, there was no honor guard standing to on the parking apron, just a staff car with a small MP escort. Likewise, none of the base's senior staff had been called away from their duties, just a single junior officer who tried futilely to shield the Argentine President from the chill downpour with an umbrella as they dashed to the waiting vehicles.

"General Arco sends his respects, Mr. President," the young Air Force man stammered as they entered the staff car. "He is awaiting you at the operations building."

"Very good, Lieutenant. Let's carry on. We haven't a great deal of time to spare."

The same sense of crisis that had been present on the flight line could be felt in the base command-and-control center. Not since the Falklands War, when Rio Grande had been at the forefront of the strike operations against the British fleet, had the facility been pushed to the limits like this. As the southernmost of Argentina's major air bases, it had been serving as the departure node for the Conquistador South supply airlift. Now it had also become the keystone in the search for the *Cunningham*.

Sparza was ushered into a briefing room immediately adjoining the operations center itself and separated from the ranked workstations and map displays by a glass wall. General Marcello Arco joined him there a few moments later.

"Good morning, Mr. President. May I order something for you after your journey? Coffee? A cup of chocolate?"

"No, thank you, General," Sparza replied, shedding his damp raincoat and draping it across the conference table. "I am required back in Buenos Aires this afternoon, so I regret our meeting must be brief. Is there anything new to report?"

"No, sir. We still have not developed a fix on the North American warship. There have been no contacts since 1700 hours yesterday evening."

"And our lost satellite?"

"Nothing new to report there either. San Martin Base verifies that the Aquila B was on schedule as it passed over the Antarctic. However, when our tracking station at Comodoro Rivadavia endeavored to acquire the satellite for a data download, it was gone. A possible sighting report from the Brazilian Space Agency indicates that it may have deorbited and burned up during reentry over the Andes."

"An inconvenient accident, General?" Sparza said, drawing one of his chairs back from the table and seating himself in it.

"Unlikely," Arco replied. "The safe assumption is that the Aquila B was shot down by the North Americans as it passed over Drake Passage."

"Indeed?"

"It is open knowledge that the United States has antisat weapons. What was not known is that they had the ability to deploy them aboard their naval surface units."

"And they elected to reveal this secret capacity to us," Sparza mused, reaching into his inner coat pocket for his cigarette case. "They must have had reason to fear the Aquila."

"Its thermographic cameras may have been the only sensors we had capable of detecting the *Cunningham.*"

Sparza paused for a moment to light a Players. "The North Americans' stealth technology. It is truly that good . . . or bad?"

"It is," Arco replied flatly, turned to face the glass wall of the briefing room, and gestured toward the CIC beyond it. "Since last night, we have conducted two full surface-search sweeps within the sectors of Drake Passage that must contain the North American vessel. We used a mixed force of our best radar aircraft, Aeronaval's Atlantiques, our 737s, and the Prefectura Naval's Dessault Falcons. Nothing.

"If the *Cunningham* was detectable using conventional resources, we would have found her. Of that I am certain, Mr. President."

Sparza gestured with the tip of his cigarette. "I fully accept your statement, General. Sit, and let us discuss what options we may now have."

Arco accepted Sparza's invitation, dropping into a chair across from his Commander in Chief. "Operationally," the Air Force man continued, "we have been taken back to the 1930s. Visual search during daylight hours only. And, as you experienced on your way in, we are losing the weather.

"Heavy cloud cover over the Antarctic Convergence is forcing our aircraft down to almost wave-top altitude, cutting into their range and search coverage. They are also encountering rain, snow, and heavy fog. We can expect that the North Americans are taking maximum advantage of this kind of environment."

Sparza produced a brief grunt of ironic laughter. "Only the day before yesterday I said that the weather was on our side. General Winter is proving to be a fickle ally."

"I regret the situation, sir," Arco replied, failing to suppress his own sensation of irony. "My aircrews are doing their best."

"I do not doubt it, General. Nor do I need to be reminded that it was my decision that committed us to this course of action. Now, for a moment let us assume that you do locate your target. Aeronaval was hit hard when they tried to take her on yesterday. What will your plan be?"

"We have moved our entire Rafale force south. Grupo Two and Eight are here at Rio Grande. Grupo Six is up at Río Gallegos with what's left of our tanker force. All three squadrons are holding a full eight-plane antishipping strike on cockpit alert. If we can find her, we will kill her, but we have got to find her first."

Sparza tilted his chair back and snubbed out his cigarette in the conference table's pristine ashtray. "Arco, I am fully aware of the doubts you have had about Conquistador South. However, I also believe that for the moment, you are the man in the best position to save this operation. You have told me of all of the conventional things that you are doing. Well and good. But what about the unconventional things that might be done?"

Ironies upon ironies. "There is . . . something, sir," Arco began slowly. "I have been in communications with some of my technical specialists, people involved in stealth-technologies research. They say that there may be a way to penetrate the kind of antiradar defenses the North Americans are using, but it will require a great deal of manpower and equipment."

"Ah."

Sparza tilted his chair forward again. "Maybe we can have that coffee now, General. And then you can tell me what you will need, and why."

OFF THE ANTARCTIC SEA ICE PACK
FORTY-FIVE MILES NORTHWEST OF CAPE LLOYD
1545 HOURS: MARCH 26, 2006

She knelt down once more in the narrow aisle beside the sick-bay bunk.

"How's it going?"

Erikson gave a weak thumbs-up. "Pretty good, Captain. I think I'm doing a little better."

Amanda glanced back to where Chief Robinson stood in the ward doorway. The Corpsman gave a minute shake of her head.

"That's good. That's why I came around. I was hoping to hear something like that."

"Yes, ma'am. I've been telling everyone who's come through that I'll be back on duty soon."

"A lot of visitors today?"

"Yeah, a couple of my buddies from Deck Division. My chief, Mr. Nichols. Even the new lieutenant that came aboard at Rio. The helo pilot."

"Lieutenant Arkady?"

"Yes, ma'am. And I don't even know him."

Amanda mentally cocked an eyebrow. "Well, I guess he was saying hello while he had the chance. The fleet will be coming up with us in a few more days and we'll be shifting you over to a carrier."

"Just getting used to this ship, ma'am."

"Well, don't worry. We're going to get you back."

"Good. Like it here."

His voice trailed off and his eyes closed. Amanda rested her hand on his shoulder for a moment, then got to her feet. Moving forward into the sick-bay office, she met the eyes of Chief Robinson again.

"So?"

"I'd like to think that I'm holding him stable, Captain, but I'm afraid I'd be lying to myself."

"Understood, Chief. Carry on."

Amanda stepped out into the corridor and started. Arkady was there, his arms crossed and his back against one side of the passage-way. He had one boot raised and braced on the farside grab rail, wedging him in place against the increasing pitch of the ship.

"Any change?" he asked.

"Not for the good. I helped to set up the projected crew roster for the Cunningham class, and it never occurred to me or to anyone else that a doctor would be an absolute necessity for a ship intended for independent operations. Damn, damn, damn! How could I have missed that?"

"We got spoiled. The surface navy's gotten used to looking back over its shoulder and seeing that big old flattop out there, serving as the font from which all blessings flow."

It was a good analysis.

"You're right," Amanda agreed, leaning back against the bulkhead beside him. "Unfortunately, there's nothing we can do about it now."

"Beyond the best we can with what's available? Nope."

"More Arkady honesty?"

"Yep. There's always plenty of that to spread around."

Amanda smiled in spite of herself. There were other places she could have been just then, not the least of which was topside, looking into the way the weather was kicking up. But she elected to stay and stretch out this exchange of words for a few moments more.

"Erikson said that you'd been in to visit him," she commented. "Why? Do you know him from somewhere?"

"Can't say that I do. But he's a point of concern for the ship and the mission. I've got a hunch decisions are going to have to be made about this kid, and I figure I should at least get to know him well enough to say hello."

Amanda glanced sideways at Arkady. Could he know that this was the same way she felt about Erikson? She'd learned that this man had the knack of being able to touch her emotionally. Now she suspected that he could also read her the same way, and she wasn't sure if she was as pleased about that. Again she found herself wondering just what might have happened back there in Rio, given a little more time.

She turned to face her Air Division leader, one shoulder still resting against the bulkhead. "When I came into my first command," she said slowly, "I learned that it was like inheriting a family. A family of strangers mostly, but the sense of responsibility is there."

Arkady nodded an agreement. "At OCS they kept harping about how a good officer must maintain a degree of detachment from their personnel. I gather the concept is that the more personally involved you are, the tougher it is to send your hands into a high-risk situation."

"I was fed the same line at Annapolis," she replied, "and I've known a great number of our profession who stick to it religiously. It always seemed to me, though, that the best commanding officers I ever had were the ones who had the guts to give a damn, even when it cost them."

"I concur."

Amanda suddenly realized that Arkady was studying her again, using the same look of frank, level-eyed admiration he had used back on the beach at Ipanema. Only this time, it was her emotional clothing he was stripping away, momentarily making her feel very naked indeed.

The Duke lifted heavily into an oncoming swell, and with her attention diverted, Amanda missed the shift of the deck. She stumbled against Arkady and his arm came around her waist, catching and supporting her. She caught a whiff of him, the mix of aftershave, healthy male, and aviation fuel. The warmth of his body jolted her like a charge of electricity. She jerked back, Arkady's arm resisting for a moment before releasing her.

She backed away a couple of steps and caught the grab rail. Looking into his face, she could see that he had felt the same sensation.

Only, he hadn't been afraid of it.

She started to speak again, not quite knowing what she was about to say, when the raucous blaring of the klaxons cut her off.

"General quarters! General quarters! All battle stations close up and rig for surface and ASW engagement!"

They split apart, bolting for their duty stations.

"Captain on the bridge!" Ken Hiro sang out as she brushed past the light curtain behind the center console.

"As you were." She shot her first look forward, over the heads of the helmsmen and out the windscreen.

She'd been right to come up here instead of to the Combat Information Center. You could fight men off a CRT screen, but the weather you had to go face-to-face with.

The seas were running at least Force Five: steep-sided gray combers with twenty-five knots of wind peeling spray off their crests. A roiling overcast hung low over the ship and hazed into a dense bank of sea smoke to the north.

The sky was brighter to the south, but it was with that odd, yellowish pale tint that denoted what polar hands called "ice blink," refracted sunlight trapped between the cloud cover and the frozen sea. Not far out that way was the outermost fringe of Antarctica's icy armor.

The more immediate problem lay straight on beyond the *Cunningham*'s bow. To the west, an ominously dark smear ran across the joining of the sea and sky.

A glance at the meteorological repeaters verified that she was looking at a squall line running vanguard to a mean-looking localized cold front.

"Okay, Ken," Amanda said to her exec. "We're going to be keeping the con up here. Get us a line on the squawk box to Combat Information Center and keep it open."

"Aye, aye, Captain. Glad to have you with us."

She circled the helm station and took a position leaning into the grab rail that ran just beneath the curved row of battle data repeaters at the front of the bridge. Most of the strike damage had been repaired. A new thermoplastic door had been inset in the portside bridge-wing access and the shattered flatscreens had been replaced. Only the shrapnel scarring on the decks and bulkheads and the stark white bandaging on the side of Hiro's face served to recall what had happened here the day prior.

"Okay, CIC. This is the Captain. What do you have for me?"

Back aft, freezing air boiled into the hangar as the helipad elevator sank down to accept Retainer Zero One. At their equipment lockers at the head of the bay, Arkady and his SO geared up quickly, survival suits over flight suits and Mae West life jackets over both.

Snagging up his helmet, Vince reached over and slapped the actuator key on the flight-status board inset in the bulkhead. The bar graphs of the pitch-and-roll inclinometers and the wind-velocity gauge shot up their scales and began to blip an ominous red as they intermittently drifted above their safety levels.

"Hey, Lieutenant," Grestovitch asked uneasily. "We're not actually gonna launch in this shit, are we?"

"The fates will decree, Gus. Let's saddle up."

"It was a single thirty-second signal intercept off a low-powered surface-search radar." Christine Rendino's filtered voice filled the bridge. "Bearing about fifty degrees relative off the starboard bow. Range indeterminable but pretty close. Couldn't make the system signature, maybe a Terma.

"The thing is that the signal broke intermittently and there was a lot of output waver, like maybe you had waves breaking over the emitter head."

"Like we might have a sub out there who stuck his radar mast up to have a look around?"

"Exactly, boss ma'am. He didn't get us, though. McKelsie reports that his signal strength was way below anything that could get a return off of us."

"Oh, he's got us, Chris. He probably picked us up on his passive sonar arrays, then he executed that radar sweep to verify who we are. When he failed to get a radar return off us, that would give him his positive ID."

Amanda called back over her shoulder to the control stations. "Lee helm. Rig for silent running. All stop on main engines and feather your propellers. All power rooms to idling output. Activate Prairie Masker and convert to hydrojet propulsion, one hundred percent power."

"Aye, aye, converting to hydrojet propulsion. Prairie Masker is on-line. Ship now rigged for silent running."

In acknowledgment of the fact that the modern submarine was possibly the single deadliest enemy the surface warship must face, the *Cunningham*'s stealth defenses extended below the waterline. Her power plants were "rafted" in heavy sound-suppressive insulation and she was equipped with a Prairie Masker compressor system that could sheath her hull in further layers of noise-killing air bubbles.

In addition, she mounted a set of auxiliary pumpjet drives in her propulsor pods, a silent propulsion option that did not produce the churning cavitation of conventional ship's screws.

"Tactical Officer, bring up your V-ROC flights."

Down on the sweep of the Duke's long foredeck, a series of small, hexagonal doors snapped open on the upper surfaces of the three Mark 42 Vertical Launch Systems. Beneath each door was a watertight plastic cap sealing a missile silo, and beneath that, a V-ROC, a vertically launched antisubmarine rocket, the fleet's premier long-range sub killer.

They just needed something to use them on. The tactical displays showed only empty water.

"Sonar, are you getting anything at all?"

"Nothing passively, Captain. Conditions in the surface sound duct are deteriorating due to the weather, and we're getting some background noise from the ice pack."

Christine's voice cut in on the circuit. "If this is that Argentine Kockums 471 we lost track of a few days ago, we're not talking about a submarine as much as we are a large chunk of solidified silence."

Amanda gave a nod that her friend could not see. Of all of the weapons in the Argentine arsenal, those Swedish attack boats were probably the closest to being on a par with the *Cunningham*'s technology. One of them was out there now, hovering in the deepwater darkness, listening, trying to line up a killing shot.

"What do you think, Ken?"

Hiro gave the bill of his officer's cap an uneasy tug. "I'd say that without putting a helo up, we don't have much chance against this guy."

"I agree." Amanda hesitated a moment and again scanned the clouded horizon. "We'd really be stretching the air-operations envelope, though."

A wind-driven slash of spray across the glass in front of her made her decision.

"Let's hold off on the helo launch. Helm, come left to two six zero. Let's open the range a little and see if we can sneak past this guy."

Minutes passed. Amanda frowned down into the tac displays as they remained obstinately empty. Snapping the jack of her headset into an access point on the console, she called up the direct sound feed coming from the hydrophones. Bypassing the cascade display, she used the computer filters to separate out the different movements of the Antarctic sea's life song.

On the surface, the hiss-and-break turbulence of wave action was dominant, the boiling intermix of ocean and air being whipped up by the oncoming storm. Beyond that, Amanda could make out the soft sizzling of a bank of krill, running deep just off the bottom. And then there was the rolling, over-the-horizon rumble of the pack, the accumulated sound of a billion tons of ice, butting and splintering in its glacial-speed dance around the southern continent.

Whatever noise the Argentine sub was producing was being lost in that acoustic environment—as was the *Cunningham*'s trace, Amanda hoped.

Amanda unplugged the jack with an impatient yank.

"It's a pain when some other stealthy bastard turns the tables, isn't it," Hiro remarked with grim humor.

"Tell me about it," she replied, lifting herself into the captain's chair to take advantage of the couple of extra inches of vision height it gave her. Almost at once, just off the bow she caught a paler flash against the gray of the sea.

"Watch it! Ice to starboard! Come left to two four oh!"

A bergy bit the size of an automobile swept slowly past the destroyer's flank, drifting away aft.

"Return to previous heading. Damn, Ken, if we angle south much more, we're going to start having some real ice problems."

"I agree, Captain. Helm! Steady as she goes! Watch your course line!"

"Ship's fighting the helm, sir. I'm having trouble holding the heading."

The hydrojets were low-powered units, not designed for fighting a sea like this, and the Duke was beginning to wallow sluggishly in the growing force of the storm.

Amanda could feel the snowball starting to build. A number of different tactical factors were converging to produce the potential for disaster. Swiftly, she called up the Global Positioning Unit display on her chair-arm screen and confirmed another fear.

"Ken, this is no good. Bucking this weather, we're barely making any way over ground at all. We're just hanging in this guy's sights."

"Captain, may I make a suggestion?"

"Of course."

"What about turning away to the east and running with the weather for a while, then circling north?"

She considered her exec's counsel for a moment, then shook her head.

"It's a temptation, but if we start running in front of this storm, we could get blown clear out into the South Atlantic before we could come about again. I am not going to be driven off station, Ken, by either the weather or the Argentines."

"Lee helm, bring up your power rooms," Amanda said, lifting her voice to key the overhead microphones. "Sonar and CIC, look alive. I'm going to try and pull us out of here."

"Aye, aye."

"Lee helm, maintain one hundred percent power on the hydro-jets. Main engines ahead slow. Make turns for ten knots. Trim screws for minimum cavitation."

The Duke shuddered and then steadied as she began to drive cleanly against the sea again. Amanda accessed the hydrophone output again, now dominated by the swishing rumble of the destroyer's own accelerating propeller beats. Two minutes passed. Three.

Then, from somewhere out in the wet dark, there came a single, piercing tone.

"Ranging ping! Bearing zero six zero relative off the bow!"

Amanda lunged forward out of the captain's chair to the tactical displays as the sonar operator continued to call off the situation.

"Transitories on the bearing! Possible outer door opening . . . Possible fish swim-out! Torpedo in the water!"

"Sonar, initiate active sweep!"

The time for stealth was over. The *Cunningham*'s sonar transducers began slamming their own sound waves out into the water, lifting echoes off the hunting sub. In moments a target hack and a bearing line appeared on the tactical display, a torpedo track sliding along it toward the Duke's position.

Amanda's hands flew across the display keyboards again, calling up the data annex of the torpedo recognition and alertment processor.

*WEAPON INDENT: (SWED) TYPE 613   533MM   SURF-SUB
              60 KTS
              MULTI-MODE   GUIDANCE;   WIRE\PASSIVE\
              ACTIVE

Only a single shot in the water. They must be using the wire guidance. A spinneret aboard the racing torpedo would be unreeling a hair-thin metallic filament in its wake, back-linking to the fire-control systems of the submarine itself. The sub's weapons officer would literally steer the fish into the belly of its target with a joystick controller.

* RANGE TO PRIMARY TARGET: 8500 YDS+

* PROJECTED TIME TO INCOMING WEAPON IMPACT: 3:41

"Lee helm, all engines ahead full!"

"Engines answering all ahead full, Captain!"

The Duke lunged forward with a palpable surge of acceleration. A steam turbine warship might take twenty minutes to work up to flank speed; a gas turbine vessel like the *Cunningham* could do it in four.

"CIC, prepare to drop LEAD decoys."

"LEADs prepped to drop."

The big destroyer struck a seventh wave and bucked through it in an explosion of spray, gaining way with each turn of her screws. Up on the bridge, Amanda tightened her grip on the grab rail and continued to stare down into the flatscreens with a fierce and total concentration.

Come on, friend. Listen to all that beautiful noise my props are making. You don't need to switch that torpedo over to active pinging, not yet.

"We have a firing fix on the sub," Dix Beltrain declared over the squawk box. "Ready to launch V-ROC."

"Time in flight to target?"

"Projected forty-five seconds."

"Right. Set LEAD decoys for ... ninety-second activation delay."

"Decoys set, Captain."

"Drop LEADs."

Back aft, a pair of Launched Expendable Acoustic Devices slid down their deployment chute and into the *Cunningham*'s boiling wake.

"LEADs deployed."

"Launch V-ROC."

There was a muffled thump up forward and a white cylinder shot up and out of its cell in the number-three Vertical Launch System. It seemed to hover for an instant over the deck, then its booster spewed flame, kicking it up into the sky and away toward the enemy.

*PROJECTED TIME OF INCOMING WEAPON IMPACT: 2:50

*LEAD SET 1 ACTIVATION: 0:65

Amanda tracked the V-ROC's flight path both on the tactical display and in her mind: the long curving trajectory, the separation of the payload from the booster and the deployment of its drogue parachute, its dolphinlike dive into the sea, the shedding of its nose and tail shrouds, and the power-up of the deadly little Mark 50 Barracuda torpedo.

"Our round is in the water," Beltrain announced over the circuit. "It has gone active and is circling to acquire target."

Okay, out there. Now it's your turn to do some ducking and dodging. Break that wire! Cut that fish loose!

"Sonar is now getting prop cavitation and warble from the Argy. He's increasing speed and turning."

Yes!

Forcing the Argentine sub to maneuver would force it to break its control link with the torpedo. The human aspect would be cut out of the loop, leaving the weapon operating on its own resources. That shifted the odds, for so-called smart weapons were frequently stupid enough to be decoyed.

God grant enough time and sea room.

*PROJECTED TIME TO INCOMING WEAPON IMPACT: 2:15

*LEAD SET 1 ACTIVATION: 0.20

"Losing sonar discrimination due to flow noise."

"Secure transponders, Mr. Beltrain. Cease active pinging."

*LEAD SET 1 ACTIVATION: 0.10

"Stop all engines! Power down!"

*LEAD SET 1 ACTIVE

The trick had been to try to catch the incoming torpedo in its moment of confusion between the breaking of its control wire and its independent reacquisition of its target. The LEAD decoys, now well astern of the Duke, were producing an acoustical clamor in the same range as a ship's propellers. With the *Cunningham*'s own engines still, the torpedo should veer off after the new sound source.

At least that was the theory. With their sonar deafened by the turbulence of their own passage through the water, they would know for certain when the explosion came.

Ignoring the savage bite of the wind through her work khakis, Amanda stepped out onto the starboard bridge wing and looked aft. Hiro followed her out, coming to stand at her shoulder as she keyed her interphone.

"All hands, this is the Captain. We've been playing tag with an Argy sub and he's thrown a torpedo at us. I think we've got it foxed, but we'll know for sure in a minute. Just in case, brace yourselves and stand by."

She surprised herself with the casualness of her own voice. Glancing over at her exec, she noted that Ken had removed his wallet from his pocket and was carefully studying the picture of his family.

This was the difference between a missile and a torpedo engagement. Missiles didn't give you a chance to think, just experience. With torpedoes, though, you had time enough to wonder.

Unbidden, Amanda found her thoughts returning to Vince

Arkady. She relived the encounter that had occured outside of sick bay just a few minutes before: that momentary contact with the warm strength of him, leading to the memory of the gymnasium and the knowing touch of his hands, and on to the texture of that one swift kiss back before it all had counted.

There was a heavy thud, more felt than heard, and looking up, they saw a thick column of water lift out of the sea well behind the ship. Hiro flipped his wallet shut with a decisive snap.

"All hands, this is the Captain again. That was the torpedo, and we're still in business. Now it's our turn to ruin the other guy's day."

They ducked back into the bridge. "Helm, resume heading of two seven zero. Lee helm, bring up your hydrojets again. Resume silent running."

"This brings us right back to where we started," Hiro said, trying to rub the chill out of his arms.

"I'm afraid it does. CIC, this is the bridge. What's happened with the V-ROC?"

"We've just reacquired the passive scan, ma'am," Beltrain replied. "Our fish is still circling around out there, running a search pattern. For a second, just before we lost imaging, I thought that it might have acquired a target. I guess I was mistaken."

"What about the Argy itself?"

"He's gone. Contact broken. But there was something else, ma'am."

"Yes?"

"Back just before our passive arrays dropped out, the Argy momentarily went active with another sonar system. We couldn't get an ID on it, but it wasn't anything standard, maybe a low-powered mine-hunter set. I don't know what this guy is up to, but I think he might be working something on us."

"Speculations?"

"None at this time, ma'am."

"Acknowledged. Keep your ears open."

Amanda leaned against the captain's chair and looked out through the windscreen, acutely aware of the several sets of eyes focused on her back. That storm front was rolling down on them fast. When it hit, they'd have to use their main engines again. This deadlock had to be broken, now, before they were laid open for another attack. Abruptly, she keyed a new address into the interphone.

"Retainer Zero One, this is the bridge."

The Sea Comanche balanced on her landing gear, a dunking sonar pod and a magnetic abnormality detector on the inboard hardpoints of her snub wings, air-droppable torpedoes on the outboard. Her rotors were deployed and turning, and deck hands, cowering against the freezing rotor wash, hunkered near the tie-down points, ready to release on command. A hardline was plugged into a jackpoint beneath the cockpit rim, linking the helo's systems with those of the mother ship and the crew with the phone net.

"Arkady, I need a fast, straight answer on this," Amanda's voice sounded in his earphones. "The weather is bad and it's going to get worse. Can you launch and conduct an effective ASW sweep under the current conditions while maintaining any kind of margin of safety?"

"Hang on a second, bridge."

Arkady toggled over to the aircraft intercom and twisted around to look into the rear cockpit.

"Hey, Gus, the Lady wants to know if we can go find that Argy sub. No shit, man, this one's a volunteer job. What about it?"

"What happens if I say no, sir?"

"Then I go after this guy by myself."

"Begging the Lieutenant's pardon, and with all due respect to his rank, but the Lieutenant couldn't find his own ass with both hands and a flashlight. Tell the Lady we're doing it."

"Okay, Gus, thanks. Bridge, this is Zero One. We can do it. Ready to launch."

"Acknowledged, Zero One." She was using her ultra-professional tone. Total control. "I'm putting the ship across the wind at this time. Launch at your discretion. You are weapons clear and you are authorized to break EMCON to prosecute contacts and for recovery."

The Duke began to turn. Lifting one hand up under the canopy top, Arkady gave the spin-up gesture to the deck chief. The ordnance hand danced back and clear of the helo, holding the orange safety streamers of the torpedo safety pins over her head to prove they had been pulled. The tie-down hands followed, dragging their chocks and belaying the straps with them. The deck chief was the last, pulling the hardline and giving the side of the cockpit a farewell slap.

Keeping the ground brakes locked, Arkady fed power to the turbines and brought up the rotor RPM, all the while gauging the motion of the helipad. At the next lift of the stern, he pulled pitch and let the rise catapult the helo into the air.

The Sea Comanche staggered under the impact of the wind, but Arkady fought her through the transition and got her nose down, gaining speed and altitude. Bucking the weather, he paid off to the north, heading for the datum point on his navigational display that marked the last known position of the enemy.

On the *Cunningham*'s bridge, Amanda heard the droning roar of Retainer Zero One's lift-off and her eyes followed the helo as it pulled away, the cold, moisture-laden air sheathing its rotors in a disk of compression vapor.

Damn you, Vince Arkady. . . .

"Damn, Lieutenant. This guy is good."

"Nothing, Gus?"

"Beyond the sound of the shrimp fucking, I'm not picking up a thing."

For a third time, Retainer Zero One held a low hover over the wave crests, the dome of her dunking sonar deployed down 350 feet into the depths at the end of its tether cable.

Arkady scowled as he fought to hold the helo on station with his pitch and collective. "Hell! Even the Swede boats can't be completely silent."

"I know, Lieutenant. If he was maneuvering, I'd at least hear some flow noise around his hull, and if he was station keeping, I'd hear his trim pumps as he maintained depth. Thing is, I'm not hearing anything at all. This guy couldn't have bottomed his boat, could he?"

Arkady considered for a moment and then gave his head a shake. "No way. We're beyond the continental shelf out here with a couple of thousand feet of water under us. All of the Kockums subs are Baltic designs. They don't have enough hull to go that deep."

"I can't figure where else he could have got to, then."

"Could he have found a thermocline down there to sit on?"

"I'll check it out, sir."

Grestovitch called up the sonar-control menu on one of his multimode telepanels and selected the "Extend" command. More dome tether, a light, braided Kevlar cable with an insulated coaxial core, peeled off the reel within the SQR/A1 pod, and the sensor head plunged deeper into the wet dark.

"At full extension ... seven hundred feet ... bathythermo-graph does not indicate a thermocline. There's nothing down here for him to hide under or sit on, and I'm still not hearing anything."

"Okay, Gus. Up dome. Let's try it again."

Arkady shifted Zero One a thousand yards west to the next station on the sonar line he was building between the *Cunningham* and the last known position of the Argentine. As he did so, he found his thoughts projecting past the mechanics of flying the weather-racked helicopter.

This guy's beating us, babe. I'm not sure how he's doing it, but he is. A wind burst snagged the helicopter, ripping away ten feet of its altitude and making its rotors flex to a dangerous extreme. *The old-timers had it easy. If they wanted to impress a lady, all they had to do was to drag some damn old dinosaur back to their cave before dinnertime.*

He grinned mirthlessly as he coaxed back the ten feet. It must be getting a little tight if he was turning his own warped sense of humor back on himself.

"On station and going to hover. Down dome to three fifty and resume passive search."

"Down dome to three fifty, aye, sir."

Using the autohover setting of the autopilot was out of the question. In fact, Zero One wasn't hovering at all as much as she was maintaining a forward flight that paced the wind. A very interesting way to make a living.

"Dome down. Commencing passive search."

Arkady fought the control grips and, as the minutes passed, tried to pretend that the turbulence wasn't getting worse.

"Come on, Gus! Let's not take all day about it here!"

"The fucker just isn't out here, sir."

"Repeat the sweep."

The SO leaned forward over his console again, feverishly using his accumulated skill to try to nurse a little more performance out of the system.

"Negative contact ... negative contact ... neg ... Sonovabitch!

There he is! Clear as a bell! He's descending out of the surface sound duct. Hull-popping noises and ballast tanks venting, bearing one six zero relative. I can't figure how I could have missed him before."

"To hell with that, Gus. We got 'im now! Go active and get us a range."

"Initiating active pinging . . . got a return! Target range five thousand yards, still bearing one six oh relative, bearing holding stable."

"Attack sequence!"

"Attack sequence start, sir. Master arm on! Torpedo select, position one! Torpedo is spinning up now!"

"Acknowledged," Arkady clipped back. "Set your preselects. Set fish for active homing. Set initial depth for one five zero. Set snake-pattern acquisition."

"Preselects set."

"Okay, coming around on bearing. We'll take the shot from here."

Arkady tried for a pedal turn and swore savagely as the helicopter fought him, trying to weather-vane back into the wind. From his station in the aft cockpit, Grestovitch continued to call out the track.

"Target is still holding on bearing, no lateral movement noted. . . . Wait a second, target is moving on vertical axis. He's blowing negative. . . . Target has gone active. . . . Target is pinging."

"Come *on*, your crank-tailed bitch! Get your ass around!"

"Target is changing depth. . . . Target is reentering surface sound duct. . . . Target has disappeared, sir."

"Damn!" Arkady let the helo back into the wind. "What happened, Gus?"

"I don't know, Lieutenant." The SO's voice carried his perplexity and frustration. "I had positive locks both active and passive and he just plain-ass disappeared. I'm not getting anything again."

"Did you lose him up in the weather slop?" Arkady demanded.

"I shouldn't have. I was lifting good active returns off of him. I shouldn't have lost the lock."

Arkady had flown with Grestovitch long enough to know that this likely wasn't operator failure. This particular Argentine was stacking the deck somehow.

"Gus, you said that this guy had gone active. Was it his attack system?"

"No, sir. It was a low-powered unit. He only ran a couple of pings off of it. Might have been a fathometer."

A fathometer?

"I've been thinking, Lieutenant," Grestovitch continued. "I heard this guy put a shot of air into his tanks just before he disappeared. Now, figuring that he knows that we've been running radar silent, and granting that he's a real ballsy dude, could he be lying doggo on the surface out there in that fog bank?"

Arkady looked out toward the ragged wall of mist off to starboard. "Yeah. That's how the U-boats used to evade the Brits during the early days of World War Two, back when they had asdic but no surface-search radars. You just may have something, old man. Up dome."

As the sonar transducer clicked into its mount under the Sea Comanche's snub wing, Arkady applied power and began a climbing turn. "Reconfigure for surface search and bring up the APG-65. Scan across the last sonar bearing we had."

"Aye, aye."

Grestovitch called up the radar display on his flatscreens and energized the system, watching intently as the sweep defined the surface.

"Negative! No surface contact. Not even a periscope return. Nothing."

"Damn, Gus. If he's not on top of the water and he's not under it, then where is he?"

"I dunno. There's nothing out there."

His own words suddenly made something click in the SO's mind.

"Hey, there really isn't anything out there."

Intently, Grestovitch ran the brightness gain up and down on his display screen.

"Lieutenant, you've heard guys talk about 'a hole in the water,' haven't you?"

"Yeah."

"Well, I'm looking at one right now. I'm getting traces of wave return all over the screen, except for right around where that Argy sub should be. There's nothing there at all, just a big dark area on the scope."

"I've never seen a black hole before, Gus. Let's go have us a look."

Retainer Zero One nosed gingerly into the fog bank. "Fog bank" was actually a misnomer, as it was more of a fast-flowing river of sea smoke, driven by the growing winds. Only a few moments' exposure to the wavering, misty streamers flowing around his cockpit made Arkady feel the potentially lethal tug of vertigo. Firmly, he fixed his eyes on his instruments and FLIR display.

"Walk me in, Gus."

"Continue to steer zero four zero true. Range to datum point, five hundred yards. Cross-referencing GPU positioning with datum point . . . and we're there."

"Okay. Hovering down. Keep your eyes open."

There was already something on the Forward Looking Infrared scanner, but the contrast was poor. As the altimeter steadied at one hundred feet, Arkady risked a look down over the cockpit rail.

White, not fog white, but ice white. They were holding over a great sheet of sea ice, more than half a square mile in area. It lay almost flush with the ocean's surface, riding too low to cause a radar return. But as the storm combers reached the edge of the floe, they collapsed in an explosion of spray and flattened out across its surface, causing Grestovitch's "hole in the water" effect.

"I will be damned. Hey, Gus. Could that funny-sounding ping the Argy produced have come from a vertical-scan sonar?"

"An ice machine? Maybe. But who ever heard of an ice machine on a diesel-electric boat?"

"Maybe the Argentines. This guy could be using it to position himself under this ice pan like a big old bass hiding under a log. Extend the MAD stinger."

Arkady circled wide to come at the floe from downwind, calling the readout from the Magnetic Abnormality Detector up onto his own repeater. Slowly he began to weave over the ice, seeking for a response.

One wasn't long in coming. The sensor pod began to react to the magnetic field being produced by a large mass of ferrous metal.

Arkady tightened the weave, maneuvering slowly until the readings maximized. Returning to a hover, he looked down on the frozen surface of the flow.

"Hello, fishie."

In the *Cunningham*'s Combat Information Center, Vince Arkady's static-spattered voice issued from the radio link speakers. "Gray Lady, Gray Lady, this is Retainer Zero One. We have a solid contact out here, but the setup is a little unusual. Breaking EMCON to request strike assist."

"Retainer Zero One, proceed," Commander Garrett responded coolly from topside.

"Roger. Zero One to TACCO, do you copy?"

Dix Beltrain toggled his own headset. "I'm here, Retainer. Whatcha all got, old buddy?"

"The reason we've been having such a tough time tracking this damn Argy sub. He's ice-picked to the bottom of a big free-floating ice pan out here. We can't get him on the passive arrays because he can power down completely, and we can't get him by active pinging because we lose his return against the floe."

Beltrain could readily visualize the setup. "Yeah, acknowledged. And whenever he wants to take a shot at us, all he has to do is to drop straight down out of the surface duct, take his bearing, and throw his fish."

"You got it, Gray Lady," Arkady replied. "I just spooked him back up into his hidey-hole again a few minutes ago. The problem is, our ASW torps won't work in this tactical situation. We can't acquire a targeting lock. We have to try something different."

"You have any ideas, Retainer?"

"Yeah, I want to go after this guy with a Sea SLAM."

Beltrain exchanged glances with some of the CIC team who had been listening in. The Sea SLAM was a marvelously versatile precision-guided munition, but no one present had ever heard of it being used for antisubmarine warfare.

"Please repeat that, Retainer?"

"Listen." Arkady's radio voice sounded aggravated. "I have this guy's position exactly fixed with my MAD gear. I'm hovering about fifty feet over him right now. I figure that this ice is about two or three feet thick and that he has the top of his conning tower butted right up against the bottom of the floe. If we can drop a SLAM in on him close enough, we should be able to give him a headache, or at least flush him out into open water."

Beltrain grinned as the concept came clear, and he snapped his fingers and pointed to the SLAM control station. A weapons technician dropped into the seat in front of the panel and began heating up the system.

"I got it now, Retainer. How do you want to work this?"

"We'll need the Captain's clearance to radiate with the fire-control radars for a few seconds—"

"Bridge to CIC, you've got it," Amanda Garrett cut in, the intentness of her voice indicating the way she had been following the exchange.

"—then I'll activate my IFF transponder and you get a lock on me for your initial targeting datum point. Once you've acquired that, I'll drop a smoke float onto the ice and get out of the way. You launch and bring your round in on the thermal flare of the float."

"We copy, Retainer! Captain, did you get all that?"

"Yes, Dix. You are authorized to proceed with the strike."

"Aye, aye. Aegis operator, energize your starboard arrays, prepare to scan the northern sector."

"Standing by to energize, sir."

"Retainer Zero One, we're ready for your transponder."

"Roger, Dix. Transponder is up for a ten count. Ten . . . nine . . . eight . . ."

"Aegis systems, execute your sweep and acquire locks on the helo."

"Aye, aye, sir. We have acquired locks and we have established the datum point."

"Right. Cease radiating and shut down."

Beltrain keyed back into the radio circuit. "Retainer, we've got the fix. Pop smoke and get the hell out of Dodge."

"Roger D, Roger D, smoke is down and we are outa here."

Beltrain took two fast steps across the deck of the CIC and peered over the shoulder of the SLAM operator.

"System is up, sir," the gunner's mate reported, her hand poised on her joystick controller. "Missile selected. Passive targeting interfaced with Aegis control and active guidance is ready to acquire. The launch cell is open and visually verified. Final-phase safeties are off and all prechecks are green."

"Shoot."

From up forward came the thud-rumble of a cold-fire launch.

The SLAM (Standoff Land Attack Missile) had been one of those off-the-shelf improvisations that had turned out more successful than even its designers could have imagined. Intended to provide naval aviation with an interim, standoff PGM for striking at heavily defended targets, it was a bastard mating of two different missiles: the airframe, engine, and warhead of the Navy's antiship Harpoon, and the infrared guidance system of the Air Force's air-to-surface Maverick.

So effective did the air-launched weapon prove that the design turned full circle and a surface-to-surface variant was produced. Armed with the Sea SLAM, a destroyer or frigate could deliver the firepower of a battleship with the precision of a sniper's rifle.

As the missile came over the top of its booster arc, the thermographic television camera in its nose activated, scanning the sea below it, picking up the ice pan almost at one. On the targeting screen back in the Duke's CIC, it appeared as a dark, irregular mass of no-heat afloat on the slightly lighter backdrop of the sea. A single bright star blazed near the center of the floe, the thermal energy radiating from the burning smoke float.

The systems operator deftly centered the targeting reticle of the guidance system on the flare and squeezed the actuator trigger, committing the missile.

To the north, the SLAM blazed down out of the sky and the smoking star fixed in the crosshairs grew until it filled the screen. Abruptly, the television image broke up and went to static as the transmitter ceased to exist.

"Now, that looked about right," Beltrain said with some satisfaction.

From their position, station keeping just east of the floe, Arkady and Grestovitch couldn't see the spray of shattered ice lift into the sky, just a flash of blue light through the mist.

"Down dome, Gus. Set depth three-fifty."

The transducer hit the waves and Grestovitch watched his depth gauge as the tether paid out. Setting the reel lock, he listened intently for results.

The local acoustic environment was still reverberating from the explosion, and it took a couple of minutes before he could hear past the echoes: the slamming and creaking of metal, the bubbling of air, and the *sush-sush-sush* of a fast-turning screw, all suddenly undercut by an urgent, throbbing hum.

"I got him. Propellers bearing three five zero true and opening the range. Numerous metallic transitories, and he's just cut in a bilge pump. We hurt him, Lieutenant! We hurt him and he's running!"

"Yeah!" Arkady exclaimed fiercely. "Mark one up for the home team. Good work, my man!"

The aviator thumbed the transmit button on the end of the collective controller.

"Gray Lady, Gray Lady, this is Retainer Zero One. The strike was effective. We confirm that the Argy has been damaged and is attempting to disengage to the northwest. Do you wish us to continue to prosecute the target?"

Amanda Garrett's answer crackled back almost instantly. "Negative, Retainer! I repeat, negative! Return to the ship for immediate recovery. Expedite!"

The Lady was sounding worried.

OFF THE ANTARCTIC SEA ICE PACK
FORTY-SEVEN MILES NORTHWEST OF CAPE LLOYD
1720 HOURS: MARCH 26, 2006

Under way again, the *Cunningham* was cutting into the outermost fringe of the cold front, and a fine, hard snow was hissing across the facing of her windscreen to fuse with the droplets of freezing spume being whipped off the wave tops.

"Ken, you keep the con," Amanda called back over her shoulder as she pulled an issue parka out of a gear locker. "I'm going aft to monitor the recovery. I'll feed you bell and steering commands as needed. For now, steer three zero zero and keep us quartering into the sea. That'll both put the wind across the helipad and get us some sea room away from the pack."

"Will do," the exec replied, assuming the command chair.

"And kill the Black Hole Systems. That'll give Arkady a thermal plume to follow home."

"Will do again. You watch yourself out there on deck, Skipper. It's getting nasty."

"Just worry about the ship, Ken. I'll be fine."

The main passageway on the weather-deck level of the superstructure was jammed with Air Division personnel, all hands made bulky and clumsy by a combination of cold-weather gear and emergency equipment.

"Coming aft! Make a hole!" Amanda slid along the grab rail until she reached CPO Muller at the hatchway. "We set to go, Chief?"

"Yes, ma'am," the burly aviation man replied, "but it's going to be a bitch of a recovery. We're at Force Six now and we're beyond the book limits clear across the board."

She accepted the safety belt Muller passed to her and cinched it around her waist. Removing her light mobile headset, she replaced it with a heavier-duty mike-and-earphone combination that used a hard link. She ran a quick communications check with the bridge and then snapped the end of her safety belt's jackline onto the hardpoint beside the hatch frame.

"Set, Captain?"

"Set. Let's go."

"Right. Crash and Salvage teams! Aviation Fuel Repair team! RAST crew! Move out!"

The hatch slammed open and they streamed through, Amanda cutting over to the starboard rail while the helipad crew deployed to their stations.

The *Cunningham*'s RAM decking, tolerable when dry, was ominously slick under the rubber soles of Amanda's sea boots, and the wind, once merely freezing, now was cold flame. When she gripped the nylon strap of the railing, she could feel the ice crystals that had worked into the fabric, their bite making her wish for a heavier pair of gloves.

No time to worry about it now. Clawing her hair out of her narrowed eyes with a quick swipe of her hand, she peered forward, sighting along the Duke's flank in the failing polar twilight.

"Bridge," she said, cupping her palm over the lip mike, "forget the load limits and bring the stabilizers up full. Then give me a couple of extra revs on the starboard propulsor pod. It'll help us hold the course line against this weather."

Years before, when she had been attending the Naval Surface Warfare School, she'd had a run-in with a senior captain on the faculty. This individual had apparently believed that the female officers assigned to his class should serve double duty as a personal harem. Amanda had corrected this misconception with a sharp backhand across the face.

Afterward, she suspected he'd tried to derail her career by having her diverted to duty aboard a Fleet ocean tug instead of the surface combatant that she'd wanted. Now, however, she blessed the name of that fanny-pinching son of a bitch. For in the two years she'd commanded the *Piegan,* she had learned more about this brand of down-and-dirty seamanship than she had during all the rest of her tours combined.

"There he is!"

The Sea Comanche's low-vis camouflage made it almost invisible against the overcast, but Amanda could make out that Arkady had already jettisoned his torpedoes in preparation for a rough-weather landing. On the *Cunningham*'s end, the crash barriers had already been deployed and the RAST hands were standing by to accept the helo's line.

In heavy seas, it is almost impossible to simply set a helicopter down on a small-surface platform. The fantail of a ship, rising and falling in a twenty-foot arc in response to wave action, can literally swat a hovering helicopter like a fly. That was why the RAST (Recovery Assistance Securing and Traversing) system had been developed.

The helicopter dropped a cable that would be connected to a deck winch that, in turn, would pull the aircraft down out of the sky. This permitted the helo pilot to flare back against the tension of the line, maintaining a controlled separation between the copter and the deck until touchdown.

Angling in across the Duke's helipad, Zero One lowered its landing gear and then popped the reel of RAST line out of a belly niche. A deck hand dashed after it and snared the light steel cable with a grounded catch crook, the static charge accumulated by the helo arcing brightly at first touch.

It took only moments for the RAST team to clear the cable from the reel and to feed it into the winch pickup. The wand man passed the ready-to-haul sign up to the helo and Arkady flashed his landing lights in acknowledgment.

Zero One came back on her line like a recalcitrant puppy on the end of a leash and the winch began bringing her down.

Amanda had looked on as these evolutions had taken place. Now she glanced forward again to read the seas they would be encountering for the next few critical seconds.

The sky had changed. It was as if the misty atmosphere off the *Cunningham*'s bow were coagulating into something solid. A wall of darkness was rushing down upon the ship.

"Slack off!" she screamed. "Slack off! Slack off!"

Too late. The squall line hit them like the expanding wave front of an explosion.

The destroyer reared like a startled stallion under the impact, and almost everyone on deck was taken down and inundated by the spray that geysered over the railings. The wall of water that had been pushed ahead of the storm rolled back under the *Cunning-*

ham's keel, lifting the aft end of the ship and then letting it drop with savage force.

Amanda heard a sharp crack, like a small-caliber rifle shot, and then a yell over the wind and rotor roar. "Jesus! The RAST line's carried away!"

Looking up, she saw Retainer Zero One flailing off into the storm like a kite with a broken string.

Aboard the helicopter, Vince Arkady snarled in survival fixation as he battled to keep his suddenly berserk aircraft away from the ocean's surface. There had never been a simulator scenario drawn up for this kind of situation. Given this set of parameters, the experts would simply say that you'd die and have done with it.

That left Gus Grestovitch, reduced to the status of a helpless passenger, to look on as the *Cunningham*'s outline faded away into the blizzard.

"We're screwed!" he whispered hoarsely.

"Bridge! Illuminate the ship! Running lights, anchor lights, work lights, everything! Full up now!"

The near-night that had fallen across the destroyer was broken by the sudden, acknowledging glare. Pulling herself back to her feet, Amanda ran across to the RAST station through a curtain of red-lit snow.

CPO Muller and the recovery team were clustered around the winch in its recessed compartment, already struggling with what looked like a titanic fishing-reel snarl.

"Chief, how bad is it?" she yelled over the wind roar.

"As bad as it gets. The cable snapped right at the connector on the helo's belly. There's no line left to bring 'em down on, and there's sure no way in hell we can recover him in this kind of weather without the RAST gear."

Peering into Muller's face, Amanda could read the deadly finality there. With any of the Navy's other LAMPS-class helicopters, it would have been easy enough to drop another line from the cabin. The Sea Comanche, with its cramped, fighter-type cockpits, had no such second-chance option.

Twin beams of white light lanced down out of the darkness and panned forward to play across the Duke's stern. Zero One was back under control and coming up on the ship again, forging ahead slowly through the blizzard.

"Captain, this is the CIC," a voice sounded faintly in her headset. "Lieutenant Arkady is requesting permission to talk to you, ma'am."

"Okay. Patch him through on this deck circuit."

Click!

"Gray Lady, this is Zero One. Looks like we have kind of a mess here."

Amanda hunkered down beside Chief Muller and tried to shield the headset mike from the booming wind gusts.

"Acknowledged, Zero One. We can confirm that your RAST line has carried away completely. We are assessing the situation."

"Not much to assess, Gray Lady. We're not getting this aircraft back aboard tonight." Vince Arkady's reply was laced with the same kind of finality that Muller's had been.

Down inside, where she lived, the knot began to tighten.

"Let's not get ahead of ourselves, Retainer. If we have to, we can write off the helo. You can execute a controlled crash inside the containment barriers."

"Negative, negative! If we bust a fuel cell, we could have a major deck fire. If we go over the side, we could damage a propulsor pod. I won't place the ship at that kind of risk."

"That decision is my responsibility, Retainer."

"No, Captain," Arkady repeated grimly over the radio link. "As aircraft commander, this one is my call."

Amanda gritted out one of those phrases that a lady shouldn't use but a naval officer sometimes has to.

"Chief, there has to be some kind of alternative procedure here!" she said, flipping the lip mike back.

"Maybe if he could hover in close enough for us to get a line on his cargo-transfer shackle . . ."

The destroyer's deck lurched as she came off the slope of a quartering sea, and another wave crest exploded over the rail, marking the futility of Muller's tentative proposal.

"Gray Lady, this is Zero One. Our just hanging around up here isn't going to accomplish anything. I'm going to break off and head for the Antarctic Peninsula. We'll set down at either the Russian or Polish station and ride the storm out there. We can set up a rendezvous when we get the weather again."

"What? No! Stand by, Zero One."

Muller had been listening in on the circuit as well. The CPO reached over and grabbed Amanda's shoulder.

"He'll never make it! He doesn't have the fuel reserves to fight this kind of weather. Even if he did manage to find one of those installations, odds are that even the Lieutenant wouldn't be able to make an unassisted landing in one piece. If he's going to get down anywhere, ma'am, it's gotta be here!"

She nodded an acknowledgment. If the wind and rotor roar was making it hard to hear, the cold was making it hard to think. Even the best arctic gear in the world would begin to fail when wet, and there was an inch of freezing seawater curtaining across the warship's decks.

"Gray Lady, do you copy?" Arkady's voice insisted, requesting permission to abandon hope.

"Negative, Zero One. That is not an option. I repeat, that is not an option. Hold on station until we can come up with something else."

"Gray Lady, I don't have time for this shit!" Arkady snapped back, a tension edge on his voice. "If I'm going to have any chance at all of finding a place to set down, I have to take departure now! I don't have the gas to fuck around!"

"Lieutenant Arkady! You will hold on station for two minutes more! That is an order!"

There was no reply, but the lights of Retainer Zero One continued to dance erratically in the murk above the fantail.

Amanda knelt on the deck, trying to ignore the pain and the chill creeping up her limbs, and trying to force some kind of possible solution from a mind that suddenly seemed to be growing clouded and empty.

A shepherd's crook rig of some kind . . . Not likely with the deck dancing around like this. A line gun up to the cockpit? No! Not up into a rotor arc. Come on . . . come on!

Locking her jaws to keep her teeth from chattering, she leaned forward and slammed her fist into the deck, both out of frustration and to drive some feeling back into her hand.

"Gray Lady." The two minutes were gone, and Arkady's voice was level again, controlled or resigned. "Taking departure for Bellingshausen Base. Good luck. We'll see you guys after the blow."

"Arkady, you don't have enough fuel!"

"Don't sweat it, Gray Lady. I can stretch what we've got. I'm jettisoning the MAD pod and the dunking sonar—"

Amanda's head snapped up. "Wait! Hold it! The dunking sonar! Arkady, hold on to that sonar pod and maintain station for one more minute!"

She turned to Chief Muller. "Chief, could we recover Zero One on the transducer tether of the dunking sonar?"

"Hell!" Muller exclaimed. "I've never heard of anyone trying it before."

"Neither have I, Gray Lady," Arkady added over the circuit, "but all of a sudden it sounds better than dropping in on the Russians for a long weekend. Are you set to receive the tether?"

"Acknowledged, Zero One. Bring it in now."

Amanda scrambled to her feet and lifted her voice over the gale. "Recovery crews, stand by! Watch yourselves, because we'll be doing a pickup on a sonar dome. Chief, get that winch clear! You, the guy with the heavy wire cutters! Stand ready! We're going to be needing you."

The Sea Comanche was nosing in again, gingerly trying to avoid the backsweep of the mast array while positioning to lower the transducer onto the helipad.

They could see the teardrop-shaped sound head swinging pendulously beneath the aircraft. Unlike the dedicated RAST line, it packed enough mass to shatter bone should anyone fail to get out of its path. The handling crew huddled back against the superstructure as Arkady centered the helo. Then the tether reel was released and the dome crashed down within the confines of the crash barriers with enough impact to crack the deck tiling.

"Go!"

The brawniest of the deck hands dove across the helipad and piled onto the transducer as if it were an opposing quarterback, containing it before the wave action could flip it away over the side. The sailor carrying the wire cutters followed them in, clipping through the tether just short of the dome. Another Aviation Division rating cradled the severed device in his arms like an infant and struggled back to the deckhouse with it.

Arkady dumped more line and backed away, giving both himself and the recovery crew marginally more room to work. The recovery hands hogged the cable back across the deck to the winch, looking as if they were engaged in a tug-of-war with the helicopter. It was a contest they would have had no chance of winning. One bad move on the pilot's part, or one exceptional wave or wind burst, and the tether would be whipped away over the side, probably taking one or more of its handlers with it.

They got the line to the winch and they clustered around it. They remained there for too long.

"Chief, what is the problem now?" Amanda yelled, coming to stand at the CPO's shoulder.

"The friggin' winch guide won't accept the tether! The cable's the wrong diameter!"

"Damn, damn, damn!"

"We'll have to rig another winch, Captain!"

"We don't have that kind of time!"

Wildly, she looked around the deck. Alternatives! The aircraft tie-downs wouldn't do it. Nor was there anything that would work in the winch compartment. For the first time, Amanda cursed the starkness mandated by the Duke's stealth design. Then she saw the personnel hatch just forward of the elevator.

Dropping down beside it, she tore up the recessed dogging lever and threw the hatch open onto its holdback latch.

Down below in the brightly illuminated hangar bay, startled Air Division hands looked up at her.

"Get me two four-by-four shoring spars from the damage-control locker and a heavy cable shackle," she screamed. "Move!"

At the other end of the tether, Vince Arkady maintained his precarious balancing act, his eyes flicking from the Sea Comanche's instrumentation to the hazy constellation of ship's lights beneath its nose. In the odd moments he could spare for the FLIR display, all that could be seen were an endless series of green and black storm rollers arcing across infinity.

"Lieutenant," Grestovitch reported levelly. "Just letting you know that we're starting to get ice buildup in the air intakes."

"I know, Gus. I can feel the power loss."

Lift loss too. The rotors were icing as well. Occasionally there was a soft, clicking impact on the outside of the cockpit as a fragment was flung free of the blades. Soon the Sea Comanche would grow weary of its burden and sink down into the sea.

"Hope those guys don't take all night about this."

That was a given. Arkady didn't bother to answer.

The copper sulfate taste of fear was starting to build in the back of his throat. A little while ago, he'd bragged in front of a lady that he'd never been afraid of any aircraft in his life. That had been an inexact statement.

All airmen fear the weather.

Most won't admit it, but the fear is there. Weather doesn't give a damn how good you are, or how well trained, or how lucky. It just fills up your sky, and if you can't escape to the ground, or get out of its way, it kills you with the bland indifference of a boulder rolling over a bug.

"Retainer, this is Gray Lady." Amanda's voice sounded in his earphones, distorted by wind roar and the feedback from the helo. "We have a further complication. The RAST system won't take the tether. You'll have to bring yourself down with your pod winch. We'll give you the word just as soon as we get things secured on this end."

Out of the corner of his eye, the aviator followed the undulating snake of the cable down from his wing until it disappeared into the red glow of the helipad.

"Why not?" he sighed.

The cable end was bent around the center of the two shoring spars and a wrench flashed as the bolts of the shackle were tightened.

"All secure, Captain!" the AC hand yelled up from the deck of the hangar bay.

"Right. Everyone down there stand clear! Way clear!"

Amanda returned her attention to deck level. "All hands! Turn loose of that cable and get back up against the superstructure!"

As she waited for her order to be obeyed, she called in to the bridge. "Ken, we're bringing him down now. Stand by."

"Aye, aye. We're set."

"Retainer Zero One. We're ready to recover. Stand by."

"Roger, Gray Lady. Let's get it done."

She took a final look around to make sure the pad was clear, then she scrambled back herself.

"Retainer, commence recovery now!"

"Executing approach. Up dome!"

The tether went taut and the shoring beams whipped upward and jammed across the hatch frame with a crash that made the deck shudder. Riding that pull, the shadowy outline of the Sea Comanche began to sweep down out of the storm rack.

"Up dome!" Arkady was pushing his flying skill beyond consciousness, adapting and responding to a multitude of different factors simultaneously, with each second. Wind, power settings, rate of descent, the movement of the deck, the need to keep the undesigned load from stripping the gears of the reel drive.

The helipad target grew larger rapidly, then too rapidly, as the *Cunningham* bucked like a mustang trying to rid itself of a horsefly.

Arkady flared back, heaving taut. However, as the ship fell away once more, he felt Zero One twist in midair. Shit! The off-center drag from the sonar pod was now rolling them onto their side. Instead of trying to correct, Arkady dumped pitch and dove, followed the deck down. An instant later, the undercarriage hit with a crash that took up every millimeter of the shock-absorber play.

Arkady's hands flew around the cockpit. Fuel flow off! Battle damage switches on! Ground brakes locked! Rotor brake engaged!

"Gus, lock the winch reel!"

"Got it!"

Master power off!

"Let's get out of this thing!" Arkady yelled.

"No shit, Lieutenant!"

The canopies swung open and the freezing blast from outside erased the pocket of warm air they had contained in a microsecond. As the two aviators swung down from the cockpit, the tie-down crew moved forward, waiting for the windmill of the rotors to slow before approaching the helo.

"Glad you made it, sir," Chief Muller yelled, coming up to Arkady. "Real rough night out."

"Tell me about it, Chief."

Looking forward, Arkady saw a figure, still slender in her cold-weather gear, standing outlined in the glare of the red work arcs.

Up on the bridge, Commander Ken Hiro shifted his vision from one bank of video monitors to another. One set was focused aft, covering the events developing on the helipad. The others, aimed forward, were operating in low-light mode. Scanning the sea ahead of the ship, they granted the bridge crew and the lookout team vision in the now near-total darkness of the failing day.

One of those lookouts now sang out. "Object in the water. Bearing five degrees off the port bow, sir."

More than an object. Hiro saw a small hill's worth of ice rolling down on them, a berg fragment being driven into the destroyer's path by the force of the storm.

"Hard to starboard! Come right to zero zero zero degrees!"

There was just barely enough time to get on the MC-1.

"Beware on deck! We're going into the trough!"

Amanda felt her ship turning across the weather even before Hiro's warning call thundered out of the deck speakers. The only constructive thing she could do in the seconds she had was to knock the open deck hatch off its holdbacks and slam it partially shut on the helo tether. A moment later, a wall of dark water curled up over the portside rail and collapsed down upon everyone on deck.

As with the others of the recovery team, Amanda had been suffering from the slow, invasive chill coming on from the freezing spray and wind. The shock of this glacial-temperature inundation, though, made the heart stagger and slam in the chest and vision gray out.

Amanda clung to the hatch frame until the liquid avalanche had passed. Shaking the salt water out of her eyes, she looked up and around. The majority of the other deckhands had been scythed down by the wave as well, and now, literally looming over them, was a new threat.

There had been no chance to get Retainer Zero One's tie-downs secure. Its only hard connection with the deck was the single point of the sonar dome tether. Now, as the ship wallowed broadside on to the gale, the helicopter began to pivot around that hard point, skidding wildly across the slick decking with the force of the roll.

In the bloody deck lights, the angular form of the helo resembled some insectoid horror from a 1950s science-fiction film, striving to break out of the pen of the containment barriers. As Amanda looked on, the sweeping Fenestron flattened two hands who had failed to get clear in time. Then she saw a third figure riding the side of the copter's fuselage like a cowboy trying to bulldog an outsized steer.

It was Arkady.

"No!"

She tried to scramble to her feet but found that she was fouled in the tangle of her lifeline and headset lead. Frantically, she struggled to kick clear as the ship reached the farside of its roll to starboard.

Arkady bailed off the helicopter as it began its reverse swing. Dragging the two injured men to their feet, he shoved them forward toward the safety of the superstructure. Instead of following, though, he recovered one of the nylon restraint straps they had been carrying and snubbed one end through a tie-down. The aviator was not going to allow his aircraft to kill itself.

Amanda tore off her headset and hit her safety-belt release, freeing herself, but too late to intervene.

Another deluge raked the destroyer's decks. This time, no one topside could even feel the searing cold of it. As Zero One began its new wild arc across the helipad, Arkady threw himself flat, letting the low-riding tail boom sweep over him. As the helo hesitated at the neutral point between waves, he rolled over onto his back and reached up, snapping the free end of the restraint to a hardpoint under the fuselage.

Captured, Zero One jerked up short.

A moment later, Chief Muller led the general charge to surround the helo and complete the tie-down. Amanda saw a set of wheel chocks adrift at her feet and she caught them up. Joining the rush, she dropped down beside one of the landing-gear trucks and pounded the rubber wedges into place on either side of the tire.

A third wave sluiced across the deck, but without the intensity of the first two. With her turbines outscreaming the wind, the *Cunningham* was coming around again, clawing her way out of the trough to face the storm once more.

It took a while longer to finish battening down the helipad. A dozen more restraint straps had to be linked between Zero One and the deck tie-downs and ratcheted tight. Her rotors were folded back and secured as well, all by men and women who were beginning to stagger as much from exhaustion and exposure as from the movement of the ship.

A growing sense of dull unreality was beginning to fall upon Amanda. So much so that she failed to recognize the symptoms of her own critical loss of body heat. The only thing that seemed to catch in her mind were momentary flashes of Arkady's face as he worked around his aircraft. When she finally led her people back toward the shelter of the superstructure, the glowing oval of the watertight door seemed to be a hundred miles away.

OFF THE ANTARCTIC SEA ICE PACK
SIXTY MILES NORTH OF SEAL ISLAND
1810 HOURS: MARCH 26, 2006

The weather-deck hatch slammed shut, locking out the night and leaving the interior passageway crowded with sodden, snow-encrusted figures too weary to move.

"Well, that was a bit of a chore," Arkady commented, leaning into the grab rail. "Think she'll be okay out there, Chief?"

"Probably, just as long as we don't get crossways to the weather again. Sorry about having to leave her topside, sir. Trying to hog her down on the elevator tonight just wouldn't have been such a good idea."

"Yeah, I know. You guys did good work out there, Chief."

"Thank the Lady. She figured out how to get you down. Speaking God's honest, Lieutenant, I had you figured as turning up missing next muster."

"Me too."

Arkady lifted one hand from the rail and studied it judgmentally. Yep, he was going to have a real good case of the shakes here presently. Probably at least as good as after that dogfight the other day.

"Get these people thawed out." Amanda Garrett was leaning back against the bulkhead a couple of feet down the passageway. Her eyes were closed, her voice hoarse and a little unsteady. "Forget water restrictions and get them under a hot shower for as long as it takes. Guelette and ... the other guy who was knocked down out there. Go to sick bay and get checked out. Let's move."

The recovery teams began to disperse, shuffling back down toward their berthing spaces. Gus Grestovitch was sitting on the deck, his head cradled in his arms. Arkady reached down and pulled him to his feet.

"Come on, buddy. You heard the Lady. Up off your ass and fly."

Grestovitch managed a wan grin as his pilot aimed him down the passageway.

After a few moments, only he and his captain remained in the corridor. The day had turned full circle. Only now they were wet, half frozen, and trembling on the edge of collapse. What hadn't changed was that Arkady found himself thinking that she was still one of the most desirable of women. As for what Amanda thought, he wasn't quite sure. She was watching him now with that same look of almost fearful wariness that he'd seen outside of sick bay.

She turned away from him and started forward. As she reached the passageway ladder up to the next level, her legs nearly buckled.

"Hey, are you okay?" Hell, his own weren't all that solid as he hurried to her side.

"I'm all right," she said thickly, clinging to the ladder railing. "I just need to get to the bridge."

There was an unfocused haziness in her eyes that spooked him, and a pallor to her skin that went beyond mere exposure to cold.

"Captain, you'd better obey your own orders and get under a hot shower for a while. You don't look so good."

"I'm fine and I am needed on the bridge!" She tried to pull herself up the ladder, but slipped and went down hard with one knee on the riser.

"Begging your pardon, ma'am, but I think you're going into hypothermic shock!"

"Leave me alone, Lieutenant!"

Something cracked inside Arkady. Reaching out, he grabbed the hood of her parka and literally shook her by the scruff of the neck. "Jesus, Lady, will you please think about yourself for five goddamned minutes!" he roared, groping for words that would reach her. "What happens to the ship if you go down? Who's going to get us out of here?"

That did it. A degree of awareness snapped back into her eyes. "All right, all right! Help me to my cabin!"

With his arm around her waist, they made it up the ladder and forward to her quarters, moving as unsteadily as if they'd split a full bottle of bourbon. Once inside the door, he yanked down the zips of her parka and peeled the mass of wet fabric off her shoulders, letting it drop to the deck.

She jerked away from him. "I can manage for myself, Lieutenant!" she said tightly.

"Fine! Do it!" He started to leave but found himself turning back to meet her gaze head-on. "And I'm not Lieutenant! I'm Arkady!"

The cabin door slammed behind him.

He stood out in the passageway for a few moments, riding with the pitch of the deck, and then looked up toward the overhead.

"Now, why in the *hell* did I say that!"

He slammed his flight helmet against the opposing interior bulkhead, producing an oilcanning boom and leaving a considerable dent in the sheet metal. With his forearm tingling from the shock of the blow, he stalked down to his own quarters.

Amanda made her way to the cabin's head. Without attempting to undress, she kicked off her sea boots and climbed into the shower, turning on the hot water full force.

It was almost a minute before she even began to feel the steaming warmth.

She held her hands up to the flow from the shower spigot and worked her fingers until they eventually began to regain a degree of their flexibility. Then, slowly, she began to undress.

Now that she was starting to recover, she could realize just how bad a shape she'd been in. Arkady had been right about her physical condition. How right was he about the other things?

Since Annapolis, many of the men she had been involved with had been fellow naval officers. With some, she'd developed friendships. Others, she'd dated. With a select two or three, she had had affairs. What she had never done was to allow herself to become drawn to anyone in her chain of command. That was dancing on the edge of professional disaster. She had sworn that she would never leave herself so vulnerable.

Unfortunately, along had come one Lieutenant Vincent Arkady, quietly demanding the right to care for her.

In the cold environment, Amanda had been wearing one of her leotards under her uniform. Peeling out of this second skin, she dropped it to her feet. Her bra and briefs followed. Sinking down to the bottom of the cramped stall, she let the hot spray play over her shoulders.

The overt answer was easy. She needed to end this, right now, before they both made fools of themselves.

Unfortunately, the real world doesn't work on easy answers. This was going beyond a simple tug of physical desire. Out on that deck tonight, she had felt fear for him. Not just the sense of responsibility she felt for everyone under her command, but a deeper, personalized fear. One that radiated up from the core of her being. One born out of the realization of all the lost possibilities there would be if this man was taken from her.

She kneeled on her discarded clothing. "Damn you ... damn you ... damn you ..."

Only, this time she couldn't say if it was aimed at Arkady or herself.

The *Cunningham* scissored steadily ahead through the storm rollers, the repetitive explosions of spray around her bow showing up as the faintest of pale flashes in the night.

"How's she doing, Ken?"

Hiro looked around to find Amanda standing at his shoulder, clad in fresh work khakis and with her still-damp hair pinned up on the back of her neck. She waved away the traditional call announcing her presence on the bridge.

"We're doing okay, Captain. She's running tight and all boards are green. The helo looks like it's riding all right too."

"Good enough. Let's take a look at the course."

They stepped across the darkened bridge to the glowing surface of the chart table.

"Still steering two nine oh, and we have resumed full blackout and EMCON. I've also bent on turns for a couple of extra knots. It'll eat into our fuel a little, but I figured that we'd want to get well clear of that last contact point before first light."

"I concur." Amanda drew her nail across the surface of the chart tank. "We'll hold this heading and get back into the center of Drake Passage. Hugging the pack just isn't going to work for us."

"Yeah. There's more drift out there than we were told to expect."

"That, plus it gives the Argys a fixed geographical line they can hunt along for us. Going out into the Passage will put us closer to the Argentine air bases, but we'll just have to live with it. How about the weather?"

"Latest metsat download indicates that we should be through the worst of this heavy stuff by about zero four hundred."

"Good. We'll call up a work crew and strike the helo below just as soon as the seas moderate." Amanda straightened from the chart table. "Sorry about taking so long to get back up here," she said, rubbing the small of her back. "After that session on the helipad, I had to defrost a little."

"No problem," Hiro replied sympathetically. "It didn't look like much fun on the monitors. Want me to keep an eye on things tonight?"

"No, I'll take it for a while. You can have the middle watch. Go get some rest and be back up here at twenty-four hundred."

"Aye, aye. Good night, ma'am. Captain has the con!"

Amanda made the circuit, checking with each of the duty watch and with the rows of data repeaters. That done, she settled into the captain's chair, wincing slightly. She'd just discovered a few aches and bruises that her shower had failed to erase. Deliberately, she kept her eyes away from the glowing screen faces, letting her natural night vision develop.

"Earl Grey, one creamer, two sugars," a voice said quietly.

The cup materialized from over her shoulder. After a moment's hesitation, she accepted it.

"Thank you, Arkady."

"No. Thank you." She felt his weight come onto the back of her chair as he leaned against it. "I never would have made it to that Russian base tonight. I was running scared because I couldn't figure out anything else to do. You did. Gus and I are alive because of it. I owe you, Captain."

"No, we're even," she replied, looking out into the night. "If you hadn't shaken some sense into me, I wouldn't have made it up to this bridge. And my only excuse would have been that I'd started to buy in to the myth that a commanding officer is supposed to be all-enduring and indestructible."

"Yeah, well, I guess we all have our moments. Tell you what, though. If you bale me out of any further bonehead stunts that I might get involved in, I'll do the same for you."

Amanda sipped the tea. It was just as she liked it, and its comforting warmth began to radiate through her. She closed her eyes and let her breath trickle out in a protracted sigh.

"Deal," she said.

BUENOS AIRES
1440 HOURS: MARCH 27, 2006

Dr. Towers pushed aside the curtain and peered out.

"That's funny," she commented.

"What, Doctor?" Steve Rosario inquired from across their sitting room/office.

"Pardon me if I'm making a cultural assumption here, but I'd always believed that South Americans were a bit more . . . volatile in matters of politics and statesmanship. I was expecting to see something like the anti-British demonstrations during the Falklands War. But for us, nothing. No rock throwing. No 'Yankee go home!' The streets are almost deserted."

"There's a reason for it."

The State Department man joined her at the window. "Take a look at the roof of the building down at the corner. The one on the other side of the intersection."

Dr. Towers spotted the two men crouched down behind the

roof parapet. One was armed with a scope-sighted assault rifle. The other was systematically scanning the surrounding area with a pair of binoculars.

"National Police antisnipers. There's one on every facing block around the Embassy."

Rosario smiled grimly. "I took a little walk earlier this afternoon. I saw at least ten plainclothes officers down at ground level, and I probably missed about twice that number. There's a SWAT team and a couple of armored cars stationed over on the other side of the park, and if you go out a little farther, you start to see the Army patrols. Sparza's brought in an entire airborne regiment equipped for antiriot work. The entire city is locked down tight."

"I didn't think we were that scary."

"I think it's being done for our benefit, and indirectly for the Argentine plan of operations. Sparza is smart enough to know that it's in his best diplomatic interest to maintain a state of extreme propriety when it comes to American citizens just now. If you were local, you'd probably be jumped for raising your voice on the street."

"Could that explain the very low-keyed editorial stance of most of the local media?" Dr. Towers said, turning back into the room. "Government censorship?"

"I suspect so," Rosario replied, lingering at the window. "I also suspect that's why neither we nor the Argentines have gone public with the word that we're already shooting at each other. Everyone wants a nice, quiet, little war."

A black Lincoln town car turned into the Embassy gates, preceded and trailed by a pair of mud-colored Ford Explorers, the ubiquitous "war wagons" of the Secret Service.

"Secretary Van Lynden is back."

The Secretary of State passed through the door of the suite a few minutes later. Setting his briefcase down beside one of the room's easy chairs, he sank down into it, his head cradled in his hands.

"What's the word from the United Nations, Steve?"

"Ambassador DeSantis reports that it looks as if we have a solid majority block assembled for a condemnation vote against Argentina. The downside is that the Argentines have gotten the extension on their recess. All votes on the Antarctic issue have been put off for another two days."

"Aah, God. Why not?"

"Could I get you a drink, Mr. Secretary?" Dr. Towers asked, with sympathy.

"Yes, Doctor. Thank you. You could. A rye on the rocks, please."

"How did it go, sir?" Rosario inquired.

"I've spent the past five hours sitting across the table from the Argentine Minister of State and, for all intents and purposes, we've just been staring at each other. We've hit the wall, Steve. Everybody's made their brag, and now they're stuck with it."

"What happens next?" Dr. Towers asked from the suite's small wet bar.

"Good question. Diplomatically speaking, we've entered a holding pattern. Both sides have established a set of absolute crisis parameters they won't go beyond. Until somebody yields on a point, we've got nothing to talk about. We'll just have to wait until some outside event changes the scenario and kicks the door open again."

"Like the outcome of things down south?" The scientist crossed the room and passed Van Lynden a bar tumbler.

"Exactly," he replied, swirling the glass and staring at the ice as it danced in the amber liquor.

Lieutenant Commander Carl Thomson surfaced from Main Engine Control for the first time in over forty-eight hours. The Duke's chief engineer had been living on station ever since the first Argentine attack, alternating long stretches in front of the master console with short naps taken on the deck plates beside it.

Eventually, though, even he had to get away from the incessant whining song of the turbogenerators.

"Anybody get the word on the playoffs?" he asked, coming through the wardroom door.

"Vegas over Philly by eight points," Christine Rendino murmured in reply. The intel was stretched limply out on the couch, her eyes closed and her deck shoes kicked off. Across from her, Frank McKelsie sprawled in an easy chair, eyes open but staring off into nowhere in particular. The wardroom itself was being haunted by sea poltergeists. The edges of the cloth covering the central table swayed in a slow rhythm, cabinets creaked, and the cup rack clinked in time to the movement of the ship.

"Somebody must have bribed the damn referees."

"Tell me about it."

Thomson went over and selected a battle ration from the box sitting on the serving counter. Drawing a cup of coffee from the urn, he sat down at the table and investigated the "bat rat." Little more than a sack lunch run up by the galley for distribution when the ship was holding at battle stations, Thomson tore into the processed chicken sandwich with more relish than it probably deserved. The coffee was good, though, the minute difference in flavor between the engine room and wardroom percolators being a welcome change.

"Feels like she's slacking off a little," he commented.

"Uh-huh," Christine replied, "we're getting out of the worst of it. Be nice to have the deck quit walking around for a while."

"Just as long as the Captain doesn't decide to go sunbathing again," McKelsie grunted.

"What's that supposed to mean?" the intelligence officer demanded.

"Hell, Rendino. We were caught way out of position by that first Argentine strike. The Captain left us wide open for that one."

"In case nobody bothered to mention it before, that was a surprise attack, McKelsie. Nobody expected the Argentines to pull a totally off-the-wall stunt like that. Not even the Captain . . . or me."

"She violated basic stealth doctrine. She let herself get caught outside of weather cover. She damn near got us all blown away, and if you weren't so busy kissing up after her, you'd admit it."

Christine opened one cold, blue-gray eye. "McKelsie, fa' sure medical science has discovered cures for cholera, clap, and the black plague. What are you still doing here?"

"That's enough," Thomson said. "Lieutenant McKelsie, I believe that you'll discover that bad-mouthing your superior officers is not a sound way to get ahead in this man's Navy."

"Shit, Chief! I'm stating a fact! The Captain made a mistake out there the other day."

"Maybe she did," Thomson agreed, rummaging around in the bat-rat sack again. "I've served under a lot of captains, under a lot of different circumstances. Sooner or later, every one of them made some kind of mistake or other. How they reacted to it, and corrected it, marked the difference between a good skipper and a bad one."

The engineer removed a doughnut from the sack and deliberately gestured toward McKelsie with it. "This tells me that the Lady is good."

"How's that supposed to work, Chief?"

"Simple. This tin can has fought its way through three major engagements in two days, and I am sitting here eating this doughnut and some damn fish isn't. That, sonny boy, counts for a whole lot in this trade."

DRAKE PASSAGE
0401 HOURS: MARCH 28, 2006

Amanda stirred restlessly in the lounge chair. Looking out into the darkened and deserted wardroom, she wearily recalled a rather pompous lecture she had sat through back at the Academy. It had concerned an officer's need to draw up a "sleep schedule" that would guarantee them an adequate amount of rest under all circumstances.

It was a reasonable concept. However, the lecturer never quite got around to explaining how you were supposed to keep to this schedule during a developing tactical situation. Or how you were supposed to shut your mind off during those scraps of downtime that you might find.

Recurling herself more tightly in the lounger, she suppressed a shiver. She couldn't seem to shake the aftereffects of her brush with hypothermia, and no place seemed warm. Finally her eyes grew heavy, and she began to close out the world.

"Captain to the Combat Information Center, please."

She was through the hatchway and halfway down the ladder to the CIC before she was fully awake again.

Christine Rendino and the current OOD, Frank McKelsie, were waiting for her by the center consoles. They both looked about as burned out as she probably did, and they also looked worried. Amanda shot a glance past them to the tactical displays.

Some of the secondary monitors had been dialed to exterior view on low-light television and infrared. It was still dark out there, the clock readout indicating that they had some ninety minutes to go before first light. There was nothing to be seen but rolling, oily-backed swells and a low, broken overcast. They were still at full EM-CON and the primary Aegis systems were down, the Alpha Screen currently showing a computer-generated signal intelligence display.

A flickering red air-target hack showed the position of a possible hostile some eighty miles to the northeast. Four additional air targets, each surrounded by a pinkish circle indicating an indefinite position fix on the contact, appeared to be running in line abreast ahead of it.

"What do we have, Mr. McKelsie?"

"We're not sure, Captain. We thing the Argys might be cooking up something new."

"Specifics."

"Rendino's got the dope. Her gang's putting most of it together."

"We've got multiple aircraft contacts on the Sigint monitors and they are acting in a totally wacko manner." Christine took over, nodding toward the big screen. "Target Alpha came over our horizon about fifteen minutes ago. He's at twenty-five thousand feet, cruising at three hundred knots. However, he's weaving so his actual speed-over-ground is about one hundred and seventy. He's conducting a continuous air search with a fairly low-powered multimode radar. I'm pretty sure he's one of those converted 737s the Argentines use as a kind of half-assed AWACS."

"Yeah," McKelsie added, "nothing we have to worry about at this range."

"The thing is," the intel continued, "that bird seems to be acting as a command-and-control node for some other kind of setup. According to my people over in Raven's Roost, he's got data downlinks going with at least four other systems in that immediate area. We're also getting a lot of voice traffic, mostly station-keeping stuff and intermittent UAF reflections off him from multiple sources below our horizon. I think probably they're Atlantique ANGs."

"It looks like they might be running a very tight antisubmarine sweep," Amanda commented. "Maybe they think we have underwater reenforcements."

"It looks like it, but I don't think it is. The leakage we've been able to read off their data-link sidelobe doesn't look like any sonar sweep I've ever seen. Matter of fact, it doesn't look like anything I've ever seen before, period."

"Yeah, Captain," McKelsie added. "Rendino and I are both tight on this. The Argys have something new going and they're going to hit us with it."

Interesting, Amanda thought, put a load on these two and they dropped their bristling antagonism for each other and became a pretty good team.

"Okay, Mr. McKelsie. What are you doing about it?"

"The Argys are sweeping from east to west, so I figured our best bet was to get out of their immediate line of advance. I've brought the ship around to a hundred eighty degrees true and increased speed to twenty-five knots to open the range. I haven't gone to full general quarters, but helm control has been shifted to CIC and both the bridge and CIC duty watches have been put on alert. Maintaining full EMCON and full stealth and all passive sensors are up full."

"Very good, Mr. McKelsie. I have the con," Amanda replied, dropping into her command chair. "How soon before we know anything more?"

"Pretty quick, I'd guess. Just as soon as those low-riders come over our horizon."

They waited in the blue-lit semidarkness. The Combat Information Center was warm and quiet, the low voices of the systems operators almost soothing. Amanda found her head sinking back against the padded seat rest. Paradoxically, now the urge to slip back into sleep was overwhelming.

No! She snapped her eyes open and gave her head an angry shake. These were the last hours before dawn. The hours when the body's resources were at their lowest ebb. Traditionally, the hours when a military unit was at its most vulnerable to surprise attack. She would not yield to her traitorous biological rhythm now.

Abruptly, the graphics on the Large Screen Display altered. The four possible target hacks of the hypothetical aircraft were replaced by the sharp, red, vee symbols of hostile air targets, each with a yellow conical scan pattern radiating ahead of it.

The patterns overlapped and the *Cunningham*'s position point marker was engulfed by the southern edge of the sweep. Christine and McKelsie stiffened and each peeled off toward their respective subsystems bays.

"Confirm multiple radar-emission sources," Christine called out a moment later. "Confirm aircraft type as Atlantique ANG Two. Confirm radar type as Ignasie B, surface-search mode, maximum output. Frequencies and scan rates appear to be synchronized. The range is closing!"

"Shit!" McKelsie snarled from his side of the compartment. "They're running a bistatic search on us!"

Amanda's jaw tightened. Stealth technology was built around the concept of reducing the target's radar image by either absorbing the incoming radar beam, or by widely and erratically dispersing it so that a clear return or "echo" was not reflected back to the receiver. Hence the Duke's coat of Wetball metallic-polymer paint and her sleekly angle-less design.

However, such a shield could potentially be broken by bistatic radar. Have several powerful radar systems sweep the same block of space while operating on the same frequency and at the same coordinated scan rate. Anything within that block of space would be hit simultaneously by several different beams, all converging at slightly different angles, producing a vastly larger number of fragmentary returns than would be produced by a single beam.

Have multiple radar receivers tuned to pick up these returns, again far more than could otherwise be detected by a single receiver. Data-link your output from all of the systems into a central point where a computer would analyze and reassemble these fragments like a cybernetic jigsaw puzzle until a true, composite image was produced. If your transmitters were powerful enough and your receivers were sensitive enough and your computer processors fast enough, you might just catch yourself a stealth.

"Mr. McKelsie, do they have a return off us yet?"

"Negative, we're still below the limits, but their signal strength is building rapidly."

"Can you phase us in to the wave clutter?"

"I can try, but this is the flattest sea state we've been in for days. I don't have a helluva lot to work with."

"Do what you can."

The Argentines must have had every hacker south of Venezuela working around the clock to cobble together the software for this. The question was what to do about it. Should they make a fight of it now, or should they try to huddle under the rags of their cloak of invisibility? Slowly and deliberately, Amanda tapped the nail of her right forefinger against the plastic arm of the command chair three times.

"Helm, all engines ahead slow. Make turns for five knots."

"Aye, aye, ma'am. Engines ahead slow. Making turns for five knots."

"Left standard rudder."

"Aye, aye. Steering left standard rudder."

Amanda lifted her voice slightly, letting it fill the CIC. "We're going to try and evade. Aegis operator, put a tactical overlay up on the helm's navigational monitor."

The *Cunningham* paid off in a wide turn to port, her wake fading as her speed bled away, her slowed propellers producing drag instead of thrust. Inboard, Amanda listened as the helmsman called off the bearing of the turn.

"Coming left to one hundred and ten degrees . . . one hundred degrees . . . ninety degrees . . . eighty degrees—"

"Okay, helm," Amanda interrupted. "I want you to minimize our radar cross-section by holding us bow-on to those search planes. Aim us right at that nearest aircraft and turn with him as they sweep past. If you need more engine, just ring it up. You've got the ship."

"Aye, aye, Captain. Will do."

Reduce speed to reduce contrast and turn bow-on to the enemy to reduce aspect. There was nothing else to be done passively. Amanda caught the eye of the duty tactical officer. "If we have to go active, I want two LORAINs on the nearest ANG and two more on that command-and-control aircraft. Don't wait for a formal launch order. Salvo fire the second you get locks."

He nodded a silent reply. CIC discipline called for the maintenance of a low sound level, but it was going to extremes now. Voices were lowered to a whisper in the ancient, instinctive reaction to the presence of an enemy. Huddled in their blue-lit techno-cave, the men and women of the *Cunningham* waited out the passage of the wolf pack.

Amanda looked across to the stealth-systems bay. "How are we doing, McKelsie?" she inquired.

The countermeasures man didn't voice a reply, nor did he take his eyes from his telepanels. Instead he held out a hand, flat and palm down, and rocked it in an ominous so-so manner.

The point of closest approach would be fifteen miles.

Just for an instant, as the Duke's bow came around due north, one of the exterior cameras picked up the distant flicker of aircraft strobes wedged in between the sea and sky. Then they were gone, and on the tactical display the *Cunningham* passed out of the Argentines' scan zone.

"Enemy radars are no longer painting us, Captain," McKelsie reported.

"Confirm that. No variance in scan rate, course, or commo traffic. They are history and we are livin'!"

Christine's restrained scream broke the tension, and all hands in the CIC unclenched their muscles and grinned at the wonder of being alive.

"For Crissakes, Rendino. Grow up!" McKelsie growled, rubbing the back of his neck.

That was back to normal too.

"Okay, people," Amanda said. "We've foxed them for now, but they'll be back. Helm, very well done. Now bring her back around to three-forty degrees true and bring up all engines ahead standard. Make turns for twenty-five knots. I'm going to park us in the safest place I can think of at the moment—right in the middle of that patch of water they just swept.

"Mr. McKelsie, I'm keeping the con. You get to work with your people and start analyzing this new setup the Argentines have."

"Aye, aye."

"Chris, have intelligence section feed McKelsie's gang anything and everything you picked up on the systems they're using. O Group in one hour. I want a countertactic!"

Amanda rubbed her eyes and settled back into her command chair. Slipping a comb from her pocket, she began to order her tousled hair. "Oh, and by the way, everyone, good morning."

DRAKE PASSAGE
1451 HOURS: MARCH 28, 2006

"Anything yet?"

General Marcello Arco leaned over the shoulder of the systems operator and peered down into the round, meter-wide screen. Edging in from the other side was the radar specialist from Naval Technical Command. All three men were absorbed in watching the steady trudge of their teamed search planes across the scope.

They were aboard the Fuerza Aérea 737-400 command aircraft

as it orbited five miles above the western approaches to Drake Passage. Below them, at wave-top altitude, Argentina's latest reconnaissance in force was under way.

"Nothing on the screen or on the data links, sir."

"We must have patience, General," Commander Fillipini, the Navy tech man, said in a conciliatory manner.

"Patience we have, time we don't, Commander. We need a fix on that ship."

"We will get one eventually, sir. As I said at the briefing, the best of stealth technology can't make something the size of a destroyer totally radar-invisible. At close range there must be some faint return, and our bistatic search procedures multiply our radar power many times over. We are practically scouring the surface of the sea. If she is down there, we will get her."

Arco grunted noncommittally. The theory seemed sound, but as to whether it would work operationally, God only knew.

Moving abruptly, Arco donned a headset and stabbed a finger at a key on the communications panel.

"Halcon Command to Halcon One. Do you copy?"

"Acknowledged, Halcon Command." An electronics-filtered voice echoed up in response from somewhere below the cloud deck.

"What is your situation, Commander?"

"Situation nominal. Nothing to report, sir. Holding course at three hundred meters as per ops plan."

"What is your sea state and visibility?"

"Sea state three with winds gusting out of the west. We are operating beneath the primary overcast, but there are snow flurries and many patches of sea smoke. For the moment, I can just make out Halcon Two's strobes to the south. A poor day for sightseeing, sir."

Arco half-smiled at the pilot's faintly apologetic tone. "We will keep that in mind, Halcon one. Command out."

Poor devils. Autopilots would be no good in the turbulence they must be bucking down there. Twelve hours straight in the air, fighting the control yoke every second from wheels-up to touch-down, and no relief crew because they would be needed to fly the next sweep.

Aeronaval or Fuerza Aérea, Arco felt for the pilots. Perhaps that was why he was out here this afternoon. Stalking around the operations bay of this command-and-control plane wasn't much of a contribution, but at least it was better than sitting on his ass back at Rio Grande.

His musing was interrupted by a sudden excited call from the operator of the bistatic radar display. "Contact! We have a surface contact!"

Instantly Arco was back over the scope, almost bumping heads with Fillipini. "There!" the naval officer said, pointing to a small smudge in the southwestern quadrant of the screen. About forty kilometers beyond Halcon Four. Very faint, bearing almost due north, speed about twenty knots."

Arco glanced aft to the Elint monitor. "Are you getting anything, Sergeant?"

"No radar or radio emissions detected on any bearing, sir."

The General returned his attention to the radar specialist.

"Any chance it could be some kind of small craft?"

Fillipini shook his head. "Not at that speed in this kind of sea state," he replied jubilantly. "We have got her!"

"Correction, we have found her. Now we try and get her. Commence targeting data downlink to all aircraft. Inform Rio Grande Base that we believe we have located the enemy. Give them our position and inform them we are going in to attack."

The General cut his own mike in again. "All Halcon aircraft, this is Halcon Command. Enemy in sight. Target confirmed as North American warship. Attack data coming up on your screens now. All aircraft arm torpedoes, assume closure bearings, and commence descent to drop altitude. Let's finish this!"

Down deep in the slop below the blue skies and billowing cloud tops, the four chunky, French-built patrol bombers configured for the kill, twin turboprops spooling up to full war power and bomb-bay doors swinging open. Crewmen stared into their sensor screens for the first hint of their prey, the excitement and tension growing within them sounding plainly in their voices as they spoke over the static-dusted radio band.

"Halcon Four to Halcon Command. Range closing to twenty kilometers. No visual fix on target. There is a large snow squall dead ahead. She is apparently hiding inside it. Threat boards are clear, no enemy response yet.... Wait a moment.... Onboard radar has a fix. We are coming up on drop point...."

Arco frowned over at Fillipini. "Why are they not reacting to us?"

"Possibly they do not realize we can detect them. Or perhaps our multiple scans have them confused momentarily. Whichever, it is all to our advantage."

Arco nodded and returned his attention to the dialog issuing from Halcon Four.

"Still no enemy reaction, Command. All torpedoes armed and set for independent proximity homing.... We are at initial drop point...."

There was a soft crunching sound in Arco's headset and then silence.

"Halcon Four? Halcon Four, do you copy?"

"Halcon Four has disappeared from the screen, General," the systems operator reported. "The datalink has gone down as well."

Arco and Fillipini exchanged stares. "What happened?" the Air Force man demanded.

"I don't know. They're just gone. Perhaps they hit the water. An accidental crash?"

Arco keyed his mike. "Halcon Three, did you see what happened to Halcon Four?"

"Negative, negative. Visibility is closing in down here. Heavy snow. Visual range less than one kilometer now."

"Halcon Three, check your threat boards."

"All radar detectors are clear. I have activated our counter-measures systems. Target is now on our onboard screens and we have a firing solution. . . . Arming torpedoes now. . . . Approaching drop point. . . . Torpedoes away! . . . We have a good drop—"

The pilot of Halcon Three screamed, just once.

"General, Halcon Three has dis—"

"I see it! Fillipini, what the hell's going on?"

The tech expert had no answer. His features were shocked and sallow in the greenish scope glow. Arco suspected that he probably looked much the same. It was the enlisted systems operator who kept his brain working.

"The target is accelerating, sir." Swiftly he enabled a highlighting circle around the enigmatic blip and started clocking it. "Sixty knots . . . Now eighty . . . One hundred . . ."

Ghostlike, the contact faded completely from the screen.

Something cold and slimy rolled over in Arco's guts. Suddenly he understood exactly what was happening. He smashed his hand down onto the transmitter key.

"Halcon One and Two, abort the attack! Abort the attack! Go full EMCON and reverse out of the area!"

Arco hit the kill switches for the radio and the main radar console. "Shut down!" he yelled to the other operators in the bay. "Shut down everything! Pilot, activate your antimissile defenses! Take full evasive action, now!"

Arco and Fillipini grabbed for handholds on the workstations and seat backs as the deck tilted up and to port. The pilot was pitching his aircraft up and out into a steep, climbing turn. He pulled power from the engines, and the airframe of the converted jetliner began to shudder softly as he popped his flaps and spoilers. He continued to roll through into a tight descending spiral, a series of soft bangs coming from back aft as the countermeasures dispensers kicked out chaff blocks and anti-IR flares. The group of men on the windowless operations deck could only hold on, wait for something to happen, and fear for what it might be.

Finally it came, a distant concussion that was felt more than heard. Five thousand feet above and a couple of miles away, a foxed missile had self-destructed after losing track of its intended prey.

The Boeing plunged into the heavy overcast and its decks leveled as it pulled out of the dive. The engines resumed their whispering roar as the pilot lined out to pull clear of the area. General Arco released his grip on the chair back and tiredly flexed his fingers.

"Commander, inform the pilot we are returning to base. As soon as we've opened the range a little more, contact Halcon One and Two and tell them to do the same."

"But, General, we know that the Norteno destroyer must be somewhere in this area. Should we not—"

"No, Commander. We have squandered quite enough good men's lives for one day."

DRAKE PASSAGE
1840 HOURS: MARCH 28, 2006

Amanda knelt down quietly beside the bunk in sick bay. Erikson's eyes were shut, and he didn't react at first, giving her a chance to fully take in his condition. He'd been a young man in good shape when he came aboard. That had changed. There was an ominous slackness to his body and a sallow tint creeping in under his fading tan. Even without a stethoscope she could hear the rales in his labored breathing.

"Hi, sailor," she said gently. "How's it going?"

He opened dulled eyes and tried for a smile. "I'm doing okay, Captain. Was that a missile launch I heard a while back?"

"It was. The Argys came hunting us again and we had to show them the error of their ways. Knocked two down and scared the daylights out of a third."

"Way to go."

It obviously hurt him to talk, and Amanda winced inwardly.

"I just dropped around for a second to keep you posted on what's been happening," she continued, carefully keeping her voice under control. "I also wanted to check with Chief Robinson about how soon we can expect you back on the duty roster. We need every good hand we can get."

He could only nod a reply. The pain, leaking past the analgesics he had been given, showed in his eyes. Amanda rested her hand lightly on his shoulder for a moment, then got to her feet and left the ward.

Chief Corpsman Bonnie Robinson was waiting for her out in the dispensary. Silently Amanda tilted her head toward the passageway door. They needed to talk beyond Erikson's hearing.

"He's failing," Amanda said flatly after the soundproof door had closed behind them.

"Captain, he's dying," Robinson replied with equal finality. "The antibiotics have prevented infection so far, but that's about all. There's a fluid buildup in his lungs, and I'm going to have to put him back on oxygen pretty soon. I suspect that there's still some low-grade internal bleeding going on in there. What's worse, that piece of shrapnel isn't stable. The last set of X rays indicates that it's shifted position. This man needs surgery now."

Amanda shook her head. "It'll be at least four more days before we can rendezvous with the task force."

"In four days he'll probably be dead."

"Just what am I supposed to do about it, Chief?" Amanda snapped, her growing sense of frustration boiling over. "The only port open to me is in the Falklands. Going there draws me way the hell and gone off my blockade station. The Brits can't come out to us because that pulls them off their station. I can't even radio for help without compromising the safety of this ship. What am I supposed to do? I'm open to any suggestions!"

"I really don't have any for you, ma'am," the young woman replied quietly. "I'm just reporting the situation as I see it."

Amanda was instantly ashamed and angered with herself. *Brilliant, Amanda, go ahead and kill the messenger bearing the bad news. God, gold oak leaves or not, Dad would take you over his knee for this and you'd deserve it.*

"So you are, Chief. Sorry I blew my stack. This thing with Erikson is getting to me a little."

"It's okay, ma'am. I've never handled anything like this before either. It's kind of scary."

"You're doing good work, Chief. Just keep him going a while longer. I'll figure something out."

Deep in thought, Amanda headed forward beyond the CIC and into officer's country, seeking out her intelligence officer's quarters. She knocked quietly on the door that bore not only Christine's official white-on-black Bakelite nameplate but a second, gold-lettered "Resident Genius" plate.

"Somebody's home. C'mon in."

Christine's cabin was a small shrine to human individuality within the ordered structure of the *Cunningham*. Science-fiction art posters and beefcake photography dominated whatever bulkhead space was not taken up by her personal stereo and state-of-the-art video game system. Her desk terminal was mounded with papers, books, and magazines that threatened with every roll of the ship to cascade down onto the collection of paperback-stuffed cardboard boxes parked on the deck.

Christine was sitting cross-legged on her bunk, surrounded by such a concentration of disordered hard copy that it was difficult to say whether she had been working or trying to build a nest. "Hi, boss ma'am," she said cheerily. "Sit and stay awhile. By the way, you look like hell."

Amanda smiled tiredly. "Thanks, Miss Rendino, I love you too." She removed half of a Milky Way bar from the seat of the cabin's only chair and dropped into it. "I need some input. What are the odds of our being spotted if we break EMCON to contact Second Fleet?"

The intel shrugged expressively. "Heck, you know the answer to that as well as I do. No matter how tight a beam we squirt or how short a burst we transmit, there's bound to be some sidelobe. If somebody happens to be in the right place at the right time and with the right equipment, they could get a bearing on us. We run that risk every time we query a weather or a recon sat. If you actually want to talk two-way with someone, the risk increases with every exchange.

"You could eliminate that risk," Christine continued, "by using laser-com, but that means we have to come out from under weather cover to get a clear line-of-sight on a satellite.

"My bottom line is this. If we're careful, and given the resources the Argys have available, we might be able to pull it off safely ... but I can't give you a carved-in-granite guarantee on that."

Amanda sighed and crossed her arms over her stomach. "That's how I figured it. Chris, that boy in sick bay is going to die if I don't get some help for him soon."

"Ah, so that's what's sticking it to you."

"Yes, and unfortunately the smart move is to just eat the loss and let him die. To do anything else is to risk the ship, the rest of the crew, and the mission."

"That isn't what you're going to do, of course. You're going to get on the blower and scream, yell, and put all of our necks on the line until you get that kid some help."

Amanda cocked an eyebrow. "What makes you think that, Lieutenant?"

"Because in certain areas you are very predictable. Just now, you're in a conflict between what's right and what's smart, and, fa' sure, smart don't have a chance. You'd made your decision before you even walked in here. You just had to sit around for a while and talk yourself into it."

"Well, that's interesting. Do you often go around forecasting my future intentions?"

"Sure," Christine grinned, "anytime you want to know what you're going to think about something, just ask me."

The intel swung her feet down off the bunk and reached across to her desk. She shoved aside a mixed stack of *Playgirls* and *International Defense Reviews* and revealed her interphone. Flipping the handset out of its cradle, she passed it to her captain.

Amanda accepted it and felt a little of her burden ease.

"Radio shack, this is the Captain. Heat up your systems. We're going to be breaking EMCON."

Chief Robinson went alert as the Duke's trudging propeller beats suddenly accelerated. When the change wasn't followed by the blare of the general quarters alarm she relaxed again and returned her attention to her sick-bay paperwork. They must only be doing a sprint to a new location. After a moment, the interphone at her elbow buzzed.

"Sick bay, aye?"

"Chief, this is the Captain." Amanda Garrett sounded relieved and pleased. "We've got it worked out for Erikson! We're going to rendezvous with the British ice-patrol ship *Polar Circle*. They not only have a doctor on board, but they have a full medical team and a surgical suite. The problem is that the Brits will have to swing out wide to the south and east to stay out of the range of the Argentines.

"Tonight we're going to work over to the east side of our patrol area. Then, tomorrow, as soon as the *Polar Circle* reports that she's in position, we'll execute a second high-speed run to the east to get within range of their helicopter.

"With a little luck, the Argys will never even know we've been gone. We're just going to need a little more time to pull this off. Can you keep Erikson going another twenty-four hours?"

"You just bet we can, ma'am! May I tell him what we're going to try and do?"

"Negative, Chief. I'll be down in a little while. I'd like to do that myself."

"It was an ambush," General Arco stated flatly. "The surface contact we detected was one of their stealth helicopters, flying slowly at very low altitude and using a blip-enhancer device to simulate the return we would have gotten from the ship. The destroyer itself presumably lay hove to in one of the nearby snow squalls.

"We detected the decoy target and maneuvered to engage it. As we did so, the North Americans launched what we believe were LORAIN surface-to-air missiles set in antiradiation mode. They homed in passively on the radar emissions of our aircraft. There was no warning."

"These damned fancy radar tricks did not work, and in proving it, you cost me two of my patrol planes!" Admiral Fouga spat.

"It did work, Admiral. That is why the North Americans sought out the system and destroyed it."

"Remarkable," President Sparza mused. "A surface warship turning on, and hunting down, the aircraft that are supposedly pursuing it. That is hardly a conventional tactic."

"This is not a conventional ship," Arco responded grimly.

Sparza had again summoned his military Chiefs of Staff and his Minister of State in his private office. During their past conferences on the Antarctic crisis, there had often been tension. Now there was open strain, stemming from the growing sensation that events were slipping more and more beyond their control.

"We are modifying two more of the remaining Atlantique aircraft for bistatic search operations," the Fuerza Aérea general continued. "We are also revising our tactics, so we will not be so vulnerable to this kind of ambush again. By this time tomorrow we should be able to resume the search."

"And what do we do until then? Sit around with our thumbs up our ass!"

"It is irrelevant what else we do, Fouga! When they downed our spy satellite, we lost the only other viable reconnaissance asset we had. During the past four days we have flown more than three hundred conventional search sorties over Drake Passage with every kind of aircraft we have in our inventory. We have not produced a single solid fix on the enemy's location. The North Americans' stealth systems work! Combine them with the deteriorating weather conditions over the Antarctic convergence and they are rendered effectively invisible. The bistatic radar is our only hope!"

"Possibly," Sparza interjected quietly, "but we may not have time to wait for it. Gentlemen, just before the two of you arrived, General Orcho was giving the latest intelligence updates from the Malvinas. I suggest that we hear him out."

The Army commander glanced at his notes in the manner of a man who knew all too well what they contained.

"With the assistance of the United States Air Force Transport Command, the British have completed their defense buildup. Currently, they have two full squadrons of F-model Tornadoes flying out of their military field at Mount Pleasant.

"In addition, VTOL fighter and helicopter units are operating out of satellite fields at Port Stanley, Goose Green, and Pebble Island. Signal intelligence also indicates that mobile air-search radars and Patriot and Rapier 2000 antiaircraft missile batteries have been deployed and are operational.

"The Royal Marine ground garrison has been augmented by the British Army's Parachute Regiment, plus light armored and artillery elements.

"At sea, the British have shut down and secured their offshore drilling operations. They have evacuated the civilian rig crews and the drilling platforms have been manned by Royal Marine commandos, armed with Stinger and Starstreak antiaircraft missiles. In addition, the Royal Navy has been basing ASW patrol helicopters off them. There is also evidence that CAPTOR mines are being deployed in the vicinity of the rigs. The liquid natural-gas storage facilities at Low Bay have also been successfully vented and shut down."

"What is the latest information on the naval forces?" Fouga demanded.

"Maintaining course and speed. They will arrive within strike range in approximately seventy hours. It is believed that both the British and American carrier groups have nuclear submarines running about a day ahead of the surface ships. This is not the most immediate threat, however."

The General removed a folder from his briefcase and began to pass around the photographic prints it contained.

"This first print is a freeze-frame still taken from a CNN news broadcast out of Mount Pleasant. In the background you can see the tail of a United States Air Force KC-10 tanker/transport, and a number of ground personnel, also identified as North American.

"This second print is a computer-enhanced blowup taken by the Brazilian Geo-Resources satellite of Wideawake Field on Ascension Island. The three straight-winged aircraft are P-3E Orion patrol planes of the United States Navy. There is also a second KC-10 and what appears to be a B-1C heavy strategic bomber.

"We believe that with the completion of the British defense buildup, the United States and Great Britain are preparing to escalate their level of aggression. We believe that they are preparing to forward-deploy long-range reconnaissance and strike aircraft into the Malvinas to support their blockade. If this is done, our situation will become . . . more difficult."

"How long do we have before they become operational?" Sparza asked.

"Possibly two days at the most."

The Argentine President returned his attention to his Air Force commander. "Arco, what can we do about this?"

The aviator looked down at the carpeting for a moment, wearily trying to assess the situation. "Well, we could try and knock out Mount Pleasant. It would mean taking our best aircraft off of their current antishipping mission. Even at that, I could not make any guarantees. Hardened airfields require a lot of killing, and they are ready and waiting for us. We would be bound to take heavy casualties."

"You cannot sink a solitary ship! You cannot destroy an airfield! Sweet Christ, why do we bother to have an air force?"

"That is enough, Fouga!" Sparza snapped. "I will be the judge of who is performing adequately and who is not. To date, I have found no fault in General Arco's actions, or in the performance of his service."

Fouga subsided, brooding, and Sparza turned his attention to his Minister of State. "Aldo, what of the diplomatic situation?"

"Things are not good, Mr. President," Salhazar replied. "At the United Nations, it appears that we are caught between North American diplomatic power and British diplomatic finesse, much as it was during the Malvinas conflict. A few of the traditional anti-Western states have responded favorably, but as more of a reflex action than a declaration of solid support. We hold the ABC block and our immediate allies. Not much more."

"What about the Antarctic Treaty conference?"

The Minister shook his head. "We have problems there as well. The other Treaty states are not reacting as we had hoped. The decisive action on the part of the United States and Great Britain is having an effect. The divisiveness and controversy we had hoped to create has not taken place. Again, we can be sure of only the ABC states. Most of the other member nations seem to be taking a wait-and-see attitude pending the outcome of the blockade."

"I am rather curious about that myself, Aldo," Sparza replied, drawing his cigarette case. He took a moment to kindle a Players with his desk lighter before continuing. "Gentlemen, the window of opportunity for this project is closing, and the situation is critical. We must act decisively if Conquistador South is to be salvaged. Our only other option is to abort and accept the resulting diplomatic and political repercussions. Now, what can we do?"

There was a long moment of silence.

Finally Admiral Fouga spoke. "The linchpin of this entire operation has always been the supply convoy and the necessity of getting it through. Very well, then, let us get it through! Now, before we are totally cut off!"

"We are already cut off, Fouga," Arco said irritably. "The *Cunningham* would be on top of you before you cleared the harbor."

"Good enough, let them come. Your ghost ship is good at hiding, but to stop us, it will have to come out of the shadows and fight!"

The Fleet Commander leaned forward intently in his chair. "Mr. President, our best escort group will be covering the transports, and our best destroyer squadron will be providing distant cover for the convoy. With that kind of firepower available to me, I am certain that I can defeat any single warship that might attempt to engage us."

"You sound as if you intend to take this personally," Sparza said.

"I do, sir. I intend to command the task force myself, should you order it to sail."

"I see. Gentlemen, are there any further suggestions?"

Sparza glanced around the small circle of men in his office. There was no response.

"Very well, then. Admiral, you will sortie the supply convoy and proceed to San Martin Base with all possible speed."

"Yes, sir! At once, Mr. President." Fouga began to hastily lever himself out of his chair.

"One moment more, Admiral." Sparza's voice caught him. "Your primary mission is to get that convoy through, not to hunt

United States warships. Be certain that you are clear on your priorities."

"Yes, sir," Fouga replied pompously and saluted, "the Fleet will not fail you."

The heavyset naval officer picked up his briefcase and cap and started for the door.

"Fouga" —General Arco did not turn in his chair to look after the Admiral— "for the sake of your men, don't take the North Americans for granted, not for a second."

DRAKE PASSAGE
0210 HOURS: MARCH 29, 2006

Retainer Zero Two, her rotors folded back parallel to her tail boom, sank down out of the night and into the red-lit pool of the hangar bay. As the elevator descended with a howl of heavy-duty hydraulics, Arkady let his head go back against the seat rest and closed his eyes. They were burning and gravelly from too many hours spent staring through a night-vision visor.

Straightening again as they reached deck level, he released his safety harness and popped the canopy latches, breaking away the rime of refrozen snow along the frame.

"How'd it go, sir?" Chief Muller asked as he helped to swing the Plexiglas panels open and to the side.

"Not too bad. A pleasant night out under the stars."

"That's only by comparison, Chief," Grestovitch cut in from the system operator's station. "Anywhere else but here and it would have been hell with the heaters busted."

"Negativism, rampant negativism, that's all I'm hearing out of that backseat anymore. That's a terrible attitude to have, Gus, even if you are telling the truth."

Arkady lifted off his helmet and painfully stood up in the cockpit. "What's the word on our ops status, Chief?"

"That depends, sir, on whether or not you still want Ensign Delany to make another sweep later this morning."

"Yeah. Why?"

"In that case, we got problems. Zero One's still down. We found ice erosion on the blades of the Fenestron, as well as cold fractures in a couple of the panels of the boom shell. We had to tear the whole fantail assembly apart again. I don't know if we can get her back together by zero four hundred."

"Okay, then she'll have to use this bird," Arkady said, swinging down over the canopy rails. "Get her prepped for a fast turnaround."

"Lieutenant, Zero Two is right up to the red-line limit on transmission time. We really need to have a look inside that gearbox before we send her out again."

"Ah, fuck it!" Arkady hooked his thumbs into his belt and scowled down at the deck. "All right, try this. Move Delany's scheduled launch time back to 0430. Any later than that and she won't be able to do anything constructive before the pixies come out at first light. If Zero Two isn't ready to fly by then, we'll just shit-can the whole operation."

"Aye, aye, sir."

"Inform Ensign Delany of the situation and the schedule change and keep me advised."

"Will do."

Grestovitch stiffly dropped down beside his pilot. "I got the mission log and the sensor records downloaded, sir," he said, patting the data cassettes in his sleeve pocket.

"Good enough. I'll touch base with the Captain while you drop those off with the duty watch in the CIC. After that, consider yourself free to crawl off somewhere and lose consciousness for a couple of hours."

"Thanks, Lieutenant. That sounds real good."

"Thank you, Gus. Given the past couple of days, I find it a little bit amazing that you're still flying with me."

"Aw hell, sir. After a while, you sort of get used to being crazy."

Amanda Garrett was alone in the wardroom, unaware when Arkady entered. She was slumped forward at the mess table with her head resting in the curve of her arm. A cooling mug of tea and a half-eaten sandwich had been pushed to one side, showing how the need for sleep had won out over hunger.

Nonetheless, when Arkady quietly lowered his helmet and flight harness to the deck, the faint click of metal against Fiberglas snapped her awake like a cat. She jerked upright, looking around wildly.

"The ship is okay, Captain," Arkady said, choosing the words he knew would calm her the most readily.

She blinked and came back into herself. "Oh, hi, Arkady. When did you get in?"

"We recovered just a few minutes ago."

She glanced at her wristwatch and rubbed her eyes with the back of her hand. "I haven't been out of it for too long, then. How did it go?"

"Not too bad," Arkady said, pulling out one of the mess-table chairs and seating himself. "We swept out about eighty-five miles to the east and didn't kick up anything on the surface except for neutral commercial traffic. I can't be as sure about subsurface contacts, but I ran a couple of sonobuoy lines and spot-checked with the dunking sonar. I think we've got clear water out there."

"I'm glad to hear it. How about the sea states?"

"Still holding at Force Three. Ceiling's down to around five hundred. The surface fog has thinned out, but we're still hitting occasional patches of freezing rain or snow."

"Is it going to give us any problem with the helicopter rendezvous?"

Arkady shrugged. "Not if the Brits know their stuff. Besides, we won't be within range for that until this afternoon. Daylight'll make things a whole lot easier."

"That's good. Now, what about Nancy? Are you still sending her out tonight?"

"Well, that's kind of problematical at the moment. I'd like to get one more sweep off before dawn, but it looks like we may not have an operational helo. We've got some servicing problems."

"God, that had to be next." She leaned forward again on the table and rested her forehead on her crossed wrists, her hair flowing down to curtain her face. "How bad is it getting with your people, Arkady?"

"It's starting to back up on us a little. This semipolar environment makes for a lot of extra man-hours of maintenance work, and we just don't have the men to produce the hours.

"I think we can keep things glued together for a couple more days while maintaining an adequate safety margin. Beyond that, we're going to have to start cutting back on flight time."

"Give me that couple of days more, Arkady," she asked, her voice muffled. "That's all I'll need."

"How are you doing, Captain?"

She straightened and looked across at him sharply. A spark of anger flared in her eyes, an instinctive denial of her own weaknesses. Arkady met her gaze levelly. *Yeah, dammit, I am going to ask.*

After a moment, she softened and produced a slight wry smile. "Fraying a little around the edges, but still all here. It's been kind of a heavy-duty few days. Beating that bistatic search system took care of our most immediate tactical problem, though. Now, if I can just get Erikson out . . ." She let her voice trail off.

"You sound like you're taking this kid personal, Skipper."

"That's because I am, Arkady. If I'd just stuck under weather cover like I should have on the day of that first Argentine air strike, he'd never have been wounded."

"And if your aunt had balls, she'd have been your uncle. The past is the past, good, bad, or indifferent. Monday-morning quarterbacking is a great way to drive yourself crazy with no concrete return out of it."

"No, Arkady. Sometimes the past hangs on, just like that boy is doing down in sick bay."

NORFOLK, VIRGINIA
1430 HOURS: MARCH 29, 2006

Much to his disgust, Admiral Elliot MacIntyre found that his backlog of hackwork had been accumulating in direct proportion to the time he was spending on-line with the Antarctic crisis. In the end, it forced him, muttering and snarling, away from Operations and to his desk for a few hours to deal with the worst of it.

Accordingly, he was rather grateful when the toning of his desk intercom interrupted the chore.

"Admiral, do you have a second?" his Chief of Staff inquired.

"Not really, but don't let that stop you. What's up, Maggie?"

"An unusual situation. I've just received a call from main gate security. Wilson Garrett is down there requesting to see you, sir."

MacIntyre wasn't exceptionally surprised. To hell with the paperchasing for a while.

"Clear him through, Maggie. VIP treatment."

MacIntyre waited for his guest in the operations-room access corridor. When he finally appeared, striding along at Captain Callendar's side, the CINCLANT found himself flashing back to certain old days in the Pacific. Wilson Garrett had been his immediate superior then, the man who had taught him just how a real skipper went about running a taut ship.

Garrett's brush cut was whiter now, but his spine was still as straight, his eyes just as sharp, and his nylon windcheater was worn like a suit of blues. Somewhere, someone had royally screwed up when this tough and capable little man had failed to get his second star.

"Welcome aboard, sir," MacIntyre said, extending his hand.

"Sir?" Garrett responded with a short, strong handclasp. "You're doing better than I ever managed, Eddie Mac."

"I don't know about that. You were smart enough to get out while you could still fly your flag off of a ship and not a brick shithouse."

Garrett smiled and replied wryly, "Maybe so. The hacks up in D.C. will probably want to put the whole fleet up on blocks one of these days. They'll figure to save some money."

The retired officer grew serious again. "Look, I know you people are busy, so I'll get right down to it. I'm here to pull strings, demand privileges, and beg favors. I'd like to find out what's happening to my kid, Eddie Mac."

"I figured as much. Come on, let's go down to Fleet Ops."

A few minutes later, Wilson Garrett was standing at the rail of the command balcony looking down appreciatively at the Large Screen Display and at the ordered ranks of workstations down in the worry hole.

"I wouldn't knock this setup. I would have killed to have this kind of C3I available back when I was trying to run CruDesRon Four from the flag plot of the old *Callahan.*"

"You get the output, all right," MacIntyre replied. "Frequently, more than you want. We're still developing an analysis-and-utilization doctrine that'll allow us to make the best possible use of the data flow. This system can put you right in the hip pocket of your task force commanders. You really have to buck the urge to micromanage. If you're not careful, you can find yourself playing them like they were characters in some kind of a video game. Now, what do you know?"

"About as much as your average civilian puke," Garrett replied. "The Argentines have invaded the South Pole and we don't like it. We're blockading the Argentines and they don't like it. The Brits are gearing up for 'The Falklands, Part II,' and we've got a carrier group burning a hole in the water trying to get south. There's also scuttlebutt that the shooting is either about to start or has already started, but that nobody is ready to admit it yet."

Garrett ran a worried hand through his short-trimmed hair. "Hell, I'm not even sure if Mandy's ship is involved. I just know that the Duke was in Rio, and that she caught a sortie order. The only other thing that I'm certain of is that I've got a CNN camera crew camping in my front yard, waiting for the casualty-notification team to show up."

MacIntyre decided that there was no reason to beat around the bush. "The shooting has started and your daughter is right in the middle of it, Wils. Truth be known, at the moment she's damn near all we've got down there."

"Hell!"

"That's the bad news," the CINCLANT continued. "The good news is that she and that hypertech tin can of hers have been fighting the whole damn Argentine military establishment to a standstill."

"Yeah?" Something bright and hot flared in the older man's eyes. "Well, that's not surprising. Mandy never did have much back-down in her."

"So the Argentines are finding out," MacIntyre said dryly. "To date, she's closed down their sea lines of communication with the Antarctic and damn near put their naval aviation wing out of business. Eight confirmed surface-to-air kills so far. She's also knocked down their only military reconnaissance satellite and taken a chunk out of a sub they sent after her. She's more than holding her own, Wils."

"Has she taken any damage?"

"A little, during the Argentines' first strike on her. The

Cunningham's still fully operational, though, and they've only taken one serious casualty. I understand they're currently trying to set up some kind of medivac for him through the British."

Garrett looked intently across at the Large Screen Display.

"What's her current position?"

"Good question. Half the time we can't spot her ourselves. This stealth business is more effective than even we expected. Generally, we get our best fixes when she interrogates a reconsat for an intelligence download."

MacIntyre glanced over to his Chief of Staff. "Maggie, when's our next bird due in over the Drake Passage area?"

"We should have a realtime link with Key Hole Thirteen Charley in just a couple of minutes, sir."

"Sounds good." The Admiral returned his attention to Garrett. "We'll be able to get a position on her for you then."

"Thanks, Eddie Mac. Now there's just one other thing I'd like to know."

"Sure."

"How in the hell could you send my daughter into that shooting gallery without adequate support!" Garrett exploded.

MacIntyre had been expecting that question; it was one that had every right to be asked. The CINCLANT was just glad that he was comfortable with the answer he had to give.

"For the same reason you would have, Wils," he replied evenly. "Because we have three oceans' worth of responsibility for one ocean's worth of fleet. Because the Duke was all we had to work with. And because that's the job, Wils."

There was a long moment of strained silence, then Garrett tiredly shook his head. "Yeah, yeah, please excuse the fatherly outburst. If Mandy had been here she would have kicked my butt for that."

"Don't sweat it. You should have seen me the first time my oldest daughter stayed out after midnight. I was a basket case."

A phone shrilled in the background and Captain Callendar

took the call. "Thirteen Charley is coming in over the Antarctic Peninsula, sir. Data download commencing through Milstar linkage."

"Thank you, Maggie. Check out the main screen, Wils. This is impressive as hell."

On the huge map display on the far wall of the room, a series of two-meter-wide outlines began to appear. Partially overlapping one another, they began to march northward, up the image of the polar continent, each square representing an area of the Earth's surface being scanned by the orbital reconnaissance platform.

The data from the reconsat's extensive sensor suite—visual and thermographic high-definition imaging, synthetic-aperture surface-scan radar, wide-spectrum EM signal receivers, and a number of other more esoteric systems—all flowed into Fleet Command Headquarters through half a dozen satellite communications channels. Some was intended for long-term storage and analysis by the intelligence sections, some for realtime usage through the workstations in the operations center.

"From what you've said, Mandy's been tangling mostly with their air and submarine elements," Garrett commented. "What about the rest of the Argentine navy?"

"They haven't come out. Oh, they've been using some of their second-line stuff to make faces at the British around the Falklands, but we haven't seen a serious challenge by their surface forces yet. They seem to be massing their best ships and a transport group at their southernmost fleet base at Ushuaia. We've been told that they may attempt a convoy run to their Antarctic garrisons."

"She'd have to go after them if they tried it, wouldn't she?" Garrett pressed.

"Hopefully the situation won't come up. The *Roosevelt* group is a little over two days out and we're setting up to forward-deploy some Orions and B-1s into the Falklands. If she can hold out just a little bit longer, the cavalry will come riding in over the hill."

On the big screen, a small set of crosshairs blinked into

existence just off the ice-pack line near the South Shetlands. Flanking it were the glowing figures 'DDG 79.' "

"Okay, there she is. She's just tapped Thirteen Charley herself. She's alive and well, Wils."

Garrett nodded. "Yeah, so she is. Thanks, Eddie Mac. I appreciate this."

"Forget it."

"I'm not planning to." Garrett straightened and squared his shoulders. "Well, there's no sense in me cluttering up your quarterdeck more than necessary—"

"Admiral," Captain Callendar cut in, the phone still lifted to her hear, "the duty officer reports a situational change at Ushuaia."

"Have them put it on the main screen."

The computerized map image on the primary display was replaced by a ghost-toned overview of the southernmost Argentine fleet base. The coastline and the land area surrounding the narrow bay were a dim grayish-green, the sea almost black. The heated buildings of the base itself and the surrounding town were a series of uneven geometric patterns in white. Clear of the harbor mouth, near the bottom of the screen, was another pattern of pale glowing dots.

"Can we get this in visual spectrum video?" MacIntyre demanded.

"No, sir. The area is socked tight under very heavy overcast. Infrared imaging only."

"Very well. Have them zoom in on that ship formation."

Eight thousand miles away and 140 miles up, a fantastically sophisticated mirror and lens system responded to the CINCLANT's command. The dot pattern grew until it filled the screen, resolving into three blunt-ended ovals running bow to stern. Four additional hull silhouettes with the finer lines of warship design held formation on this trio at the two, four, eight, and ten o'clock positions.

"Thermographic analysis indicates three diesel-powered transport types being covered by two large gas turbine and two small diesel escorts," Maggie Callendar reported. "Speed eighteen knots, bearing one seven nine degrees. The two turbine escorts are probably Meko 360s. No positive ID yet on the smaller ones."

"That matches part of the available Argentine force pool." MacIntyre frowned. "Check Ushuaia anchorage. What about the Animosos—their First Destroyer Squadron?"

The image scanned north and settled on the offshore moorage of the naval base. Three slender hull forms were still present there. However, even as they watched, the midships section of each vessel began to glow more brightly.

"Analysis reports that the ships of the First Argentine Destroyer Squadron are lighting off turbines. Apparently they're powering up to get under way."

"And it's a sure-money bet as to where they're headed. Maggie, dispatch a situation update to the Pentagon War Room and to the Royal Navy liaison group. Then get a sighting report off to the *Cunningham.* Inform them that the Argentine fleet has sortied and request an acknowledgment! They're probably picking this up on their own download, but we've got to be certain they know what's coming at them!"

MacIntyre thought he heard Wilson Garrett say something, but when he turned back to the retired officer, he realized that the man was speaking to someone else a long distance away.

"There's seven of 'em, angel," he was whispering, his hands tightly gripping the balcony rail. "For God's sake, be careful."

Ken Hiro gestured awkwardly with the communications hard copy. "Uh, Captain, we've just received a Flash advisory from CINCLANT. . . ."

"I know, Ken. We see them."

Amanda leaned, stiff-spined, over the chart table in the Intelligence bay of the CIC, her impassive features underlit by the coldly glowing surface. Christine Rendino stood by quietly, her usual ebullience extinguished. In the darkness, neither officer could see how tightly their captain's fists were clenched, how deeply she had driven her nails into the palms of her hands.

Finally, Amanda took a deliberate deep breath. "Chris, notify all division heads that there will be an operations group in fifteen minutes.

"Ken, acknowledge CINCLANT's advisory. Inform them that we are proceeding to intercept the enemy with intent to engage. Also, please request that they contact the HMS *Polar Circle* for us. Inform them that we will not be making rendezvous."

Amanda pushed away from the table and started slowly for the hatchway. "If you need me, I'll be down in sick bay."

The *Cunningham*'s RPV control station was located at the far end of the cramped Elint bay, and Amanda Garrett and Christine Rendino were forced to squeeze in around the operator's chair to see the display screens. During those odd moments when his attention wandered, Arkady found the close, warm presence of the two women rather disconcerting, Amanda's clear-water-and-wildflowers scent mingling with Christine's muskier cologne.

With a side-stick controller in his right hand and a throttle in his left, Arkady was "flying" one of the Duke's Boeing Brave 2000 reconnaissance drones, a small, stealthy, Remotely Piloted Vehicle that resembled a stumpy cruise missile. On his head he wore a bulbous virtual-reality helmet with its display visor flipped down over his face.

A whole different world existed inside that helmet. It was as if he were sitting in a cockpit aboard the drone itself, a three-dimensional, computer-graphics simulacrum of its surrounding environment being projected on the inner curve of the visor. He could look "down" and see the surface of the ocean represented by a glowing white-on-blue grid pattern marching beneath the "nose" of the RPV. He could look "up" and see the cloud cover represented by a wider-hatched gray grid overhead. He could sweep the "horizon" with a turn of his head, and a blip of thumb pressure on a control-stick button would materialize a systems-status display or a navigational readout in front of his eyes.

Pilot and drone were connected via a tight-beam UHF relay through an orbiting Milstar communications satellite. The data link was a violation of stealth protocols; however, Amanda had wanted to see her enemies as something more than a symbol on a screen.

"Navicom readouts indicate you're coming in on the primary search zone," Christine murmured. "Keep your eyes open."

"I got 'em already. I'm acquiring multiple air-search radars bearing zero off the nose."

Within the VR program, radar waves could be made as readily visible to the human eye as the beam of a flashlight. Arkady could "see" the convoy's search systems on his horizon, sweeping and pulsing in pale red like a cluster of lighthouse beacons.

"Okay, that's them. Stay alert for the distant covering force. Satellite scan indicates they're running out ahead of the main body of the convoy."

"Roger, I'm taking her down to the deck."

Arkady rolled the controller forward, and two hundred miles to the north the RPV dipped its nose in response and sank toward the surface of the sea.

To Amanda and Christine, there was something rather eerie in the alert, watchful movements of Arkady's head as he peered about with his distant telepresence eyes. After a few moments, his attention fixed on something.

"Okay, I've got the covering force. Three of 'em, running in column."

Christine reached forward and tapped a series of keys, activating the drone's camera turret. A flatscreen came on, displaying a televised view of blurred gray wave tops. Using a trackball controller, she slewed the camera around to the bearing Arkady had indicated. In the visual range, nothing could be seen but a curtain of sea smoke. The touch of another key, however, switched the system over to thermographic imaging.

The horizon snapped clear, presenting a vista like a photographic negative: three ghostly pale ships sailing against a dark sea and sky.

"Ladies and gentlemen, I'd like to introduce you to the Argentine First Destroyer Squadron," Christine murmured, "genus *Animosos italianos*. About five thousand tons' displacement each, a single five-inch gun forward, three OTO Melara seventy-six-millimeter Super Rapid point defense mounts, Aster surface-to-air missile system, two tubes for type B-515 dual-mode torpedoes, and an eight-cell Exocet launcher. The guy in the center there with the enlarged helicopter hangar aft and the slightly different bridge silhouette will be your task-force flagship."

Amanda leaned forward to study the screens, her shoulder brushing unthinkingly against Arkady's. He had noticed that she'd been unusually quiet, and now, through the touch of her, he could feel her tension.

"They're being a bit slow on the uptake, aren't they, Chris?" she commented.

"They don't know we're out there yet, boss ma'am. These guys aren't radiating at all. Total radio and radar silence. They've been running that way ever since they cleared the coast."

"Any change in their positioning?"

"Not really. They've been holding out here about ten miles off the port or starboard bow of the convoy. Probably they're station keeping on the convoy's radar emissions."

"Do they seem to be favoring either side?" Amanda pressed.

"No. According to the reconsat data, about once a watch they tack on a little extra speed and cross over the course line from one side to the other. It seems to be a set operational pattern."

They watched as the trio of missile destroyers drifted away aft on the screen.

"Do you want me to circle back, Skipper?" Arkady asked.

"Negative. Let's have a look at the convoy itself."

"Aye, aye. Going on in."

The cruise drone cut swiftly across the distance to the second Argentine formation. In less than a minute, the boxy outline of a Meko-class destroyer materialized on the screens. Simultaneously, the signal intelligence display on the RPV control console began to trill urgently.

"Heads up, Arkady," Christine warned. "Their radar is starting to get a return off you."

"Rog. Better bring up the gyrostabilizer on the camera

platform. I'm going to have to dazzle 'em with my fancy footwork here in a second."

To Arkady, the enemy vessel was a yellow outline sketch on the blue and white cross-hatch sea, its air/sea search sweep a wide-angled pink floodlight radiating from its masthead. Suddenly the Argentines' fire-control radars lit off, tight, angry, scarlet beams that lashed out and tried to engulf the drone. Asterisk patterns in bright orange began to dance around the drone, denoting the shells that had started to burst around it.

On the thermal imager, Christine and Amanda saw pulsing white gouts of flame appear fore and aft on the destroyer as its 40mm turrets opened fire.

"Nothing wrong with this guy's reaction," Amanda commented grimly. "Get around him, Arkady."

He was too busy to verbalize an answer. He shaved a few more feet off his already perilously low altitude and threw the drone through a series of violent scissoring maneuvers to shake the flak. Then he cut hard right across the stern of the Meko. Another hard turn to port pulled it back onto the course line, and a few seconds later the RPV was streaking down the convoy's starboard flank.

One after another, its camera panned past the ships in the transport column. The big, modern-looking freighter with its aft-mounted superstructure and its decks stacked high with prefab housing modules. The bulkier, more massive vessel with the distinctive M rigs of a naval oiler. The smaller tank-landing ship, one-third of the displacement of the others and yet with its topside crowded with a miscellany of stores and equipment. Then they were past and the air around the drone again filled with the hot flare of airbursting shells.

"I'm taking flak again," Arkady reported.

"We see it," Christine replied. "It's coming in from the nearside trailing escort. One of the little guys."

"I want a look at them too," Amanda ordered.

"Okay, we'll be coming up on the nearside ship in a second."

The intel peered intently into the monitor. "Yeah, there he is. An A-69 corvette. French-built. A real golden oldie."

"Old or not," Arkady cut in, "this guy has an Argentine Annie Oakley in that bow turret. This gunfire is getting too close to be funny."

"Let's get the eyeball verification on those farside escorts," Amanda began. "Come right . . ."

The image on the repeater screen jarred wildly and broke up. Within the VR helmet, Arkady saw red damage-alert warnings flash past in front of his eyes too rapidly to be read. The drone slewed wildly and the graphics sea surface rushed up toward him. His world went abruptly black.

"Damn, damn, damn!" Amanda's fist struck the back of his chair with a soft thump.

He lifted off the VR helmet and shook his head, striving also to shake off the sensation that he had just died in a plane crash.

"Sorry, ladies. They busted me."

"Such is life, pal. At least your little bod wasn't out there to get perforated too," Christine replied, backing out of her corner of the station. "Ah well, at least we know pretty much what the setup is. Good enough for government work."

"It isn't good enough, Lieutenant!" Amanda snapped. "I am taking this ship into a combat situation, and I cannot afford to rely on toss-off guesswork!"

Christine's eyes widened and she recoiled slightly under the impact of the words.

"I beg your pardon, ma'am," she replied quietly. "We have verified one Meko 360–class destroyer and one A-69–class corvette with the convoy close-escort group. Signal intelligence has also identified the emissions signature of a second 360-class vessel. As to the remaining light escort, sat-scan verifies that it's less than three hundred feet long, diesel-powered, and it displays the emission signature of the standard Argentine light surface forces systems package.

"Possibly it could be one of their Meko 140–class corvettes or a Sparviero fast-attack craft, but, as the Argentines usually operate their naval vessels in two- or three-ship squadrons of like types, my best estimate is that it is a second A-69."

As she spoke, she watched the burst of anger drain out of Amanda to be replaced by a look of deep weariness. Christine had always thought that her friend had looked young for her age. Just for the moment, though, the reverse was true.

"We could get another drone up there in another twenty minutes, Captain," Arkady said from the control station. He had listened quietly throughout the exchange, not turning in his chair.

"No. We might need those last three Braves later, and I want to get back under EMCON. We'll go on Christine's assessment. Secure the drone systems, Arkady. Chris, have your people run a detailed analysis on the signal intelligence we've recorded off this mission. See if there might be anything out of the individual ship-emission patterns we can make use of."

"Aye, aye."

Amanda departed the bay. Lieutenant Rendino waited until her captain was well clear before she leaned back against a side console. She produced a soft, thoughtful whistle.

"She's cool, sis," Arkady said, starting to power down the workstation.

"I know. She's getting flayed worse than all the rest of us put together. It's just that I've been running with the Lady for some time now, and I've never seen the load hit her this hard before. It's kind of spooky. Sort of like God getting a migraine."

"She's cool," Arkady repeated evenly, gazing into the empty screens of his station. "She's just calling the ball for the first time and learning about all the shit they don't put in the books."

The little case clock in President Sparza's private office chimed softly as Harrison Van Lynden was ushered through the door. The Argentine leader rose from behind his desk and nodded a greeting.

"Good evening, Mr. Secretary. Please be seated. May I offer you a cup of coffee?"

"Yes, I'd like that, Mr. President. Thank you."

They were alone in the room. Sparza himself poured and served the steaming beverage from a silver serving set that had been placed on a side table. It was good coffee, a Colombian blend brewed strong, "fighting coffee" intended for a long, sleepless night. Van Lynden knew that a pot full of a similar grade waited for him back at the United States Embassy.

"Now, Mr. Secretary," Sparza said, resuming his seat, "how may I help you?"

"Well, the problem at hand is fairly obvious. Your ships are at sea and so are ours. In the near future, possibly tonight, they are going to meet and there is going to be a battle."

"I know. I am waiting here for the reports to come in."

"We still have time to stop this, Mr. President. That's why I came this evening in this rather semiofficial mode. I'd like to ask if there is any way at all we can cut this thing off before we take any more casualties and before the relationship between our nations is further scarred."

Sparza stared down at his desktop for a long moment. "I do not know what I can say, Mr. Secretary, except that I believe the actions we have taken are necessary and right for the future of Argentina. My people have a destiny on the Antarctic continent, and I will not deny it to them. We will not back away from this."

"Then we have to stop you. One of the things I have learned over the past few days is that there is a destiny in Antarctica, but it's one for the entire human race, not for any single nation. The United States will not be backing down either."

"Then, Mr. Secretary, there will be a battle."

"Apparently so."

Both men were quiet for a moment, both sensing that with that final declaration, their role in these developing events had passed. They had become onlookers now, no more involved in the outcome than the rest of the world.

"It's a peculiar thing," Van Lynden said finally. "There's an old truism about two wrongs never making a right. Well, I fear that our two 'rights' are about to make a cataclysmic wrong."

"Possibly. The problem with the profession of statesmanship is that other men pay for your errors and failings with their blood." Sparza leaned forward intently. "Please believe me. When we initiated planning for Conquistador South, we did not intend for there to be a loss of life. We did not desire a conflict with the United States."

"I regret, Mr. President, that you have one." Van Lynden gave the softest and briefest of laughs. "That shoots down another old truism. The one about two democracies never going to war against one another."

Sparza shrugged. "That is an unrealistic expectation. Conflict between men and nations stem from deeply held beliefs and desires. This will remain a constant for as long as men and nations have differing beliefs and desires. The mere structure of the governments involved is an irrelevancy."

"I suspect you are right, Mr. President."

Van Lynden set his cup and saucer on the edge of the desk and rose from his chair. "If you will excuse me, I'll be returning to my embassy. I think we've both got a long night ahead of us."

"We do. I shall be here if you need to communicate with me, Mr. Secretary."

"I'll be standing by as well, although I doubt there'll be much for either us to do until it's time to start picking up the pieces."

DRAKE PASSAGE
2021 HOURS: MARCH 29, 2006

"Ken, what's your assessment of their tactics?"

It wasn't a full Operations group, just a call-up of the key tactical officers into the wardroom to assess battle options. Ken Hiro and Dix Beltrain had drawn chairs up to the big table; Christine Rendino sat curled up on the couch with her feet tucked under her. Amanda paced slowly, trying to burn off the sickening residue of the day's adrenaline load.

"They have their escorts divided into a close and a distant covering force," her exec replied. "That's a classic package for convoy escort, but it seems a little bit fancy to me for this setup."

"I agree with Mr. Hiro," Beltrain added. "If I were running the Argys' show, I'd pull all my escorts in tight around the transports. Then I'd charge right down the middle with all radars blasting. I'd trust in my concentrated point defenses and ECM to break up any attack a single raider could launch."

"That makes sense," Amanda said, crossing her arms. "You might lose a couple of escorts that way, but you'd have a very good chance of being able to eat the strike and still get your convoy through. So, are the Argentines just being stupid, or do they have something else on their agenda?"

"They do," Christine said flatly. "Like your head served up on a silver platter. Those distant escorts aren't just escorts. That's a hunter-killer pack out there, targeted right on us. You can bet on it. Those guys know they've got to get in close to get at the Duke, so they're using the convoy for bait."

"I can see that," Amanda said, nodding to herself. "The Argentines are the ones playing stealth games now. We're operating under EMCON, so their hunter-killer group does too. That way, neither of us can get a fix on the other. However, to make a run on the convoy, they know that we'll have to light off our fire-control radars. They'll wait for that moment, then they'll plaster us with Exocets set in homing antiradiation mode."

"Either that, or they'll drop back and catch us in a cross fire between the distant and the close escort groups," Christine finished.

"Just a second!" Ken Hiro made a sharp negative motion with his hand. "That compromises the principles of mass and mission intent. These guys are pros. We can't assume that they'll put the convoy at risk just to go head-hunting."

"Sure we can," the intel responded. "All the evidence points to it. Look, Mr. Hiro, we're dealing with a traditional Latino culture here. Macho to the max. For the past few days the Duke has been kicking over their toys and pissing in their sandbox. What's worse, it's been a woman who's been sticking it to them. They've probably got officers out there who would cheerfully flush their whole damn merchant marine down the toilet in exchange for one clear shot at us!"

"It still doesn't make sense."

"No, sir, it doesn't, but we're talking glands here, not brains."

"Let's leave their motivations in abeyance for the moment," Amanda cut in, "and concentrate on what we're going to do about it. Any suggestions?"

Her people didn't have a fast answer. Finally Hiro said, "I'd say our best angle of approach would be from astern. That sector is covered by their two smallest escorts and their weakest sensors. We could come in up their wake, kill their two trailers, then engage the transport line. They'll probably be focusing most of their attention ahead and not behind them. With a little luck, we should be able to work in fairly close before we get spotted."

"Begging your pardon, sir, but that's a crappy tactical setup," Dix Beltrain said emphatically. "For one, coming in from astern like that will reduce our rate of approach by forty percent. They'll have a whole lot longer to spot us. For two, attacking that ship column from astern will make for a real bad targeting template. Minimum radar cross-sections, target overlaps at varying ranges, mutual countermeasures support . . . I'll be trying to designate into one gigantic blob of chaff and jamming. Before I could guarantee you kills on all three of those transports, the lead escorts and the distant covering force would have more than enough time to swing wide and get a line of fire on us."

"Well, what would you suggest, Lieutenant?" Hiro countered.

"We've got a bad hand here. Let's shuffle the deck again and go for a redeal."

"What's that supposed to mean?"

"I mean, let's change some of the tactical parameters here, sir," Beltrain replied heatedly. He looked over to Christine Rendino. "Chris, do we have any more reconsat passes tonight?"

"Hmm, sure. One at about 2400 hours and another at 0430."

"Okay, now our Stealth Cruise Missiles outrange the Argentines' Exocets by a whole lot. I suggest we stand well off the Argy formation and shotgun it with all twelve of the SCMs we've got aboard." Beltrain shrugged. "Heck, we're bound to hit something. Even if we don't get the transports, we might be able to thin out their escort force and blow a hole in their formation. Then we can use the next sat pass to reassess the situation and plot a followup strike."

"We can't assume that we'll get the luxury of a second strike, Lieutenant!" Hiro responded. "Without specific target designation, we can't be certain we'll do enough damage to disrupt their formation. We also can't be certain we'll have enough time to develop another favorable tactical situation. We may only get one shot at this, so we've got to be sure."

"He's got a point, Dix," Christine added from the couch. "Come daylight, the Argy Air Force will be covering that convoy like a coat of paint. By the time we get the dark again, they'll have made rendezvous with their icebreakers and they'll be in the pack, beyond our reach. We gonna do it, we gotta do it now. And we better do it right first crack out of the box."

"I know that, Chris, but I still stand by firing on bearing at long range. By my assessment, it has as much chance of working as Mr. Hiro's coming-in-the-back-door plan and it doesn't put the ship as much at risk."

Dix looked up at his captain, waiting for her to make the call. All three of her officers were. Amanda stepped off a pace or two, deliberately positioning herself so she would not have to meet their eyes. She didn't have a decision for them.

Belatedly, Amanda realized that she was in no kind of condition for effective mission planning. By rights, she should have been the one putting her own concepts and ideas forward for analysis here. Instead, she found that her tactical awareness was gone. She couldn't hold the full mental image of the developing situation she was confronted with. Her thoughts wouldn't track properly, angling off and chasing around in circles. She could recognize the symptoms; somewhere along the line she had passed a critical level of personal exhaustion.

Come on, Mandy! For half of your life you've worked and built and prepared for this day, and when it comes at last, you crap out because you're short a few hours' sleep.

She rubbed her dry and aching eyes, then glanced at her wristwatch. She'd learned her lesson on the night of the submarine engagement. She didn't have much time left, but she would use a little of what was available to try to get herself back into some kind of shape for decision making.

"Thank you for your input," she said noncommittally, turning back toward her officers. "I'll take it under consideration. It's now 2035 hours. At 2200, there will be a full O group and we'll make a strike commit. Ken, make sure all hands have a chance to take a break and get something to eat. Beyond that, try and get some rest yourselves. It's going to be a long night."

It wasn't what her people were hoping to hear from her, but at the moment it was all she had.

Amanda left the wardroom, heading aft for the companionway ladder that led up to officers' country. She hesitated at its foot, momentarily too tired to climb. Leaning against the side of the passage, she rested her head against the cool steel.

Through that contact, she could feel the living vibration of her ship: the tension and release of the hull working with the sea, the white-hot whisper of the turbines as they fed power into the drive system, the heartbeat-steady thudding of the propellers as they cut dark water. She could recognize each and every movement of that symphony. It was a soothing and steadying thing, something to draw strength from. Amanda did so for a few moments before straightening again and going on her way.

In quarters, she began to work through an old ritual. She ignored water-use restrictions and granted herself a ten-minute shower and shampoo. Toweling off lightly, she pulled on a fresh pair of cotton briefs and a uniform shirt, then turned her attention to her music collection. Selecting a mild instrumental version of *South Pacific*, she dropped it into her CD player and set the volume to low. Dousing the cabin lights, she stretched out on the top of her bunk. The clock alarm was set to grant her an hour's worth of rest, enough maybe to clear her mind and let her think again.

It was a vain hope. Her pet formula for getting to sleep failed her. Exhausted or not, her mind refused to shut down. Random fragments of thought ricocheted through her mind, prodding her back into wakefulness.

Both Ken Hiro and Dix Beltrain had come up with good concepts. The problem was that somewhere, buried under her blanket of weariness, something kept whispering that they weren't quite good enough.

After half an hour's futile pursuit of sleep, Amanda gave up. Rolling over onto her stomach, she tucked her pillow under her chin and stared into the darkness. Damn, damn, damn, just what was the best way to go about killing a convoy? Maybe she should consult with some experts on the subject.

Those experts would be men like "Red" Ramage, Otto Kretschmer, and Gunther Prien, the great submarine aces of both sides of the Second World War. In her search for doctrine that could be applied to stealth-ship operations, Amanda had studied them extensively. She knew what they would say.

"*You have to get inside! Maneuver directly into the convoy's line of advance, then dive. Go deep and rig for silent running. Lie doggo and let the convoy run over the top of you. Then surface right in the middle of them and open up with everything you've got, torpedoes and deck guns both. Fire on anything and everything that moves! Flow with the developing tactical situation. Take advantage of the confusion. Blow them to hell!*"

"A proven and valid way to do the job, gentlemen," Amanda replied to the shades of the men who shared the darkness with her. "The only problem is that I can't dive this damn barge."

Get in close without being spotted, yes. Fifteen, maybe even ten miles, on full stealth and with a good sea running. Just close enough to get caught cleanly between the convoy and the distant covering force.

Figure eight Exocet cells on each of the five big Argentine warships and four on the two smaller ones. Forty-eight heavy antiship missiles, not counting gun mounts and torpedo tubes—too many. Amanda might have been willing to match her countermeasures and point defenses against one group of escorts or the other, but not both simultaneously.

Well, what about trying to lure some of the escorts off somehow?

Not likely. Amanda had already played the decoy gambit once before with the Aeronaval patrol planes. The Argentines were angry and aggressive, but not stupid. They must know that the Duke had to come to them sooner or later. They wouldn't readily abandon a sure thing to go off chasing will-o'-the-wisps.

Okay, then what about a diversion? Something that would scramble the Argentine defenses just long enough for the *Cunningham* to get across that last ten miles and inside the convoy perimeter. Maybe the helos? Configure them for surface attack with Hellfire and Penguin missiles and send them around to hit the far flank of that covering force . . .

No. Drop it. Too risky.

Wait a minute. Was it really all that risky, or was it so just because a certain Lieutenant Vincent Arkady would be flying one of those helicopters?

Examine that thought, Mandy. Turn it over in your mind and look at it carefully from all angles.

Somewhere over the past few hectic days, Arkady had become a larger presence in her mind. More so than any man had in a long time. Twice she had sent him out, and twice he had nearly died carrying out her orders. Was the thought of doing it a third time making her freeze?

This is why you aren't supposed to cross the line, the risk to your objectivity and professionalism.

With great deliberation, she closed her eyes and played it out like a hand of cards. The hard outline of the mission parameters against his knowing touch. The grim risk probabilities versus his relaxed, lazy-panther slouch against a convenient bulkhead. The cold consideration of the gains and losses against his comfortable and comforting presence when the load was on.

When she opened her eyes again, she was pleased to find that her soul was still her own. The simple truth was that it was irrelevant who might be flying the mission. No helicopter, not even a Sea Comanche, could hope to survive inside the area defenses of a modern surface warship, and Amanda Garrett did not believe in suicide missions, not for anyone.

She rolled back onto her side. For the first time she wished that the old *Boone* had been invited along on this cruise. What she really needed was another ship to provide a diversion while the

Duke made her run in on the convoy. Either that, or a way for the Duke to be in two places at the same time.

Well, why couldn't she be?

Amanda abruptly sat upright. For almost five full minutes she stared into the darkness, her mind functioning with sudden crystal clarity. Then she reached for the interphone at the head of her bunk.

"Ken, this is the Captain. Cancel the schedule I gave you. I want all operations officers in the wardroom immediately. We're going to do this thing right now!"

DRAKE PASSAGE
0031 HOURS: MARCH 30, 2006

"Fire twelve!"

The warning horn blared and the last Stealth Cruise Missile punched out of its launch cell. Holding the peculiar tail-down attitude of its breed, it arced away from the *Cunningham*, booster pack streaming a curtain of golden flame. Its razor-blade wings snapped open and the small turbojet power-plant spooled up to power. Completing conversion to flight mode, it kicked free of its exhausted booster, leveled out, and raced for the horizon.

Onboard the SCM, an almost miraculously precise guidance system began tracking on the distant impulses of a NAVSTAR satellite. The cruise missile had been carefully programmed to swing wide along a circular course and to deliver itself to an exact point in space at an exact moment in time. Nothing short of a massive systems failure or total destruction could stop it.

"All SCMs launched, Captain. All missiles running hot and straight on designated headings," Beltrain reported from the tactical console.

"Very well, Dix. Give us a time to target."

In the bottom right corner of the Alpha Screen, a second digital readout flashed into existence over the standard time hack and began counting down.

"There you go, ma'am. First missile estimated in over point item in T minus fifty-one minutes and thirty seconds."

"Okay. Helmsman, are we ready to initiate the speed run?"

"Yes, ma'am," the seaman called back over his shoulder from the battle helm station. "Course to point item is up and in the system. Navicom and autopilot read green and ready to engage. Projected time to point item, fifty minutes."

"Very well. Helm, you will engage on my mark."

Amanda leaned forward in the captain's chair, regarding the time hack through narrowed eyes.

"Stand by to take departure. Coming up on T minus fifty . . . three . . . two . . . one . . . mark! Engage!"

The helmsman keyed in the autopilot and the light patterns on his console shifted. Without human influence, the helm controller spun to a new heading, and smoothly the *Cunningham*'s bow began to come around in response. On the lee helm pedestal, the power levers and throttles flipped forward against their stops with an audible click. On the propulsion system's repeaters, the glowing green bars of the engine-output gauges crawled up their scales until they reached their limits and flared bloodred.

A soft rushing roar with shrill metallic overtones began to fill the background. The Duke's huge gas turbines were spinning up to their peak RPM, sucking a tornado of cold air down the intake ducts and into their shimmering blades. Like the cruise missiles she had just unleashed, the destroyer herself was now a computer-guided projectile aimed and launched at a specific target.

Amanda pushed herself up and out of the captain's chair and joined her tactical officers at the chart table. A moment later, Arkady ducked through the aft hatchway and joined the group. He'd watched the SCM launch from the weather decks and he wore a heavy navy parka over his flight suit. As he brushed past her, she could feel a clean trace of the topside cold caught in its fabric. He moved into his slot around the table and gave her a nod and a sober smile.

"All right. Let's go over this one last time, just to be sure." Amanda called up the latest satellite photo image of the Argentine convoy onto the chart-table flatscreen. "The enemy task force is continuing to hold a course of one nine zero degrees true and a speed of eighteen knots. The distant covering force has executed its latest cross over the line of advance, and is currently holding on stations some ten miles off the starboard bow of the main formation. Given our current course and speed, and granted they don't make any changes, we will be making intercept on the convoy in about . . . forty-seven minutes."

Amanda picked up a data wand and drew a glowing line across the screen, converging on the convoy's heading. "We're steering zero degrees true, due north. That will bring us in on the bow of the formation at a shallow angle. Adding their eighteen-knot rate of advance to our own forty-knot speed will give us a cumulative rate of closure of about fifty-eight knots. That should get us across the ten-mile gap between stealth integrity failure and the convoy perimeter in about eight minutes."

"That'll also put us damn near alongside the distant covering force when our stealth crashes," McKelsie interrupted.

"So it will," Amanda agreed. "That's what that cruise-missile stream we just launched is all about. The roundabout course they're flying will bring them in over point item at approximately the same time as we and the convoy arrive there. We'll be coming in from the south. The SCMs will be coming in from the west at thirty-second intervals. Not only will we be catching the Argys in a cross fire, but hopefully we'll also be confusing them as to where the attack is actually coming in from and how many of us there are out here. With a little luck, by the time they sort things out, we'll have gotten at the transports."

"I still don't know about setting the cruisers to come in at two hundred feet, though," Beltrain commented, leaning forward against the chart table. "That high, they're going to be a whole lot easier to spot and hit with point defense."

"I know," Amanda replied, "but the whole idea is for them to provide a distraction while we make our run in. If they actually happen to hit anything, it'll be chocolate frosting on sugar pie. Oh, and by the way, Dix, the discriminator circuits on those SCMs should reject lock on anything with a radar cross-section as small as we have. Just in case, make sure our IFF beacons are set to go in case we have to wave one of them off."

"Will do, ma'am."

"To continue, the intent is to get within the convoy perimeter. To do so, we'll kill this nearside forward escort the second we lose stealth. That'll blow us our hole. Once we're inside, between all the grass and garbage being put out by our countermeasures and those of the transports, the Argentines won't be able to be sure of their target designation. They won't be able to fire inward without running the risk of hitting their own ships. We, on the other hand, will be able to blaze away at anything that moves. We'll take down the transports, blow ourselves another hole out the back of the escort perimeter, then beat it out of there. Any comments?"

"It still strikes me," Ken Hiro said slowly, "we're counting an awful lot on the Argys doing exactly what we want them to do. What if they've thrown a course change in on us?"

"That's a point. In fact, if you or I had been running the show, I'd have bet we'd have been throwing in random variances in course and speed all along, especially after each satellite pass. They haven't, though. They've held this heading and speed steadily for the past sixteen hours, and there is no visible reason for them to change for at least another eight or ten. I think those are solid enough odds to bet on.

"If they do throw a major course change in on us . . . well, we'll sheer off and think of something new. We won't be any worse off then than we are now. One way or another, we'll know pretty soon. Anything else?"

Amanda scanned around the table, meeting the eyes of her people. She was satisfied with what she saw.

"Okay, Ken, I'll be keeping the con down here. You've got the bridge. It's safe to assume that if the CIC goes down, the ship will have received heavy damage and I will be dead or otherwise out of it. If that's the case, your primary concern will be the survival of the ship and the crew. Break off the mission and get the Duke out of there."

"Aye, aye, ma'am. You've got it."

"Very well, then, let's go to stations."

Her people dispersed out from the chart table, all except Arkady. He moved closer in the blue-lit dimness, and Amanda smiled to herself. He had good shoulders, she noted, and just now it would have been rather nice to be able to bury her face against one of them for a few minutes.

"You didn't have too much to say, Arkady."

"Not too much to say. It's a good plan. It's comparatively simple. It makes the best possible use of our available resources. It matches our strengths against the enemies' weaknesses, and like every other military plan of operations since year one, it'll dissolve into elephant snot the second we make contact with the enemy."

"That's a stark assessment."

The corner of his mouth quirked up. "I'm the guy who does honest, remember? In the end, it's all going to boil down to whoever is riding the captain's chair, and how good they are at gluing things back together again after they start falling apart."

"I know," Amanda replied quietly. She crossed her arms across her stomach and hugged herself lightly to suppress a shudder. "God, please don't let me screw up!"

"If I were him, I think my reply would be, 'Don't sweat it. This is what I made you for.' "

Arkady took a step back and saluted crisply. "Captain, request permission to observe the engagement from CIC."

Amanda straightened and answered the salute. "Permission granted, Lieutenant."

From up forward, the Aegis systems operator called out, "Multiple surface-radar sources coming up over the horizon. Position bearing and number consistent with enemy force projection."

Someone else, possibly Christine over in Raven's Roost, whispered, "Show time!"

NORFOLK, VIRGINIA
0110 HOURS: MARCH 30, 2006

"Yo?"

"Admiral Garrett? This is Captain Callendar, Admiral MacIntyre's Chief of Staff. Sorry to disturb you at this hour, sir, but the Admiral thought that you would like to know that they are going in now. We will keep you advised as the situation develops."

"Thank you, Captain. I appreciate it. My compliments to Admiral MacIntyre."

Wilson Garrett replaced the phone in its wall cradle and returned to the living room. Impatiently, he scooped the television remote control up off the low, golden-pine coffee table and killed the cable news broadcast issuing from the entertainment center across the room. Dropping back onto the couch, he picked up his sketch pad and tried to return his attention to the concept drawings he had been working on. He found, however, that the images of Empress Augusta Bay that he had been seeking had become entwined with the visualization of a much more current and personally meaningful battle.

Sliding his pencil into the wire coil atop the pad, he angrily swiped at his eyes with the back of his hand. And when he resumed his drawing, it was not of a naval engagement. It was a sketch of a young woman, an idealization of girl as remembered by a father.

A number of the secondary monitors in the Combat Information Center had been switched over to the exterior low-light television system. Through them, it appeared as if the ship were a projectile fired through the narrow slot between the wind-whipped sea and the low overcast. Her prow tore through intermittent veils of mist and rain, and once, off to port, an ominously large pan of drift ice flashed past.

Jane's All the World's Warships for 2006 listed the Cunningham-class destroyer as having a top speed of "thirty knots plus," the "plus" being a modestly well-guarded secret. This night, bucking Force Five seas, the Duke's iron log registered a clean forty-two.

The twin prop wakes streaming aft from the propulsor pods met right astern and kicked up a thundering rooster tail that rose above the level of the well deck. The normal pitch and roll of her cruising state was gone, replaced by an unsteady floating sensation as the huge, 80,000-ton hull tried to lift and plane. She was no longer riding up and over the waves; rather, she was driving through them, her sharp-edged clipper bow smashing into each oncoming roller like an ax into soft wood, the jolting impacts radiating back along her frames.

"How are we doing, McKelsie?" All hands in the CIC wanted to ask that question, because over in the countermeasures bay, the battle had already been joined.

With all stealth protocols closed up, the Duke had the radar cross-section of a small cabin cruiser. However, even a small cabin cruiser could be tracked at ranges of up to twenty-five miles by a good surface-search system, and the Argentines had good surface-search systems.

Working in close would require that the enemy's own technology be turned back against him. In high sea states, search radar would frequently pick up "wave clutter," annoying random contacts and ghost targets brought about when the radar sweep reflected off the moving surface of the sea. Modern radars had electronic filters built into them to eliminate most of the phenomenon.

McKelsie and his spook team were counting on that. They were using a vast block of processing capacity to produce a continuously updating computer model of the surface wave patterns that surrounded the *Cunningham.* Then, employing that model, they manipulated the "mutability envelope" of the ship's Wetball stealth skin, phasing its radar return into the surface clutter being produced around it.

In effect, she was a chameleon, camouflaging herself by matching the color and pattern of its background. In theory, the Argentine radar systems would discard the *Cunningham*'s return along with the rest of the trash.

Of course, there was always the risk that some technology-distrusting curmudgeon on the other side might just switch his filters off and take a real look around.

"So far, so good, Captain," McKelsie reported. "No shift in enemy scan rate or frequency. No fire-control radars coming up."

Amanda eyed the Alpha Screen critically. The convoy was right where it was supposed to be, almost dead-on beyond the *Cunningham*'s bow. However, the distant covering force was still designated as an outlined block of empty space off to port, a best-guess estimate of their position.

"You know, boss ma'am," Christine's voice sounded in Amanda's headset, "if the distant covering force has reversed back over to this side of the convoy's course line for any reason, this heading is going to have us plowing right into them. We could end up being exposed worse than I was the day my bikini broke at Waikiki."

Amanda smiled in spite of herself. "You aren't likely to enjoy it nearly as much either, fa' sure," she replied into her lip mike. "I'll take it under advisement, Chris."

Amanda called the thermographic imaging from the mast cameras up onto her own flatscreens and mentally demanded that they show her the presence of her enemies. Arkady looked on as well, from the station he had taken for himself behind the command chair. He was quiet, saying nothing, but she could sense his presence on the fringe of her personal space and catch that scent of Old Spice and kerosene that she had come to associate with him.

"Direction-finder arrays are picking up make-and-break static off multiple targets," Christine reported, suddenly businesslike. "Triangulating now."

How easy it was to forget how to breathe.

"Yeah! Confirm the distant covering force! Right where they're supposed to be! Passing down the port side at a seven-mile range! We're getting RSM reflection off them now."

Breathe.

A trio of target hacks replaced the empty block of space on the Alpha Screen and Arkady's hand appeared in the corner of Amanda's vision, a clenched fist with an upraised thumb that gave an emphatic shake. The time-on-target display for the cruise missiles ticked down past four minutes.

"Helm, return helm and lee helm to full manual control. Maintain current speed and heading."

"Aye, aye, helm and lee helm answering on manual."

Amanda keyed her headset over Main Engine Control. "Chief, we're in the groove and on final approach. If you've got any more revs in your pocket, I can use them right now."

Thomson's response was the slow quivering of the iron log up toward forty-three knots.

For a moment, she considered switching over to the MC-1 circuit and addressing the crew. Then she discarded the notion. She had either made them ready for this moment or she hadn't.

The time hack wound down to three minutes.

"Dix, set up a triple-deuce pattern on that nearest DD in the escort perimeter."

"Aye, aye, ma'am."

"Don't wait for my order. Lock up on him and launch the second we go active."

"Will do."

Dixon Beltrain's voice was completely level, totally confident. Whatever specters of personal weakness that might have haunted him at one time had been exorcised.

Two minutes.

"Enemy scan pattern changing!" McKelsie called out from his systems bay. "The lead, nearside destroyer."

"Does he have a lock on?" Amanda demanded.

"Negative, but his primary system is tight-sweeping this sector. He thinks he sees something out this way, but he's not quite sure what."

"Any fire control coming up?"

"Negative."

"Chris, anything on his talk-between-ships circuits?"

"All channels still clear. He isn't yelling yet."

A few miles away, on the other end of that radar beam, an Argentine skipper was mentally flipping a nickel, just as she was.

"Let's wait him out," Amanda ordered.

Sixty seconds.

Amanda started at a touch. Concealed in the low-lit dimness of the CIC, Arkady's hands had come down off the back of the command chair and were now resting on her shoulders. It was a good place for them to be, and she leaned back and braced herself against their warm pressure.

The time hack came up triple zero.

"SCM target-acquisition radars just went active on the western horizon!" Christine yelled. "Argentine search-and-fire control systems coming up all across the board!"

"Light off all radars! Initiate full-spectrum jamming and ECM! Commence firing!"

Topside, the RBOC mortars thumped as they hurled their aluminum-strip payloads into the sky, while back aft, decoy projectors tossed foxer pods into the sea. The Aegis system came fully on-line and Dix Beltrain's tactical screens blazed with targeting data. The TACCO's hands did their death dance across the keypads, making the designations and locking them down.

"Hot birds coming off the rails!" he yelled, striking the launch sequencer.

Thunder and lightning blazed on the *Cunningham*'s foredeck and the internal monitors glared with illumination overload. Six missiles, four Harpoon IIs and a pair of Standard HARMs, salvoed from the VLS cells. The rocket-driven Standards climbed away in high flaming parabolas, while the turbojet-powered Harpoons followed a shallower arc and leveled out ten feet above the wave crests. Set to short-range, "sprint" mode, they fired their afterburners and punched through the sound barrier en route to their target. At this range, the Argentine destroyer *Heroina* had only seconds to respond.

It was almost enough. Her captain had already started to turn toward and in to the faint ghost bogey they'd detected and her countermeasures men had been sitting with their hands poised over their systems controls. They buried their ship under a blanket of chaff and their jammers blared out a squall of electromagnetic white noise. Both of the *Heroina*'s forward Dardo forty-millimeter twin mounts and her bow five-inch turret hosed their firestreams into the flight paths of the oncoming missiles.

In all, they managed to destroy or divert five out of the six rounds. It was one of the Standard HARMs that got through, fixing on the guidance radar of the Dardo mount that had been trying to kill it.

It came blazing down almost vertically, smashing through the top of the Fiberglas turret shell and exploding as it impacted against the gun actions. The blast of the 214-pound fragmentation warhead drove the turret down into its own magazine like the blow of a titanic sledge-hammer, leaving a flaming, twenty-foot-wide crater torn in the deck.

Every man on the bridge was killed or critically wounded as shrapnel riddled the superstructure, and all power was knocked out in the forward half of the ship. With her rudder locked into the final turn set by her decapitated helmsman, the *Heroina* began to circle aimlessly.

Aboard the *Cunningham*, there was only a faint flicker on the low-light monitors.

"Nailed him!" Beltrain exulted. "Single explosion blossom on the target and a pronounced thermal flare!"

"I confirm that!" Christine called from the intelligence bay. "Initial target's EM suite has just crashed. He's no longer radiating."

"Target is turning. . . . Whoa!" Beltrain interrupted himself. "Blossom on the lead transport! Looks like one of the Harpoons the Meko diverted just found a home."

The *Alferez Mackinlay* had bad karma three times over. The Antarctic operations transport lacked point defenses or countermeasures beyond the elementary protection of chaff launchers, and as the lead ship in the transport column, she was denied the cover of the other vessels' foil clouds. Lastly, her decks were stacked high with aluminum-skinned housing modules, almost doubling the size of her radar signature.

The Harpoon II had been lured off by a jamming ghost produced by the *Heroina*'s ECM. After bypassing its intended target, it had reverted to hunting mode. In microseconds, it had located and fixed on the unfortunate *Mackinlay*, five miles inside the escort perimeter. Flashing in over her bow, the missile buried itself in the deck cargo. The explosion that followed showered the freighter from bow to stern with shredded sheet metal and fragments of burning plywood.

The *Cunningham* continued her headlong charge. The crippled Argentine destroyer loomed up momentarily through the sea smoke, a distorted silhouette outlined in the light of its own flames. Then the Duke was past, crossing the escort line and racing on toward the heart of the enemy formation.

Aboard her, voices were starting to rise all around the CIC as training and discipline struggled with the surge of combat adrenaline. Systems operators were absorbing the raw data off their screens, analyzing it and relaying their findings on to their division officers. The officers distilled it down further, using it to make operational decisions within their own fields of responsibility and passing that which they judged to be truly critical on to the command chair.

"Exocet launch from second Meko!"

"Any lockup, McKelsie?"

"Negative, Captain. Missile trending aft down the port side. Second launch now . . . also trending aft. I think he's designating on a chaff cloud or one of our decoy pods."

"Right. Chris, what's the distant covering force up to?"

"The covering force appears to be concentrating on the cruise-missile stream. No fire-control emissions coming in from that bearing."

"Stay on them! McKelsie, keep those decoys coming!"

It was a critical, fragile structure built up out of fast judgment calls made under awesome pressure loads.

Arkady was out of the immediate command loop, so he could afford to concentrate on her. She was leaning forward now, her head turning constantly between the Alpha Screen and her reporting officers, demanding and absorbing the information she needed for her decision making.

There was an edge and a vibrancy to her voice that he had never heard before, an aliveness he had never seen in any woman. Amanda was the junction point of the staggering technological capacity of the *Cunningham* and the skill and dedication of her crew. She was the diamond lens that focused that potential into a searing beam that she turned upon her enemies. She burned bright.

The deck bucked and slewed underfoot, and he grabbed for the chair frame to keep himself upright. *Vince,* he said to himself grimly, *this is one hell of a time to start feeling horny.*

"Captain, do we follow up on the initial target?"

"Negative, Dix. Dead one, drop him. Shift fire to the lead transport."

On the Large Screen Display, a designation box blipped into existence around the lead ship of the convoy column. Two more Harpoons pumped out of their launch cells, this time aimed with deliberation.

The *Mackinlay*'s firefighting parties were unreeling their hoses forward along the ship's weather decks when they saw the missiles burning in like wave-skimming meteors. The lead Harpoon center-punched the hull, exploding deep within the midships holds. Her crewmen felt her decks shudder underfoot for an instant before the plating buckled upward and tore open like the capsule of an erupting volcano, casting them down into the flames below. The second round struck aft, at the base of the transport's superstructure, the quarter-ton warhead blowing it apart like a gasoline-soaked house of cards, destroying alike the propulsion and steering systems and those who operated them. A headless leviathan with the fires of hell glowing within her, the *Alferez Mackinlay* began to fall off and lose way.

Headless also was the entire Argentine naval force. Fate had decreed that the first ship hit had also been the command ship of the close escort group. Its captain, an experienced and capable officer, had been almost the first man to die in the engagement, ripping a massive hole in the Argentine command structure.

The remainder of that structure was now decoupling under the shock of the assault. Those voice communications channels and data links not yet taken out by the Duke's cascade jammers were loading up with calls for help, demands for targeting data, and pleas for someone to, for the love of God, tell them what was going on!

The man who should have been bringing order to this chaos was Admiral of the Fleet Luis Fouga, the man who less than twenty-four hours before had claimed overall command of the task force in his President's office. However, Fouga was a political officer. He had never seen a minute of combat in his thirty-year military career. More important, he had never truly prepared himself for that first critical minute.

Now, with his command under attack and his own flagship struggling to survive against the cruise-missile stream it had encountered, he was incapable of coherent speech, much less effective leadership.

Despite that, and despite the panic and disorganization, the Argentines were beginning to fight back.

"Dix, what's happened to that nearside trailing escort?"

"Escort three . . . Shit! It's gone!"

"Check your Alpha Screen replay. Find him!"

Amanda dropped her eyes to her own flatscreens and called up the computer-recorded imaging from the Aegis system, cursing herself twice over. That starboard-side close escort had been the one she had not been able to get a positive identification on, and now, in the flurry of the strike, she had lost positional awareness of it. She found herself recalling the old fighter pilot's dictum, "The thing that you miss is frequently the thing that doesn't miss you."

Amanda initiated the high-speed replay from the point where the Duke had activated her radars. Watching intently, she saw the Argentine ships begin their antimissile zigzag ballet and the strike blossom on the lead Meko. Then she saw the trailing escort make its move.

From its slot at the four-o'clock position off the convoy's stern, it accelerated sharply, better than tripling its speed in what must have been a matter of seconds. It sheered inward toward the transport line, closing the range with it and merging into the purple blobs of chaff trailing back in the wake of the cargo ships.

"Hydrofoil!"

Someone with more cunning than common sense had ordered a thin-skinned coastal craft out into the wildest stretch of sea miles on the planet, and some crew with chrome-steel guts had obeyed—just on the chance that it might screw up someone's attack plan, just as it was doing.

"Where is he, Dix?" Amanda demanded.

"I can't pick him out. He's swung around on the farside of the transports and he's being masked by their countermeasures."

"Can you get a fix on radar emissions?"

"No, ma'am, he's gone EMCON."

Amanda lifted her voice. "Chris, Argentine hydrofoils, what do you have on them? Right now!"

"Sparviero missile corvette, twelve hundred tons' displacement, composite and aluminum construction, submerged tripedal foil system, hydropump propulsion! Sixty knots plus speed! Single OTO Melara seventy-six-millimeter forward, twin Breda forty-millimeters aft, four Exocet cells amidship!"

"Torpedo tubes?"

"None!"

"Right. Helm, maintain intercept heading on the transport line. Dix, what's that second Meko doing?"

"He's increased speed and has come around to port. It looks like he's cutting across the convoy course line back over to where we were. He's off the port quarter and looks to be passing us astern. I think he's still fixated on our first decoy cluster. Shall I engage?"

"Negative. If the fool hasn't figured out what the score is yet, don't point out the scoreboard. Target that hydrofoil the second he comes out from behind the freighter's chaff screen. He's up to something."

"Aye, aye, ma'am, but it's going to be tight. We're running out of range."

"So is he. Gunnery stations, stand by to engage surface targets!"

Amanda and her TACCO stared at the primary display, waiting for something solid to materialize out of the haze of chaff and ghost jamming.

He came, appearing around the bow of the now-leading fleet oiler, cutting the turn so close that he likely panicked every man on the bride of the larger ship. Search and fire-control radars activating, the corvette raced away from the convoy line, aiming himself dead-on at the onrushing destroyer.

"Captain, target bearing zero degrees relative off the bow. Combined rate of closure ... goddamn, one hundred and ten knots!"

For a moment Amanda was touched by admiration. This kid had been born of the same breed as the *Jervis Bay* and the "Little Boys" off of Samar. He was outmatched in technology and in firepower, and he had no hope of organized support. Yet, when the ships he was charged to protect were endangered, his response was a flaming, death-or-glory dive right into the guns of his enemy.

"Take him, Dix."

"Can't do it! He's come inside the arming perimeter of the Harpoons. They won't have enough time to come down out of boost mode and unsafety ... Exocet launch!"

On the exterior monitors, a double streak of orange burned overhead through the fog, wobbling unsteadily. One of the Phalanx mounts burped out a startled responding burst. The closing range had pulled the fangs of the corvette as well.

"We're going to guns," Amanda ordered. "Gunners, action to starboard, set for full autofire. We'll rake him as we pass. Helm, ten degrees left rudder."

She had made the decision to angle off and open the range almost without thinking, an instinctive move to provide the Duke with a safety margin in this head-to-head standoff. It was impossible to know that less than two miles away, another captain was issuing the exact mirror to her command at almost the same instant for the same reason.

"Captain! Target altering course to starboard! Collision bearing!"

The Navicom system came to the same conclusion as the tactical officer a split second later. Collision alarms warbled at both the helm and command stations.

"Helm, emergency hard left rudder! Crash turn!"

Throwing a destroyer into a tight, minimum-radius turn while she's running flat out at flank speed is not generally considered to be a good idea. You could pop seams, crack frames, and shear years off her hull life. You could buckle the rudder post or tear it out altogether. Given a heavy sea state and a little bad luck, you could even capsize a ship as large and well found as the *Cunningham*.

Amanda had no choice. To try to reverse out of the turn to starboard meant having to fight the growing momentum of the swing to port they had already begun. To back engines and lose their speed meant probable death at the hands of the Argentine defenses. Survival meant turning inside of the collision point and praying that the Argentine captain could do the same.

The CIC crew felt the deck tilt ominously beneath their feet, and the blaring of a second set of alarms almost drowned out the moaning of overloaded metal that echoed up out of the ship's structure.

"The roll inclinometer is approaching red-line limits, Captain!"

"I know, helm. Keep pushing her. She can take it."

Amanda was venturing into that unknown territory beyond listed design specifications. She was trusting to her mariner's instincts and to the years she had spent helping to create this ship. Going by the book would not save them now.

—————

If it was bad in the CIC, it was terrifying topside. As the big ship leaned, Ken Hiro and the bridge crew were forced to brace themselves against whatever was available. Peering down and out of the starboard side of the windscreen, they could see the first wave curling green along the full length of the weather-deck railing.

Then it grew worse.

The Argentine corvette came into sight, tearing a furrow through the sea smoke. In the manner of hydrofoils, she was pitching into her turn as steeply as the American destroyer was listing out of hers. The tip of her stern foil was lifting out, slashing open the surface of the sea, and the twin horizontal geysers of her hydrojet drive thundered in her wake. She was attempting to avoid the impending collision as desperately as *Cunningham* and, just for the moment, the American destroyer hands were wishing her well.

"Okay, helm," Amanda said quietly. "Start bringing your rudder amidships. Not too fast or you'll lay her right over on her side. Let her get her head up."

The inclinometers shifted back into the safety zone and with a heavy, shuddering roll the Duke came upright on her new heading. A meager two hundred yards away, the Argentine corvette was running parallel to her, almost matching her course and speed. Muzzle flashes began to flare rhythmically at its bow and stern, and tracer rounds began to arc out at the *Cunningham.*

"Gunners, take him! All mounts traverse right and fire as you bear!"

Amanda could feel the shell hits, heavier and more muffled than the discharge of the Duke's own weapons. The first faint scent of burning plastic and hot metal began to seep in through the ventilators.

Back aft at the damage-control stations, the DC officers began calling down the warning lights appearing on their panels.

"I'm showing skin damage above the waterline between frames nineteen and twenty-two."

"Confirm that. We've got shell hits opposite number-two Vertical Launch System. Damage-control team Alpha Bravo responding."

"Roger, inform the TACCO that number-two VLS is going down. I'm pulling the safety breakers."

"Shell hits astern. Frame forty-one. I'm showing skin penetration and a high-temperature warning light."

"Confirm that. Team Alpha Delta responding. Fire in the hangar bay!"

Arkady gave Amanda's shoulder a parting squeeze and then he was gone, racing aft.

The Duke was not passively accepting the attack. She was repaying in kind. Danny Lyndiman, the same young gunner's mate who had been on-line the day of the first Argentine air strike, was at his new duty assignment at number-one gun-control station. Both of the Oto Melara Super Rapids were slaved to his hand controller, with both turrets firing to the same aiming point. Laying the crosshairs of his targeting screen on the Plimsoll line of the hydrofoil, he squeezed the trigger.

The Oto Melaras raged, each slamming out its stream of 76mm projectiles. They weren't tracer rounds, but their superheated steel glowed green in the thermographic sights, marking their flight. As the converging shell streams touched the Argentine's hull, skin shredded and hellfire spilled out. With the precision of a metalsmith wielding a cutting torch, Lyndiman began to draw the stream of shell-bursts across the length of the corvette's hull.

Simultaneously, dazzling white points of light began to dance across the hydrofoil's upperworks. The Duke's second duty gunner had placed the starboard Phalanx mount under manual control and had brought it into the engagement, the vicious little tungsten penetrators stitching through the superstructure of the smaller craft like a needle through tissue paper.

The Argentine vessel couldn't stand it. The two vessels thundered along side by side, exchanging broadsides like two Napoleonic ships of the line. They were trading a near-equal amount of fire, but the American vessel had almost eight times the displacement to absorb it with. The destroyer was being hurt, but the corvette was being torn apart. Her captain, in a desperate bid for survival, accelerated and veered off, trying to open the range.

"He's bugging out!" Dix yelled joyfully. "He's running for it! Gunners, stay on him! Stay . . . Jesus, sweet Jesus!" The TACCO's voice sank to an awed whisper. The voices of every other person within sight of an exterior monitor were stilled as well.

One of the Duke's Oto Melara rounds had found and damaged the main spar of the corvette's forward hydrofoil assembly. Under the load of the turn, it had sheered off.

Dropping ten feet off the plane, the corvette's narrow forehull had dug into the face of an oncoming wave. At sixty knots, the water might as well have been concrete.

The hydrofoil's immense momentum drove its bow under the surface while its stern was lifted into the air. Its keel whipped like a willow wand, tearing loose hull framings and smashing them out through the Fiberglas skin like bone splinters through the flesh of a compound fracture.

Aghast, the men and women of the *Cunningham* watched as the stern of the corvette angled higher, fifty, sixty, seventy degrees, hesitating for a long moment at the high point of its arc. Amanda had an instant's hellish vision of what must be happening inside that hull. Ammunition raining down out of magazine racks, tons of kerosene spilling out of bunkerage tanks, white-hot turbines tearing loose from their bedplates and crashing forward through thin bulkheads . . .

The length of the Argentine's hull split open like the petals of a blossoming flower, disgorging a single, titanic golden-orange fireball. The Duke's deck plates rang under the impact of the shock wave as she swept past the explosion. Then the monitors went empty and dark and she was in the clear, barring a single fragment of smoking metal that came spinning down out of the mists to rattle off the upperworks. From somewhere over near number-one gunnery station, a quietly exultant voice exclaimed, "Yeah! Free game!"

Amanda shook off the effects of the spectacle and returned her attention to the main situational display. Their evasive turn had brought them around more than ninety degrees from their previous course of due north, to a heading of west-southwest. The following firefight with the hydrofoil had carried them clear across the bow of the Argentine transport column from its port side to the starboard.

It had also cost them the initiative of the attack. Dead or not, that gutsy hydrofoil skipper might still kill them.

"Helm, left standard rudder! Bring us back around to zero one zero degrees."

What was worse, the Duke's invisibility had been compromised. The battle damage to her sensitive stealth skin would multiply her radar cross-section several times over.

"Mr. McKelsie, give me a maximum-density RBOC screen and a full decoy pattern."

"Captain, we've only got one decoy set left in the launchers, and the RBOC magazines are getting low."

"Then give me all of what's left. Now, McKelsie! Kill all radars! Cease radiating!"

The *Cunningham* completed the foaming circle she had begun, coming about more than a full 360 degrees. She was attempting what in an aerial dogfight would have been called a turn and burn, the creation of a knot of radar and thermal clutter that might serve as a false target to draw enemy fire.

"Steering zero one zero, Captain."

"Very well. Steady as she goes. Hold us parallel to the convoy line."

With their sensors disabled and their communications links cut by the Duke's jamming, the two surviving Argentine transports were blindly holding to their original course and speed.

"What's the status of those last two operational close escorts?" she asked Beltrain.

"The undamaged Meko looks like he's going to assist his shot-up partner, and the A-69 is hanging back behind the convoy. He's having trouble getting a burn-through, but he's trying to target on something . . ."

The exterior monitor covering the stern arc flamed brightly. Half a mile back along the *Cunningham*'s wake, in the heart of the chaff node, a futile Exocet salvo boiled the sea and tore up the sky.

". . . and I guess he just did," Beltrain finished.

"Right. Secure EMCON! Radars back up!"

The screens reactivated. Amanda could see the A-69–class frigate turning away, its bolt spent and its missile cells empty. The three ships of the distant covering force still appeared to be milling around in confusion some fifteen miles ahead of the convoy. A glance at the infrared scanners indicated the continuing, intermittent flicker of weapons fire and at least one steady-state glow out along that bearing.

"Dix, what's going on out there?"

"I'm not sure, ma'am. The SCMs should be long gone by now. Maybe we pinked somebody."

Beltrain's assessment was correct. Fate had guided the distant covering force almost directly into the path of the *Cunningham*'s diversionary cruise-missile strike. The cool cybernetic intellects that dwelt within the guidance packages of the SCMs had recognized the Argentine destroyers as worthy targets, and they had swarmed the warships like a school of hungry barracuda.

The Argentines had fought back and had fought back well. Those rounds not decoyed off target were destroyed by a barrage of gun and missile fire. The captain of the fleet flagship *Nueve de Julio* did not make his fatal error until literally the final minute of the strike.

Seeking to evade the last of the incoming weapons, he had ordered a turn away from the cruise missile stream. But, in doing so, he had unmasked the broad rear facing of his ship's helicopter hangar to the SCM's search radar. The missile was drawn in by this high-RCS target like a moth to a flame. The high-sided structure also blocked a few key degrees of coverage for the Oto Melara point defense mounts, and the twelfth SCM rode in through this narrow free-fire zone and struck the hangar doors with dead-center precision.

Punching through, it had slammed into the tightly parked cluster of helicopters within, bulldozing them into a crumpled jumble against the front of the hangar bay. The cruise missile's engine module had disintegrated, spraying flame and white-hot shrapnel throughout the compartment, while the half-ton warhead had torn loose from the airframe and crashed forward through three more bulkheads before finally exploding.

The blast shattered the midships superstructure of the big Animoso-class destroyer. Both funnels and the mainmast toppled over the side with a hollow metallic scream, the flashback down the stack ductwork demolishing the engine rooms and decimating the engineering watch. Dead in the water, she began to roll broadside on to the force of the waves, while back aft, the burning and bursting fuel cells of her own aircraft turned her stern into a self-consuming inferno.

Dead also was the last Argentine hope for reorganizing into any kind of effective fighting force. Admiral Luis Fouga would never have to face his failure. He had been crushed between the crumpled bulkheads of his flag plot. From this point on, control of this conflict would rest solely aboard the spectral killer that was systematically ripping the heart out of the Argentine dreams of Antarctic empire.

"Coming in on the oiler, Captain!"

"Turrets traverse right and engage the target! Dix, arm starboard torpedo bays. Range safeties to minimum. We don't have time to fool around with wire guidance, so set all fish for independent proximity homing. Salvo-fire all tubes as you get a solution!"

The night-bright optics swiveled to cover the new target along with the gun mounts. Both acquired it simultaneously as the big, slab-sided tanker loomed up out of the sea smoke. The autocannon began to hammer again and golden shell bursts danced along the tanker's deck line, followed by a fiery series of secondary explosions among the replenishment stations and fuel-transfer heads.

On the Alpha Screen, a cone of yellow illumination radiated out from the flank of the *Cunningham*'s position hack, designating the effective firing arc of her starboard bank of fixed torpedo tubes. The cone enveloped the Argentine oiler.

"Opening outer tube doors. Solution is set."

Just above the Duke's waterline amidships, a series of pocket-panel hatches sliced open, revealing a row of blunt, polyethylene-capped warheads.

"Firing on bearing now. Torpedoes away!"

With the peculiar, sequential *thump-kisss* of an above-water launch, five Mark 50 Barracuda torpedoes shot out of their tubes and into the sea. Unlike World War II–vintage tin fish, these stumpy little weapons had only a secondary surface-attack capacity. Their comparatively small, shaped-charge warheads had been intended to crack the shell of a deep-diving nuclear submarine, not cave in the side of a merchant vessel. On the other hand, 110 pounds of high explosives detonating against one's hull plates could not be casually shrugged off either.

Four of the Barracudas found a home. Four thin plumes of spray kicked up along the flank of the *Luis A. Huergo*. With her decks aflame and black oil bleeding from her ruptured belly, she began to lose speed.

Amanda gave a curt nod. "Helm, come right to zero four five. Cut back across the bow of the third transport. Dix, stand by your portside tubes. Same setup. We'll go for a down-the-throat shot as we cross his course line. Gunners, action to port. Shift fire to new target."

There was an uneven stammer to the firing of the Oto Melaras now. Both turrets had expended their entire base load, and the shell humpers down in the magazines were having trouble shoving ammunition into the feeder belts fast enough to fully satisfy the voracious appetite of the guns. The mounts were still capable of dealing damage, though.

The forecastle of the tank-landing ship *Piedrabuena* shattered under the impact of multiple hits. Danny Lyndiman rocked his hand back minutely and the firestreams walked up the front facing of the deckhouse to focus on the bridge, chewing the structure away. Then the torpedoes arrived. Three of them, a triple sledgehammer blow against her hull. Spray exploded out from beneath her forefoot and the entire bow structure distorted and collapsed like a wet cardboard box.

No surviving human eye witnessed the end of the *Piedrabuena.* The *Cunningham* had already swept past on her way to the open water northeast of the ruined convoy. The LST's propellers had continued to race after the torpedoes had hit and the mangled bow doors had acted like a gigantic scoop, channeling a thousand tons of ocean into the overloaded vehicle deck that ran almost the full length of the ship's hull.

As smoothly and swiftly as a crash-diving submarine, the *Piedrabuena* began to slide beneath the waves. The men who could have ordered the engines stopped were dead in the wreckage of the wheelhouse. The others followed swiftly as icy seawater exploded into their compartments. Carrying her entire crew with her, she began her final voyage, two miles down into the chill wet dark of Drake Passage.

"There goes the LST, ma'am," the TACCO reported. "She's a goner."

"I can also confirm that one of the Animosos is out of it. Dead in the water and all electronics are down," Christine called in from Raven's Roost. "We got these dudes up a tree."

Amanda agreed. She ruled this battlefield now. Her tactical

officer had solid locks on the two surviving close escorts. With one word from her, he could kill them both in seconds. She could then double back among the drifting hulks of the convoy. Using them for cover, she could defy or destroy the last surviving elements of the Argentine distant covering force. She could make it a clean sweep if she so desired, and go home with a broom tied to her mast-head. At this moment, she was the queen of the polar seas.

"Do you want to reengage, ma'am?" Dix inquired.

"Negative. Check fire, all systems. Maintain course and speed and pull clear of the area. We've done our job."

BUENOS AIRES
0211 HOURS: MARCH 30, 2006

President Antonio Sparza sat alone in his work office, listening to the faint pulse-beat ticking of the case clock. He was here respond-ing to something more than nervous tension. It had denied him sleep and had driven him to this place where he had reached the high-water mark of his life.

The desk phone warbled softly.

"Yes."

"Mr. President, this is Admiral Valleo at the Naval Ministry." The officer was speaking with a deliberate conciseness, like a man giving a well-thought-out testimony at a trial. "The convoy has been intercepted."

"Go on."

"The corvette *Catamarca* and the tank-landing ship *Piedra-buena* have been sunk. The fleet oiler *Huergo*, the Antarctic opera-tions ship *Alferez Mackinlay*, and the destroyer *Nueve de Julio* have all been heavily damaged and are currently burning and dead in the water. At this time it has been considered advisable to remove the crews from these vessels. The destroyer *Heroina* has also been damaged, but it is believed that she can be saved."

"What about the North American warship?"

"The convoy escorts engaged the attacking vessel with gun and missile fire. The results are unknown at this time. We are not in current contact with the enemy."

"I see."

There was a silent pause that the officer on the other end of the circuit was almost hesitant to break.

"Mr. President, we are out of communication with Fleet Admiral Fouga. It is believed that he may have been killed aboard the *Nueva de Julio*. The senior surviving convoy captain is requesting instructions. What should we tell him, sir?"

"Tell him to come home, Admiral. Tell him to save whatever he can and come home."

Sparza set the phone back into its cradle. Getting up from his desk, he went out into the richly carpeted corridor beyond his office. A short distance down that corridor, glass double doors opened onto the balcony that extended across the front of the Casa Rosada and faced the Plaza de Mayo.

The Plaza was the soul and the voice of the Argentine people. For a century, they had gathered here to cheer for their leaders or to scream for their downfall. The Plaza was empty now, streetlights illuminating it beneath the darkness of a fall night, the pavement shining blackly from a recent shower.

Sparza slipped a cigarette between his lips and kindled it with a quick flare of his lighter. Ignoring the chill, he leaned against the balustrade and stared out across the Plaza. When next the people would gather, it would be to judge him. He would be here waiting for them.

"Comrades, I give you us. We have met the enemy and they are history." Christine Rendino gestured grandly as if she held a glass of champagne instead of a mug of six-hour-old, reheated coffee.

"No shit? Hey, somebody call the President and tell him that we can all go home now. Rendino says so."

Even McKelsie's sneering sounded mellow. As the tactical officers gathered around the CIC command chair, they were savoring a multitude of euphoric sensations. The residual adrenaline that was keeping exhaustion at bay, the feels-good-because-it-has-stopped sensation of released tension, the ancient warrior's joy of discovering that the battle was over and that they were still alive. They had passed through the fire and had proven themselves.

"I speak the truth, Chaff Breath," the intel responded. "The key to this entire setup has been whether or not the Argys could get a supply convoy through to their Antarctic garrisons. After tonight, the operative word is 'not.'

"Even if the Argentines had assembled another logistics block, which they haven't, and had another transport group and escort force ready to sortie, which they don't, our carriers and subs would be in position in time to cut them off. Like, rewind it and put it back in the box, guys, 'cause it's over. Am I right, Captain?"

"I think that's a fair assessment." Amanda nodded thoughtfully. "In a strategic sense, anyhow. Tactically, we're still deep in enemy territory, and we've still got a lot of people out there who now have even more reason not to like us. The ship's company is tired. If we let ourselves get complacent as well, we could still get burned. This fight is still on. Now, Dix, what's the ordnance situation?"

"Six Harpoons and two Standards expended along with all of the SCMs and torpedoes," he replied. "We've burned about forty percent of our available Oto Melara ammunition and about another four hundred rounds of twenty-five-millimeters for the Phalanx. We're fat on missiles, but the number-two Vertical Launch System is still off-line. We took some shell hits in the area and we had some water sloshing around up there. The boards read green, but I'd like to do an individual diagnostic and an eyeball inspection of each round and cell in the array before I bring it back up again."

"Very well. Make it so, but make it fast. Mr. McKelsie, what do you have to say?"

"The skin damage we took is going to increase our radar cross-section down the starboard side by at least twenty percent, maybe more. I'll need to make ranging tests with one of the helicopters to be certain just how bad it is. The big bitch is that we've expended all of our foxer decoys and we're down to one full magazine load left for the RBOCs."

"Nothing to be done about that. As soon as we get a patch job done on the hull and a low sea state, we'll see about getting a coat of retinal schiff base paint on over the damaged areas. That'll help some.

"Chief," she said, shifting her attention to her senior engineer, "thank you. The black gang came through magnificently. How are things going down there?"

Thomson nodded in quiet acknowledgment. "The plant's okay. No problem during the speed run except for a couple of minor overheat warnings. Just the same, I figure to run a Charley-grade systems-maintenance package, just in case. The only thing is, ma'am, that we burned a whole lot of fuel these last few hours. We're down to twenty-seven percent of bunkerage."

Amanda bit her lip. There was nothing to be done about that, either, except to try to tighten their maneuvering belts a little more.

"Okay, Ken, damage-control report?"

"Two seventy-six-millimeter hits forward. They were above

the waterline, but, like Lieutenant Beltrain said, there was minor flooding from wave action. That's been taken care of and we should have patches in place within the hour. Four forty-millimeter hits aft, one of which penetrated the hangar bay. There was a minor fire, but that was successfully suppressed.

"Some of the aviation service gear was damaged, as well as one of the helos. Retainer Zero Two is nonoperational and is probably going to be down for the rest of the cruise."

Amanda took a mental deep breath. "Any crew loss?"

"We took some fire casualties in the Air Division."

Her guts cinched up tighter.

"Nothing serious, though," Hiro continued. "Minor burns and smoke inhalation mostly. Lieutenant Arkady is down in sick bay now with his people. He'll probably be able to give a more detailed report when he gets up here."

"Good enough. I guess we got through it, then." Amanda exhaled deeply and shot a quizzical look across at her exec. "Tell me, what was it like up on the bridge?"

Hiro let his usual reserve slip a little and his smile was tugged offside by the bandaging on his face. "Well, I'll tell you this. It'd make an interesting ride at Disneyland."

It felt good to be able to laugh. Amanda could feel herself coming back down off the edge. Along with the relaxation, however, there was a growing sense of unreality to her surroundings and an unsteadiness that had nothing to do with the sea motion of the deck. Her state of accumulated exhaustion couldn't be shrugged off for much longer. Regardless, there were still things that she had to see done.

"Ken, as soon as we've hauled off a little more from the engagement area, I want to go off EMCON and see if we can contact the *Polar Circle* directly. Our top priority now is to set up that rendezvous again with all possible speed—"

"Captain." They hadn't heard Arkady enter the compartment. He was standing back aft near the hatchway, his flight suit smoke-

and water-stained. For the first time in the short span of days he had been aboard the Duke, he looked uncertain.

"I've just come up from sick bay," he said quietly. "Erikson's dead. It was some kind of massive internal hemorrhage. Chief Robinson said it happened while we were going in on the strike. There wasn't anything she could do."

The silence became an almost tangible thing with dimension and texture. Then, with great care, Amanda set her mug down on top of her console.

"Mr. Hiro, keep the ship moving to the northeast and set fuel-conservation protocols. Hunt for a low sea state to expedite repairs, but keep us under weather cover. Break EMCON only to issue a sitrep and a casualty report to CINCLANT."

She rose from the command chair and left the Combat Information Center, stepping past her officers without speaking. Arkady's whispered "I'm sorry" didn't register on her consciousness.

Amanda went up one level to the thwartship passageway aft of the wardroom, the one with the weather-deck hatches to port and starboard. She chose the one to port, the side of the ship away from the damage-control parties. Struggling with the dogging latches, she forced the hatch back against the pressure of the wind. Stumbling across the ice-slicked tile of the deck, she clutched at the railing with numbing fingers.

At her feet, the dim gray foam of the *Cunningham*'s passage boiled along the destroyer's flank. Beyond that, Amanda could sense the black vastness of the world ocean. She let the sleety spray and the ice-borne wind scourge her through her clothing.

After a moment or two, the first choking sobs came. Alone with the darkness and the sea, Amanda Lee Garrett cried as a mother might weep over her lost firstborn.

Vince Arkady had spent the last couple of hours back aft in the hangar bay, working with the Air Division on cleanup and repair and knocking off only when nothing more could be done in the short term.

Somewhere out there it was dawn, although it couldn't be proved by going up on the weather decks. The Duke lay hove to in a thick bank of sea smoke, her sluggishly turning propellers giving her barely enough steerageway to hold position. It was as if she were packed in black cotton wool, with visibility near zero and with all topside sound muffled out of existence.

Things were eerily quiet belowdecks as well. The conventional plan of the day had gone by the board. All hands not actually on watch or involved in damage-control duty were racked out, recovering from the past night's action. Arkady fully intended to join them just as soon as he'd done something about a twelve-hours-empty stomach.

Even the wardroom was dark and abandoned, lit only by the dim, blue night-illumination panel over the pantry door. Arkady glanced at the coffee urn and shuddered. One more swig of Navy-issue coal tar and he'd heave his guts out. Instead, he hunkered down in front of the small built-in refrigerator under the serving counter, rummaging around in it for something more palatable.

His search produced a quart of milk. Kneeing the refrigerator door shut, Arkady popped open the foil-and-plastic cap of the carton and took a long pull. Ignoring the flat, faintly metallic taste of radiation-preserved sea stores, he poured the beverage down his throat, drinking for the bulk and the soothing coolness.

He'd worked pretty well down the quart before he realized that he wasn't alone. Amanda Garrett was across the compartment, curled up in her favorite recliner. She had been so quiet that he hadn't noticed her in the shadows. For a moment he thought that she might be asleep, then he caught the glint of her eyes in the night light.

"Hi, Skipper." He nodded to her. "How's it going?"

"All right, I guess," she replied softly. "I've just been sitting here considering a few things that I've learned about myself recently."

She wanted to talk with someone. Arkady could sense that. She desperately wanted to talk with someone. A problem with command was that although a captain could take reports, make inquiries, ask opinions, and confer with fellow officers, they tended to be short of people with whom they could simply talk, barring God. And God, as Arkady had learned, was frequently a sleep-on-it-and-work-things-out-for-yourself kind of guy.

"Come up with anything interesting?" he inquired, crossing the compartment and dropping into a nearby chair.

"Yes, I have. I've found that after a lifetime of preparing to be a professional military officer, I don't particularly enjoy having to kill people."

"That's nice," he replied, slouching down on the base of his spine. "It's always a comfort to learn that your commanding officer isn't a certifiable psychopath."

"I'm serious, Arkady."

"So am I, Skipper. These last couple of days, I've seen what this gray lady of ours can do when she's running loose with her hair on fire. Frankly, the thought of some gung-ho, kill-'em-all-and-let-God-sort-'em-out type pushing her buttons would scare the hell out of me.

"A very astute person once observed, 'As the lethality of the individual weapons system grows, so must the responsibility of the individual who controls that weapons system in a geometric proportion.' "

She chuckled softly. "I wrote that."

"Yep, good words. They make sense."

"I didn't know what I was talking about."

"Sure you did. You had the concepts down, you just lacked the direct hands-on experience. It's kind of like sex, I guess. Everybody has a general idea about how it's supposed to work, but until you actually get involved, you have no idea how complicated things can really get."

"Are you trying to get me to laugh it off?"

"Nope, just sort of trying to encourage your sense of perspective."

Amanda sighed. "I had to do the same thing with one of our other people a while back. I pointed out to him that there were some things a combat simulator just couldn't simulate. At the time I think we were talking about fear. It didn't occur to me then that the same thing could be said about killing."

She shifted around in the recliner to face the aviator. "Arkady, how many casualties do you think the Argentines took tonight?" she asked.

"Hard to call. Damn near nobody got off that LST or the hydrofoil. Those four other ships were hit hard too. With the combination of the bad sea state, low temperatures, and rotten visibility, rescue operations are going to be a bitch. I'd say two to three hundred KIA, if they're lucky."

"I concur. If your intent was to try and make me feel better, you're not doing a very good job of it."

Arkady set the milk carton on the deck. "Look, I could sit here and play Little Mary Sunshine all night and it wouldn't signify. What seems like a long time ago, I said something about honest working best with a class act. I think that's still applicable here.

"We've just come out of a classic knife fight in a phone booth with a bunch of guys who would have cheerfully blown us away if given one-eighth of an opportunity. Now, they weren't monsters and they didn't go around cutting babies up on their morning

Cheerios, but they were professional warriors in the service of a nation that had broken international law. We were the cops on the beat who caught the call, and it turned out we had to use deadly force to stop the execution of the crime in progress. I can live with that."

"Not all of us will, though. Erikson died and he didn't have to. I could have gotten him out, I just had to make the decision." Amanda's voice sank back toward a whisper. "I promised I'd take him home."

"Begging the Captain's pardon, but that was a promise you *damn* well didn't have the right to make! This is a warship in the service of the United States of America. You do not have the right to promise any of us a round-trip ticket! What you do have the right to do is to expend our lives like rounds of ammunition, if necessary, to get the job done.

"Erikson wasn't dumb. I went down there and talked to him myself a couple of times. He knew that you couldn't just abandon the mission, no matter how badly you wanted to get him out. You didn't let him down. If he could come back and tell you anything, it'd be that this was just the way it was."

Amanda sat up angrily. "This wasn't 'just the way it was'! I have the command responsibility here! For Erikson and for every one of those Argentine boys who died out there last night! I will not try and rationalize things away like that!"

"Okay, then," Arkady replied levelly, "you're responsible. But not just for Erikson's death. You're also responsible for the survival of this ship and for the successful execution of this mission in the face of what can honestly be called overwhelming odds. You are taking the bulk of your crew home alive, Captain, and that is an impressive performance."

He settled back into his chair. "So that's both ends of the stick. Now, you decide what you're going to do about it. It's like me and my carrier qualification. You can either stand, or you can walk away. What's it going to be?"

She didn't answer; rather, she sat for a time gazing off into the shadows and into her future. Arkady understood what that was about. On the night he'd abandoned his dream of becoming a fighter pilot, he'd done some staring into the dark himself. In the end, he'd walked.

He didn't regret it. It was the right choice made for all of the right reasons. But still, deep down in his guts where he lived, he knew that he wasn't the same man afterward. He found himself praying that this lady wouldn't have to make the same kind of discovery.

"I'll stand," she said finally.

Amanda didn't notice the exultant thumbs-up Arkady gave the universe.

"You're right," she continued. "This is what I am and, despite all of what's happened, this is still what I want to be. I won't give the Duke up, Arkady. It's just that for all of my adult life, I've studied and theorized about the abstracts of war. Now, probably like a hell of a lot of other people before me, I find that there are certain realities beyond all of that theorizing that I'm going to have to confront."

She looked across at the shadowy outline of her father's painting on the bulkhead and murmured:

> *"The strength of twice three thousand horse,*
> *That seeks the single goal;*
> *The line that holds the rending course,*
> *The hate that swings the whole . . .*

"I am the chooser of the slain, Arkady, and that's a rather heavy thing to learn to live with."

"I won't give you an argument."

Amanda curled up again on the recliner. "What do you think? Was this snowball fight really worth all of the fuss?"

She'd made her decision and was already sounding a little more like herself again.

"I'm not sure," Arkady replied. "I think we're all still too close to this thing to be able to call it."

"What do you mean?"

"We might need a little more time between it and us before all of the causes and effects shake down and we can see just exactly what we've accomplished."

"The judgment of history?" she inquired drowsily.

"Exactly. I think it's going to be something like the Vietnam War. We backed out of it in 1972 with our tails between our legs. It wasn't until about twenty years later, when we could put it in perspective with the rest of the Cold War, that we began to realize that we'd actually won the damn thing and just hadn't noticed. We might have to ask our grandchildren about this one."

"Our grandchildren, Lieutenant?"

"Speaking figuratively, Captain."

Things went quiet after that. Arkady sat in the dark and listened as Amanda's breathing slowed and evened. He was almost sure that she was no longer awake when she spoke again.

"Arkady, when we get clear of this, do you think we can find ourselves another beach somewhere?"

"Why not?"

And then she slept.

Arkady resisted the temptation to reach out and touch her. There would be other, better, times and places. Instead, he edged his chair around a little so that he could look at her more easily, and then, content, he watched over the still form on the recliner until sleep claimed him as well.

"I suppose we won," Dr. Towers said, glancing at the glowing television screen across the embassy dining room from the table she shared with Harrison Van Lynden.

"Apparently," the Secretary of State replied, buttering his last piece of toast. "There's been no official word from the Ministry of State yet beyond Sparza's press release, but I think it's only a matter of time."

Dr. Towers shook her head. "We've still lost, though. Antarctica was special in that the only lives that had ever been lost there had been lost in the quest for knowledge. It was the one place on Earth where man had never slain man. Now it's just another piece of ground to fight over. It will never be the same."

"All the more reason to ensure that the fighting never starts again. That brings up the topic I've been meaning to speak to you about, Doctor. Would you be interested in taking a sabbatical from the National Science Foundation?"

"A sabbatical? To do what?"

"As a result of this incident, the President has instructed the State Department to form a special task force to resolve the remaining questions concerning Antarctic territoriality and to oversee United States participation in the international park project. We'd like for you to head that task force."

"Me?"

"Most definitely. Some might say that this is locking the barn door after the horse has been stolen, but I think you'll agree that there's still a lot of work to be done."

"I do agree, Mr. Secretary, but I'm a scientist, not a diplomat."

"You've done good work with us here and you know the area and its problems inside and out. That's more than a number of our ambassadorial cadre can claim. Believe me, Doctor, I think you're the right person for this job. I wouldn't have asked you otherwise."

"First Ambassador to Antarctica?" she mused with a frown. "Well, there are definitely some things I'd like to see get done. Some of us in the scientific community have had a tendency to sit up in our ivory towers and sneer at the politico-diplomatic process. Maybe that's been part of the problem."

"So?"

"How much time do I have to decide?"

"We'll be heading back to Washington in the next day or two. I'll need to know by then."

"You will, Mr. Secretary."

Steven Rosario entered the dining room and paused at their table. "We've just received a call from the Argentine Ministry of State, sir. President Sparza is requesting a meeting with you at your convenience."

Van Lynden tossed his napkin across his plate. "Very good, Steve. Return my compliments to President Sparza and inform him that I will be available to meet with him at ten this morning."

Rising from his chair, Van Lynden inquired, "Would you care to join us, Doctor?"

"Yes, I would. Very much so." She glanced again at the television screen. "Do you think he's going to be able to survive this?"

"I don't know. They won't pull him down easily. He's an able politician and a fighter. I think that he's also basically a good man. It's just that his dreams didn't quite match up with the rest of the world's."

Across the room, the CNN newscaster droned on. ". . . In the release issued by his Ministry of State, Argentina President Antonio Sparza is quoted as saying, 'We have brought our justifiable concerns over the fate of the San Martin Peninsula to the attention of the world community. Accordingly, we will now withdraw our forces and seek to resolve these questions via diplomatic means.'

"This statement comes, however, amid growing rumors of a clash or series of clashes between the naval and air forces of the United States and Argentina in the icy, mist-shrouded waters beyond the Antarctic Circle. . . ."

NORFOLK, VIRGINIA
0831 HOURS: MARCH 31, 2006

Captain Margaret Callendar deftly manipulated the small trackball controller on the balcony railing. Across the operations room, a designator circle danced across the Large Screen Display in response.

"The USS *Sea Serpent* has entered the eastern approaches to Drake Passage with another attack boat, the Royal Navy's HMS *Victorix* running about four hours behind her. . . . The British *Ark Royal* carrier group is also just arriving on station southeast of the Falkland Islands. . . . On the Falklands themselves, patrol squadron VP-4 has completed deployment and is currently running Orion sweeps south to the ice line beyond South Georgia Island, and west to the South Shetlands. Air Combat Command also reports that they have four B-1Cs operational out of Mount Pleasant. They're configured for antishipping strike duties and are on call to launch as needed."

Elliot McIntyre took the first sip of his first on-watch mug of coffee. "What about the *Roosevelt* group?" he inquired, leaning back in the observation chair.

"They've successfully transited the Straits of Malvinas and are proceeding on course south. There have been no contacts with Argentine forces."

"And the *Cunningham?*"

"Running northeast to rendezvous with the *Roosevelt*. She's had a combat air patrol over her since first light, and she should be joining up with the Teddy at about noon our time."

"Very good. As soon as she's finished replenishing, relieve her on station. Instruct Captain Garrett to proceed independently to Norfolk at best possible speed."

"Aye, aye, sir. As soon as they had air cover, the *Cunningham* came out of EMCON. They've executed a postengagement data dump to our computers, and it's undergoing analysis and processing at this time. By midwatch we should have a pretty good idea of just what all went on down there."

"That's likely to be some interesting reading."

"Yes, sir. Another interesting piece of reading came in as well. Captain Garrett's transmitted a commendations and decorations list."

"Let's have a look at it."

Captain Callendar retrieved a sheaf of hard copy from her desk. Balancing his coffee mug on the chair arm, MacIntyre accepted it and flipped through the first few pages:

Lieutenant Commander Kenneth A. Hiro . . . Silver Star and Purple Heart; Lieutenant Christine M. Rendino . . . Silver Star; Lieutenant Frank R. McKelsie . . . Silver Star; Lieutenant Dixon L. Beltrain . . . Silver Star; Lieutenant Commander Carl M. Thomson . . . Silver Star; Lieutenant Vincent M. Arkady & AC 1st Gregory Grestovitch . . . Distinguished Flying Cross; Seaman Lucas S. Erikson . . . Bronze Star for Valor . . .

"Rubber-stamp everything that I can authorize and pass on everything that I can't with my strongest possible endorsement. You can also tack a couple more on to the end of the list. I'm requesting that the *Cunningham* be considered for the Presidential Unit Citation and I'm putting Amanda Garrett up for the Navy Cross."

Margaret Callendar smiled. "Yes, sir. My pleasure."

"They deserve it, Maggie. We've just fought, and won, the most intense fleet action since the Second World War, and our 'fleet' consisted of a single ship. Damn, I'm proud of those people."

"You won't be the only one, sir. May I relay the word to Captain Garrett's father?"

"Be my guest, Maggie," MacIntyre replied, reclaiming his mug. "That's one medal I wouldn't have minded presenting myself, but I guess Wils really deserves first call on that job. Now, what are the Argentines up to?"

"They seem to be standing down. No aggressive moves anywhere across the board for the last twenty-four hours. Hardly any activity at all except for on the Antarctic Peninsula itself."

"What's happening there?"

"They appear to be abandoning the British stations. They're pulling their garrison units back into San Martin Base. Sigint and satellite imaging indicate that they've started airlifting personnel and equipment out to the Argentine mainland."

"Has this been verified?"

She nodded. "It looks solid, sir. They're going home."

The CINCLANT nodded to himself and took another sip of coffee. It was over. He could feel it. The figurative hairs that had been standing up on the back of his neck ever since he had sent his people into this campaign were lying down again. For one last time he studied the great graphic representation of the near-juncture of the South American and South Polar continents and the passage of ocean between them.

Well done, thou good and faithful servants.

"That's it, then," he said. "I guess we can put this one to bed."

"So it appears, Admiral, and it's a good thing too."

"Now what?"

"We've just caught a Flash Red from the State Department. The situation in Mauritania has just gone critical. Rioting between Arabic and Black African factions is going into its third day, and there are reports of mutiny within some elements of the military. State is sniffing coup fever in the air, if not an outright civil war.

"The airports and borders have been closed, and they'd like fleet units standing by in case it becomes necessary to evacuate both our citizens and the other foreign nationals who are currently in-country."

MacIntyre smiled wryly and drained his mug. "Two international crises within the space of one cup of coffee. Okay, Maggie, let's see who we have in the neighborhood."

SOUTH ORKNEY ISLANDS
1045 HOURS: APRIL 7, 2006

The British are a people who frequently prize sentiment above cold logic. It is one of the secret strengths of that race. Thus, the final act was played out on a snow-shrouded hill overlooking the last moorage of the motor ketch *Skua*. The Royal Navy had responded to the pleas of a small group of college students and one grieving woman. They had brought Evan York home.

The grave had been blasted out of the frozen shale with abandoned Argentine explosives, and a marker had been made from a piece of the *Skua*'s mahogany decking that had been found washed ashore along the edge of the bay. That bay was frozen solid now. Out beyond the entrance, the ice-patrol ship *Polar Circle* stood by in the last lead of open water. She had executed the dash in to restock Signy Island Base and to return the wintering-over team. She had also carried the burial party.

The ceremony itself was brief and small. There were only the scientists from the base, Evan York's crew, and a navy chaplain whose words were torn away by the gusting winds. Then the others moved back and allowed Roberta Eggerston to say good-bye to the man she loved.

She knelt at the grave and carefully placed a flash of color at the base of the marker, a small handful of flowers husbanded from a

Port Stanley greenhouse. She pinned the stems to the ground with a small stone, then rose to her feet and walked away. She would never again return south. There would be no more flowers for Evan York's grave.

Nor would any really be necessary. Before they could even begin to wilt, the blossoms had been flash frozen in the searing, dry chill of the polar winter. They would remain fresh and unchanged for as long as there was an Antarctic.

The burial party departed, the ship disappeared into the sea smoke, and the katabatic winds began to scatter snow crystals across the flowers and the bare stones of the grave, slowly sheathing them in ice and eternity.

AEGIS   A mating of a sophisticated cybernetic battle-management system with a series of advanced planar-array radars, giving a surface warship a sea- and air-control capacity out to a 250-mile radius.

    The augmented SPY-2A variant deployed aboard the Cunningham-class DDG combines increased range and fire-control capacity with improved definition and simplicity of operation.

AEW (AIRBORNE EARLY WARNING)   The doctrine of mounting a high-powered search radar aboard an aircraft to enhance its coverage area. The Boeing AWACS is the premier example of this technology.

    In *Choosers of the Slain,* the Argentine Air Force utilizes the Israeli Elta Phalcon phased-array radar mounted aboard a 737-400 airframe, while the *Cunningham*'s Sea Comanche helicopters can mount a podded version of the British-built Clear Water III radar.

ASW (ANTISUBMARINE WARFARE)   The delicate and deadly art of submarine hunting.

ATLANTIQUE ANG   A twin-turboprop maritime-patrol aircraft produced by Dessault-Breguet of France. Equipped with a wide variety of sophisticated weapons and sensor systems, it is capable of flying both ASW and surface strike missions.

BLACK HOLE SYSTEM   A combination of anti-infrared technologies used to reduce the heat signature of a military vehicle.

Aboard the Cunningham-class destroyer, blowers mix cooler outside air with the ship's engine-exhaust gases before they are vented outboard, reducing the thermal plume from the turbines. Likewise, seawater is circulated through cooling jackets surrounding the ship's funnels to prevent "hot spotting," which could provide a target for home-on-heat guided munitions.

BSA   British Antarctic Survey.

COLD FIRE LAUNCHING SYSTEM   A vertical-launch technology that utilizes a charge of inert gas to project a missile out of its launch cell for a midair ignition. Utilized aboard the Cunningham-class DDG to protect the RAM decking from exhaust-flame damage.

ECM (ELECTRONIC COUNTERMEASURES)   Jamming and decoy systems used to confuse and degrade search sensors and weapon-guidance systems.

ELINT (ELECTRONIC INTELLIGENCE)   The collection of battle-field intelligence (target location, system type, nationality, force strength, etc.) via the analysis of emissions produced by radars and other electronic systems.

EMCON (EMISSION CONTROL)   An operational state in which a naval vessel or aircraft maintains complete radio and radar silence, rendering them undetectable to signal intelligence systems.

ESSM (ENHANCED SEA SPARROW MISSILE)   Uprated follow-on to the current NATO Sea Sparrow system. A medium-range, surface-to-air system using radar guidance, it can be fired either from its own dedicated launcher or from a quad-pack fitted into a cell of a Mark 41 or 42 VLS array.

EXOCET   Produced by France, it is one of the first and most successful of the antiship missile designs. It is radar guided, and powered by a solid-fuel rocket motor; air-, surface-, and submarine-launched variants have been produced. The AM-44 model mentioned in the novel is a projected version with an extended range and a multimode seeker head.

FENESTRON   Literally, "fan in tail," an advanced helicopter technology that replaces the conventional tail rotor with a ducted fan inset into the tail fin, reducing noise, vibration, and radar cross-section.

LORAIN   Next-generation naval surface-to-air missile. A long-range, hypersonic, area defense weapon, utilizing multimode guidance and an exotically fueled ramjet propulsion system.

OTO MELARA SUPER RAPID   A 76mm, water-cooled autocannon produced by the Oto Melara corporation of Italy. A dual-mode weapons system with an exceptionally high rate of fire, it is capable of engaging both air and surface targets with a wide variety of munitions types. A popular and efficient design, it serves as the primary gun armament of the Cunningham-class destroyer.

RAFALE   A fifth-generation fighter-bomber produced by Dassault of France. A single-seat, single-engine, supersonic aircraft with delta wings and a forward canard. It is night and all-weather strike capable.

RAM (RADAR-ABSORBENT MATERIAL)   A family of composite materials used in the creation of stealth weapons systems. They work by "soaking up" incoming radar waves, converting them into thermal energy within their structure rather then reflecting them off.

RAM (ROLLING AIRFRAME MISSILE)   A missile crossbreed of the Sidewinder airframe and the Stinger guidance system. A light maritime surface-to-air defense system, it is utilized aboard the Cunningham-class destroyer as an adjunct to the ship's Phalanx antimissile cannon.

RAVEN'S ROOST   Shipboard nickname for the intelligence systems bay. Because of their stealth capacity, the Cunningham-class destroyers have been given an enhanced capability to perform "Raven" missions—i.e., to act as a Sigint (Signal Intelligence)- and Elint (Electronic Intelligence)-gathering platform.

RBOC (RAPID BLOOMING OVERHEAD CHAFF) PROJECTOR   A shipboard antimissile defense system. Originally intended to protect vessels against radar-guided missiles by screening them with clouds of metal foil.

In recent years, however, additional projectiles have been developed for the system, including flare and multispectral smoke rounds that can provide protection against infrared and laser-guided munitions.

SAH-66 SEA COMANCHE LAMPS (LIGHT AIRBORN MULTI-PURPOSE SYSTEM)   The original RAH-66 Comanche was intended as an Army scout/gunship helicopter utilizing low-radar-visibility technology. The SAH-66 Sea Comanche is a naval variant produced to complement the stealth capacity of the Cunningham-class guided-missile destroyer. Intended for ASW and surface search/recon operations, the Sea Comanche mounts a powerful APG-65 radar in its nose. It can also be equipped with a number of different pod-mounted sensor systems, including dunking sonars, Magnetic Abnormality Detectors, and the Shearwater AEW system.

In addition, the SAH-66 can be armed with a broad spectrum of torpedoes, missiles, depth charges, and gun pods.

SCM (STEALTH CRUISE MISSILE)   The follow-on to the Tomahawk sea-launched cruise missile. A sophisticated, long-range strike weapon incorporating low radar visibility in its design. A multimode weapon, it can be configured for either antishipping or land attack.

Sea SLAM   A ground-attack variant of the Harpoon anti-shipping missile. Utilizing an infrared, electro-optical targeting system developed for the Maverick air-to-surface missile, it is a sea-launched weapon, primarily intended for precision strikes against land targets.

Sigint (Signal Intelligence)   The collection of battlefield intelligence via the interception and decryption of enemy radio and land-line communications.

Standard HARM (Homing Antiradiation Missile)   A derivative of the Standard surface-to-air missile. The Standard HARM is designed to seek out and destroy enemy land- and sea-based radio and radar systems by homing in on their EM emissions. The missile is equipped with a memory system that allows it to prosecute the kill even if the target transmitter is shut down.

Tornado   A twin-engine, swing wing fighter-bomber produced by the European Panavia consortium. An extremely sophisticated, two-place aircraft with full day/night and all-weather capability, a number of specialized variants have been produced, including interceptor, intruder, recon/Wild Weasel, and maritime strike.

USARP   United States Antarctic Research Program.